MW01075491

STEVE MARTIN WRITES THE WRITTEN WORD

ALSO BY STEVE MARTIN

Cruel Shoes

Kindly Lent Their Owner: The Private Collection of Steve Martin

Born Standing Up

An Object of Beauty

The Ten, Make That Nine, Habits of Very Organized People. Make That Ten.: The Tweets of Steve Martin

A Wealth of Pigeons: A Cartoon Collection (with Harry Bliss)

Number One Is Walking: My Life in the Movies and Other Diversions

So Many Steves: Afternoons with Steve Martin

STEVE MARTIN WRITES THE WRITTEN WORD

COLLECTED WRITTEN WORD WORKS BY STEVE MARTIN

NEW YORK BOSTON

The following pieces were originally published in *The New Yorker* magazine: *A Public Apology; Writing Is Easy; Yes, in My Own Backyard; Changes in the Memory After Fifty; Dear Amanda; Times Roman Font Announces Shortage of Periods; Taping My Friends; The Sledgehammer: How It Works; The Paparazzi of Plato; Side Effects; How I Joined Mensa; Drivel; The Hundred Greatest Books That I've Read; The Y3K Bug*

The following was originally published in *The New York Times Magazine: The Nature of Matter and Its Antecedents*

The following was originally published in *The New York Times* Op-ed section: *Mars Probe Finds Kittens*

Jacket design by YY Liak. Jacket photo by Joe Pugliese/August Image. Jacket copyright © 2025 by Hachette Book Group, Inc.

Grand Central Publishing
Hachette Book Group
1290 Avenue of the Americas, New York, NY 10104
grandcentralpublishing.com
@grandcentralpub

First Omnibus Edition: May 2025

Articles from *Pure Drivel* were first published by Hyperion in book form in 1998. *Shopgirl* was first published by Hyperion in 2000. *The Pleasure of My Company* was first published by Hyperion in 2003.

Grand Central Publishing is a division of Hachette Book Group, Inc. The Grand Central Publishing name and logo is a registered trademark of Hachette Book Group, Inc.

The author gratefully acknowledges permission to reprint excerpts from the following lyrics and poetry:

"Heat Wave" copyright © 1933 by Irving Berlin. Copyright renewed. International copyright secured. All rights reserved. Reprinted by permission.

"I Feel Pretty" from *West Side Story*. Music by Leonard Bernstein. Lyrics by Stephen Sondheim, copyright © 1956, 1957 by The Estate of Leonard Bernstein and Stephen Sondheim. Copyright renewed. Leonard Bernstein Music Publishing Company LLC, Publisher, Boosey & Hawkes, Inc., Sole Agent. Reprinted by permission.

"Love Poem" by Mick Gowar © Mick Gowar, used by permission.

Print book interior design by Sheryl Kober.

Library of Congress Cataloging-in-Publication Data has been applied for.

ISBNs: 9780306835735 (hardcover); 9780306837890 (signed edition);
9780306837883 (B&N signed edition); 9780306835742 (ebook)

Printed in the United States of America

LSC-C

Printing 1, 2025

CONTENTS

INTRODUCTION

My entire career is based on an unlikely math. As a kid, I loved comedy, and I loved curtains (the kind in theaters). So add those two loves together, and you can see that I might like to stand in front of a curtain and do comedy. The curtain was only an aspiration, because initially I stood in front of brick walls, basketball stanchions, and salad bars.

At first, my material was written down in my head or shorthanded on a set list: "cat handcuffs," "candle bit." As I matured, writing nouns with verbs became essential. Early on, I did have a love of language. In high school, the romantic spiel of *Cyrano de Bergerac* had me swooning, hoping I, too, could eventually woo Roxanne with sly linguistic persuasion.

When fortune wafted me from the streets of Hollywood to a writer's desk at CBS Studios in Los Angeles, I had to write entire sentences: "Ladies and gentlemen, Judy Collins!"

For sketches on *The Smothers Brothers Comedy Hour* (and Glen Campbell's spinoff summer show and *The Sonny and Cher Comedy Hour*), I had to write dialogue as well as stage directions.

SONNY ENTERS
SONNY
Hi, Cher.
CHER
Hi, Sonny.

When I was forced to write my own screenplays—hang on, nobody forced me, but if I wanted to be in a movie, I'd better, since no one was offering me anything—real, believable dialogue was needed. Here, I was definitely unfit. I barely had dialogue in my own life, being shy and taciturn (poetically so, I thought), but draft after draft of *The Jerk*, and able assists from cowriters, eventually produced a semblance of humanity, even if exaggerated.

But first, here's a partial routine from my stand-up:

> I've gotta get a pair of cat handcuffs, and I've gotta get 'em right away. Just the little ones that go around the little front paws... or maybe the manacles of four that get all four paws. But what a drag:
>
> I found out my cat was embezzling from me!

When I performed it with pauses, exasperation, indignation, and rising anger, it all made sense.

However, when I started writing sentences, in essays at first, I knew that this was a different animal from a handcuffed cat. The pauses, exasperation, and indignation had to be present in the words alone. I couldn't add: "—he said, after pausing with exasperated indignation." Now, clarity and concision were prized. Like in comedy, I never wanted the audience to be lost. "What does the reader know and when do they know it, and if they do know it, how long can they remember it?"

I realized, eventually, that grammar could be my friend, rather than the inhibitor of my grand emotions. If I were to woo Roxanne, *she had to understand what I was talking about,* rather than her having to say, "Wait, go back. Huh?"

The works I present here are complete, but also represent the ghostly mechanics of a writer in process.

PURE DRIVEL

In *Pure Drivel*—collected essays from the *New Yorker*—I first dabbled with prose, producing enough work to become comfortable, applying my editing sense from movies and plays to the essay. Certain works still seem relevant—"A Public Apology," "Side Effects," and "Dear Amanda"—though I would tweak them if I had the energy. I'm proud of these short pieces, but they rarely strayed from a comic format, the twisted premise, and the funny line. In my next effort, *Shopgirl,* I dared to leave the artist's comforting friend, irony (*Oh, I don't really mean it*), behind.

SHOPGIRL

I started writing *Shopgirl* after I emerged from a complicated romantic relationship and asked myself, "What just happened?" The book represents my dip into a river of melancholy. It poses as a roman à clef, but it's not. It is only disguised as one. I was single at the time of its writing, and I probed not only my own psyche but the psyches of others, both living and literary, about romance, breakups, and heartache. The book blends myriad misguided relationships—and their subsequent lessons—into a resolution. The story is made up but is true enough to warrant a dedication to a single person.

When it was published, I was anticipating rejection. After all, a comedian should never, *ever* write something serious. But the expected knee-jerk criticism didn't happen, and the book coasted just slightly under the backlash radar. I was told by those who had experienced similar uneven situations that it helped them to understand the reason for their own dead end.

A line from the novella *The Pleasure of My Company*, published three years later, answers the questions posed by *Shopgirl*:

> It is hard to find that the person you love loves someone else.

THE PLEASURE OF MY COMPANY

The Pleasure of My Company began when a friend, a creative friend, suggested, "You ought to write about 'that guy.'" I knew exactly what she was talking about. "That guy" was the darker shadow of a comic persona I had done onstage, and sometimes as a comic premise with friends: a benign liar and modest egomaniac with his views of life distorted by—oh, let's just say it—pain. The book was written in the haze of another bust-up, so here the humor is infused with some of that water from the risky river of melancholy.

The book presages my own life, too. Its ending is my ending. If you read it, you'll find out why.

When it comes to my movies, television appearances, and live performances, I never look back. Why, I almost can't tell you, because I almost haven't figured it out. The best explanation is that between the viewer and me, there is no interface. Wait, poor word, because there's only *my face*. In movies and television, I'm always looking at *my face*. It's *me*, and I can't avoid myself. But on the page, there is no face. There are the words that once meant something to me and hopefully still do. So, occasionally, I will revisit the books I've written, sometimes reading the entirety, sometimes opening to a page and seeing what comes up. Unlike performed works, rife with spontaneity, false starts, and quick recoveries, sentences are set in unchanging circumstances. The words are there because their neighbors are there, because the paragraphs are there, because the chapters are there. And they're not dependent on how my delivery was that day. No, my writing doesn't have tired eyes or a bad haircut. When I look back at my performance-based output, I think, *That was then*. Even the costumes are dated. But rereading these few books, they are still fresh to me, and I accept them as "This is still now."

STEVE MARTIN WRITES THE WRITTEN WORD

A PUBLIC APOLOGY

Looking out over the East River from my jail cell and still running for public office, I realize that I have taken several actions in my life for which I owe public apologies.

Once, I won a supermarket sweepstakes even though my brother's cousin was a box boy in that very store. I would like to apologize to Safeway Food, Inc., and its employees. I would like to apologize to my family, who have stood by me, and especially to my wife Karen. A wiser and more loyal spouse could not be found.

When I was twenty-one, I smoked marijuana every day for one year. I would like to apologize for the next fifteen years of anxiety attacks and drug-related phobias, including the feeling that when Ed Sullivan introduced Wayne and Shuster, he was actually signaling my parents that I was high. I would like to apologize to my wife Karen, who still believes in me, and to the Marijuana Growers Association of Napa Valley and its affiliates for any embarrassment I may have caused them. I would also like to mention a little incident that took place in the Holiday Inn in Ypsilanti, Michigan, during that same time. I was lying in bed in room 342 and began counting ceiling tiles. Since the room was square, it was an easy computation, taking no longer than the weekend. As Sunday evening rolled around, I began to compute how many *imaginary* ceiling tiles it would take to cover the walls and floor of my room. When I checked out of the hotel, I flippantly told the clerk that it would take twelve hundred ninety-four imaginary ceiling tiles to fill the entire room.

Two weeks later, while attempting to break the record for consecutive listenings to "American Pie," I realized that I had included the *real tiles* in my calculation of imaginary tiles; I should have subtracted them from my total. I would like to apologize to the staff of the Holiday Inn for any inconvenience I may have caused, to the wonderful people at Universal Ceiling Tile, to my wife Karen, and to my two children, whose growth is stunted.

Several years ago, in California, I ate my first clam and said it tasted "like a gonad dipped in motor oil." I would like to apologize to Bob 'n' Betty's Clam Fiesta, and especially to Bob, who I found out later only had one testicle. I would like to apologize to the waitress June and her affiliates, and the DePaul family dog, who suffered the contents of my nauseated stomach.

There are several incidents of sexual harassment I would like to apologize for:

In 1992, I was interviewing one Ms. Anna Floyd for a secretarial position, when my pants accidentally fell down around my ankles as I was coincidentally saying, "Ever seen one of these before?" Even though I was referring to my new Pocket Tape Memo Taker, I would like to apologize to Ms. Floyd for any grief this misunderstanding might have caused her. I would also like to apologize to the Pocket Tape people, to their affiliates, and to my family, who have stood by me. I would like to apologize also to International Hardwood Designs, whose floor my pants fell upon. I would especially like to apologize to my wife Karen, whose constant understanding fills me with humility.

Once, in Hawaii, I had sex with a hundred-and-two-year-old male turtle. It would be hard to argue that it was consensual. I would like to apologize to the turtle, his family, the Kahala Hilton Hotel, and the hundred or so diners at the Hilton's outdoor café. I would also like to apologize to my loyal wife Karen, who had to endure the subsequent news item in the "Also Noted" section of the *Santa Barbara Women's Club Weekly.*

In 1987, I attended a bar mitzvah in Manhattan while wearing white gabardine pants, white patent-leather slippers, a blue blazer with gold buttons, and a yachting cap. I would like to apologize to the Jewish people, the State of Israel, my family, who have stood by me, and my wife Karen, who has endured my seventeen affairs and three out-of-wedlock children.

I would also like to apologize to the National Association for the Advancement of Colored People, for referring to its members as "colored people." My apology would not be complete if I didn't include my new wife, Nancy, who is of a pinkish tint, and our two children, who are white-colored.

Finally, I would like to apologize for spontaneously yelling the word "Savages!" after losing six thousand dollars on a roulette spin at the Choctaw Nation Casino and Sports Book. When I was growing up, the usage of this word in our household closely approximated the Hawaiian *aloha*, and my use of it in the casino was meant to express "until we meet again."

Now on with the campaign!

WRITING IS EASY!

Writing is one of the most easy, pain-free, and happy ways to pass the time in all the arts. For example, right now I am sitting in my rose garden and typing on my new computer. Each rose represents a story, so I'm never at a loss for *what* to write. I just look deep into the heart of the rose and read its story and write it down through *typing*, which I enjoy anyway. I could be typing "kjfiu joewmv jiw" and would enjoy it as much as typing words that actually make sense. I simply relish the movement of my fingers on the keys. Sometimes, it is true, agony visits the head of a writer. At these moments, I stop writing and relax with a coffee at my favorite restaurant, knowing that words can be changed, rethought, fiddled with, and, of course, ultimately denied. Painters don't have that luxury. If they go to a coffee shop, their paint dries into a hard mass.

LOCATION, LOCATION, LOCATION

I would recommend to writers that they live in California, because here they can look up at the blue sky in between those moments of looking into the heart of a rose. I feel sorry for writers—and there are some pretty famous ones—who live in places like South America and Czechoslovakia, where I imagine it gets pretty dreary. These writers are easy to spot. Their books are often depressing and filled with disease and negativity. If you're going to write about disease, I would suggest that California is the place to do it. Dwarfism is never funny, but look at the result when it was dealt with out here in California. Seven happy dwarfs. Can you imagine seven dwarfs in Czechoslovakia? You would get seven melancholic dwarfs at best, seven melancholic dwarfs with no handicapped-parking spaces.

LOVE IN THE TIME OF CHOLERA: WHY IT'S A BAD TITLE

I admit that "Love in the time of..." is a great title, so far. You're reading along, you're happy, it's about love, I like the way the word *time* comes in there, something nice in the association of *love* and time, like a new word almost, *lovetime*: nice, nice feeling. Suddenly, the morbid *cholera* appears. I was happy till then. "Love in the Time of the Oozing Sores and Pustules" is probably an earlier, rejected title of this book, written in a rat-infested tree house on an old Smith-Corona. This writer, whoever he is, could have used a couple of weeks in Pacific Daylight Time.

I did a little experiment. I decided to take the following disheartening passage, which was no doubt written in some depressing place, and attempt to rewrite it under the influence of California:

> Most people deceive themselves with a pair of faiths: They believe in *eternal memory* (of people, things, deeds, nations)

> and in *redressibility* (of deeds, mistakes, sins, wrongs). Both are false faiths. In reality the opposite is true: Everything will be forgotten and nothing will be redressed. (Milan Kundera)

Sitting in my garden, as the bees glide from flower to flower, I let the above paragraph filter through my mind. The following new paragraph emerged:

> I feel pretty,
> Oh so pretty,
> I feel pretty and witty and bright.

Kundera was just too wordy. Sometimes the Delete key is your greatest friend.

WRITER'S BLOCK: A MYTH

Writer's block is a fancy term made up by whiners so they can have an excuse to drink alcohol. Sure, a writer can get stuck for a while, but when that happens to real authors, they simply go out and get an "as told to." The alternative is to hire yourself out as an "as heard from," thus taking all the credit. It is also much easier to write when you have someone to "bounce" with. This is someone to sit in a room with and exchange ideas. It is good if the last name of the person you choose to bounce with is Salinger. I know a certain early-twentieth-century French writer, whose initials were MP, who could have used a good bounce person. If he had, his title might have been the more correct "Remembering Past Things" instead of the clumsy one he used. The other trick I use when I have a momentary stoppage is virtually foolproof, and I'm happy to pass it along. Go to an already published novel and find a sentence you absolutely adore. Copy it down in your manuscript. Usually that sentence will lead you naturally to another sentence; pretty soon your own ideas will start to flow. If they don't, copy down the next sentence. You can safely use up to three sentences of someone else's work—unless they're friends; then you can use two. The odds of being found out are very slim, and even if you are, there's no jail time.

CREATING MEMORABLE CHARACTERS

Nothing will make your writing soar more than a memorable character. If there is a memorable character, the reader will keep going back to the book, picking it up, turning it over in his hands, hefting it, and tossing it into the air. Here is an example of the jazzy uplift that vivid characters can offer:

> Some guys were standing around when in came this guy.

You are now on your way to creating a memorable character. You have set him up as being a guy, and with that come all the reader's ideas of what a guy is. Soon you will liven your character by using an adjective:

> But this guy was no ordinary guy, he was a red guy.

This character, the red guy, has now popped into the reader's imagination. He is a full-blown person, with hopes and dreams, just like the reader. Especially if the reader is a red guy. Now you might want to give the character a trait. You can inform the reader of the character trait in one of two ways. First, simply say what that trait is—for example, "But this red guy was different from most red guys, this red guy liked frappés." The other is rooted in action—have the red guy walk up to a bar and order a frappé, as in:

"What'll you have, red guy?"
"I'll have a frappé."

Once you have mastered these two concepts, vivid character writing combined with adjectives, you are on your way to becoming the next Shakespeare's brother. And don't forget to copyright any ideas you have that might be original. You don't want to be caught standing by helplessly while your familiar "red guy" steps up to a bar in a frappé commercial.

WRITING DIALOGUE

Many very fine writers are intimidated when they have to write the way people really talk. Actually it's quite easy. Simply lower your IQ by fifty and start typing!

SUBJECT MATTER

Because topics are in such short supply, I have provided a few for writers who may be suffering in the darker climes. File some of these away, and look through them during the suicidal winter months:

"Naked Belligerent Panties": This is a good sexy title with a lot of promise.

How about a diet book that suggests your free radicals *don't* enter ketosis unless your insulin levels have been carbo-charged?

Something about how waves at the beach just keep coming and coming and how amazing it is (I smell a bestseller here).

"Visions of Melancholy from a Fast-Moving Train": Some foreign writer is right now rushing to his keyboard, ready to pound on it like Horowitz. However, this title is a phony string of words with no meaning and would send your poor book to the "Artsy" section of Barnes and Noble, where—guess what—it would languish, be remaindered, and die.

A WORD TO AVOID

Dagnabbit will never get you anywhere with the Booker Prize people. Lose it.

GETTING PUBLISHED

I have one observation about publishers: Whatever their pronouns are, they love it when you call them "babe."

Now that we've established that, you are ready to "schmooze" your publisher. Let's say your favorite author is Dante. Call Dante's publisher and say you'd like to invite them both to lunch. If the assistant says something like "But Dante's dead," be sympathetic and say, "Please accept my condolences." Once at lunch, remember never to be moody. Publishers like up, happy writers, although it's impressive to suddenly sweep your arm slowly across the lunch table, dumping all the plates and food onto the floor, while shouting, "Sic Semper Tyrannis!"

A DEMONSTRATION OF ACTUAL WRITING

It's easy to talk about writing and even easier to do it. Watch:

> Call me Ishmael. It was cold, very cold, here in the mountain town of Kilimanjaroville.© I could hear a bell. It was tolling. I knew exactly for who it was tolling, too. It was tolling for me, Ishmael Twist,© a red guy who likes frappé. [Author's note: I am now stuck. I walk over to a rose and look into its heart.] That's right, Ishmael Twist.®

Finally, I can't overstress the importance of having a powerful closing sentence.

YES, IN MY OWN BACKYARD

Last week in Los Angeles, I realized that the birdbath in my garden is by Raphael. I had passed it a thousand times; so had many producers, actors, executives, and the occasional tag-along screenwriter. No one had ever mentioned the attribution "Raphael." In fact, none of my guests had bothered to attribute it at all, which surprised me since they spend so much time discussing it. When I try to steer the conversation around to my films, my television appearances, and my early work, all I hear back is: "What a charming birdbath." To me, this is further evidence that the birdbath is a Raphael: One just can't look away.

Much has been made of the fact that Raphael never sculpted. That may be true, but what is less known is that he designed many avian objects that we today take for granted, including the clothesline and the beak polisher. A birdbath is completely within the oeuvre of the master. Mine is stylistically characteristic of his work, including triangulation (inverted), psychologically loaded negative space, and a carved Madonna holding an infant who looks fifty. Identical birdbaths appear in thirteen of his paintings; there is a Vasari portrait of Raphael painting the birdbath, and there is a scribble in his last diary that in translation reads, "Send my birdbath to Glendale," which is where I bought it at a swap meet.

In every person there's an art expert, and I'm sure the one in you wants some proof of authenticity in this age where, every day, Rembrandt van Rijns are being demoted to Rembrandt Yeah Sures.

There are two ways of confirming a work of art: scholarship and intuition. As far as scholarship goes, you can imagine that my copy of *Raphael for Dummies* is now well thumbed in my quest for authentication. But I needed to find a latter-day Berenson to put the final nail in the coffin of confirmation. The Los Angeles phone book lists two Raphael scholars, although one has a Maui area code. Both have been called in, and they are unanimous in their conclusion: one for, one against. This kind of scholarship proves something, but it can never take you the last mile; it is intuition that confirms attribution every time. How many times have I sat in my garden with the cordless, sipping on a cocktail ice of Prozac and Halcion, ignoring the masterpiece that stood before me? However, everyone has experienced that moment when our inner censor slips away and the volume of our head-noise is turned down low and we realize we are sitting in front of Raphael's birdbath. It is a swooping cloak of *sureness*, which falls from heaven and settles over you.

At that moment, I decided there was only one way to finally confirm my intuition to the rest of the world. I would visit the tomb of Raphael, who is buried in the *Pantheon* in Rome, and commune with the great master himself. (I emphasize the

Pantheon italically because, in my dyslexia, I read it as *Parthenon* and wasted money on a trip to Athens. I suggest a name change for one of them, to avoid confusion. After all, it's not like one is a river and one is an airport; they're both buildings.)

Entering the Pantheon, one cannot help but experience a feeling of awe. Looking to the left, one sees the hallowed name Pesto, to the right, a series of popes and pope wannabees. Unfortunately, they are not buried in alphabetical order, so finding Raphael was not easy. I skipped over him a couple of times, because evidently he had a last name and that threw me off. Forgive me, but if I'm looking for the grave of Liberace, I want it filed under Liberace, not Władziu Valentino, etc. Madonna, take note.

I stood before the vault where Raphael has lain for the last four hundred and fifty years. Before I relate to you the next part, I have to tell you a little bit about the Pantheon. It has the world's largest domed ceiling. A domed ceiling might be a big deal in the world of architecture, but in the world of whispering, it is definitely lousy. Everything comes back to you three times as loud, and even your diction is cleaned up. So when I whispered, "Did you make my birdbath?" everybody in the place heard me except Raphael, who was dead. I whispered again, louder, "Did you make my birdbath?" A few minutes later, a man in a trench coat came up to me and said, "Yes, but the Wide Man wants a green lawn." He then handed me an envelope containing five hundred million lire and slithered away.

The voice of Raphael did not come to me with his answer until several hours later, when I sat in a café within sight of the Pantheon, sipping a synthetic low-fat coffee mixed with a legal (in Italy) derivative of Xanax and quaalude. The voice emanated directly from the Pantheon and headed across the square to where I was sitting. Raphael, who now must be in heaven and hence has access to practically everything, used Italian but subtitled it with a dialect only my sister and I spoke when we were five. It confirmed that the birdbath was his and that he wanted everyone to know he was not gay.

The Martin Birdbath, as some scholars are now calling it—I objected at first—is still in the garden, although attended by a twenty-four-hour armed guard named Charlie (he's off on the weekends), whom I have grown to like. I'm not quite sure he knows what he is guarding, but with the parade of academicians trooping through, he's got to figure that it ain't cheese. His job, in addition to keeping the birdbath from being stolen, is to keep birds away. This is hard, because to a bird, a birdbath is a birdbath, be it by Raphael or the Sears garden department.

Even though several offers have emerged, I'm not going to sell the Raphael. I'm not even going to mention it to my guests, unless I feel it's going to get me somewhere. I suppose if I see someone staring at it as though a boom has just been lowered on them, I'll take them aside and fill them in. I will tell them they are standing in the presence of a master, that they are in touch with the power of the ages, and that they deserve the overused but still meaningful hyphenation "sensitive-type." Then I will direct them to sit back in my Gauguin-designed lawn chair and enjoy the view. How do I know it's by Gauguin? It is. I just know it is.

CHANGES IN THE MEMORY AFTER FIFTY

Bored? Here's a way the over-fifty set can easily kill off a good half hour:

1. Place your car keys in your right hand.
2. With your left hand, call a friend and confirm a lunch or dinner date.
3. Hang up the phone.
4. Now look for your car keys.
   (For answer, turn to page 17 and turn book upside down.)

The lapses of memory that occur after fifty are normal and in some ways beneficial. There are certain things it's better to forget, like the time Daddy once failed to praise you and now, forty years later, you have to count the tiles in the bathroom—first in multiples of three, then in multiples of five, and so on—until they come out even, or else you can't get out of the shower. The memory is selective, and sometimes it will select 1956 and 1963 and that's all. Such memory lapses don't necessarily indicate a more serious health problem. The rule is, if you think you have a pathological memory problem, you probably don't. In fact, the most serious indicator is when you're convinced you're fine and yet people sometimes ask you, "Why are you here in your pajamas at the Kennedy Center Honors?"

Let's say you've just called your best friend, Joe, and invited him to an upcoming birthday party, and then, minutes later, you call him back and invite him to the same party again. This does not mean you are "losing it" or "not playing with a full deck" or "not all there," or that you're "eating with the dirigibles" or "shellacking the waxed egg" or "looking inside your own mind and finding nothing there," or any of the demeaning epithets that are said about people who are peeling an empty banana. It does, however, mean that perhaps Joe is no longer on the list of things you're going to remember. This is Joe's fault. He should have a more memorable name, such as *El Elegante*.

Sometimes it's fun to sit in your garden and try to remember your dog's name. Here's how: Simply watch the ears while calling out pet names at random. This is a great summer activity, especially in combination with Name That Wife and Who Am I? These games actually strengthen the memory and make it simpler to solve such complicated problems as "Is this the sixth time I've urinated this hour or the seventh?" This, of course, is easily answered by tiny pencil marks applied during the day.

Note to self: Write article about waxy buildup.

If you have a doctor who is over fifty, it's wise to pay attention to his changing memory profile. There is nothing more disconcerting than patient and healer staring at each other across an examining table, wondering why they're there. Watch out for the stethoscope being placed on the forehead or the briefcase. Watch out for greetings such as "Hello... you." Be concerned if while looking for your file he keeps referring to you as "one bad boy." Men should be wary if, while examining your prostate, the doctor suddenly says, "I'm sorry, but do I know you?"

There are several theories that explain memory problems of advancing age. One is that the brain is full: It simply has too much data to compute. Easy to understand if you realize that the name of your third-grade teacher is still occupying space, not to mention the lyrics to "Volare." One solution for older men is to take all the superfluous data swirling around in the brain and download it into the newly large stomach, where there is plenty of room. This frees the brain to house relevant information, like the particularly troublesome days of the week. Another solution is to take regular doses of ginkgo biloba, an extract from a tree in Asia whose memory is so indelible that one day it will hunt down and kill all the humans that have been eating it. It is strongly advised that if taking ginkgo biloba, one should label the bottle *Memory Pills*. There is nothing more embarrassing than looking at a bottle of ginkgo biloba and thinking it's a reliquary for a Spanish explorer.

So in summary, waxy buildup is a problem facing all of us. Only a good strong cleanser, used once or twice a month, will save us the humiliation of that petrified yellow crust on our furniture. Again, I recommend an alcohol-free, polymer-based cleanser, applied with a damp cloth. Good luck!

The car keys are in your right hand. Please remember to turn the book right side up.

MARS PROBE FINDS KITTENS

The recent probe to Mars has returned irrefutable evidence that the red planet is populated with approximately twenty-seven three-month-old kittens. These "kittens" do not give birth and do not die but are forever locked in a state of eternal kittenhood. Of course, without further investigation, scientists are reluctant to call the chirpy little creatures *kittens*. "Just because they look like kittens and act like kittens is no reason to assume they are kittens," said one researcher. "A football is a brown thing that bounces around on grass, but it would be wrong to call it a puppy."

Scientists were at first skeptical that a kitten-type being could exist in the rare Martian atmosphere. As a test, Earth kittens were put in a chamber that simulated the Martian air. The diary of this experiment is fascinating:

- 6:00 A.M.: Kitten appears to sleep.
- 7:02 A.M.: Kitten wakes, darts from one end of cage to another for no apparent reason.

- 7:14 A.M.: Kitten runs up wall of cage, leaps onto other kitten for no apparent reason.
- 7:22 A.M.: Kitten lies on back and punches other kitten for no apparent reason.
- 7:30 A.M.: Kitten leaps, stops, darts left, stops abruptly, climbs wall, clings for two seconds, falls on head, darts right for no apparent reason.
- 7:51 A.M.: Kitten parses first sentence of lead editorial in daily newspaper, which is at the bottom of the chamber.

With the exception of parsing, all behavior is typical Earth-kitten behavior. The parsing activity, which was done with a small ballpoint pen, is considered an anomaly.

Modern kitten theory suggests several explanations for the kittens' existence on Mars. The first, put forward by Dr. Patricia Krieger of the Hey You Bub Institute, suggests that kittens occur both everywhere and nowhere simultaneously. In other words, we see evidence of kitten existence, but measuring their behavior is another matter. Just when the scientists point their instruments in a kitten's direction, it is gone, only to be found later in another place, perhaps at the top of drapes. Another theory, put forward by Dr. Charles Wexler and his uncle Ted, suggests that any universe where round things exist, from theoretical spheres to Ping-Pong balls, necessarily implies the existence of a Mover Kitten. The scientific world has responded by saying that the notion of the Mover Kitten is not a concern for legitimate research and should be relegated to the pseudoscientific world. The pseudoscientific world has responded by saying that at least three endorsements from independent crackpots are needed before anything can truly be called "pseudo."

Some have suggested that the hostility of the Martian climate should be enough to seriously set back the long-term prospects of any species. However, the weakness of Martian gravity is a bonus for felines. They are able to leap almost three times as high as they can on Earth. They can climb twice as far up a carpet-covered post, and a ball with a bell in it will roll almost three times as far. This is at least equal to the distance a mature poodle can roll a ball with its nose.

Even though there could be a big market on Earth for eternal kittens, most scientists agree that the human race should not pursue a further involvement. There are those, however, who believe that having now discovered the creatures, we have a responsibility to "amuse" them. Dr. Enos Mowbrey and his wife/cousin, Jane, both researchers at the Chicago Junebug Institute for Animal Studies, argue that the kittens could be properly amused by four miles of ball string cut into fourteen-inch segments. The cost of such a venture would be:

- Four miles of string: $135
- Segmentation of string: $8
- Manned Mars probe to deliver string and jiggle it: $6 trillion

It is unfortunate that Dr. Mowbrey's work has been largely dismissed because of his inappropriate use of the demeaning term *kitty cat*.

The next time you look up at the heavens, know that mixed in the array of stars overhead is a pale red dot called Mars, and on that planet are tiny creatures whose wee voices are about to be thunderously heard on this planet, a meow of intergalactic proportions.

DEAR AMANDA

Dear Amanda,

This will be the last letter I write to you. I think we have made the right decision. Thank you for your love. We had a wonderful experience these past five months. I want you to know that our time together will live inside me in a special place in my heart. It is best if we do not phone or write.

Love always,
Joey

Dear Amanda,

I dialed you last night because the *Lucy* pie episode was on and I knew you'd want to see it. Anyway, while I was leaving a message, I leaned on the phone and accidentally punched in your message-retrieval code. Sorry about that. Who's Francisco? Just curious.

Joey

Dear Amanda,

I realized that I still had your set of six Japanese sake cups that I bought for you on our trip downtown and was wondering when it might be a good time to drop them off. You can give me a call at the usual number but maybe better at the office up till seven but then try the car or I'm usually home now by seven forty-five. I would like to get these back to you, as I know you must be thinking about them. This will be my last letter.

Regards,
Joey

Dear Amanda,

It was a lucky coincidence that my cat leapt on your speed-dial button last night, as it gave us a chance to talk again. Afterwards, I was wondering what you meant when you said, "It's over, Joey, get it into your head." So many interpretations. Just curious. Oh, I found myself on your street last night and noticed a yellow Mustang that I don't remember ever being at your apartment complex. Is this the mysterious Francisco I've heard rumors about? No big deal. Just curious. I left one of the sake cups at your front door; it happened to be in my car. What was that loud music?

With respect,
Joey

Dear Amanda,

This will be the last letter I write to you. I hate to hurt you like this, but I'm seeing someone new. You'd like her. Her name is Marisa—she has the same number of letters in her name as you! Incidentally, I heard that Francisco had or is having a tax problem. Should I meet with him? I'm over it all now and would be glad to help. Also, a word of warning: Latins. One woman is never enough. Just a thought.

Joey

P.S. Do you have my red Pentel pen? I really need it. Page me when you get this.

Dear Amanda,

This will be the last letter I write to you. I'm quite upset that you changed your phone without a forwarding number. There could still be emergencies, and I'm still in possession of those fancy upholstered hangers of yours. Marisa questioned me about them the other day, and it wasn't fun. They're probably too dear to you to throw out, as we bought them together at the swap meet the day your mother raved about me, saying I was "pleasant." *Please* come by and pick them up; they're seriously damaging my relationship with Marisa. A good time would be any Wednesday after five but not after seven, Fridays anytime except lunch, Monday is good, and the weekend, anytime. Also Tuesday. By the way, there's someone named Francisco trying to pick up girls on the Internet. Hmm . . . I wonder.

Joey

Dear Amanda,

Valentine's Day is tomorrow, and I hope you don't mind my throwing this note through your window, as the post would be too slow. The rock it's tied to came from our desert trip! I'm wondering if you'd like to get together for a quick lunch on the fourteenth—you can even bring Francisco if you want; maybe I could help him sort out his heavy urology bills. I need to get my letters back from you, and could you bring this one too? I could bring the hangers, and I also want you to have the photo of me nude skydiving. Can you let me know soon? I'm waiting outside on the lawn.

This will be the last letter I write to you.

Love you always,
Joey

TIMES ROMAN FONT ANNOUNCES SHORTAGE OF PERIODS

Representatives of the popular Times Roman font, who recently announced a shortage of periods, have offered other substitutes—inverted commas, exclamation marks, and semicolons—until the period crisis is able to be overcome by people such as yourself, who, through creative management of surplus punctuation, can perhaps allay the constant demand for periods, whose heavy usage in the last ten years, not only in English but in virtually every language in the world, is creating a burden on writers everywhere, thus generating a litany of comments such as: What the hell am I supposed to do without my periods? How am I going to write? Isn't this a terrible disaster? Are they crazy? Won't this just create misuse of other, less interesting punctuation???

"Most vulnerable are writers who work in short, choppy sentences," said a spokesperson, who added, "We are trying to remedy the situation and have suggested alternatives like umlauts, as we have plenty of umlauts—in fact, more umlauts than we could possibly use in a lifetime; don't forget, umlauts can really spice up a page with their delicate symmetry, resting often midway in a word, letters spilling on either side, and can not only indicate the pronunciation of a word but also contribute to the writer's greater glory, because they're fancy, not to mention that they even look like periods, indeed are indistinguishable from periods, and will lead casual readers to believe the article actually contains periods!"

Bobby Brainard, a writer living in an isolated cabin in Montana, who is in fact the only writer living in an isolated cabin in Montana who is not insane, is facing a dilemma typical of writers across the nation: "I have a sentence that has just got to be stopped; it's currently sixteen pages long and is edging out the front door and is now so lumbering I'm starting to worry that one period alone won't be enough and I will need at least two to finally kill it off and if that doesn't work, I've ordered an elephant gun from mail order and if I don't get some periods fast, I'm going to have to use it..." The magazine *International Hebrew* has issued this emergency statement: "We currently have an oversupply of backward periods and will be happy to send some to Mister Brainard or anyone else facing a crisis!" period backward the in slip you while moment a for way other the look to sentence the getting is trick only The

The concern of writers is summed up in this brief telegram:

Period shortage mustn't continue stop
Stop-stoppage must come to full stop stop
We must resolve it and stop stop-stoppage stop

Yours truly,
Tom Stoppard

Needless to say, there has been an increasing pressure on the ellipsis...

"I assure you," said the spokesperson, "I assure you the ellipsis *is not*—repeat, *is not*—just three periods strung together, and although certain writers have plundered the ellipsis for its dots, these are deeply inelegant and ineffective when used to stop a sentence! ¿An ellipsis point is too weak to stop a modern sentence, which would require at least *two* ellipsis periods, leaving the third dot to stand alone pointlessly, no pun intended, and indeed two periods at the end of a sentence would look like a typo...comprende? And why is Times Roman so important? Why can't writers employ some of our other, lesser-used fonts, like Goofy Deluxe, Namby-Pamby Extra Narrow, or Gone Fishin'?" In fact, there is movement toward alternate punctuation; consider the New Punctuation and Suicide Cult in southern Texas, whose credo is "Why not try some new and different types of punctuation and then kill ourselves?" Notice how these knotty epigrams from Shakespeare are easily unraveled:

Every cloud engenders not a storm ☺
Horatio, I am dead ☹

Remembering the Albertus Extra Bold asterisk embargo of several years back, one hopes the crisis is solved quickly, because a life of exclamation marks, no matter how superficially exciting, is no life at all! There are, of course, many other fonts one can use if the crisis continues, but frankly, what would you rather be faced with, Namby-Pamby Extra Narrow or the bosomy sexuality of Times Roman? The shortage itself may be a useful one, provided it's over quickly, for it has made at least this author appreciate and value his one spare period, and it is with great respect that I use it now.

SCHRÖDINGER'S CAT

A cat is placed in a box, together with a radioactive atom. If the atom decays, a hammer kills the cat; if the atom doesn't decay, the cat lives. As the atom is considered to be in either state before the observer opens the box, the cat must thus be considered to be simultaneously dead and alive.

—Erwin Schrödinger's Cat Paradox, 1935

WITTGENSTEIN'S BANANA

A banana is flying first class from New York to LA. Two scientists, one in each city, are talking on the phone about the banana. Because it is moving in relationship to its noun, the referent of the word *banana* never occupies one space, and anything that does not occupy one space does not exist. Therefore, a banana will arrive at JFK with no limousine into the city, even though the reservation was confirmed in LA.

ELVIS'S CHARCOAL BRIQUETTE

A barbecue is cooking wieners in an airtight space. As the charcoal consumes the oxygen, the integrity of the briquette is weakened. An observer riding a roller coaster will become hungry for wieners but will be thrown from the car when he stands up and cries, "Elvis, get me a hot dog."

CHEF BOYARDEE'S BUNGEE CORD

A bungee cord is hooked at one end to a neutrino, while the other end is hooked to a vibraphone. The neutrino is then accelerated to the speed of light, while the vibraphone is dropped off the Oakland Bay Bridge. The cord will stretch to infinite thinness, the neutrino will decay, and the vibraphone will be smashed by the recoiling bungee. Yet an observer standing on the shore will believe he hears Tchaikovsky's second piano concerto performed by Chef Boyardee's uncle Nemo.

SACAGAWEA'S RAIN BONNET

Lewis and Clark are admiring Sacagawea's rain bonnet. Lewis, after six months in the wilderness, wants to wear the rain bonnet, even when it's not raining. Clark wants Sacagawea to keep wearing it and doesn't want to have to deal with Lewis, who conceivably could put on the bonnet and start prancing. However, an observer looking back from the twenty-first century will find this completely normal.

APOLLO'S NON-APPLE NON-STRUDEL

Imagine Apollo running backward around the rings of Saturn while holding a hot dish of apple strudel. In another universe, connected only by a wormhole, is a dollop of vanilla ice cream. The vanilla ice cream will move inexorably toward the wormhole and be dumped onto the strudel. Yet wife swapping is still frowned upon in many countries.

JIM DANDY'S BUCKET OF GOO

Jim Dandy is placed in a three-dimensional maze. His pants are tied at the ankles and filled with sand. Every time he moves to another dimension of the maze, he must review the movie *Titanic*, first with one star, then with two stars, then with three, while never mentioning its box office take. If he completes the maze, he will then be able to untie his pantlegs, and the spilling sand will form a bowling trophy that Jim Dandy may take home.

THE FEYNMAN DILEMMA

A diner says to a waiter, "What's this fly doing in my soup?" And the waiter says, "It looks like the backstroke." Yet if the same scene is viewed while plunging into a black hole at the speed of light, it will look like a Mickey Mouse lunch pail from the thirties, except that Mickey's head has been replaced by a Lincoln penny.

GEORGE HAMILTON'S SUN LAMP

George Hamilton is dropped into an empty rental space next to a tanning salon on the dark side of the moon. There is no way into the salon except through an exterior door, but if George exits, it could mean dangerous exposure to deadly gamma rays. George could open his own tanning salon by tapping the phone lines from next door and taking their customers. And yet George is cooked when he exits the rental space while using a silver-foil face reflector.

CATCHING UP ON MY READING

I was skimming the *Times Literary Supplement* when I glanced at an article about Jane Austen, and I realized I had never actually flipped through *Sense and Sensibility.* This was a shortcoming in my literary education that I could no longer afford, especially with the new company I was keeping. I went to the bookstore and picked up a copy—heavy! I was in the classics section, so I added *Jane Eyre* (never read it—weird), *Animal Farm,* and *Lord of the Flies.* I felt especially noble, as every one of them is a movie, which could have saved me a ton of time.

I opened *Sense and Sensibility* and leafed through the pages back to front. So far I liked it. I read the last paragraph. It was good! Made me want to read the title page. I was intrigued, so I went to the front. It read, *Sense and Sensibility.* Honestly, I was slightly bored. "Sense and . . ." was fine. But, I don't know, it just slowed down for me at "Sensibility." I laid it aside.

I picked up *Animal Farm.* I was interested, but the book seemed short. Almost too short to even riffle through. If I'm going to read a book, I want it to be long. I want it to unfold methodically, like a gas station map. But what a surprise: I read the last paragraph—man, this is a great book! I couldn't wait to read the title. I creased open the first few pages and folded them back, ready to nestle in to one of the classics. I read, "Animal . . ." and fell asleep. About twenty minutes later, I woke up and read, "Farm." Zonk. Out for two hours. I'm wondering, is it me? Or are these books not what they're made out to be?

I then picked up *Lord of the Flies*. It felt, honestly, lightweight. Was it the paper, or the content? I think the test of a good book is when you can randomly open it to any page and find oneself interested. So, I casually flipped open the cover and landed on the first set of endpapers. There was no writing on them, just a few small designs. I know that Golding is a great writer, etc., but really, this is no way for him to begin a book. With nothing? No words at all? Just some designs? Please, I'm a reader. When I sit down with a book, I want to read it, not look at it.

Somehow, though, I felt satisfied. I had riffled, browsed, or thumbed through three classic books. That night, at my book club meeting when asked who had read that month's book, I raised my hand up halfway.

A thought occurred to me. Perhaps today's writers are every bit as good as the so-called greats. Perhaps, when I go to the bookstore, I should do more than go to the new releases section and absorb them by waving my hand over them. Perhaps I should give them a chance and read a one-line synopsis.

SHOPGIRL

for Allyson

CONTENTS

When you work in the glove department at Neiman's, you are selling things that nobody buys anymore. These gloves aren't like the hardworking ones sold by L.L. Bean; these are so fine that a lady wearing them can still pick up a straight pin. The glove department is adjacent to the couture department and is really there for show. So a lot of Mirabelle's day is spent leaning against the glass case with one leg cocked behind her and her arms splayed outward, resting on her palms against the countertop. On an especially slow day she might lean over the case on her elbows—although this position is definitely not preferred by the management—and stare through the glass at the leather and silk gloves that lie on display like pristine, just-caught fish. The overhead lights reflect in the glass countertop and mingle with the gray and black of the gloves, resulting in a mother-of-pearl swirl that sometimes sends Mirabelle into a shallow hypnotic dream.

Everyone is silent at Neiman's, as though it were a religious site, and Mirabelle always tries to quiet the tap-tap-tapping of her heels when she walks across the percussive marble floors. If you saw her, you would assume by her gait that she is in danger of slipping at any moment. However, this is the way Mirabelle walks all the time, even on the sure friction of a concrete sidewalk. She has simply never quite learned to walk or hold herself comfortably, which makes her come off as an attractive wallflower. For Mirabelle, the high point of working at a department store is that she gets to dress up to go to work, as the Neiman's dress code encourages her to be a model of precision and style. Her problem, of course, is paying for the clothes that she favors, but one way or another, helped out by a generous employee discount and a knack for mixing and matching a recycled dress with a 50 percent off Armani sweater, she manages to dress well without straining her budget.

Every day at lunchtime she walks around the corner into Beverly Hills to the Time Clock Café, which offers her a regular lunch at a nominal price. One sandwich, which always amounts to three dollars and seventy-five cents, a side salad, and a drink, and she can keep her tab just under her preferred six-dollar maximum, which can surge to nearly eight dollars if she opts for dessert. Sometimes, a man whose name she overheard once—Tom, she thinks it is—will eye her legs, which show off nicely as she sits at a wrought iron table so shallow it forces her to angle them out into the aisle. Mirabelle, who never takes credit for her attractiveness, believes it is not she he is responding to but rather something independent of her, like the lovely line her fine blue skirt makes as it cuts diagonally across the white of her thigh.

The rest of the day at Neiman's sees her leaning or bending or rearranging, with the occasional odd customer pulling her out of the afternoon's slow motion until 6:00 P.M. finally ticks over. She then closes the register and walks over to the elevator, her upper body rigid. She descends to the first floor and passes the glistening perfume counters, where the salesgirls stay a full half hour after closing to accommodate late buyers, and where by now, the various scents that have been sprayed throughout the day onto waiting customers have collected into strata in the department store air. So Mirabelle, at five-six, always smells Chanel number 5, while someone at five-two is always treated to the heavier Chanel number 19. This daily walk always reminds her that she works in the Siberia of Neiman's, the isolated, landlocked glove department, and she wonders when she will be moved around in the hierarchy to at least perfume, because there, in the energetic, populated worlds of cosmetics and aromatics, she can get that which she wants more than anything: someone to talk to.

Depending on the time of year, Mirabelle's drive home offers either the sunny evening light of summer or the early darkness and halogen headlights of winter in Pacific standard time. She traverses Beverly Boulevard, the chameleon street with elegant furniture stores and restaurants on one end and Vietnamese shops selling mysterious packaged roots on the other. In fifteen miles, like a Monopoly game in reverse, this street dwindles in property value and ends at her second-story apartment in Silverlake, an artists' community that is always bordering on being dangerous but never quite succeeding. Some evenings, if the timing is right, she can climb the outdoor stairs to her walk-up and catch LA's most beautiful sight: a Pacific sunset cumulating over the spread of lights that flows from her front-door stoop to the sea. She then enters her apartment, which for no good reason doesn't have a window to the view, and the disappearing sun finally blackens everything outside, transforming her windows into mirrors.

Mirabelle has two cats. One is normal, the other is a reclusive kitten who lives under a sofa and rarely comes out. *Very* rarely. Once a year. This gives Mirabelle the feeling that there is a mysterious stranger living in her apartment whom she never sees but who leaves evidence of his existence by subtly moving small, round objects from room to room. This description could easily apply to Mirabelle's few friends, who also leave evidence of their existence, in missed phone messages and rare get-togethers, and are also seldom seen. This is because they view her as an oddnik, and their failure to include her leaves her alone on many nights. She knows that she needs new friends but introductions are hard to come by when your natural state is shyness.

Mirabelle replaces the absent friends with books and television mysteries of the PBS kind. The books are mostly nineteenth-century novels in which women are poisoned or are doing the poisoning. She does not read these books as a romantic lonely hearts turning pages in the isolation of her room, not at all. She is instead an educated spirit with a sense of irony. She loves the gloom of these period novels, especially as kitsch, but beneath it all she finds that a part of her identifies with all that darkness.

There is something else, too: Mirabelle can draw. Her output is small in quantity and size. Only a few four-by-five-inch drawings are finished in a year, and they are infused with the eerie spirit of the mysteries she reads. She densely coats the paper with a black waxy crayon, covering everything except the image she wants to reveal, which appears to be floating up through the blackness. Her latest is a rendering of a crouching child charred stiff in the lava of Pompeii. Her drawing hand is sure, trained in the years she spent acquiring a master of fine arts degree at a California college while incurring thirty-nine thousand dollars of debt from student loans. This degree makes her a walking anomaly among the perfume girls and shoe clerks at Neiman's, whose highest accomplishments are that they were cute in high school. Rarely, but often enough to have a small collection of her own work, Mirabelle gets out the charcoals and pulls the kitchen lamp down low, near the hard surface of her breakfast table, and makes a drawing. It is then properly fixed and photographed and stowed away in a professional portfolio. These nights of drawing leave her exhausted, for they require the full concentration of her energy, and on those evenings she stumbles to bed and falls into a dead sleep.

On a normal night, her routine is very simple, involving the application of lotion to her body while chattering to the visible cat, with occasional high-voiced interjections to the assumed kitten under the sofa. If there were a silent observer, Mirabelle would be seen as a carefree, happy girl who is preparing for a night on the town. But in reality, these activities are the physical manifestations of her stillness.

Tonight, as the evening closes, Mirabelle slips into bed, says an audible good night to both cats, and shuts her eyes. Her hand clicks off the lamp next to her, and her head fills with ghosts. Now her mind can wander in any landscape it desires, and she makes a nightly ritual of these waking dreams. She sees herself standing on the edge of a tropical lagoon. A man comes up from behind her, wraps his arms around her, buries his face in her neck, and whispers, "Don't move." The image generates a damp first molecule of wetness between her legs, and she presses her bladed hand between them, and falls asleep.

In the morning, the dry food that had been laid out in a bowl the night before is now gone, more evidence of the phantom cat. Mirabelle, sleepy eyed and still groggy, prepares her breakfast and takes her Serzone. The Serzone is a gift from God that frees her from the immobilizing depression that would otherwise surround her and seep into her body like a poisonous fog. The drug distances the depression from her, although it is never out of sight. It is also the third mood elevator that she has tried in as many years. The first two worked, and worked well for a while, then abruptly dropped her. There is always a struggle as the new drug, which for a while has to be blended with the old one, takes root in her brain and begins to work its mysterious chemistry.

The depression she battles is not the newly acquired symptom of a young woman now living in Los Angeles on her own. It was first set in the bow in Vermont, where she grew up, and fired as a companion arrow that has traveled with her ever since. With the drug, she is generally able to corner it and keep it separate from her daily life. There are black stretches, however, when she is unable to move from her bed. She takes full advantage of the sick days that are built into her work allowances at Neiman's.

In spite of her depression, Mirabelle likes to think of herself as humorous. She can, when the occasion calls, become a wisecracker and buoyant party girl. This mood, Mirabelle thinks, sometimes makes her the center of attention at parties and gatherings. The truth is that these episodes of gaiety merely raise her to normal, but for Mirabelle the feeling is so exceptional that she believes herself to be standing out. The power at these parties remains with the neurotically spirited women, who attract men whose need it is to tame them. Mirabelle attracts men of a different kind. They are shyer and more reticent. They look at her a long time before approaching, and when they do find something about her that they want, it is something simple within her.

JEREMY

At twenty-six, Jeremy is two years younger than Mirabelle. He grew up in the slacker-based LA high school milieu, where aspiration languishes and the lucky ones get kick-started in their first year of college by an enthused and charismatic professor. He had no college dreams and hence no proximity to the challenge of new faces and ideas—he currently stencils logos on amplifiers for a living—and Jeremy's life after high school slid sideways on an imperceptibly canted icy slope, angling away from center. It is appropriate that he and Mirabelle met at a Laundromat, the least *noir* dating arena on earth. Their first encounter began with "Hey," and ended with a loose "See ya," as Mirabelle stood amidst her damp underwear and jogging shorts.

Jeremy took Mirabelle on approximately two and a half dates. The half date was actually a full evening, but was so vaporous that Mirabelle had trouble counting it as a full unit. On the first, which consisted mainly of shuffling around a shopping mall while Jeremy tried to graze her ass with the back of his hand, he split the dinner bill with her and then, when she suggested they actually go inside the movie theater whose new neon front so transfixed Jeremy, made her pay for her own ticket. Mirabelle could not afford to go out again under the same circumstances, and there was no simple way to explain this to him. The conversation at dinner hadn't been successful either; it bore the marks of an old married couple who had very little left to say to each other. After walking her to her door, he gave her his phone number, in a peculiar reversal of dating procedure. She might have considered kissing him, even after the horrible first date, but he just didn't seem to know what to do. However, Jeremy does have one outstanding quality. He likes her. And this quality in a person makes them infinitely interesting to the person who is being liked. At the end of their first date, as she stepped inside her apartment and her hand was delivering the door to its jamb, there was a slight pause, and they exchanged a quick look of inexplicable intent. Once inside, instead of forever losing his number in her coat pocket, she absentmindedly stuck it under her phone.

Six days after their first date, which had cut Mirabelle's net worth by 20 percent, she runs into Jeremy again at the Laundromat. He waves at her, gives her the thumbs-up sign, then watches her as she loads clothes into the machines. He seems unable to move, but speaks just loudly enough for his voice to carry over twelve clanking washing machines, "Did you watch the game last night?" Mirabelle is shocked when she later learns that Jeremy considers this their second date. This fact comes out when at one abortive get-together, Jeremy invokes the "third date" rule, believing he should be received at second base. Mirabelle is not fooled by any such third date rule, and she explains to Jeremy that she cannot conceive of any way their Laundromat encounter, or any encounter involving the thumbs-up sign, can be considered a date.

This third date is also problematic because after warning Jeremy that she is not going to pay half of its cost, she is taken to a bowling alley and forced to pay for her own rental shoes. Jeremy explains that bowling shoes are an article of clothing, and he certainly can't be expected to pay for what she wears on a date. If only Jeremy's logical mind could be applied to astrophysics and not rental shoes, he would now be a honcho at NASA. He does cough up for dinner and several games, even though he uses discount coupons clipped from the newspaper to help pay for it all. Finally, Mirabelle suggests that if they have future dates, he should take her phone number, call her, and they could do free things. Mirabelle knows, and she lets this be unspoken, that all free things require conversation. Sitting in a darkened movie theater requires absolutely no conversation at all, whereas a free date, like a walk down Hollywood Boulevard in the busy evening, requires comments, chatter, observations, and with luck, wit. She worries that since they have only exchanged perhaps two dozen words between them, these free dates will be horrible. She is still willing to go out with him, however, until something less horrible comes along.

Jeremy's attraction to Mirabelle arises from her passing similarity to someone he had fallen in love with in his preadolescent life. This person is Popeye's girlfriend, Olive Oyl, whom he used to swoon over in a few antique comic books lent to him by his uncle. And yes, Mirabelle does bear some similarity, but only after the suggestion is made. You would not walk into a room, see her for the first time, and think *Olive Oyl*. However, once the idea is proposed, one's response might be a long, slow, "Ahhhh . . . yes." She has a long thin body, two small dark eyes, and a small red mouth. She also dresses like Olive Oyl, in fitted clothes—never a fluffy, girly dress—and she holds herself like Ms. Oyl, too, in a kind of jangle. Olive Oyl has no breasts, but Mirabelle does, though the way she carries herself, with her shoulders folded, in clothing that never accentuates her curves, makes her appear flat. All this in no way discounts her attractiveness. Mirabelle is attractive; it's just that she is never the first or second girl chosen. But to Jeremy, Mirabelle's most striking resemblance to Olive Oyl is her translucent skin. It recalls for him the pale skin of the cartoon figure, which was actually the creamy paper showing from underneath.

Jeremy's thought process is so thin that he has the happy consequence of always ending up doing exactly what he wants to do at all times. He never complicates a desire by overthinking it, unlike Mirabelle, who spins a cocoon around an idea until it is immobile. His view of the world is one that keeps his blood pressure low, sweeping the cholesterol from his relaxed, freeway-size arteries. Everyone knows he is going to live till age ninety, although the question that goes begging is, "For what?"

Jeremy and Mirabelle are separated by a hundred million miles of vacuum space. He falls asleep at night in blissful ignorance. She, subtly doped on her prescription, time-travels through the terrain of her unconscious until she is overcome by sleep. He knows only what is right in front of him; she is aware of every incoming sensation that glances obliquely against her soft, fragile core. At this stage of their lives, in true and total fact, the only thing they have in common is a Laundromat.

MIRABELLE'S FRIDAY

She stands over the glove counter, and from her secluded outpost looks far across the hall toward the couture department. When the view is reversed, and a couture girl bothers to glance toward her, Mirabelle looks like a puppy standing on its hind legs, and the two brown dots of her eyes, set in the china plate of her face, make her seem very cute and noticeable. But pointlessly so, at least today. For this Friday is what she has termed the day of the dead, when for some reason—usually an upcoming Beverly Hills dress-up event—the couture department fills with women who are unlikely to notice the slender girl standing at one end of their hallowed hall. They are the Wives of Important Men.

The metamorphosis most wanted by the wives of important men is that they become important in their own right. This distinction is achieved by wielding power over any and all and is characterized by an intense obsession with spending. Without spending, there would be thirty to sixty empty hours per week, to be filled with what? And not only is there the spending itself, there is the organization and management of spending. There is hiring and firing, there is the discernment of what the spending needs to be on, and there is the psychological requirement that the husband be proud of the wife's spending. The range of the spending can go from clothes and jewelry to furniture and lighting, dishes and flatware, and catalog seeds and firewood. Sometimes it is fun to spend economically. Of course, economic spending is not intended to save money, but is a practice of ethics.

Along with the desire to spend comes a desire to control what is coming back at them from the mirror. Noses are bobbed into a shape that nature never knew, hair is whipped up with air and colored into a metallic-tinted meringue, and faces are pulled into death masks. The variety of alteration is vast, except when it comes to breasts. Breasts are made large only—and in the process misshapen—and the incongruity of two bowling balls on an ironing board never seems to bother anyone. In Beverly Hills, young men, searching for young women who remind them of their face-lifted mothers, are stranded and forlorn in a sea of natural-looking twenty-five-year-olds.

Today, as she stares hypnotically at these tribal women, one clear thought emerges to Mirabelle: how different this place is from Vermont. Then, out of the idleness that permeates every day at work, she shifts her weight from one foot to the other. She scratches her elbow. She curls her toes, then angles her leg to give her calf a stretch. She flicks a paper clip several inches across the glass of the countertop. She runs her tongue along the back of her teeth. Footsteps approach her. Her automatic response is to straighten up and look like she is an ever-ready force in the Neiman's sales team, for the sound of footsteps could mean *supervisor* as likely as *customer*. What she sees, though, is a rare sight in the fourth-floor glove department. It is a gentleman, looking for a pair of ladies' dress gloves. He wants them gift wrapped and could they do that? Mirabelle nods in her professional way, and then the man, sharply dressed in a dark blue suit, asks her opinion on which is the finest pair. Being a sharp dresser herself, she actually does have an opinion on the merchandise she offers, and she gives him the lowdown on smart glove purchasing. There is some conversation about what and who they are for. The man gives her some embarrassed, vague answers, often the case when men shop for women, and in response she suggests that the silver satin Diors are the best. He purchases the gloves with a credit card, smiles at her, and leaves. Mirabelle watches him walk away. Her eyes go to his shoes, which she understands and knows something about, and her inner checklist gives him full marks in all categories. Mirabelle catches herself in the countertop mirror, and realizes she has blushed.

There are a few late browsers that day, and they punctuate the tedium like drops from a Chinese water torture. Six o'clock, and she is down the stairs rather than the elevator, which can become clogged at closing time, and out onto the main floor. Several customers linger at the fragrance counter, a few in cosmetics, surprisingly light for a Friday. Mirabelle thinks the salesgirls in these departments overuse their own products, especially the lipstick. With their inclination toward the heavy application of a greasy burgundy, they look like Man Ray's disembodied lips floating over a landscape of boxed perfumes.

It is six-fifteen and pitch dark on the drive home down Beverly Boulevard. It is drizzling rain, which causes the traffic to move like sludge in a trough. Mirabelle wears her driving glasses as she grips the wheel with both hands. She drives in the same posture as she walks, overly erect. The glasses give her a librarian quality—before libraries were on CD-ROM—and the '89 Toyota truck she drives indicates a librarian's salary, too. The rain splashes on the roof and Garrison Keillor intones on the radio, creating a warm, fireside feeling in this unlikeliest of circumstances. All this coziness sends her into a little ache and she swears that she will find someone tonight to hold her. This is an extremely rare decision for Mirabelle. The last time she was even mildly promiscuous was in college, when it was the thing to do and she was feeling her bohemian oats. She decides that when she gets home, she will pick up the phone and call Jeremy.

SLEEPING WITH JEREMY

In calling Jeremy, Mirabelle knows that she is making a devil's bargain. She is offering herself to him on the outside chance that he will hold her afterward. She feels very practical about this and vows not to feel bad if things don't work out. After all, she tells herself, she isn't really involved with him emotionally or otherwise.

For Mirabelle, there are four levels of being held. The first, and highest, is the complete surround: He will wrap his arms around her and they will spoon as he whispers how beautiful she is and how he had been transported to another plane. The odds of this particular scenario unfolding from the youthful Jeremy are slim, in fact, so slim that they could slip out the door without opening it. There are, however, other levels of holding that for tonight would suit Mirabelle just fine. He could lie on his back and she would rest her head on his chest, while one of his arms holds her tight. Third best would involve Mirabelle lying on her back with Jeremy alongside her, resting one hand on her stomach while the other plays with her hair. This position requires the utterances of sweet nothings for her to be fully satisfied. She is aware he has barely spoken a sentence that didn't end in "you know" and then trail off into a mumble since they have been together, which makes the appearance of these sweet nothings unlikely. But this could be a plus, as she can interpret his mumbles any way she wants—they could be impeccably metered love sonnets for all she knows. In fourth position, they are lying on their backs, with one of Jeremy's legs resting languidly over one of hers. This is the minimally acceptable outcome, and involves a commitment of extra time on his part to compensate for his lack of effort.

Coming out of her reverie, which was so specific she could have been a lawyer formulating a contract, she picks up the phone and dials. It rings a few times, and the thought that he might not be home sends a shiver of relief through her. However, just as she is about to hang up, she hears the clatter of the phone being picked up. But instead of hearing his voice on the other end of the line, she hears what she makes out to be Jeremy's TV set filtered through the telephone. She keeps waiting for him to say hello or yeah or anything, but the TV continues. Eventually she hears him walk across the room, open the refrigerator, walk back to the living room, and flop himself down on the sofa. She can hear the laugh track of the television, and a few moments later, Jeremy's vociferous nose-blow. Mirabelle stands there, wondering what to do. She thinks surely he will see that the phone is off the hook. Surely he heard it ring. Now committed, she worries that if she hangs up, she will get a busy signal for the rest of the night, as it is already clear that the phone doesn't lie in the path from sofa to refrigerator, and that that particular route is the only one he will be taking that evening. She presses the speakerphone button and cradles the handset. Jeremy's TV is still present in her house, but at least she has her hands free.

In her small apartment she is never far from the speaker, and she gets out of her shoes and takes off her skirt and blouse, throws on an oversize shirt, and walks around in her underwear. She completes several chores that are left over from the weekend. A couple of times she screams Jeremy's name into the speakerphone, with no effect. She catches herself midscream and thinks how it must look and swears never to do something so humiliating again for any reason, ever, in her life. Then, with the TV still squawking through the telephone, she sits back on her futon and starts to laugh. The laughter causes a few tears to appear at the corners of her eyes, which sets her off on a crying jag. Then a hiccup gets her laughing again, causing her to fall over sideways on the futon, and at one point she is actually laughing and crying at the same time. She finally burns herself out and after resting for several minutes, goes over to hang up the phone. As she is about to press the hope-ending speaker button, she hears Jeremy's footsteps coming across the hardwood, increasing in volume, clearly walking toward the phone. Her hand hesitates. Then she hears the touch-tones of Jeremy dialing the phone. She waits. Suddenly his voice says, "Hello?" Mirabelle picks up the receiver and says hello back.

"It's Jeremy."

She responds, "Do you know who this is?"

"Yeah. Mirabelle."

"Did you just call me?" she says.

"Yeah."

It is at this point that she understands that Jeremy knows nothing about what has occurred over the last twenty minutes. He thinks he has just walked over to the phone and dialed

Mirabelle, and she has answered. Mirabelle decides not to ask what happened, afraid that they might enter an infinite loop of explanation. It turns out that he wants to see her that night, so she invites him over and everything falls into place.

Jeremy arrives thirty minutes later and leans against the wall with a slouch so extreme that he appears to have left his skeleton at home. He carries a paper bag containing some vile-smelling fast food, which she immediately recognizes as French fries because the grease stains have made the bag transparent. But at least he's had the courtesy to bring something over, an offering to her for what he is about to receive. Mirabelle hastily constructs a fifth option, which is to get him to simply snuggle with her, so she won't have to put out. This option is hastily discarded because it is the afterglow she wants, and she begins her process of seduction wordlessly, naturally set into motion by the blush of her skin, and the willingness of her legs, and her readiness, which she knows a man can sense. If only Jeremy were a man.

Instead, she practically has to spell it out for him. Mirabelle longs to have a *Wuthering Heights* movie on tape that she can throw on, point to, and say, "Get it?" Jeremy's instinct for love-making turns out to be all right, once the idea has been writ large by Mirabelle with oils and candles and incense and music and some two-bit scotch that neither has drunk before in their lives. But because Jeremy fails to fully arouse Mirabelle, her ardor never peaks and she therefore fails to fully arouse Jeremy, resulting in a see-saw condom battle that is waged this way: She works Jeremy up into a nice little erection, but by the time they get the condom on, with its dulling insulation, there is a loss of stature. Mirabelle is not exactly relaxed and wet either, which causes

Jeremy's penis to bend and fold as he tries to enter her. Then they have to start all over. She removes the condom, works him up by kissing him on the mouth and stimulating him with her hand. Occasionally, the cat jumps on the bed and bats at Jeremy's testicles as if they were hanging balls of catnip, causing a disastrous delay in the action. Then they struggle with the condom and the cycle begins all over again. This goes back and forth several times, with Mirabelle rubbing him vigorously, then flopping herself speedily back on the bed and spreading her legs instantly, until the inevitable happens again. There are three entities in the room that night, Mirabelle, Jeremy, and an animated penis that expands and contracts like an anesthesiologist's oxygen balloon. Finally, his youth prevails, and Jeremy successfully dwells for a few moments in paradise. The life expectancy of a radial tire: This is the thought that races through Jeremy's mind as he tries to delay his impatient ejaculation.

Eventually, the deed is done and all the thrashing comes to an end. The two of them, not touching, lie there in the shadowy darkness, and everything is silent. The distance between them is awful. But then Jeremy snakes his arm around her shoulder, sliding it just under her neck, and reaches his hand up into her hair and gently pulls her near him. He brings his body in close. Mirabelle feels her perspiration mix with his, and she likes that. Her senses refocus on the room and she smells the vanilla of the candle. She sees herself in the bedroom mirror and notices that her breasts have filled from his touch, clumsy as it was, and she likes the way she looks. Jeremy glistens in the low light. Mirabelle stares into her own eyes. And she feels all right.

Then a terrible thing happens. Jeremy uncoils himself from Mirabelle, stands in his underwear at the foot of the bed, and begins to talk. More than talk. Orate. And worse, he talks in a way that requires Mirabelle to respond with periodic uh-huhs. What he talks about is a range of topics loosely categorized under the heading Jeremy. He talks about Jeremy's hopes and dreams, his likes and dislikes, and, unfortunately, a lot about amplifiers. This includes Jeremy's perspective on amplifiers, and cost analysis, and how his boss's view of amplifiers contrasts with his own. This is the topic that requires most of the uh-huhs, and only by staring straight at him and forcing her eyes open a tiny bit wider can Mirabelle appear somewhat interested. Unlike his penis, his stream of chatter does not rise and fall. It maintains a steady flow, and Mirabelle begins to question whether William Jennings Bryan still deserves to be known as America's most grandiose public speaker. Jeremy booms and bellows opinions and observations for a full thirty minutes, none of which ever leave the sphere of Jeremy. Eventually, he sputters out, returns to bed, and puts an arm around her, in a position yet uncategorized by Mirabelle that gives her some more of what she wants. Even with the ignoble flailing that took place earlier, she feels as though she has been wanted, and she knows he has thought her beautiful, and that she has made him happy and energized him, and that the expenditure of his energy on her has sent him into a deep, deep sleep.

THE WEEKEND

It is 9:00 A.M., and for the second time that morning Mirabelle is awake. The first time was two hours earlier when Jeremy slipped out, giving her a kiss goodbye that was so formal it might as well have been wearing a tuxedo. She didn't take it badly because, well, she couldn't afford to. She also is glad he's gone, not looking forward to the awkward task of getting to know a man she's already slept with. A little eye of sunlight forms on her bed and inches its way across her bedspread. She gets up, mixes her Serzone into a glass of orange juice, and drinks it down as though it were a quick vodka tonic, fortifying herself for the weekend.

Weekends can be dangerous for someone of Mirabelle's fragility. One little slipup in scheduling and she can end up staring at eighteen hours of television. That's why she joined a volunteer organization that goes out and builds and repairs houses for the disadvantaged, a kind of community cleanup operation, called Habitat for Humanity. This takes care of the day. Saturday night usually offers a spontaneous get-together with the other Habitat workers in a nearby bar. If that doesn't happen, which this night it doesn't, Mirabelle is not afraid to go to a local bar alone, which this night she does, where she might run into someone she knows or nurse a drink and listen to the local band. As she sits in a booth and checks the amplifiers for Jeremy's signature stencil, it never occurs to Mirabelle to observe herself, and thus she is spared the image of a shy girl sitting alone in a bar on Saturday night. A girl who is willing to give every ounce of herself to someone, who could never betray her lover, who never suspects maliciousness of anyone, and whose sexuality sleeps in her, waiting to be stirred. She never feels sorry for herself, except when the overpowering chemistry of depression inundates her and leaves her helpless. She moved from Vermont hoping to begin her life, and now she is stranded in the vast openness of LA. She keeps working to make connections, but the pile of near misses is starting to overwhelm her. What Mirabelle needs is some omniscient voice to illuminate and spotlight her, and to inform everyone that this one has value, this one over here, the one sitting in the bar by herself, and then to find her counterpart and bring him to her.

But that night, the voice does not come, and she quietly folds herself up and leaves the bar.

The voice is to come on Tuesday.

MONDAY

Mirabelle awakes to a crisp LA day with an ice-blue chill in the air. The view from her apartment is of both mountains and sea, but she can see it only by peering around her front door. She feeds the cats, drinks her potion, and puts on her best underwear—although it is unlikely anyone will see it today, unless someone bursts in on her in a changing room. She had a nice day on Sunday because her friends Loki and Del Rey finally called back and invited her to brunch at one of the outdoor cafés on Western. They gossiped and talked, about the men in their lives, about who is gay and who isn't, about who is a cokehead and who is promiscuous, and Mirabelle regaled them with the Jeremy story. Loki and Del Rey, who were obviously named by parents who thought they would never not be infants, told similar stories and the three of them cried with laughter. This buoyed Mirabelle, as it made her feel normal, like one of the girls. But when she went home that night, she wondered if she had betrayed Jeremy just a little, as something in her believed that he would not have told about their exploits over lunch with the guys. This little thought was a tiny foundation for Jeremy's tiny redemption, and it made part of her like him, if only just a little bit.

* * *

The day at Neiman's plods along, made extra viscous by the promise of a fun evening with the girls. It is Art Walk night in Los Angeles, when the town's galleries stay open and offer free "wine" in plastic cups. Most of the local artists will be spotted tonight at one gallery or another. Mirabelle's own talent for drawing makes her feel comfortable and confident in this group, and having recently placed several of her recent works with a local gallery makes her feel that she is an equal.

Finally, six o'clock. Tonight's walk past cosmetics and perfumes has special fascination for Mirabelle. Being Monday, there are no customers and the she-clerks are idle. Mirabelle notices that when they are in motion, these perfume nymphs look breezy and alive, but when they are still, their faces become vacuous and frozen, like the Easter Island of the Barbie Dolls. She then retrieves her truck from the dungeon of the parking garage, slams it into fourth, does her thing down Beverly Boulevard, and is home in nineteen minutes.

At eight minutes after seven, she hits the Bentley Gallery on Robertson where she is to meet Loki and Del Rey. The joint is not jumping but at least it has enough people in it so everyone is forced to raise his voice, giving the impression of an event. Mirabelle wears her tight maroon knee-length skirt over low heels and a smart white sweater that sets off her blunt-cut nut-brown hair. Loki and Del Rey aren't there yet, and Mirabelle has the annoying thought that they might not show. It wouldn't be the first time they'd left her stranded. As Mirabelle never shows her distress, it is assumed she is fine in all circumstances and Loki and Del Rey never figure that their failure to show is really a thoughtless ditching. She gets a plastic cup of wine and does the thing she always does at these openings, something so odd that it sets her apart from all the others. She looks at the paintings. It is a perfect disguise. Holding the wine dictates her posture so she doesn't have to think about where to put her hands, and the pictures on the walls give her something to focus on while she stands sentry for Loki and Del Rey.

Twenty minutes later, the two women appear, snag Mirabelle, and head two blocks up to Fire, an avant-garde gallery—or at least one that thinks it is. This opening has more of the party atmosphere that everyone is looking for, and some of the revelers have even spilled out onto the street. For Loki and Del Rey, this is the warm-up party for their final landing spot, the Reynaldo Gallery. The Reynaldo Gallery, representing the big-money artists, is set in the heart of Beverly Hills and needs the prettiest girls and the most relevant people to populate its openings. After getting enough alcohol at the Fire Gallery to hold them—they know the bar at Reynaldo's will be impossible—they drive into Beverly Hills, park and lock, and cross Santa Monica Boulevard to the gallery. They push their way in and finally slink through the crowd and into the heart of the matter. The party needs a volume control but there isn't one, and everyone would be straining to hear each other except they are all talking simultaneously. Loki and Del Rey decide to brave the tumult at the bar, and at first Mirabelle hangs loosely by them, but eventually the chaos separates them and she finds herself in the vacant narrow rim that circles the room between the crowd and the paintings. Only this time, she is less intent on the pictures and more intent on who and what is going on in the room. In a sea of black dresses, she is the only one wearing any color, and she is the only one wearing almost no makeup, including the men. Her eyes scan the room and spot several celebrities dressed in the latest nomad/wanderer fashion and several very handsome men who have learned to give off the seductive impression that they would be consummate fathers.

One in particular attracts her, one who looks as though he does not know he is handsome, who looks slightly lost and like an actual working artist, whom she dubs the Artist/Hero. She sees him notice her staring, so she skillfully moves her eyes away, where she sees the absolute opposite of his pleasure-giving radiance. It is Lisa. Lisa is one of the cosmetics girls at Neiman's, and Mirabelle can't help but recoil. What is she doing here? This girl does not belong at an art opening. She is on Mirabelle's turf, where an eked-out high school diploma is just not enough. But Lisa holds her own, and here's why. Lisa, thirty-two, can be counted among the very beautiful. She has pale red hair that hangs in soft ringlets against skin that has never seen the sun. She is slender and oval faced, with shapely legs that pin themselves into a pair of provocative high heels. Her breasts, though augmented, rise above the line of her dress and seem to beckon, successfully keeping the secret of their artificiality. She appears sunny, a quality that Mirabelle can call upon only for special occasions.

Lisa wears high heels even to lunch. In fact, she overdresses for every occasion, because without the splash that her wardrobe makes, she believes that no man will like her. She fools herself by thinking that in some way she is pursuing a career by making important contacts with successful men, and that the sex is tangential. The men play along, too. They think that she likes them, that her hand jobs aren't bought. These men allow her to feel interesting. After all, aren't they listening to every word? She believes that only in her body's perfection can she be loved, and her diet focuses on five imaginary pounds that keep her from perfection. This weight anxiety is not negotiable. No convincing makes it otherwise, even from the most sincere of her lovers. Lisa's idea of fun is going to bars and taunting college men by making them believe she is available. A good time is measured by the abandon she can muster; the more people who are crammed into a Mercedes heading to a party in the hills, the more valid the proof that she is having fun. At thirty-two, Lisa does not know about forty, and she is unprepared for the time when she will actually have to know something in order to have people listen to her. Her penalty is that the men she attracts with her current package see her only from a primitive part of their brains, the childish part that likes shiny objects that make noise when rattled. Older men looking for playthings and callow boys driven by hormones access these areas more easily than the clear-thinking wife seekers of their late twenties and early thirties.

There is a third category of men who like Lisa. These are the men whose relationship to women is driven by obsession and possession, and she will be the ugly target of more than one such man in her lifetime. To Mirabelle, the idea of being an object of obsession is alluring and represents a powerful love. She fails to understand, however, that men become obsessive over beautiful women because they want no one else to have them, but they fall in love with women like Mirabelle because they want a certain, specific part of them.

Mirabelle turns away, refusing to be intimidated by this crimson Marilyn. She is staring at the surface of a picture when she overhears voices in conversation next to her. Two men are trying to remember the name of the artist who uses words in his paintings. She quickly discounts the New York artist Roy Lichtenstein, as the conversation is on the wrong coast.

"Are you thinking of Ed Ruscha?" says Mirabelle.

Both men snap their fingers and begin a conversation with her. After two sentences, she realizes that one of them is the impossibly perfect, lost-looking Artist/Hero that she had spotted only minutes earlier. This provokes a certain eloquence in Mirabelle, at least in terms of LA art, which she keeps up on through gallery visits and reviews, and she presents herself to the Artist/Hero as formidable and worthwhile and smart. So Mirabelle doesn't flinch when Lisa walks over, and she accepts her into the group, giving Lisa a generous benefit of the doubt. She isn't really aware that Lisa has already taken over the conversation with her flashing eyes and pointed laughter, and has slipped in between the cracks of the Artist/Hero's brain with the subliminal suggestion that she likes him, and likes him a lot. By appealing to his absolute worst side, Lisa eventually dominates him, and later the Artist/Hero is seen taking her phone number. Mirabelle is not affected by a man's failure to approach her, as her own self-deprecating attitude never allows the idea that he would in the first place.

Mirabelle does not understand that Lisa's maneuvering is not directed at the Artist/Hero but at her. She does not see that she has been defeated by an opponent who wants to see the glove girl in retreat. In Lisa's mind, she has once again established the superiority of the cosmetics department over the glove department, and by association, the couture department itself.

Mirabelle participates in several other good conversations throughout the rest of the evening. The thoughtful nature of these exchanges makes her feel that this is exactly what she should be doing and that she couldn't be doing anything better. After being dropped off by Loki and Del Rey at gallery number one to get her car, she drives home, her head filled with recapitulations of the evening's finest arguments in order to find out whom she agrees with most.

She slides into bed at exactly midnight, after amusing herself by feeding her cats with a bowl that says "Good Dog." She closes her eyes and taps her finger on the lamp switch. A few moments later, as she lies quiescent in her bed, she feels something terrible enter her brain, stay for a fleeting second, then disappear. She does not know what it is, only that she doesn't like it.

TUESDAY

It is now the middle of November, and the smell of Thanksgiving is in the air, which means that Christmas is waiting in the oven. The increasing number of browsers forces Mirabelle to forgo her favorite position of leaning over the counter on her elbows, something she can get away with only when there are absolutely no customers in sight.

She skips lunch because she has to visit Dr. Tracy to renew her Serzone. He asks her several questions that she correctly answers, and he writes out the prescription. She feels relieved, as her supply seems dangerously low, and is glad to have the prescription overlap by several weeks instead of four days. She worries about unforeseen events like the doctor suddenly having to be out of town, leaving her short. She also renews her prescription for birth control pills, which she takes not especially for birth control but more for her period, which in the past has been uncomfortably nonperiodic.

The rest of the day at Neiman's seems like purgatory, as tonight there is no Art Walk to look forward to; there is nothing. Her plan is to read, perhaps draw, or find an old movie on the classics channel. Maybe she can put together a phone call between herself and Loki. By the end of the day, her lower back aches and her soles burn. She prepares the register a full half hour before closing, knowing there are to be no more customers. All she has to do when six o'clock strikes is press one button and the register is closed. She is satisfyingly out minutes early, and in her car.

The streets of Los Angeles are starting to crowd regularly now in anticipation of the holidays. Even the shortcuts are clogging up, and Mirabelle uses the time in her car to plan the coming months. From Christmas Day to New Year's Day she will be in Vermont visiting her parents and brother. She already has the airplane ticket, bought months earlier at a phenomenally low price. Thanksgiving is still open, and she knows it needs to be filled. To be alone on Thanksgiving is a kind of death sentence. The year before it had been commuted at the last minute by a visiting uncle who happened to be in town and who invited her to a small gathering at a restaurant, and then hit on her. This had been a particularly grim evening, as the dinner company had also been lousy. They were a stuffy group who were having steaks and cigarettes, who were united by a rare quality on this day: They were thankless. The seldom-seen uncle on the mother's side then drove her home, high as a kite, and under the pretense of fingering her pretty necklace, laid the back of his hand on her blouse, then asked if he could come in. Mirabelle looked at him dead in the eye and said, "I'll tell Mom." The uncle feigned ignorance, drunkenly walked her to the door, returned to his car, put it in reverse when he intended drive, and fled.

Mirabelle suddenly finds herself home, having no recollection of any detail of the drive from Neiman's. She parks her car in the spot reserved for her in the clapboard garage. She lugs a bag of groceries, her purse, and an empty cardboard box up the two short flights to her insular apartment, which hangs in the air over the city of Los Angeles. At the top of the steps, she fumbles for her key, and as she sets the bag down to get it from her purse, she sees a package propped against her front door. It is wrapped in brown paper, sent parcel post, and sealed with wide packing tape. It is the size of a shoebox.

Mirabelle uses her shoulder to jar open the front door, which has been sticking slightly from the week's rain. She puts the package on the kitchen table, double dips some dry cat food into a bowl, and checks her messages. She has none. She sits at the kitchen table and with a pair of scissors cuts off the package's dull outer wrapping. Inside is a pale red gift box, wrapped in an expensive white bow. She cuts the ribbon, opens the box, and sees a layer of tissue paper. There is a small note card on top, sealed in an envelope. She holds it up and studies the front, then turns it over and looks at the back. There are no revealing marks or brand names.

She parts the tissue, and inside is the pair of silver satin Dior gloves that she sold last Friday. She opens the note and reads, "I would like to have dinner with you." The bottom of the note is signed, Mr. Ray Porter.

She leaves the box on the kitchen table in a disarray of tissue. She backs out of the room and circulates nervously through the apartment, returning several times to the vicinity of the box. She doesn't touch it for the rest of the night, and she is afraid to move it because she does not understand it.

MONOTONY

Mirabelle's ambition is about one-tenth of 1 percent of what would be called normal. She has been at Neiman's almost two years without moving one inch forward. She considers herself an artist first, so her choice of jobs is immaterial. It doesn't matter to her if she is selling gloves or repainting apartments, as her real work is done in the evening with artists' crayon. Thus, she has zero ambition in these day jobs, and she tends to leave it to chance when it comes to getting and changing them. She is not aware that some people fight like alley cats for desirable situations. She presents a résumé, fills out an application, waits, and finally makes a call to see if she got the job. Usually, a confused secretary will answer and say that the position had been filled weeks ago. This aimlessness in presenting herself contributes to her feeling of being adrift.

She is, however, motivated to visit galleries and present her drawings to the dealer. She has established a relationship with a gallery on Melrose who will take a drawing and, six months later, sell it. But this does not produce enough outside income to set her free from being a shopgirl, and the inspiration required for a drawing exhausts her. And besides, she actually enjoys the monotony of Neiman's. In a way, when she is standing at the glove counter with her ankles crossed, she is perfect, and she likes the sense of accomplishment she gets from repetitive work.

So when she runs into Lisa at the Time Clock Café, she finds herself sitting across from her exact inverse. It is as though her every thought, trait, and belief had been turned inside out and decorated with a red wig. Lisa, idly curious about Mirabelle in the same way that a cat is curious about a dust mote, invites her to sit down. But Lisa's curiosity has talons, and she knows that in her approach to the glove girl, she must appear to be as benign as Mirabelle in order to casually extract the maximum information. If Immanuel Kant had stumbled across this luncheon after his noon Beverly Hills shrink appointment, he would have quickly discerned that Lisa is all phenomena and no noumena, and that Mirabelle is all noumena and no phenomena.

Mirabelle has a knack for discussing the mundane, at length. In this sense, she is Jeremy's blood brother. She can talk about glove storage nonstop. How her own ideas of storage are much better than the current system at Neiman's, and how her supervisor had become upset when he discovered that she had re-sorted them by size rather than color.

Today, she talks to Lisa about the intricacies of working at Neiman's, including the personality aberrations of her many bosses. This takes a while, as practically everybody at Neiman's is her boss. These comments come from Mirabelle not as criticisms but as polite observations, and Lisa is confounded because she cannot discern an ulterior motive. Tom, the regular lunchtime Mirabelle-watcher, has spotted the two of them and is having his sandwich while trying to read their lips. He has also noted that Mirabelle's legs are slightly ajar, creating a wee wedge of a sight line right up her skirt. This keeps him at the lunch table a little longer than usual, ordering a dessert loaded with calories that he cannot afford. However, the periodic shifting of her legs creates a high anticipation in Tom that generates a compensating calorie-eating adrenaline. Suddenly, Lisa takes over with a breast-jutting arch of her back, and Tom's resulting caloric burn puts him back at even.

Mirabelle tells her about the mysterious glove delivery, mistakenly bringing Lisa into her inner circle of one. Lisa keeps an amused look on her face, but inside, this story sickens her, because it happened to someone else. Lisa can only think that this man's footpath had fallen just outside her orbit. She then gives Mirabelle advice that is so foreign to her that Mirabelle actually cannot comprehend it. The advice ranges from playing aloof, to looking up his credit card information, to returning the package unopened. The topic so excites Lisa that she forgets all her careful posturing with Mirabelle and blurts out her deepest and darkest:

"When a man approaches me, I know exactly what he wants. He wants to fuck me."

Mirabelle's back tenses and her legs reflexively close, prompting Tom to ask for his check.

"And if I like him, I fuck him a lot, until he gets addicted. Then I cut him off. That's when I've got him."

This is the extent, depth, and limit of Lisa's philosophy of life. Mirabelle stops midsip and stares at her as though looking at the first incoming pictures of an alien life-form. She maneuvers the topic elsewhere, a few exchanges are made on other subjects, allowing Lisa to land on earth, and they finally split the check.

Lisa has taken all her intelligence and intuition, which is not meager, and focused a Cyclops eye on the soap operas of four square blocks of Beverly Hills, closing off her life. Mirabelle's outward-facing intelligence is gathering information, which is still coalescing and might not gel for several years. But she has always felt that her thirties were going to be her best decade, and since she is still lingering in her twenties, there is no hurry.

The rest of the day, and the next two days, rock to a lethargic syncopation. Moving too slowly to be counted by the clicks of a metronome, time is measured by lunches and closing times and customers, broken only by an occasional surge of curiosity about the intriguing package and her memory of the man who sent it. The mornings are sometimes busy, relatively, even producing a few sales in between the browsers, who generally scan the glove department as though they were looking into a stereoscope to view some antique photo. Mirabelle's brain activity, if it could be plotted by an electroencephalogram, drops to a level that most scientists would interpret as sleep. On Thursday afternoon, she is brought back to life by an enthusiastic Japanese tourist who can't believe she has lucked upon the glove department, and who buys twelve pairs to be shipped back to Tokyo. This involves taking the address, calculating mailing costs, wrapping, and inscribing gift cards. The woman wants the Neiman's name on everything, including the gift cards, and Mirabelle calls around the store to find the old variety with the name embossed. In Mirabelle's world, this is the equivalent of running the three-minute mile and it leaves her worn out, complaining, and ready for an early night. Finally completing the last detail of the global transaction, she thanks the woman with the one foreign word that Neiman's requires its employees to know: *arigato*. The woman picks up her receipt, slips it in her shopping bag already crammed with previous purchases, cheerfully thanks Mirabelle with an engaging bow, and walks backward twelve steps until she turns and heads west toward couture. This is when Mirabelle becomes aware of a man standing to one side, who turns her with his voice. "So will you have dinner with me?" And then, because Mirabelle doesn't reply, he says, "I'm Mr. Ray Porter."

"Oh," she says.

"I'm sorry if I was forward," he says, "but I'm practicing a new philosophy of life that involves being more forward."

While Mr. Ray Porter explains his presumption in sending her the gloves, Mirabelle sizes him up. Her intuition, rusty as it is, absorbs him in one single clinch, and no alarm bells sound. He is dressed for business—though without a tie—in a sharp blue suit. In every respect, size, height, weight, he is normal. Again, she checks out his shoes, and they are good. It is then she first notes, in the split second that has passed, that he is probably fifty years old.

Mirabelle forgets all about Lisa's complicated instructions and simply asks Mr. Ray Porter who he is. He tells her he lives in Seattle, but has a place in Los Angeles because he does business here. She asks if he is married and he says he is four years divorced. She asks if he has children and he says no. The question she does not ask, but is foremost in her mind, is "Why me?" As these subtle negotiations proceed, it is determined that they will meet at a Beverly Hills Italian restaurant at 8:00 P.M. on Sunday. She declines to have him pick her up, and Mr. Ray Porter easily agrees. This keeps her free of all worries she might have about going to dinner with a total stranger: She can drive herself home. He has an easygoing manner that relaxes her, and they exchange exactly one semihumorous line each. Both glance around to see if anyone is watching, and he seems to be aware that employees should not be seen chatting up customers, although vice versa is common. He backs away with an aside that he will need a map to find the glove department again, then he says something about how glad he is that she is coming to dinner, then he faintly blushes and disappears around a corner.

MR. RAY PORTER

There is nothing too mysterious about Ray Porter, at least in the usual sense of the word. He is single, he is kind, he tries to do the right thing, and he does not understand himself, or women, or his relationships with women. But there is one truth about him that can be said of a man who asks a woman to dinner before he has ever exchanged one personal word with her. Mr. Ray Porter is on the prowl. He does not know Mirabelle, he has only seen her. He has responded to something visceral, but that visceral thing is only in *him*, not between *them*. Not yet. He only imagines the character that unites her clothes, her skin, and her body. He has imagined the pleasure of touching her, and imagined her pleasure at being touched. She is a feminine object that tweaks him at his animal best.

Extrapolating from Mirabelle's wrist, he understands the terrain of her neck, he can imagine the valley of her breasts, and he knows that he can lose himself in her. He does not know his further intent with her, but he is not trying to get what he wants at any expense. If he thinks he would harm Mirabelle, he would back away. But he does not yet understand when and how people are hurt. He doesn't understand the subtleties of slights and pains, that it is not the big events that hurt the most but rather the smallest questionable shift in tone at the end of a spoken word that can plow most deeply into the heart. It seems to him that nothing in the world of relationships proves to be generally true, that nothing follows a logical sequence, and that his search for cohesion leaves him empty of answers.

His attraction to Mirabelle is not random. He is not out and about sending gloves all over the city. His action is a very spontaneous and specific response to something in her. It may have been her stance: At twenty yards she looks off-kilter and appealing. Or maybe it was her two pinpoint eyes that made her look innocent and vulnerable. Whatever it was, it started from an extremely small place that Mr. Ray Porter never could have identified, even under torture.

His small house and furnishings in the Hollywood Hills tell one simple story; Mr. Ray Porter has money. Enough that there is never a problem, any time or any place. The giveaway is the lighting. Little hidden spotlights alternate with warm lamplight, creating a soft yellow glow that implies "decorator." The house, being a second home used for business only, isn't strewn with personal objects. It is this anonymous quality, like being on vacation in an expensive hotel room, that makes you want to take off your clothes and start fucking. In the bedroom, there is a fireplace opposite an antique four-poster bed, with books piled high on either side, all nonfiction and all stuck with three or four bookmarks. The house focuses on the view of the city that Mirabelle is so casually denied.

Neatness, which the house displays on every coffee table and bathroom countertop, is not a characteristic of Ray Porter.

Neatness is a quality that he admires, however, and therefore buys, by hiring an obsessive maid.

In the garage are two cars. One is a gray Mercedes, the other a gray Mercedes. The second gray Mercedes is used for hauling his sports equipment, so he won't have to load and unload every time he feels like a bike ride. A rack hangs incongruously on the back, and in the trunk are rollerblades and a tennis racquet. When Mr. Ray Porter tempts fate by exercising in traffic, he wears a twenty-first-century version of armor, which offers similar protection but not the romance: a beaked plastic bicycle helmet, elbow pads, and knee pads. He dons this getup whether it is winter or summer, meaning for three months out of the year he wears large black knee pads while wearing shorts. When he is astride his bicycle, tooling down a Seattle main street and sporting this outfit, the only visible difference between Ray Porter and an insect is his size.

The kitchen is the most unused part of the house. Since his divorce, the kitchen has become like a middle-American living room: for display only. Usually he eats out, alone, or tries to fill the evening with friends or a date. These dinner dates, which function mainly to fill a vacuum of loneliness between the hours of 8:00 P.M. and 11:00 P.M., cause him more grief than a year of solitary confinement. For even though they look like dates and sound like dates, and sometimes result in a liaison, to him they aren't exactly dates. They are friendly evenings that sometimes end in bed. He incorrectly assumes that whatever is his understanding of the nature of one of these evenings, his date is thinking it, too, and he is deeply shocked and surprised when one or another of these women, whom he has seen over the past several months and with whom he has had several sexual encounters, actually believes they are a couple.

These experiences have caused him to think very hard about what he is doing and where he is going. And the result of all this thinking is that he now understands that he doesn't know what he is doing or where he is going. His professional life is fine, but romantically he is an adolescent, and he has begun an education in the subject that is thirty years overdue.

His interest in Mirabelle comes from the part of him that still believes he can have her without obligation. He believes he can exist with her from eight to eleven and enter a private and personal world that they will create that will cease to exist in the off hours or off days. He believes that this world will be independent of other worlds he might create on another night, in another place, and he has no intention of allowing it to affect his true quest for a mate. He believes that in this affair, what is given back and forth will be exactly even, and that they will both see the benefits they are receiving. But because he picked Mirabelle out by sight alone, he fails to see that her fragility, which he smelled and sensed and is lured by, runs deep in her heart and is part of her nature, and cannot be separated out for him to fuck.

Ray and Mirabelle have similar ideas about wardrobe. He likes a stylish look, though modified for his age. He has lots of suits in striking fabrics, and his money enables him to make mistakes and get rid of them. His closet has his LA clothes, which means he can travel to and from Seattle with no suitcase. The drawback to this arrangement is that he will arrive at his home, see a shirt he hasn't worn for three months because he has been out of town, and feel like he is slipping into a new look. His LA friends have an entirely different view. They see that he is wearing exactly the same shirt he wore last time.

His aversion to carrying luggage, eventually causing him to buy a house in LA so he could stock it with clothes, comes from a mildly obsessive belief in the management of his time. Standing at a baggage carousel, being jostled by passengers while scanning a hundred similar bags for a number to match his claim check, which is always misplaced, does not sit well with his logic. He has no time to be exasperated, especially if he can solve it by buying a house. This need for efficiency dictates many of his daily movements. In setting out his breakfast, he will accomplish all the tasks that occur on one side of the kitchen before starting the tasks that originate on the other side of the kitchen. He will never cross to the refrigerator for orange juice, cross back to the cabinet to get cereal, and cross back again to the refrigerator for milk. This behavior is rooted in a subterranean logic a robot programmed for efficiency might display.

Luckily, this behavior is not entirely fixed in him. It escalates during busy times and wanes during evenings and vacations. However, it translates itself into other forms so removed from the original impulse as to be unrecognizable. His attraction to Mirabelle is an abstraction of this behavior: Her cleanliness and simplicity represent an economy that other women do not have.

Ray Porter parks the car and enters the house in his most efficient way. The garage door is closed by remote control while he is still in the car gathering his papers. This saves him pausing at the kitchen door to press the indoor remote. This little abbreviation is second nature to him. Once inside, he sets his papers down in the kitchen, even though they need to be in his office. He will take them later when he has to go to the office via the kitchen. There is no point taking them to the office now, as he needs to beeline to the living room to make reservations for Sunday.

He sits on the sofa, turns on the TV news, starts reading the newspaper, and simultaneously starts dialing the restaurant. He makes reservations at a small but sweet place in Beverly Hills that is on his speed dial. La Ronde, an Italian restaurant with a French name (the culinary complement to Rodeo Drive's French chateaus with Italian porticos tacked on), offers quiet and privacy to an older man who walks in with a twenty-eight-year-old who looks twenty-four. Then, after attending to the TV and browsing the newspaper until he is absolutely bored, he begins to do what he does best. He raises his head toward the view, which by now has transformed into sparkling white dots of light set in black velvet, and begins to think. What goes through his head are streams of logical chains, computer code, if-then situations, complicated mathematical structures, words, non sequiturs. Usually, these chains will unravel into loose ends or pointless conclusions; sometimes they will form something concrete, which he can sell. This ability to focus absolutely has brought him millions of dollars, and why this is so can never be explained to normal people, except to say that the source of his money is embedded deeply in a software string so fundamental that to change it now would be to reorganize the entire world. He is not filthy rich; his contribution is just a tiny line of early code that he had copyrighted, and that they had needed.

Tonight, these mental excursions get him nowhere and finally he gets on the phone to a Seattle girlfriend, or as he really thinks of it, a woman in Seattle who is a friend he is having sex with who is fully informed that they are never going to be a couple. "Hey." "Hey," she says back. "What're you doin'?" she says. "Staring at my knees. Nothing much. You okay?" She replies, "Yeah." He senses she's upset over something and digs deeper. She responds by spilling out her woes—mostly work related—and he listens attentively, like John Gray in a nest of divorcées. The conversation finally runs out of gas. "Well, this is good, this is a good talk. So I'll see you when I get back. By the way, I think I should tell you I have a date on Sunday. Thought I should let you know." "All right, all right," she counters, "you don't have to tell me everything, you just don't, just keep it to yourself." "Shouldn't I tell you, though?" he replies. "Shouldn't I?"

She tries to explain, but can't. He tries to understand her, but can't. He knows this is an area where logic doesn't apply and he just listens and learns the lesson for next time.

This information, this anecdotal training in the understanding of women, gleaned from experience, books, advice, and mostly hurt feelings being hurled at him, fits in no previous compartment of his experience, and he has created a new memory bank just for housing it all. This memory bank is in a jumble. It is not coherent. Occasionally his more rational mind will venture in and try to arrange it, like a boy cleaning his room. But just when everything is in its place, the metaphor holds and two days later the room is a mess.

These encounters are probably the most formative experiences of his early fifties. He is collecting pleasures and pains, gathered from his relationships with ballerinas and librarians, decent females without the right pheromones, and nutballs. He is like a child learning what is too hot to touch, and he hopes all this experience will coalesce into a philosophy of life, or at least a philosophy of relationships, that will transform itself into instinct. This fact-finding mission, in the guise of philandering, is necessary because as a youth he failed to observe women properly. He never sorted them into types, or cataloged their neuroses so he could spot them again from the tiniest clue. He is now taking a remedial course in fucking 101, to learn how to handle the diatribes, inexplicable antics, insults, and misunderstandings that seem to him to be the inevitable conclusion to the syllogism of sex. But he is not aware that he is on such a serious mission: He thinks he is a bachelor having a good time.

That night, he calls a restaurant that delivers and he orders an appropriate meal for a fifty-year-old. This is easier in LA than in Seattle, as most take-out food in any part of the country involves fat and cholesterol. In LA, however, it's a snap to order a low-fat veggie burger, or sushi, delivered right to your door no matter how complicated the route to your house. In Los Angeles you can live in the tiniest apartment in the tiniest cul-de-sac with a 1/4 in your address and twenty minutes after placing an order a foreigner will knock on your door bearing yam fries and meatless meatloaf. And if Ray's solitary dinner at home were broadcast on satellite, the world would learn that millionaires, too, eat their dinners out of a white paper bag while standing in the kitchen. Even Mirabelle knows not to do that, as the self-prepared dinner is a great time killer for lonely people, and as much time should be spent on it as possible.

After the food arrives via the smallest car he has ever seen, Ray Porter turns on a small TV in the kitchen and begins channel flipping. At that moment he becomes Jeremy's soulmate; their two hearts beat as one as they eat from a sack and rapidly click their way through the entire broadcast range, with similar timing of the occasional paper rustle and periodic foot shift. They are nearly indistinguishable as they engage in this rite, except that one man stands in the kitchen of a two-million-dollar house overlooking the city, and the other in a one-room garage apartment that the city overlooked. If Mr. Ray Porter knew where to train his telescope, he might even have been able to peer down fifteen miles to Silverlake, right into Jeremy's window, and if Jeremy weren't in an impenetrable stupor, he might even have been able to wave back. And if three lines were drawn, joining the homes of Jeremy and Ray to Mirabelle's wobbly flat, the apex of the triangle would pinpoint the unlikely connection between these two wildly opposite men.

Mr. Ray Porter gets into bed and closes his eyes. He visualizes Mirabelle sitting on his chest, wearing the same simple orange cotton skirt she wore on the day he first saw her. He imagines the skirt draped over his head, so he can see her legs, her stomach, and her white cotton underwear. The lamplight penetrates the skirt and casts an orange glow over everything in his little imaginary tent. A sunset of flesh and fabric, which sends him into an onanistic fit. He is then silent and satiated, with a ghostly image of Mirabelle still lingering in his head. But soon an arbitrary array of untethered words, logical marks, and symbols rushes through his mind, sweeping away everything. Minutes later, his mind is clear and he falls asleep.

DATE

Mirabelle's first dilemma is the valet parker. She can't afford to pay someone three-fifty plus tip to whisk her car away. But parking is restricted and she will have to leave her car several blocks away if she doesn't. She decides it is inelegant to arrive on this first date looking windblown, and she slides the car to the curb and takes the check the valet hands her, praying that Mr. Ray Porter will take pity on someone who is currently carrying only eight dollars in cash. The car vanishes and she pulls on the restaurant door but it won't open, then she pushes, then realizes she is trying to open the hinged side, then she pushes on the correct side, then pulls, and the door finally gives way. She enters a darkened little cave, certainly not the hip spot in town, and sees a jury of older diners wearing gold-buttoned blazers and big shirt collars. There is a saving grace, though. A young actor from a hot television show, Trey Bryan, sits in the corner with several producer types, and his presence saves the place from being complete squaresville. The maître d', a once dashing Italian, approaches her with a "Buona sera," and Mirabelle wonders what he said.

"I'm meeting Mr. Ray Porter," she chances.

"Ah. Nice to see you again. Right this way."

He leads Mirabelle past several red leather banquettes and around a lattice. In a booth too large for two people sits Ray Porter. He is looking down at a notepad and doesn't see her at first, but he looks up almost immediately. The incandescent lighting, filtered through the red lampshades, warms everybody up, and to him, she looks better than at Neiman's. He rises to greet her and guides her into the booth, and sits her to his right.

"Do you remember my name?" he asks.

"Yes, and all the exciting times we've had."

"Would you like a drink?"

"Red wine?" she questions.

"Do you like Italian?"

"I'm not sure what I like; I'm still forming," says Mirabelle.

Ray Porter is relieved that he can desire her and like her at the same time. The waiter attends them and Ray orders two glasses of Barolo from the wine list as Mirabelle plays with her spoon.

"So why did you go out with me?" He cascades his napkin open and lays it on his lap.

"I think that's an impolite question." Mirabelle puts the right amount of coy in her voice.

"Fair enough," says Ray Porter.

"So why did you ask me out?" says Mirabelle.

The fundamentally simple answer to that question is rarely spoken on any first date ever. And the real answer doesn't occur to Ray, Mirabelle, or even the waiter. Fortunately, Ray Porter has a logical reply that prevents a silence that would have been awkward for both of them.

"If it's impolite for me, it's impolite for you."

"Fair enough," says Mirabelle.

"Fair enough," says Ray Porter.

And they sit, each in a tiny struggle about what to say next. Finally, Mirabelle succeeds.

"How did you get my address?" she says.

"Sorry about that. I just did, that's all. I lied to Neiman's and got your last name, then one call to information."

"Have you done that before?"

"I think I've done everything before. But no, I don't think I've done that before."

"Thank you for the gloves."

"Do you have anything to wear them with?"

"Yes, plaid shorts and sneakers."

He looks at her, then realizes she has made a joke.

"What do you do?" he asks.

"What do you mean?"

"I mean besides work at Neiman's?"

"I'm an artist. I draw. I can draw."

"I can't draw a line. A sheet of paper is less valuable once I've scribbled on it. What do you draw?"

"Usually dead things."

At this point, Ray Porter imagines an entirely different iceberg beneath Mirabelle's psychic waterline than the one that actually exists.

The wine arrives. The waiter pours it as they sit in silence. When he leaves, they speak again.

She asks him about himself and Mr. Ray Porter tells her, all the while his eyes drifting down the line of her neck to her white starched blouse, which, as she breathes, bellows open and closed. This half inch of space allows him a view of her skin, just above her breasts, which nestles into the white of her bra. He wants to poke his hand in and leave a light, pale fingerprint on her. His glances toward her take place between Mirabelle's own glances toward him, so that these looks to each other are effectively woven together, yet never intercepted by either.

They make it through to the end of the evening, with the conversation lasting just until the check comes, at which point they run out of topics. Then they deal with the business part of the evening, that part where phone numbers are exchanged and hours indicated when it is best to call. Ray Porter gives her his Seattle number as well, the direct line, not the office. As they leave the restaurant, he places his hand on the small of her back in a gesture of assistance as she passes through the door. This is their absolute first physical contact and does not go unnoticed by either's subconscious.

Mirabelle's car comes first, and she troops around to the open door, where she begins to fumble in her purse for a tip. "It's been taken care of," says the valet.

She drives home, not sure of what she is feeling, but filled with what is probably the first truly expensive meal of her life. When she gets home, there is a message from Ray Porter asking her to dinner next Thursday. There is also a message from Jeremy asking her to call him back, that night. Her responsibility gene kicks in, and she phones him, even though it is twenty-five minutes short of midnight.

"Yeah?" Jeremy believes this is a clever way to answer the phone.

"You wanted me to call?" says Mirabelle.

"Yeah. Thanks. Oh, hi. What are you doing?"

"You mean now?"

"Yeah, wanna come over?" says Jeremy.

Mirabelle thinks of Lisa. She wonders how he can be addicted so soon. They hardly did it and she hardly cut it off. One sloppy evening of flaccid sex and Jeremy is begging for another soggy dog biscuit. Lisa's phone must be ringing off the hook. She must have endless messages of coercion on her machine from sad-eyed lovers.

"Come on over," continues Jeremy.

This inquiry reverses every electron in Mirabelle's body, causing her attraction to Jeremy, which was at one time a weak North-South, to become a strong North-North. It is the perfect wrong time for Jeremy to do to Mirabelle what she had done to him—call him up for a quick fix—because, in a sense, she is now betrothed. Her first date with someone who treated her well obligates her to faithfulness, at least until the relationship is explored. She does not want to betray this unspoken promise to Ray Porter. But Mirabelle is polite, even when she doesn't have to be, and she thinks she owes Jeremy at least a conversation. After all, he wasn't *so* awful, and she continues:

"It's too late," she says.

"It's not too late," he counters.

"It's too late for me. I have to get up."

"Come on."

"I can't."

"Come on."

"No."

"It's not too late."

"No."

"Want me to come over there?"

"It's too late."

"I can be over there in ten minutes."

"No."

"Wanna meet somewhere?"

"I can't."

"We could meet somewhere."

"I have to hang up."

"I could come over and then leave early so you could sleep."

Mirabelle convinces Jeremy that no way, not now, not tonight, not ever, is he getting her in bed when it isn't her idea, and finally she gets him off the phone. This incident has sullied the events of the evening, and she has to concentrate to get herself back to her earlier buzz.

She putters around the kitchen, remembering this or that about her dinner with Ray Porter, also noting that this was one of the first evenings in a long time that hadn't cost her anything. She is pleased that she had been her best self, that she had entered a new world and had been comfortable in it. She had given something back to the person who took her out. She had made jokes, she had been wry, she had been pretty for him. She had turned him on. She had listened. And in return, he had put his hand on the small of her back and paid for her parking and bought her dinner. To Mirabelle this exchange seems fair and good, and next time, if he asks, she will kiss him.

Ray Porter's faithfulness ratio is somewhat different. While he also had a good time, meaning that the evening was charged with little invisible ions of attraction, this does not mean that any devotion is in order at all. What it does mean is that they will have several or many dates, and until something is indicated or promised otherwise, they are independent of each other. But this is such a routine thought for Ray Porter that he doesn't even bother to think it. He had called her from his car phone with an invitation for Thursday not only because he liked her but also because there is a riddle in his mind. Upon reflection, he cannot tell if the surface he glimpsed under Mirabelle's blouse was her skin or a flesh-colored nylon underthing. As he weighs the evidence, he decides that it had to be a nylon underthing, as what he saw was too uniform, too perfect, too balanced in color to be skin. On the other hand, if it *was* her skin, then she possesses his particular intoxicant, a heady milk bath he can submerge himself in, and soak in, and drown in. He knows that this riddle will probably not be solved on Thursday, but without it, there will be no Saturday, which is the next logical step in its solution.

He gets in bed, and instead of letting the streams of data pour through his mind, he lets the symbols of sex form their own strict logic. The white blouse implies the skin which implies the bra which implies her breasts which implies her neck and her hair. This leads to her stomach which necessarily invokes her abdomen which leads to her inner thigh which leads to her panties which leads to a damp line on white cotton that he can press on and gain a millimeter of access to her vagina. This access leads to further access and implies taste and aroma and a unification of his self made possible by the possession of his very opposite. This logical sequence is plotted against a series of intermittent days that spread over several months. The entire formula is a function of whether the square inch in question is skin or nylon, and if it is nylon, what then is the true texture of the square inch hidden beneath it?

GLOVES

Mirabelle strides confidently past the working stiffs on the first floor and heads to her sanctuary on the fourth. She takes the stairs two steps at a time, and oddly, she is in the mood to work. She is even thinking of ways to sell more gloves by laying a few out on the end tables and display cases throughout the store. Then she gets to her department, takes her post, crosses her legs at the ankles, and stands there. And stands there. No management comes by all day for her to spill her idea to. There is more for her to look at, however, as the pre-Thanksgiving nonrush means more people pass by her counter on their way to somewhere else. Lunchtime comes, and she has a definite feeling that she has not moved for three and a half hours.

She decides to take a two-hour lunch. This is accomplished through lying. She explains to her immediate boss, Mr. Agasa, that she has an appointment for a female problem and that she tried to schedule it for another time but that this is the only time the doctor can take her. Mr. Agasa stammers while she adds that things are slow and that she has asked Lisa to keep an eye on the counter, and he nods a concerned okay.

"Are you all right?" he asks.

"I think I'm okay, but I should be checked."

And she leaves the store. Hitting the flats of Beverly Hills, she pops into a yogurt shop on the premise that she can have an entire meal for three dollars, and she takes her brimming cup outside and vacations in the sun on Bedford Drive. In the hard sunlight, her hair shines a deep maroon. She angles her wire chair toward the low-rise that houses all the Beverly Hills shrinks, hoping to spot a few celebrities. This is the building where she goes to renew her medication, so she recognizes a few of the nurses and receptionists who file in and out. Next to her sits a woman so repulsive that Mirabelle has to turn her body uncomfortably so as to edge her out of her peripheral vision. The woman converses on a cell phone while shoveling in contradictory amounts of low-calorie yogurt. Her fat droops over the chair and hides all but its legs. Her hair is brassy from chemicals designed to make it look golden, and her smoker's face has a subtle gray cast. However, what she speaks about on the phone is in fact quite gentle. She is concerned about someone who is ill, which makes Mirabelle squirm a little over her lie to Mr. Agasa. The woman speaks, stops, then after what must have been a long speech by the person on the other end of the line, says,

"Just remember, darling, it is pain that changes our lives."

Mirabelle cannot fathom the meaning of this sentence, as she has been in pain her whole life, and yet it remains unchanged.

Just then she sees the heartthrob Trey Bryan enter the shrinks' building. Trey Bryan is hot as a pistol, which qualifies him for immediate psychoanalytic care. She had seen him once in Neiman's buying what looked very much like doilies for his girlfriend's shoulders. She has witnessed heartthrob shopping many times, and she knows it is a ritual that is very refined. It requires a girlfriend who, if not already famous, is comfortable with becoming famous. She has to look bored, and therein lies the purpose of the shopping trip: The heartthrob must dance around laying gifts at her feet, trying to lift her spirits. Mirabelle could never figure out why the receiver of these gifts is so bored. Mirabelle loves to get gifts.

An important part of the celebrity-couple shopping ritual is that the two shoppers appear exclusive; their world is so extraordinary, so charged, that their movement through the regular, unexclusive world scatters little dewdrops of diamonds. Mirabelle had once waited on such a couple, when she stood in at the Comme des Garçons section, and felt her own transparency. It was as though she were a chalk outline of herself, animated by an inferior life force.

Today, though, with her extra hour and fifteen minutes, and the sun beating down on her in spite of it being November, she decides to visit the competition and check out the glove departments at a few other stores. She can at least empathize with other sad, lost girls who stand in solitude behind their counters. Her first stop is Saks Fifth Avenue on Wilshire Boulevard, where she sees an impression of herself standing vacantly in the lonely distance, hovering over merchandise that no one wants. She says her name and identifies herself by job description, and the clerk is so excited to have someone talking to her that Mirabelle considers offering her a Serzone to level her out.

Next stop is Theodore on Rodeo Drive. This is a hip, sexy store and features gloves so youthful and spirited that Mirabelle longs to deal in them. She can imagine the coolest people coming to her, swapping fashion tips as they try on the merchandise. To take advice from her current customers would be fashion suicide, unless she somehow wanted to be mistaken for fifty.

As she drifts around Beverly Hills, she finds herself a block from La Ronde. This arouses no particular emotional response, it is not "the place where they rendezvoused," but it does make her feel less like an outsider in Beverly Hills. She has actually eaten in one of the actual restaurants, which is what 90 percent of the out-of-towners roaming around this afternoon haven't done. She wanders into the Pay-Less and buys sanitary napkins, because she needs some, and because it will reinforce her lie to Mr. Agasa should he see her purchase.

She goes back to Neiman's, where Lisa tells her that someone has been looking for her. "Who?" asks Mirabelle.

"Well, I don't know, a man."

Mirabelle assumes it is Ray Porter. Perhaps canceling. She will call her message machine at her first break.

"What was he like?" Mirabelle asks Lisa.

"He's a man, over fifty. Normal."

"What else?"

"A little overweight. And he asked for Mirabelle Buttersfield. By name."

Ray Porter is not overweight, she thinks.

"He said he'll come back," adds Lisa, vanishing toward the stairwell.

Mirabelle slides back into her berth behind the counter. She stands there a minute and is suddenly struck by an overwhelming wave of sadness. This causes her to do something she has never done at Neiman's: She pulls out a low drawer in the counter and sits on it for several minutes, until she recovers.

LISA

Lisa Cramer's body is good enough for any man or woman on this planet, but it is not good enough for Lisa Cramer. She believes that she has to be flawlessly pleasing to a man, and that she has to be an expert at fellatio. This talent is fine-tuned and polished through extensive conversations with other women and the viewing of selected "educational" porno tapes. She even once attended a class given by Crystal Headly, a down and going sex-film actress. She is not reluctant to roll out this expertise, either. Within several dates, and sometimes sooner, Lisa will demonstrate this skill to the lucky fella, thus making herself feel that she is the kind of woman any man would want. The men, however, feel confounded by their good fortune. Who is this person who goes down on them so easily? Lisa can only judge her success by the frequency of follow-up phone calls from the men, who are eager to take her to dinner, or a play. The fact that they are willing to take her to a play—low on the list of LA date priorities—demonstrates just how far they are willing to go. Lisa knows it is the sex they are after, but it is sex that is the source of her worth. The more they want it, the more valuable she is, and consequently, Lisa has made herself into a fuckable object.

Lisa is not interested in sex because it is fun. It is the fulcrum and lever for attracting and discarding men. They come to her because of a high hope, an aroma that she gives off, as delicious as baking bread. But when she's done with them, they are limp and drained, and ready for their own bed. She has literally absorbed all their interest, and she wants them to retreat before they discover some horrible flaw in her that will repulse them. Thus Lisa, with all her power, never feels quite good enough for anything beyond her ability to create desire in men. In fact, several prohibitive compulsions appeared in her early twenties that keep her from widening her circle of experience. She cannot get on an airplane. Fear of flying grips her so intensely that she has forever banished air travel as a possibility. She also cannot ingest any medicine of any kind. Not aspirin, not antibiotics, not even a Tums, for fear of losing her mind. And she can never, ever, be alone, without worrying that she will suddenly die.

Lisa has developed a taste for Mr. Ray Porter, even though she has never met him. There is simply a problem that he has selected Mirabelle and not her as his arbitrary object of desire, and Lisa is sure that once he lays eyes on her, correct thinking will occur. Lisa cannot imagine Mirabelle being an expert sex partner. Of course, Mirabelle's lack of advanced training might be exactly why Ray Porter wants her, but this reasoning is way beyond Lisa, because she has no idea that her own sovereignty could be usurped by one square inch of Mirabelle's skin, glimpsed under a starched blouse.

The day Lisa heard Mirabelle blab her story at the Time Clock, a vestigial memory was jarred in her head at the mention of the name Ray Porter. Lisa went home that night, concentrated, and remembered that his name had been in the air a few years ago because he had picked up and had an affair with a shoe clerk at Barneys, the fashionable department store two doors down. Then, when he came in with another woman six months after the affair was over, the salesgirl went berserk and threw two pairs of Stephane Kelian shoes at him, with one falling into an open fish tank, and she was promptly fired. Barneys has a "don't ask don't tell" policy when it comes to customers and employees, and throwing shoes clearly violates the "don't tell." Lisa also remembers that Ray Porter is powerful.

Lisa doesn't see an interposition of herself between Mirabelle and Ray Porter as unethical. In her mind, Mirabelle deserves no one, and Lisa will be doing him a favor. What would Ray Porter do with a leaden Mirabelle lying nude on his bed with her legs open? What would any man do with a soggy girl who can't assert herself, who has a weak voice, who dresses like a schoolgirl, and whose main personality component is helplessness?

SECOND DATE

Before Thursday's date, there are several formal phone conversations between Ray and Mirabelle, which establish that he will pick her up, that the time will be 8:00 P.M., and that they will go to a fun local Caribbean spot that Mirabelle knows called Cha Cha Cha. She is concerned about him seeing her apartment, which, at five hundred dollars a month, is only slightly more than the cost of their meal at La Ronde. She is also concerned that he'll have trouble finding it. The apartment is at the conjunction of a maze of streets in Silverlake, and once found, still requires complicated directions to achieve the door. Down the driveway, second stairway, around the landing . . .

When Thursday comes, Mirabelle speed cleans the apartment while simultaneously dusting herself with powders and pulling various dresses over her head. She settles on a short pink-and-yellow-plaid skirt and a fuzzy pink sweater, which sadly prohibits any of Ray's peeking. This outfit, in combination with her cropped hair, makes her look about nineteen. This look is not meant to appeal to something lascivious in Ray but is worn as a hip mode-o-day that will fit right in at Cha Cha Cha.

Then, finally prepared, she sits in her living room and waits. Mirabelle doesn't have a real sofa, only a low-lying futon cradled in a wood brace, which means that anyone attempting to sit on it is immediately jackknifed at floor level. If a visitor allows an arm to fall to one side, it will land on the gritty hardwood. If he sits with a drink, it has to be put on the floor at cat level. She reminds herself not to ask Ray to sit down.

The phone rings. It is Ray, calling from his car phone, saying he is only a little bit lost. She gives him the proper lefts and rights, and within five minutes, he is knocking at her door. She answers, and both of them scurry in to avoid the harsh glare of the bare hundred-watt porch bulb.

If Mirabelle worried about Ray seeing her apartment, her concern was misplaced. This collegiate atmosphere dislodges a musty erotic memory in him, and he feels a few vague waves of pleasure coursing just below his skin. Mirabelle asks him if he wants anything, knowing that she has nothing to give him except canned clam juice. He declines, but wants to snoop around the apartment, and he pokes his nose into the kitchen, where he sees the college-girl dish rack and the college-girl mismatched drinking glasses and the college-girl cat box. The problem, of course, is that Mirabelle is already four years out of college and has not been able to earn an income at the next level.

She asks him if he wants to sit down, which she immediately regrets, and Ray squats down onto the futon, bending himself into a crouch that for someone over fifty would be considered an advanced yoga position. After the absolute minimum conversation required to make the futon invitation not ridiculous, she suggests they leave. As Ray helps himself up, his body sounds a few audible creaks.

They leave the apartment and walk toward his Mercedes, with all the spontaneity of a prom date. Driving, he stiffly points out the features of the car, including the electric seat warmers, which prompt a few jokes from both of them. At the restaurant, they squirm and talk and wriggle until midway through the entrée, which is a chili-hot fish of some kind prepared to blast the heads off all comers. Things are wooden between them, and would have remained so for the complicated second date, had it not been for an elixir called Bordeaux.

The wine greases things up a bit, and this little relaxation, this gear slippage, makes Ray bold enough to touch her wrist. He says he likes her watch. It isn't much, but it is a beginning. Mirabelle knows that her watch is of a dullness that could arouse no opinion at all, and even though her own eyes have filled with shallow pools of alcohol, she suspects that this contact is not about her watch but about Ray's desire to touch her. And she's right. For as Ray drags the tip of his finger across the back of her hand, he measures the degree of tropical humidity that her skin delivers to his fingertip, and impulses of pleasure leap from neuron to neuron and are delivered to his receptive brain.

He slips his finger and thumb around her wrist. "Now I'm your watch," he says, boyishly. Mirabelle and Ray, not drunk but hovering, are trying to figure some way out of the conversational mess they have gotten themselves in. Ray really wants to be driving around with his hand on her thigh, but he is stuck here in Cha Cha Cha making small talk. Mirabelle wants them to be strolling down Silverlake Boulevard holding hands, getting to know each other, but she needs a closing line about the watch, or they are just going to languish forever in endless circularity.

Then Ray has a brilliant idea. He orders one more glass of wine and suggests they both drink from the same glass. Mirabelle is not a drinker, so Ray downs about two-thirds of it, and right in front of her gets out a pen and calculates his body weight versus the amount drunk minus the food eaten, and announces he is okay to drive. Which leads them to the car.

Which leads them to her porch.

Where he kisses her good night, and presses himself against her, and she feels him thicken against her legs. And neither cares about the harsh porch light. And he says good night. And as he walks away, he thinks that he cannot imagine anything better than their next date.

THEIR NEXT DATE

Mirabelle ends up at Ray's house, where, fully clothed, they get on his bed and she sits on top of him and he unbuttons three buttons on her blouse and he finds the area above her breasts and confirms that it is her skin he had seen at La Ronde and not a flesh-colored underthing. That's all they do, and he drives her home.

THE CONVERSATION

The conversation consists of one involved party telling another involved party the limits of their interest. It is meant to be a warning to the second party that they may come only so close.

Again, Mr. Ray Porter takes Mirabelle to La Ronde. They sit at the same booth and have the same wine, and everything is done to replicate their first dinner, because Ray wants to pick up *exactly* where they left off, with not even a design change in a fork handle to break the continuum. Mirabelle is not sparkling tonight, because she works only in gears, and tonight she is in the wrong gear. Third gear is her scholarly, perspicacious, witty self; second gear is her happy, giddy, childish self; and first gear is her complaining, helpless, unmotivated self. Tonight she is somewhere midshift, between helpless and childish, but Ray doesn't care. Ray doesn't care because tonight is the night as far as he is concerned, the night where everything is going to come off her. And Ray feels compelled to have the Conversation. It is appropriate tonight because of Ray's fairness doctrine: Before the clothes come off, speeches must be made.

"I think I should tell you a few things. I don't think I'm ready for a real relationship right now." He says this not to Mirabelle but to the air, as though he is just discovering a truth about himself and accidentally speaking it aloud.

Mirabelle answers, "You had a rough time with your divorce."

Understanding. For Ray Porter, that is good. She absolutely knows that this will never be long term. He goes on: "But I love seeing you and I want to keep seeing you."

"I do, too," says Mirabelle. Mirabelle believes he has told her that he is bordering on falling in love with her, and Ray believes she understands that he isn't going to be anybody's boyfriend.

"I'm traveling too much right now," he says. In this sentence, he serves notice that he would like to come into town, sleep with her, and leave. Mirabelle believes that he is expressing frustration at having to leave town and that he is trying to cut down on traveling.

"So what I'm saying is that we should be allowed to keep our options open, if that's okay with you."

At this point, Ray believes he has told her that in spite of what could be about to happen tonight, they are still going to see other people. Mirabelle believes that after he cuts down on his traveling, they will see if they should get married or just go steady.

So now they have had the Conversation. What neither of them understands is that these conversations are meaningless. They are meaningless to the sayer and they are meaningless to the hearer. The sayer believes they are heard, and the hearer believes they are never said. Men, women, dogs, and cats, these words are never heard.

They chat through dinner, and then Ray asks her if she would like to come to his house, and she says yes.

SEXUAL INTERCOURSE

With one switch, the lighting in Ray's house goes from post office to jazz nightclub. He starts fantasizing about events that are only moments away. His hours of being with Mirabelle and not having her are about to give way to unrestricted passage. The memory of her sitting on top of him, when he gave a slight squeeze of her breasts through layers of clothing, crystallizes his desire and causes it to crackle.

Ray is lured on not simply because he is a guy and she is a girl. It is just that Mirabelle's body, as he will soon discover, is his absolute aphrodisiac. His intuition sensed it, led him to the fourth floor, and has been reinforced with every whiff and accidental touch. He deduced it from the sight of her, and from the density of her hair and the length of her fingers, and from the phosphorus underglow of her skin. And tonight, he will feel the beginning of an addiction that he cannot break, the endless push and pull of an intoxication that he suspects he should avoid but cannot resist.

He puts both hands on the sides of her neck, but she stiffens. She says it makes her nervous. This takes a bit of undoing, and he breaks from her, makes a few irrelevant comments, and resumes. They get on the bed and dally, a mesh of buttons and buckles and shoes clashing and gnashing. This time, he buries his face in her neck and draws in his breath, inhaling her natural perfume. This gets the appropriate response. A few clothes are removed.

They are relaxed. They are not on a straight path to intercourse, as they take talking breaks, joking breaks, adjusting-the-music breaks. Things intensify, then ebb, then reheat. After a few minutes with Ray exploring the landscape of her bare stomach, he takes a bathroom break and disappears through a doorway.

Mirabelle stands up and methodically takes off all her clothes. Then she lies face down on the bed and smiles to herself. Because Mirabelle knows she is revealing her most secret and singular asset.

Mirabelle's body is not extravagant. It does not flirt, or call out, and that causes men who care about drama to shop elsewhere. But, when viewed at the radius of a king-size bed, or held in the hands, or manipulated for pleasure, it is a small spectacle of perfection.

Ray enters the bedroom and sees her. Her skin looks like it has faint micro lights under it, glowing from rose to white. Her breasts peek out from her sides as they are flattened against the sheets, and the line of her body rises and falls in gentle waves. He walks over and puts his hand on her lower back, lingers there, then rolls her over, kisses her neck, runs his hand down her legs and in between, then touches her breasts, then kisses her mouth while he cups her vagina until it opens, then he eats her, makes love to her, as safely as the moment allows. Again she thinks how different this is from Vermont. Then he faces her away from him and brings his body up next to hers. Mirabelle, fetal, curled up like a bug, receives the proximity of Ray Porter as though it were a nourishing stream. They wake in the morning on either side of the bed.

BREAKFAST

At breakfast, early because she has to get to work, Mirabelle becomes age seven. She sits, waiting to be served. Ray Porter gets the juice, makes the coffee, sets the plates, toasts the bread, and pours the cereal. He gets the paper. Mirabelle is so dependent, she could have used a nanny to hold open her mouth and spoon-feed her the oat bran. She speaks in one-word sentences, which requires Ray to fill the silences with innocuous queries, like an adult trying to break through to a disinterested teenager. In this snapshot of their morning is hidden the definition of their coming relationship, which Ray Porter will come to understand almost two years later.

"You like your breakfast?" Ray decides to try a topic that is in both their immediate vision.

"Yeah."

"What do you usually have for breakfast?"

"A bagel."

"Where do you get bagels?"

"There's a shop around the corner from me."

Total dead end. He starts over.

"You're in great shape."

"Yoga," she says.

"I love your body," he says.

"I have my mother's rear end. Like two small basketballs covered over in flesh, that's what she said once, on a car trip." She emits a little chuckle. Ray gets an odd look on his face, and Mirabelle reads him and she says the only funny thing of the morning:

"Don't worry, she's older than you are."

He wants to reach over and slide his hand in between the opening in the robe that he has lent her. He wants to relive last night, to trace his hands over her breasts, to analyze and codify and confirm their exact beauty, but he doesn't. This will take place on another night with dinner and wine and walking and talking, where the seduction is not assumed, and the outcome undetermined. His sexual motor is already whirring and purring for their next date.

Ray's libido is exactly twenty-four hours ahead of his reason, and tomorrow at this time he will recollect that Mirabelle became quite helpless in the morning and wonder about it (his mind works slowly when it comes to women; he often does not know that he has been insulted, slighted, or manipulated until months or sometimes years later). But since he does not know what to expect from a woman—his four years of dating have not really educated him—he accepts Mirabelle's morning behavior passively. Ray's former experience has been with tough-minded, outgoing, vital, ambitious women, who, when displeased, attack. Mirabelle's dull inertia draws him into a peaceful place, a calm female cushion of acceptance.

He drives Mirabelle home, just in time for her to get ready and be late for work.

JEREMY'S ADULTHOOD

The stencil adheres to the amplifier by manila tape, and Jeremy has learned to evenly apply the paint in one skillful squirt of the airbrush. The Doggone Amplifier Company has a logo of a dog with cartoon speed lines trailing out behind it, with the brand name laid out in a semicircle underneath. It is not easy to fill in the delicate speed lines; some of the earlier paint jobs, before Jeremy joined the ranks, are uneven and sloppy. When he works he crouches in an uncomfortable position that only someone under thirty could bear for long before he would have to seek work elsewhere. His salary is so small that his paycheck could read "so and so *measly* dollars" and no one would contradict. But it's Jeremy's work clothes that tell the story of his line of business: His jeans look like a Jackson Pollock and his T-shirt looks like a Helen Frankenthaler—he is working at the bottom end of the arts.

His boss, Chet, ambles through the warehouse with a client in tow, and their faint muffled voices waft over the stacks of amps to Jeremy's straining ears. He catches a glimpse of them and notices that the client is a sharply dressed businessman, presumably the manager of a rock band trying to make a deal for a ton of amplification in exchange for promotion. The problem in the negotiation, of course, is that Chet only wants to sell amps, and the manager only wants them for free. There is no middle ground. Chet's business is waterlogged and about to sink and he simply can't afford to ship out fifteen thousand dollars' worth of equipment for use months later. The manager slips away with a handshake and Chet stands there as the Mercedes disappears out of the lot through the chain-link fence.

For Christopher Columbus, it was the sailing of three ships that launched his life's great journey. For Jeremy, it is the sight of the sinking Chet watching the ass end of a hundred-thousand-dollar car shrink to a vanishing point down an industrial street in Pacoima. He lays down his spray gun and gets in Chet's field of vision.

"You know what I was thinkin'?"

"What was that?" Chet barely replies.

"You know who hangs out with rock musicians when they're on the road?"

"Who?" says Chet.

"Other rock musicians."

"And?"

"If you had someone on the road with one of the bands using our stuff, someone who looks sharp, like that guy does"—he thumbs in the direction of the dust of the Mercedes—"someone the musicians could relate to, I bet you could sell a lot more amps."

"Do you have someone in mind?"

"Me."

Chet looks at the specter of ineptitude that is standing in front of him. He does not see a sharply dressed businessman; he does not see a clever salesman. But he does see someone he thinks a rock musician could relate to.

"And how much would you like to be paid to do this?" says Chet.

"I could do it for . . ."

Jeremy has never, ever been asked such a question. He has always been told what he would be paid. He can't even fill out an employment form that asks "desired salary," as it confounds him: He always wants to write down one million dollars. But Jeremy has been asked, so he has to answer:

"—nothing."

"What do you mean, nothing?"

"I could do it for . . ."

Jeremy has heard only one financial phrase in his life, and he opens and closes every door in his memory bank until he finds it:

"—a finder's fee."

"And what would you find?" says Chet.

"Bands to use the amps. And if another band starts using the amps because of a band I got to use the amps, I'd like a finder's fee for them, too." And then hastily adds, "of five hundred dollars."

Chet can't see any reason not to take Jeremy up on his proposal. After all, it's a kind of commission basis, an Avon Calling of rock and roll. Since a set of amps can cost fifteen thousand dollars, it will be easy to shoot five hundred Jeremy's way. He doesn't see any problem in finding a new stenciler; in fact, his nephew is just out of high school and is looking for a job in the arts. Jeremy, overestimating his own value, is thinking the exact opposite: "I hope he doesn't realize he's going to have to find someone else to stencil."

Chet accepts the offer but does have to lay out some cash. Two hundred and twenty-two dollars for Jeremy to buy a new suit. Jeremy is enterprising enough to stretch the dough into an extra pair of pants so he won't look like a carbon copy of himself day after day. He then spends five dollars on a copy of *GQ* for his road bible on dressing and finds cool ways to manipulate his own six shirts into a weekly wardrobe. On the road, he learns to scan newsstands and surreptitiously tears pages out of magazines with ideas for style.

Jeremy's first gig is with the only professional band currently using Doggone amplifiers, Age—pronounced *AH-jay*. Age has scored some success with a one-shot hit record and Jeremy offers to accompany them for free in exchange for on-the-road amp repair. He will travel on their bus and bunk with a roadie. His real mission, of course, is to convince some other band, somewhere else, that he is a genius acoustician who has developed the ultimate amplifier and that Doggone amps are the only amps that any hip band can possibly consider.

Three days before Thanksgiving, he boards Age's auxiliary bus for a sixty-city road trip, starting in Barstow, California, heading toward New Jersey, and ninety days later, in a masterpiece of illogical routing, ending in Solvang, California.

THANKSGIVING

Ray and Mirabelle's subsequent date after the night of their consummation is as good as the first, but Ray will be out of town on Thanksgiving, so Mirabelle is forced to rely on her unreliable friends. She speaks to Loki and Del Rey several days before, who say they are going to a backyard feast in West Hollywood, but they don't know the address yet and will call her when they get it so she can come. Several days before, she lays out her clothes for the occasion so she won't accidentally wear them too soon and have nothing to wear on the big day. Mirabelle's real ache comes from not being with her family, but it is either Thanksgiving or Christmas, and Christmas is the better and longer stretch during which to get away. Because of her unimportance to Neiman's, she swings it so she can get a full five days off, assisted by a big lie that her brother's psychiatrist is going on vacation and the whole family is needed during the holidays to keep him straight. Mirabelle delivers this plaint to Mr. Agasa with a slight cry in her voice that says she is about to break down in tears. The genuine sympathy Mr. Agasa shows for Mirabelle's perfectly healthy brother embarrasses her, especially when he volunteers several book titles that link good mental health with exercise, forcing Mirabelle to dutifully write them down and file them in her purse.

On Thanksgiving morning, Mirabelle wakes with dread. She worries that there might be no call from Loki or Del Rey, which wouldn't be the first time they'd let her down and not thought twice about it. She can't dump them as friends because she absolutely needs even the slipshod companionship they give her. They are also her only source of party info, as she has been ostracized as a loner by the Neiman's girls. She waits till 10:00 A.M. to make calls to them both, leaving messages on their machines, asking for the address of the Thanksgiving dinner. At this point, Mirabelle foresees a disastrous day ahead of her unless one of these two flakes calls her with the address. First, she has no cash. Second, even if she did, she knows that everything is shut tight on Thanksgiving, except the classic diner that she would have to dig out of the Yellow Pages and perhaps drive to downtown LA to find. She opens her refrigerator and sees a Styrofoam box containing a skimpy half sandwich she had rescued uneaten from a lunch two days ago. Horrified, her brown irises narrow in on this leftover, which she sees as her potential Thanksgiving dinner.

She goes for a walk on the vacant, empty street in front of her house, hoping when she returns to see a flashing red light on her answering machine. There is absolutely nothing stirring in the short blocks around her house. She can hear activity, the slam of a car door, voices chatting, a dog barking, but these sounds are distant and disembodied. She passes the schoolyard near her apartment and hears the clanking of a chain, swinging in the breeze against a metal pole. She sees not a person.

By the time she angles her way back and up the stairs to her apartment, it is noon. From across the room, she can read that the light is not flashing, is not signaling an end to her worry. She goes back outside and repeats her thirty-minute walk.

This time, she calculates. She calculates the time it will take for Loki or Del Rey, once they retrieve the message, to actually call her. Once home, they will probably play the message within the first ten minutes of arrival. There might be other messages on their machines to return, there might be other things to do. This means that it will be a half hour from the playback to her phone call. Mirabelle knows that her walk is just a half hour long, and using a calculus discerned from Ray Porter, figures that there is going to be no new call on her machine when she gets back. So she takes a sideways turn and extends her walk by ten minutes.

When she gets home, she jiggles the door open and sees—out of the corner of her eye, not wanting to betray to herself her own anxiousness—the red light of her machine blinking at her in syncopation. She waits a minute before playback, occupying herself with a made-up kitchen chore. It is Jeremy, calling from the road, vaguely wishing her a happy Thanksgiving and simultaneously canceling out the thoughtfulness of his call by boasting that he's using the phone for free.

Mirabelle sits on her futon, knees to her chest, and sinks her head over. Her foot taps impatiently on the floor as the clock ticks over, first an hour before the party is to start, then an hour after the party is to start, then it rolls upward to 4:00 P.M., when darkness begins to creep around the edges of her windows. She gets out her drawing paraphernalia and during the next hour fills in a background of oily black and leaves the eerie, floating nude image of herself in white relief.

The phone rings. Any call will be good on this deadly day. As it rings, she glares at it, momentarily getting even with the caller for the delay, then snatches up the phone and listens.

"Hi. What are you doing?" It's Ray Porter.

"Nothing."

"Are you going somewhere for Thanksgiving?"

"Yes."

"Can you cancel it?" says Ray.

"I can try." She amazes herself with this answer. "Where are you?"

"Right now I'm in Seattle, but I can be there in three and a half hours."

Ray has felt at 4:00 P.M. what Jeremy once felt at midnight: the desire to be swimming in Mirabelle. Except that the distance is shorter from Seattle to Los Angeles than it is from Jeremy's to Mirabelle's when two people want exactly the same thing. Ray has a plane standing by, at a mere nine thousand dollars, and by the time she has hung up the phone he is out the door.

In the hours between the phone call and Ray's arrival, Mirabelle's body chemistry changes hourly, and sometimes a flash picture of deepest love coming her way bursts upon her consciousness. Mr. Ray Porter, twenty-eight thousand feet up, sees her two bright pink nipples resting on top of her cushiony flesh. But somewhere, as diverse as these two images are, Ray and Mirabelle's desire intersects, and within a narrow range, they are in love on Thanksgiving Day.

* * *

Ray brings airplane food for two, which on the private service he uses isn't bad. Shrimp, lobster, fruit dessert all wrapped in Saran. They nestle on her bed with their feast spread around them, candles burning, and he tells her how beautiful she looks and how much he loves to touch her, and later, Mirabelle takes out the gloves he has sent her, stands before him wearing nothing but them, crawls onto the bed, and erotically caresses him with the satin Diors.

They make love slowly, and afterward his hand wraps around her waist and holds her. And even though the gesture is somehow compromised by a lack of final and ultimate tenderness, Mirabelle's mind floats in space, and the five fingers that pull her toward him are received into her heart like a psalm. It is a comforting touch, a connection however tenuous, that makes her feel attached to something, someone, and less alone.

Later, as the millionaire lies next to her in the too-small bed in the too-small room, with one arm around Mirabelle and a cat lying on his chest, they talk back and forth in small packets of conversation. Ray listens to her work woes, her car woes, and her friend woes, and Ray makes up a few woes to tell her in response. They talk back and forth, but their conversation is second in importance to the contact of his hand on her shoulder.

"Holidays can be tough on single people. I generally don't like them," says Ray.

"Bad for me, too," says Mirabelle.

"Christmas, Thanksgiving . . ."

"All bad," agrees Mirabelle.

"Halloween I hate," says Ray.

"Oh, I like Halloween!"

"How can you like Halloween? You have to figure out what to dress up as, and if you don't you're a killjoy," says Ray.

"I like Halloween because I always know what to go as," says Mirabelle.

"What do you go as?"

"Well, Olive Oyl." Mirabelle implies a "stupid" after she speaks. Mirabelle says this without the slightest trace of irony, in fact, with glee that at least this one part of her life is solved.

Although he does not know it, Ray Porter fucks Mirabelle so he can be close to someone. He finds it difficult to hold her hand; he cannot stop in the street and spontaneously hug her, but his intercourse with her puts him in proximity to her. It presses his flesh against hers and his body mistakes her flesh for mind. Mirabelle, on the other hand, is laying down her life for him. Every time she jackknifes her legs open, every time she rolls on her side and pulls her knees up so he can enter her, she sacrifices a bit of herself, she gives him a little more of her that he cannot return. Ray, not understanding that what he is taking from her is torn from her, believes that the arrangement is fair. He treats her beautifully. He has begun to buy her small gifts. He is always thoughtful toward her, and never presses her if she isn't in the mood. He mistakes his actions for kindness. Mirabelle is not sophisticated enough to understand what is happening to her, and Ray Porter is not sophisticated enough to know what he is doing to her. She is falling in love, and she fully expects her love to be returned once Mr. Porter comes to his senses. But right now, he is using the hours with her as a portal to his own need for propinquity.

* * *

In the morning, at a coffee shop around the corner, Ray ruins everything by reiterating his independence, even clearly saying that their relationship is not exclusive, and Mirabelle, in a logical and rational mode and believing that she, too, is capable of random dating, agrees for both of them, then adds that if he does sleep with someone else, she should be told.

"Are you sure you want that?"

"Yes," says Mirabelle, "it's my body and I have a right to know."

Ray believes her, because he is naïve.

Ray stays in LA for three days, sees Mirabelle one more night, calls her twice, hurts her inadvertently one more time, levitates her spirit once, makes love to her again, buys her a watch and a blouse, compliments her hair, gets her a subscription to *Vogue*, but rarely, maybe twice, kisses her. Mirabelle pretends not to notice. When Monday finally comes, she goes to work, passing the perfume girls with confidence, inspired by the undeniable evidence that someone is interested in her.

VISITOR

"Can I take you to lunch?"

Mirabelle stands at her post, and before her is a man in his midfifties, a bit overweight, with short-cropped hair and dressed like someone who never thought one way or another about dressing in his life. Everything he wears is in the wrong fabrics for a Neiman's devotee—his belt is not leather, his shoes are catalog-bought. A porkpie hat sits atop his head. He wears a synthetic palm tree shirt, cotton pants, and well-broken-in work boots.

"You're Mirabelle Buttersfield?"

"Yes."

"I'm Carter Dobbs; I'm looking for your father."

Mirabelle and Carter sit at the Time Clock Café. This time, her admirer, Tom, is missing from the tableau, but most of the regulars move in and out of their spots, as though an unseen movie director has yelled, "Places, everybody."

A few minutes into the conversation and Mirabelle knows why this man does not belong, nor care to belong, in the matrix of Beverly Hills.

"I was in Vietnam with your father. I have been trying to locate him, with this address." He slides a paper toward her over the metal tabletop. Mirabelle sees that it is her home address, which has remained unchanged in twenty-eight years. "I've written him, but I never get a response," he says.

"Does he know you?" asks Mirabelle.

"He knows me well. There's never been a problem between us, but he won't answer me."

"Why not?"

"I think I know why, but it's personal, and I'm guessing he needs to talk to me."

"Well," says Mirabelle, "that's our address. I don't know why he won't get in touch with you, but I'm—"

"Are you going to see him?" Carter interrupts.

"Yes, I'm going to see him at Christmas and I can give him your card, whatever you want."

"Thanks. It's the ones that don't call back that need to talk the most."

"It was so long ago."

"Yes, sweetie. So long ago. Some do better than others, and I've just made it a mission of mine to reach my brothers, see if they're okay. Is your dad okay?"

"Not always."

Mirabelle tries to size up Carter. She has seen his type in Vermont, although Carter is clearly not from Vermont, with his Midwest nonaccent, flavored occasionally with a subtle drawl. Well-mannered, kind, moral. Like her father. Except that Carter Dobbs wants to talk.

Mirabelle's father, Dan Buttersfield, has never spoken to her about one emotional thing. She is kept in the dark about family secrets; she has never seen him angry. She has never been told anything about Vietnam. When asked, her father shakes his head and changes the subject. He is stoic like a good WASP from Vermont should be. The household was shaken when Mirabelle was seventeen when it was revealed that her father, whom she adored, had been involved in a sexual affair that had lasted for seven years. Mirabelle's emotional age was always five years behind her real age, so this information was received as if by a twelve-year-old. It struck her hard and made her bluff happiness for the next eleven years. This event fits exactly into Mirabelle's jigsaw puzzle of sadness still being assembled inside her. Having watched her mother's struggle, Mirabelle keeps a fear harbored inside her of the same thing happening to her, and when anything occurs in her life that is even similar, like a current boyfriend going back to an old girlfriend, she breaks.

Carter Dobbs walks her back to Neiman's. He gives her his card from Dobbs' Auto Parts in Bakersfield, California, and he squeezes her arm goodbye. As he turns away from her, she finally can name what disturbs her about him. He doesn't laugh.

GIRL FRIDAY

Mirabelle is tied up in Friday traffic, and this is only Thursday. She slogs along Beverly and misses every light. She fails to step on the gas at the exact nanosecond of the light change, and she gets honked at by not one but two drivers.

Locked in the darkness of her car, with the wipers set on periodic, she feels uneasy. The night scares her. Then the uneasiness gives way to a momentary and frightening levitation of her mind above her body. She can feel her spirit disconnect from her corporeal self, and her heart starts racing. She had felt its calling card months earlier, this unwelcome visitor in her body, who seemed to fly through her and then was gone. This time, it is stronger than before, and it stays longer. It is as though her body is held down by weights and her mind is being methodically disassembled.

The stairs from her impossible-to-negotiate parking space to her front door are endless; she trudges from step to step. The door is heavy as she pushes it with the inserted key. Once inside, she sits on the futon for several hours without moving. The cat nudges her for dinner but she can't get up.

Mirabelle has been through this before, but the power of the depression keeps her from remembering that its cause is chemical. As has happened several years before, her medication is failing her.

The phone rings but she cannot answer. She hears Ray Porter leave a message. She drags herself to bed without eating. She closes her eyes, and the depression helps her sleep. Sleep, however, is not relief. The depression does not go away, politely waiting to come back in the morning when she is refreshed. It stays, and tonight it works on Mirabelle even as she sleeps, poisoning her dreams.

In the morning, she calls in sick, faking a flu, which is the closest expressible illness to what she is actually experiencing. By noon she has thought to call her doctor, who wants her to come in and who suggests that she is experiencing a pharmaceutical collapse. But the chemical malaise makes her disinterested even in getting well, and she feels the value of everything that has meaning for her slip away—her drawing, her family, Ray Porter. For the first time in her life, she thinks she might rather be dead.

The hours slip along, and she might have sat on her futon all day had the phone not rung around four. This time, she answers.

"Are you all right?" It is Ray Porter.

"Yeah."

"I called you last night."

"I didn't get the message. My machine is acting funny," she lies.

"Do you want to have dinner tonight? It's my last night here for a while."

Mirabelle can't answer. Ray repeats himself:

"Are you all right?"

This time, she lets her tone speak for her. "I'm pretty okay."

"What's the matter?" says Ray.

"I'm supposed to go to the doctor."

"Why? Why do you have to go to the doctor? What's wrong?"

"No. I have to go to my . . . I take Serzone, but it stopped working."

"What's Serzone?" says Ray.

"It's like Prozac."

"Do you want me to take you to the doctor? Do you want me to come over there and take you to the doctor?"

"I probably should see him."

"I'll come and take you."

Within an hour, Ray collects her, drops her off at Dr. Tracy's, and sits in his car, waiting for Mirabelle in a no-waiting zone in Beverly Hills. He can see the stream of people going in and out of this medical building and wonders how Mirabelle can afford such treatment, but it is a Neiman's employee benefit that provides her with a local doctor, and luckily, her doctor has moved from the valley, twenty miles from her apartment, to the Conrad Medical Building two blocks from her job. Ray sees a beautiful woman in her thirties exiting the building with a broad-brimmed hat pulled low over her face, hiding two freshly enormous lips. Ray Porter guesses there is a waiting period after injection while they deflate to an approximation of actual human form. He sees a vibrant Chiquita with her ass vacuum-packed into a yellow rayon wrap, her torso perched on two tree stumps. He sees what he thought didn't exist except as parody: a leather-skinned businessman with dyed black hair, his shirt open to his waist, and his chest laden with fourteen karat. He clinks as he darts across the street.

He sees a dozen or so women who have decided that overkill is best in the breast department. He wonders if they are kidding; he wonders if the men who adore them excuse their lapse in taste and love them anyway, or see them as splendid examples of woman as hyperbole. This is what he likes about Mirabelle; her beauty is uncultivated and he can trust that what is there at night will be there in the morning, too. He wonders what it is that makes him willing to sit in his car on a street, this millionaire, waiting for a twenty-eight-year-old girl. Is it his lust for her, or is something happening inside him that makes him care for her in an unexpected, unpredictable way?

He sees a family of tourists, with a sixteen-year-old daughter who is so purely beautiful that it makes him ashamed of the lewd image he fleetingly conjures.

Ray has very loose boundaries on what he considers fair game, although rarely has he allowed himself to dip below the arbitrary twenty-five-year-old watermark. What distinguishes him from the man with dyed hair who clinked across Bedford Drive a few moments ago is that whether he knows it or not, Ray is actually looking for someone. But he needs to be killed off several times by getting in too deep with the wrong person; he needs to break a heart and know that he has caused it, and to experience the sudden loss of interest that can occur within hours of a high peak of desire.

At this point in his transition from boy to man, he does not know the difference between a woman who is feasible and one who is not. This is still to come. Meanwhile, his eye roams around and focuses his unconscious on what can be a woman's smallest desirable quanta. The back of her neck seen in the shadow of her hair. The arch of her foot resting in an open sandal. An appealing contrast in the color of her blouse and skirt. These glimpses propel his desire, yet because he won't admit to himself how small the thing is that he wants, he inflates it to include her entire self, so he won't think of himself as a bad guy. Then a courtship begins, unconscious lies are told, and an enormously complex schema is structured, all to attain the mystery of an ankle that enters seductively into an oversize jogging shoe.

As Ray Porter sits in his car in this corridor of lust, where scores of women pass through his crosshairs, a desire for Mirabelle takes root and spreads. He reminds himself that she is not feeling well, but then again, she might be in the mood later, and in fact, a good fuck might be the best thing for her.

Mirabelle emerges from the Conrad Medical Building with a prescription-size sheet of paper in her hand, comes over to the car, and explains through the lowered window that she will go across the street to the pharmacy to fill it. Ray nods and asks her if she wants him to go with her, she says no. When Mirabelle is halfway across the street, she hesitates and returns to the Mercedes. Ray lowers the window, and Mirabelle, shrinking her body like an embarrassed child, speaks:

"I don't have any money."

Ray turns off the car, goes in with her, and pays seventy-eight dollars for one hundred tabs of Celexa, the latest miracle of chemistry that should right Mirabelle's listing ship. Back in the car, he suggests that she stay at his place for the night. Mirabelle takes this as an expression of his caring, which it is. It is just that his caring is a potion, mixed with one part benevolent altruist and one part chimpanzee penis.

He drives Mirabelle up the winding roads into the Hollywood Hills as she sags lower and lower. The Celexa will take weeks to kick in and she knows it.

"Thanks for all this."

"That's okay," Ray says. "Are you feeling better?"

"No."

However, the thought that someone is taking care of her buoys her up exactly one notch from the bottom of her earlier depression. An intense headache begins to split her in half, and after Ray slots the car in the garage, he helps her to his bed.

If the headache had not appeared, Ray would have stroked his hand along her, down across a breast to her abdomen, and tried to seduce her. The headache keeps her from seeing the worst side of Ray's desire for her, and the worst side of men's desire in general. He is lucky he doesn't try, because she would have hated him for it.

Mirabelle sleeps motionlessly and silently, with her auburn hair splayed across her face and neck. Ray lies next to her, flipping the TV channels with the volume set to whisper, doing a crossword, looking at her—sometimes wondering if now would be the time to wake her up for her all-important sexual cure. But the night passes eventless, and eventually he nods off and sleeps fitfully until morning.

Breakfast is the same as usual, only this time, Mirabelle's inactivity makes sense—she is ill. Ray is leaving town for ten days, and he carefully takes her home and waits while she assembles herself for her day at Habitat. Mirabelle begins to motivate herself toward cure, and she knows physical activity will be good for her.

"Are you going to be okay?"

"Yeah."

He hugs her tightly, with his palms squarely on her sturdy back, then backs out with a wave and a goodbye.

Mirabelle vacantly labors at Habitat, lifting and hauling Sheetrock and occasionally putting on a giddy face for her coworkers that hides nothing. She declines to go out for a beer even though one of the volunteers is flirting with her. In her depression, she has accidentally put on the perfect outfit for driving Mirabelle-watchers wild. The exact right khaki shorts with the exact right T-shirt with the exact right surface tension.

Ray calls her that night to check in on her. She is feeling ever so slightly better, even if only from the placebo effect of one pill and being freed, at least for the weekend, from the monotony of the glove department. Still, she sits essentially motionless through Monday morning, separated from suicidal thoughts by only a thin veneer. She struggles all weekend to keep it from cracking.

Weeks later, Mirabelle doesn't know if she is feeling better naturally or because the Celexa is working. It feels like a natural lift, and she wonders if she needs the pills at all. But she isn't stupid, and she recalls hearing that this is a common feeling, so she keeps taking the pills daily.

VERMONT

Christmas is approaching and she is making plans for travel to Vermont. She will leave on one of the worst flights imaginable, the red-eye to New York on Christmas Eve, connecting to Montpelier on a commuter flight at 8:00 A.M. on Christmas Day, and then take a bus seventy-five miles to home. Ray gives her the cost of the ticket east, as he figures Christmas is going to strain Mirabelle's budget and why not help her. He also slips her an extra $250 so she won't be a pauper in front of her friends. She already knows what she is going to give Ray for Christmas, the nude drawing she made of herself the night of her Thanksgiving despair, in which she is suspended in black space. And he knows what he is going to give her, a handpicked blouse from Armani, which he bought for her knowing she would be absolutely crazy about it.

Mirabelle begins the nightmare of holiday travel with a phone call from Ray wishing her well, and a black sedan he sent to take her to the airport. Even flying at these inhuman hours, the sedan is the last sanctuary of calm before the holiday crowds engulf her. After several hours, the 747 to New York stinks from the perspiration of four hundred passengers being rocked and rolled in the uneasy Christmas air. She transfers at JFK and finds herself aboard a prop plane that sits on the runway a full hour before takeoff. On descent to Montpelier, the plane bounces through a snowstorm and scares even the pilot. Mirabelle has to comfort the twenty-five-year-old, six-foot-four footballer who sits next to her, who quakes with every engine downshift and every crank of the flaps. Mirabelle herself is not nervous; it just doesn't occur to her that the plane can do anything but land, and she alternates between soothing the athlete next to her and reading a book.

By morning, after retrieving her luggage without help and hauling it to a shuttle that takes her to the bus station, she looks like a college student bound for home, or a ragamuffin. The bus, warm and cold at the same time, heads through the light snow. The riders are equally divided: Some of them are like Mirabelle, exhausted travelers who had bumpy naps on interminable night flights, while the others are wide-awake conversationalists on the first leg of their exciting Christmas journey.

When the bus pulls into Dunton at 11:30 A.M., Mirabelle can see her older brother Ken standing inside the depot, wearing a bright red parka the size of an oil barrel. They say quick hellos as she runs from the bus to the car wearing her skimpy LA jacket; the freezing wind tells her that she has been in LA too long. Her brother shifts the lime-green Volkswagen into gear and mutters a "Hey, kiddo," and then drives about five miles an hour on the icy roads. Ken is a policeman with an uncanny knack for tracking down criminals in his small town, mainly because he knows everyone and has a sixth sense for adolescents who might be headed in the wrong direction. She feels deep affection for her brother, although this has never once translated into honest conversation. She asks him how Mom and Dad are, and he answers truthfully, which is that they are unchanged.

Unchanged means this: Mom cannot imagine in this world that Mirabelle is having sex, and Dad ignores the subject entirely. Even though Mirabelle is twenty-eight years old, her status as a child in the house has never changed. Father to daughter, daughter to mother, the relationships are frozen in time, and it is this containment she felt nine years ago that squeezed Mirabelle out of the house and into California, where she could start digging in fresh dirt for her real personality. California doesn't matter, though, once she walks through her parents' door.

Moderation in all things, including success. Her dad supports his family well but has not succeeded past that. The house is small and paper thin; they have two old cars, but currently her father is on a rampage of relative success selling home products à la Amway. The extra income means a few things are being refurbished, and a plastic sheet covers the entire roof of the house waiting for dry weather so it can be repaired.

Catherine and Dan have been married for thirty-five years, and the stoic construct of their relationship has been broken only once, when Dan revealed his seven-year affair with a neighbor. Catherine collapsed, then fought, then resurrected the marriage with a quiet power and sophistication that she had not shown at any other time in her life or has ever shown again. The one who was broken, who did not recover, who did not understand, and who saw the image of her father crack and shatter, was Mirabelle.

Mirabelle did not know how to rebound from this betrayal, and Dan did not know that while he was cheating on his wife, he was cheating on his daughter, too. But she still needed to be loved by this man who had committed the unspeakable, and the push/ pull she felt toward her father confused and stunted her.

Even before this episode, Mirabelle had feared her father, but she could never remember why. She does remember a shift in his manner, sometime after he returned from the war. She remembers a loving, even jovial man who became sullen and removed, and whom she learned to be cautious around. With quiet pervading the house, Mirabelle would retire to her room and read, thus beginning a lifelong relationship with books. But now all that is years ago. Now her father is much more congenial, as though something has softened, as though his resolve to be unreachable has eroded with time.

"So how're you doin' out there?" Her father sits in the easiest chair in the living room, and Mirabelle sits on the sofa, verging on relaxed.

"I'm fine, I'm still working at Neiman's."

"How's your art coming along?" Dan never sees her endeavors in art as frivolous, and as much as is possible for him, gets it.

"I'm drawing, Daddy. I've even sold some."

"Really? That's great, that's just great. What do they sell for?"

"The last one brought six hundred dollars, split with the gallery."

Mirabelle's mother brings a tray of Cokes into the room and just catches her daughter's modestly expressed boast. She looks askance at her, as if to say, "Can that possibly be true?" For some reason, she feels the need to fake naïveté about this art thing that Mirabelle is doing. She pretends she doesn't get the preoccupation with it, that it is all beyond her understanding. The source of this self-deception is a mysterious and arbitrary decision to place certain arenas outside her realm of understanding, like the man of the house being simply unable to comprehend how to wash and dry dishes. The woman who had become a firewall of protection around her family when it was threatened now feels the need to play dumb.

The three talk on, then Dad suggests the family take a walk around the neighborhood, which they do. He leads her by certain houses so he can call out to neighbors and show off his daughter, and Mirabelle becomes the daughter she was to him prior to the revelation of his affair. She hangs back behind her dad. Her pose becomes awkward, her voice weakens, she shyly says hello to familiar neighbors, and none of what she has seen and experienced in California is present in her demeanor. Catherine stands by, in wife mode, and Mirabelle looks at her and wonders where her own deep eroticism could possibly have come from.

After the family dinner, with her brother's wife Ella making it five, Mirabelle goes to her room and sits on the bed amid the relics of her childhood. Her mother's discarded sewing machine has been stowed in the room, and there are a few stray cardboard storage boxes stuffed into her closet, but otherwise everything is the same. A clock radio from the seventies, predigital, sits on her bedside table, in exactly the same spot it occupied when Jimmy Carter was president. The books that Mirabelle dove into when she wanted to vanish from the family are still in perfect order on her painted wicker bookshelf. The yellow glow from the incandescent overhead light washes over everything, and it, too, is familiar. Although she feels she is a stranger in the house, she is not a stranger in this room. This room is her own, and it is the only place where she knows exactly who she is, and whom she is fighting against, and she would like to remain in it forever.

She opens one of the storage boxes—cardboard drawers in cardboard chests—and sees piles of old tax forms, long past any purpose of being saved, a few ledgers, and some rolled-up Christmas wrapping. She kneels down, brushing dust off the floor, and slides open the lower drawer. A folded sweater and more financial flotsam. She sees an array of photos tucked inside another antique ledger. She picks it up and the photos spill onto the bottom of the box. She sifts through them and sees Christmas pictures of herself at five years old, riding on her father's neck. He is all smiles and clowning, her brother is nearby with a space weapon, and Mom is probably taking the picture. But the mystery for Mirabelle is, what happened? Why did her father stop loving her?

Mirabelle lies back on her bed holding the photos like a gin hand. Each one is a ticket to the past; each reveals a moment, not only in the faces but in the furniture and other objects in the background. She remembers that rocker, she remembers that magazine, she remembers that porcelain souvenir from Monticello. She stares into these photos, enters them. She knows that even though the same people and the same furniture are outside her door, the photo cannot be re-created, reposed, and snapped again, not without reaching through time. Everything is present but untouchable. This melancholy stays with her until sleep, and she loves being held by it, but she cannot figure out why these photos are so powerful beyond their obvious nostalgic tug.

The next day, she and her dad take a walk in the woods. In Vermont, no matter in which direction you go, you end up in the woods, so they go straight out their own backyard. The snow is crunchy and manageable. Mirabelle wears her mom's parka, which makes her look like someone has inflated her. Dad is all man in a furry vest and plaid shirt and lambskin jacket. After the "How's Mom?" discussion in which little is said and nothing is answered, Mirabelle produces from her pocket the photographs and hands them to him.

"I found these last night. Remember these?" She laughs as she presents them, to indicate their harmlessness.

After reaching clumsily for his glasses, which are inconveniently stashed under layers of insulation, Dan looks at the photos.

"Uh-huh." This is not the response Mirabelle is looking for. She had hoped for a smile or chuckle or flicker of some memory of pleasure.

"We were giggly," probes Mirabelle.

"Yeah, it looks like we are having a lot of fun."

He hands the photos back to her. She cringes at his disconnection from the events in the pictures.

Mirabelle suddenly knows why the photos have such a powerful effect on her. She wants to be there again. She wants to be in the photographs, before Easter, before the shift in his personality. She wants to be hoisted onto her dad's shoulders the way she was as a child; she wants to trust him and be trusted by him, enough that he would share his secrets with her.

"These were taken right when you came back from Vietnam, weren't they?"

Mirabelle has tried to open this door before. Today his response is the same as always.

"Not sure. Yeah, I guess."

The air bites them as Mirabelle and her father continue to walk. Then, coming to a clearing in the snowy forest, they grind to an uncomfortable halt. Mirabelle pushes a hand deeper in her pocket and fingers the card given to her by Carter Dobbs. The distance from the house gives her courage and she thinks now is the time. "There's a man trying to reach you," says Mirabelle. "He says he knows you."

She offers him the card. Taking it, he pauses in the chilling snow and looks at it, saying nothing.

"Do you know him?" Mirabelle asks.

He hands the card back to her. "I know him." And the conversation is over. But she had noticed something. When he was holding the card, he took his thumb and traced it over the name, and when he did so, he was powerfully distant from where he is now, in this snow with his daughter, in the woods in his backyard, in Vermont.

Her mother leaves the house to go babysit for her three-year-old grandchild. Mirabelle goes to her room after watching several hours of television with her now monosyllabic dad. The house is quiet, and she angles the shade on her bedside lamp and browses some of the books of her youth: *Little Women, Jo's Boys, Little Men, Jane Eyre, The Little Princess, The Secret Garden, The Happy Hollisters.* Nancy Drew. Agatha Christie. Judy Blume: *Are You There God? It's Me, Margaret. Deenie. Starring Sally J. Freedman as Herself.* But something catches her ear. Something . . . the sound of a cat? Or an injured animal in the far distance. But her mind keeps recalculating the data, inching the source of the sound closer than the outdoors. This wail, these moans, are coming from inside the house. Wearing her bunny slippers—a gift last Christmas from an aunt who underestimated Mirabelle's age by fifteen years—she opens the door to her room and steps out into the hall. She does not need to walk far to know that the sounds, which she has now identified as sobbing, are coming from her father, who is behind the closed door of his bedroom. She stands frozen like a deer with bunny feet, then guides the slippers backward into her room, noiselessly. She shuts her door without making a sound, as she had done one night twenty-one years ago after hearing the same cries coming from the same room.

The moaning has stopped, and now the house is quiet. Mirabelle sits in her armchair and sees her parka, which has tumbled off the foot of her bed and onto the floor. She retrieves Carter Dobbs's business card. She approaches her parents' bedroom and lays the tiny business card up against the doorway. Then she quietly slides her way back to her own room.

Six months pass unnoticed as Ray and Mirabelle live in a temporary and poorly constructed heaven, with him flying in and out, visiting her, taking her to fine restaurants, then back to his place, sometimes sleeping with her, sometimes not. Sometimes he takes her home and says good night. She does not like sex when she has her period. When she feels depressed, sex can sometimes leave her sullen, so during these times there is an awkward domesticity while they wait it out. He takes note of her use of expressions that linger from her adolescence—*lazy bones, sleepyhead, early bird*—and is alternately amused and annoyed by them. A toothbrush is set aside for her. Since his house is closer to Neiman's, she often stays the night with him, bringing an overlarge purse stuffed with a change of clothes so she can go directly to work from his house. When he fantasizes about sex, he thinks of her and no one else.

Ray shows up one day on Mirabelle's message machine, saying he is in town and inviting her to an event in New York next month, and yes, she'll need a dress so let's go shopping. He takes her to Beverly Hills on one of her floating days off and they spend an erotic day shopping at Prada for something suitable. Ray glimpses her changing behind the flimsy screens, and when they get home, she tries on the dress, and then he fucks it right off her. Over the next several days, Mirabelle plans the trip, makes arrangements to get off work, and silently counts the days until takeoff.

JUNE

Ray Porter can't believe how much she is crying, and he wishes he could take back what he has told her. But the letter is in her hand, just barely, and she looks away from it as she drops it onto the bed. She tilts her head down and sobs like a child. He had written the letter because he wanted to say it succinctly; he didn't want to stammer or mollify it, he didn't want to change direction in the middle of a sentence and retract what he was about to tell her because of a vulnerable look in her eye. But she wanted to know; she had asked to know and she seemed to have meant it. So he handed her the letter in person as they sat in his bedroom, at the beginning of the evening, which quickly came to a close hours before it normally would have.

Dear Mirabelle,

I suppose the only way to say it is to say it: I slept with someone. It was not romantic or intimate, and I did not stay the night with this person.

I am not telling you this to hurt you, and I'm not telling you because I want our relationship to change. I am telling you this only because you asked me to. I hope that you can find a place of understanding in you. I am sorry,

Ray

With Mirabelle turned away from him, he takes the letter and quickly slides it into a drawer so she won't have to look at the tangible evidence of what he has done. The letter represents such an awful thing to her, and Ray does right by disappearing it.

He had debated with himself for two hours while flying to Los Angeles. Tell her, or not? But she had asked him to tell her. She must have meant it. Plus, it wasn't love; it was a fuck. Plus, she had asked him to tell her. He thought this was a new feminism thing that he is honor bound to oblige; that if he doesn't, he is a pig. That he will actually come off well by telling her; no one could judge him otherwise. But whatever his thought process was, whatever he told himself was the right thing to do, was false. Because his logic is not based in any understanding of her heart, and he continues to misread her.

Mirabelle doesn't ask any questions. She rises up and drags her sweater down the hall, stumbling like a drunk. Ray does not know how to handle this girl. If only she were practical, he would handle her in a practical way, but Mirabelle is in stage one—a child who has just had her heart rearranged by someone she trusted. She mumbles a cancellation of their upcoming weekend trip to New York. He follows her to her car and watches her drive away. The next day, he gets on a plane to Seattle.

Ray waits a day, then phones her just at the moment he knows she will be walking through the door.

"How are you?"

"Okay," she says in a small voice.

"You want to talk about it?"

"Okay. Can I call you back?"

"Yeah."

And they hang up. Mirabelle lays down her things, takes off her diaphanous Gap windbreaker, and drinks some water. She has been in a daze all day. She never wants to talk to him again, yet she is glad he called. She needs to talk to a friend, an ally, about Ray's transgression, but Ray is her only friend. She goes to her bedroom and dials area code 206.

"Ray?"

"Hang up and I'll call you back," he says.

"Yeah."

This is a fiscal ritual. Whenever she calls him long distance, they hang up and he phones her back so she won't have to pay for the call.

"Are you better?" he says.

"I'm a little better," she says, not knowing what she means.

"Should we see each other?" says Ray.

"I don't think so. I changed my ticket from New York. Is that okay? I want to go to Vermont to see my parents."

Mirabelle is not going to her parents for comfort. There will be no sympathy from her mother or father, because she can hardly explain the situation to them, especially since her father is guilty of the same act. But there will be solace in her room, in her things.

"Sure. Of course," says Ray.

The conversation stumbles on, and Ray tells her he is sorry he hurt her. And he is, but inside he doesn't know what he could have done differently. He is determined not to love Mirabelle; she is not his peer. He knows that he is using her, but he isn't able to stop. And as powerful as their desire for each other remains, their conflicting goals stalemate them, and their relationship has failed to move forward, even the incremental amount necessary for it to stay alive. They mumble some goodbyes, Ray knowing it is not yet over, and with Mirabelle unable to think further than her own current pain.

PRADA

Lisa got wind of Mirabelle's Prada visit. For Lisa, Prada is the end-all be-all of courtship. Its exquisite clothes are not only expensive but identifiable. A Prada dress is a Prada dress and will always be a Prada dress. Especially a *new* Prada dress. A new Prada dress means that the trip to the shop is recent, that fresh money has just been spent, and if Lisa were wearing a new Prada dress, it would signify a big catch on her part. It would show that she has landed money and that her man has spent enough time with her to have escorted her to Beverly Hills and waited till she had tried on each and every, and then shoved a credit card thoughtlessly across the counter without even checking the price tag.

Lisa comes face-to-face with the rumor one morning when she sees Mirabelle arrive at work in a sparkling and flattering killer dress. To Lisa, Prada is as recognizable as her own mother, and seeing Mirabelle draped in the perfect Prada shift provokes in her a deep guttural growl. Lisa calls her friend at the store to get the full scoop, and yes, Ray Porter and an unknown miss did roll through. The only thing Lisa can think to do when she hears her worst fears confirmed is trim and coif her pubic hair. This is a ritualistic act of readiness, a war dance, that is akin to a matador's mystical preparations for battle. It is also done out of the belief that everything natural about her has to be tampered with for it to achieve its utmost beautiful state. Breasts, lip size, hair, skin color, lip color, fingertips and toenails, all need adjustment.

Lisa sits on the toilet as she shaves, one leg propped up on the bathroom cabinet. She can dip the razor in the toilet when she needs to wet it while she shapes and combs the furry patch to perfection. Lisa is determined to cull Ray Porter away from the Mirabelle mistake. All she has to know is where is he and what does he look like. She can easily glean this from the trusting Mirabelle, probably in one lunch, so she doesn't worry too much or make plans to connive. After the final dip of the razor in the toilet and a gentle splash of water to the now perfectly shaped lawn, Lisa stands up, stark naked, and looks at herself in the bathroom mirror. She is an hourglass with all the sand at the top. She is white and pink, and her implants pull and stretch and whiten the skin around them so her breasts glow. Her nipples are the color of bubble gum, and the silicone makes them resilient enough to chew like bubble gum, and now, between her legs, is the nicest little piece o' property west of Texas.

Mirabelle had told her parents that she was going to New York, so when she calls them and tells them she will be coming to Vermont instead, there is some explaining to do. But she bluffs her way through it, and since her parents never ask too many questions anyway, they are not aware that she can barely hold herself together.

On her arrival in Vermont, Mirabelle puts on an Academy Award face. She actually manages to appear cheery, though she occasionally retreats into her room to let the gloom from her losses with Ray Porter seep from her pores. She roams aimlessly through the house and sees on her father's desk the business card she had given him, significantly moved from the bedroom. She wonders if he has made the call that she hoped he would make.

Twenty-eight hours into her awful weekend, the phone rings and she picks it up. It is Ray Porter, calling from New York. There are awkward "How are yous," then, as he approaches his reason for calling, Ray softens his voice, giving the impression that he is leaning into her. He intones his question so apologetically it nearly brings them both to tears:

"Why don't you come to New York."

Mirabelle wants to be there, in spite of her ache, and there is no hesitation in her yes, as much as she tries to imply it. She has shown him that she is hurt, and now it is over. She wants to be in New York City, and not in Vermont.

Mirabelle tells her mother that she is leaving today.

"What on earth for?"

"I'm meeting Ray."

Mirabelle's mom and dad know that she is seeing someone named Ray Porter, but they pretend their daughter's relationship is somehow chaste. This of course requires incredible manipulations of reality and enormous blocks and blind spots. Mirabelle, to her mother and father, is simply not sleeping with anyone.

"Oh, that'll be nice for you," her mother says simply.

At this point, Mirabelle could have turned on her heels, and nothing more would have been said, ever. But 10,319 days have passed since her birth, and today for some reason, explicable only by the calculation of the stress of lying multiplied by twenty-eight years, Mirabelle adds one small truth:

"I'll be staying with him if you need to reach me."

Catherine continues scrubbing the same plate for the next few moments. "In a hotel?"

"Yes," says Mirabelle, and then, just for good measure, "but don't worry, Mom, I'm on the pill."

"Well," says Catherine. "Well," she says again.

Catherine rubs the plate, then in a modulation of voice so loaded with meaning that only Meryl Streep could duplicate it more than once, adds one more "well." With perfect theatrical timing, her dad walks through the kitchen door and she tells him the same thing all over again, just to feel the same rush of power one more time. But there is no clamor; instead, everyone sits on their churning feelings, and Dan quickly changes the subject, flips on the TV, and is then absorbed by it.

NEW YORK

She catches a plane that day and meets Ray in New York at dusk. Mirabelle doesn't have her Prada dress with her, but her quick instinct for clothes prevails and with an authoritative sweep through Emporio Armani assisted by a contrite Ray, who can't wait to atone by pushing wads of money across the countertop, she ends up swathed in a shimmering Armani silver dress that equals the Prada, and that night they head off to a dinner for fifteen hundred.

After the event, where she looks statuesque and elegant, where a few photographers' bulbs go off as they enter in spite of their noncelebrity status, where it is so challenging to Mirabelle to be sitting at a table for twelve among hundreds of tables, where she is so enthralled to be at this event that its dullness is not apparent to her, they end up at a small cocktail party for a dozen people at a smart Park Avenue apartment. The group gathers in a wood-paneled library where several Picassos look quizzically down on them. There are white-haired men older than Ray; there are sharp, young saber-toothed up-and-comers who have just cracked thirty. There are also tough businesswomen whose sexuality has somehow been packed away and left in a drawer somewhere and then, as an afterthought, stuck back on themselves and worn like a power tie.

They are a smart, agile-minded group, but they are not sure what to make of Mirabelle, who sits in the middle of them like a flower. She is the only one wearing anything lighter than dark blue. Unlike them, her white skin is a gift, rather than the result of being bleached under neon all day. Mirabelle speaks quietly and to individuals only. When someone finally asks her what she does, she says she is an artist. This leads to a discussion among the aficionados about current art prices that excludes Mirabelle from the rest of the conversation.

As the evening loosens, confounding the normal progress of a party, the conversations gel into one, and the topic, rather than jumping wildly from politics to schools for kids to the latest medical treatments, also gels into one. And the topic is lying. They all admit that without it, their daily work cannot be done. In fact, someone says, lying is so fundamental to his existence that it has ceased to be lying at all and has transmogrified into a variant of truth. However, several of them admit that they never lie, and everyone in the room knows it's because they have become so rich that lying has become unnecessary and pointless. Their wealth insulates them even from lawsuits.

All points of view are duly expressed, with nothing new forthcoming, but with nods and asides and overlaps. This rapid exchange gives the appearance of an interesting conversation but one whose actual content is flat, dull, and drunken. That is, until Mirabelle speaks. Mirabelle, sober as an angel, fearlessly breaks into the chatter midstream:

"I think for a lie to be effective, it must have three essential qualities."

The booming voices of the men fade and the trebles of the women trail off. Ray Porter quietly worries inside.

"And what are those?" says a voice.

"First, it must be partially true. Second, it must make the hearer feel sorry for you, and third, it must be embarrassing to tell," says Mirabelle.

"Go on," the room implies.

"It must be partially true to be believable. If you arouse sympathy, you're much more likely to get what you want, and if it's embarrassing to tell, you're less likely to be questioned."

As an example, Mirabelle breaks down her lie to Mr. Agasa. She explains that the partially true part is that she did sometimes need to go to the doctor. She then made him feel sorry for her because she was in pain, then she embarrassed herself by having to explain it was a gynecological problem.

The agile minds in the room click open the brain files and store this analysis away for future use. Ray Porter, meanwhile, is tilted momentarily one centimeter off axis and for the first time in almost a year wonders if it is not he but Mirabelle who is determining the exact nature and character of their relationship.

They don't make love that night, or for a while, but within a month everything resumes, and the letter and its dark information is mentioned only one more time, ever: Mirabelle tells Ray that if something similar happens again, it is better left unsaid. But the sandy foundation of their relationship has been eroded. It has been eroded by the unmentionable being mentioned; their silent agreement not to discuss Ray's devotion or dedication has been broken.

Mirabelle no longer knows what she believes about her relationship with Mr. Ray Porter. She no longer asks herself questions about it; she simply resides in it. Ray continues to see her and make love to her, with their erotic interest never waning, not even one pheromone. He pays off her credit card debt, which had whopped up to over twelve thousand dollars. Months later, he pays off her slowly accruing student loan, which has recently crossed the forty-thousand-dollar mark. He replaces her collapsing truck with a newer one. These gifts, though he doesn't know it, are given so that she will be all right after he leaves her.

He continues his quest elsewhere for a single appropriate love with occasional dates, road trips, and flirtations, but he continues to care about Mirabelle in a way he cannot explain. His love for her is not the crazy love he expects to feel, the swinging delirious rhapsody that he has promised himself. This love is of a different kind, and he searches his mind for its definition. Meanwhile, he maintains a belief that their relationship can go on undisturbed until the absolute right woman comes along, and then he will calmly explain the circumstance to Mirabelle and she will see clearly how well he has handled everything, and wish him well, and congratulate him on his reasonable thinking.

LA

"I'll have a hot dog," says Mirabelle. It must be noted that this is not an ordinary hot dog but a Beverly Hills hot dog with none of the unspeakable ingredients of a carnival hot dog. So Mirabelle is not violating the purity of the tender blood flowing under her dewy skin. Lisa, on the other hand, orders a salad that fulfills her personal view of the two main qualities of diet food: It looks ugly and tastes bad. She has not allowed that some foods, perfectly low in fat, can actually taste good. She saves ordering normal food, food that might not be so dietary, for those times when a man is watching, hoping to come off as a vixen who never gains an ounce. This is the importance of dating for Lisa; without it, she would wither away, barely able to lift a spoonload of sliced carrots.

Lisa and Mirabelle sit outside as usual, under the California sun on a perfect eighty-degree July day.

"How's your love life?" Lisa knows that her real inquiry is twenty questions away on her list, and she'd better start circling the topic early.

"It's fine."

"He doesn't live here, right?"

"He lives in Seattle."

"That must be hard."

"It's okay, we get to see each other once, sometimes twice a week, sometimes more or less." Then Mirabelle, oblivious to undercurrents and thinking that Lisa might have an interest outside Rodeo Drive, says, "Have you ever read *Idols of Perversity?*"

This question passes through Lisa like a cosmic ray: no effect. Mirabelle then does a neat and tricky little analysis of her favorite book while Lisa handles her disinterest by staring in Mirabelle's face and dreaming of makeup. As Mirabelle winds down, and as her break recedes into the land of lost lunch hours, Lisa pushes hard.

"When do you get to see him next?"

Mirabelle never, ever would betray any personal information about Ray Porter, even his name, though in this case, the fully briefed Lisa already knows it. But in her excitement she does tell Lisa that she will see him next week: "We're going to the Ruscha opening at Reynaldo Gallery." Mirabelle assumes Lisa will be there already, as no one who attends anything ever at the Reynaldo Gallery would miss the next event. In a clear instant, Lisa sees herself wrangle Ray away from Mirabelle and, with a simple toss of her lasso, utterly make him hers.

COLLAPSE

Ray Porter's quest for the right woman is not going well because he is living in the wrong eternal city. He is still in the city of his youth, where women in their twenties frolic like bunnies, and speak in high tones, and cajole him and panic him. He still believes that here he will find a china-skinned intellectual who will dazzle him with a wild laugh and a sense of life.

A bridge is being built in his subconscious. The bridge is to span from this eternal city to a very different eternal city. This new city is where his true heart will live, a heart that bears the marks of his experience, that knows how and whom to love. But the bridge is several powerful and painful experiences away from being finished, and right now he sits in his Seattle house with a woman he has no idea he isn't interested in.

Christie Richards is thirty-five and a fashion designer of some local note. She has a saucy body that given the right astrological moment and an exactly measured dose of Cabernet can arouse Ray's memory of adolescent backseat conquests. And as Christie sits across from him at his dinner for two, which has been prepared and delivered to the candlelit table by a nearly invisible chef, all the essential ingredients of lust converge on him. As he rotates her body in his mind so he can see it from all sides, Christie drones on about Seattle fashion.

"—but I want windows, because without windows you're a rack designer. I have an overweight design that sells well, but no store is going to put an overweight design in their window, they want to bury them in the basement . . ." And she talks on and on, sometimes mentioning a recognizable fashion name as she continues to drink and pour, drink and pour, finally coming to the dregs of the Cabernet, with Ray, hiding his enthusiasm for getting her steaming drunk, casually opening another bottle and filling her glass.

But by the end of dinner, Christie starts talking with a slur, a big slur, and Ray begins to wonder if he has perhaps shoveled a few too many drinks her way. He takes her outside for some refrigerated Seattle air, which he thinks will do her good. It does her good, but not him, as now she is energized with oxygen and ready to forgo the foreplay, which at this point Ray Porter needs desperately if he is going to do what a man's gotta do.

She then drags him to his bedroom, which she has been in before, but only on a polite-host guided tour. The lights are already at dim and she kneels down before him and tugs at his belt buckle with the words, "I'm gonna suck your dick."

Well, all right, thinks Ray. Christie fumbles unsuccessfully with the incredibly simple pants hook, then falls flat on her face with a kerplunk. On his wheat-colored carpet, she looks like a drunken *Christina's World* by Andrew Wyeth, except instead of the longing look toward the homestead, she is trying to focus her eyes on anything that will stay still. She brings her face to within one foot of the bed leg and gamely crosses and uncrosses her eyes, hoping to bring the swirling images into one.

Ray knows he is in the wrong place at the wrong time, even if it is his own house. He knows he shouldn't be doing this, he knows that the days of these parenthetical women appearing in his life sentence are coming to a close. He helps her up and walks her down the hallway to the living room, where he props her on the sofa, shoveling pillows under both her arms so she won't fall over. He looks into her eyes and says dumbly, "Can you drive?" He doesn't really say this to find out if she can drive, but to let her know it is time to go home. She, knowing her limits, shakes her head no, although Ray isn't sure if she means no, or if she can no longer hold up her head.

Ray can drive her home but there is the car problem. Her car is parked outside, and if he drives her home there will be the morning headache of taxicabs and meeting times.

"You can stay here in the guest bedroom."

One of Christie's eyelids droops lazily. "I want to stay with you."

Ray is not amused with her. He firmly says no and takes her to the spare bedroom. She, stunned, sees the door close on her. Then she turns, sees the bed, and falls on it face first.

Ray Porter sinks into his thousand-dollar sheets as if he were sliding into heaven. He is alone and happy about it, but he does worry that Christie will feel her way along the hallway and find him. His usual speedy calculations slow to molasses, and big thick questions blob their way down his thought tunnel: How long does this go on? Why am I alone?

Ray is asleep, and dreaming of knocking. Knocking? He wakes at the moment of deepest third-stage slumber, so groggy that only one of his senses—his hearing—is functioning. He lies there, wondering if there is a burglar in the house. He pulls himself out of bed and walks down the hall, brave only because he quickly computes that the odds of there actually being a burglar are slim. He can hear the noise in the distance . . . is it down the street? There is construction down the street; would they be working at 3:00 A.M.? He hears it again, but this time realizes it is someone knocking on his front door.

He pulls open the door and there is Christie, standing fully dressed, except she has no shoes.

"My shoes are in your backyard."

The only logical scenario is so illogical that he does not ask her what happened. She must have gone to the backyard, slipped off her shoes, decided to leave, left the house forgetting her car keys, and been forced to knock on the door rather than sleep outside, or something like that. He gets the shoes, bundles up Christie, who is underdressed for the chilly night, puts her in his car, and drives her the eleven miles to her home.

The next day, he sends her flowers.

Mirabelle puts on her pink argyle sweater and her pastel plaid short skirt to wear to the 5:00 P.M. Ruscha opening, and when she exits her car in the sheltered Beverly Hills parking lot, she looks like a rainbow refracted in the spray of a lawn sprinkler. At the far end of the lot, a car is being locked and a man steps away from it. In silhouette, he files a paper in his billfold. His suit tapers at the waist and his hair falls over his forehead. He starts to walk away, but Mirabelle is illuminated by the last remaining rays of yellow sunlight that stray into the garage, and she catches his eye.

Then he says, "Mirabelle?"

Mirabelle stops. "Yes?"

"It's me, Jeremy."

He approaches her at an angle, the light now raking across his face, and she can finally see him. Although he is the same person, this new Jeremy has nothing to do with the old Jeremy. It would take three Old Jeremys to trade in for one New Jeremy, as the New Jeremy is the sleeker, better model, with many desirable features.

"It's so nice to see you again," he says.

So nice to see you again? Mirabelle thinks, *What is he talking about?* This is not Jeremy lingo. Is she supposed to say "So nice to see you again" back? It isn't particularly nice to see him again, but it isn't unpleasant either, and she is curious about him. But before she decides what to do, Jeremy casually unbuttons his one-button suit, leans forward, and kisses a continental hello on one of her cheeks.

"Are you going to the opening?"

"Yes, I am," says Mirabelle.

"I didn't know if I'd make it back to town before it closes, so I wanted to see it tonight. Can I walk with you?"

Mirabelle nods, surveying Jeremy's sumptuous leather shoes and the precise fall of his pant legs draping over them. She wonders what happened.

What happened was this. Jeremy's three months on the road, which expanded into a year of multiple trips eastward, not only were a financial success, relatively, but were a success of another kind: Jeremy evolved from ape to man. After touring with Age for only a couple of weeks, Jeremy was invited to stay with them on their bus. After a gig, the bus would leave at around 1:00 A.M. and be driven three hundred miles or so to the next stop. Usually everyone on the bus would stay up a couple of hours, then retire to individual sleeping bunks with draw curtains that recalled a 1940s train, minus Ingrid Bergman. Inside the bunks were headphone jacks that plugged into a central sound system. One of Age's members was a Buddhist, new enough to the discipline that he went to sleep every night listening to audiotapes of books on Buddhism and meditation. Jeremy would plug in because he was bored. At first, he was sickened that he was listening to spoken-word tapes and wind chimes, but soon, after one particular meditation provoked a surreal vision in which he toured his bedroom at age four, the nightly routine became the high point of his evening and he began to listen, and listen intently. But more important, as the Buddhism tapes dwindled, new tapes from shopping mall bookstores were purchased from the same shelves that stocked the now exhausted supply of Buddhist recordings, and Jeremy was suddenly plugged into the entire current canon of self-help.

These books, listened to in the hypnotic rolling darkness of his Greyhound bunk, taught Jeremy about the Self, inner and outer, Jungian archetypes, the male journey and rites of passage, the female journey and rites of passage, the care of the soul, and Tantric sex. He got a heavy dose of relationship books, beginning with *Men Are from Mars . . .* and ending with a parody book called *Loving Someone Dumber Than You* (Jeremy identifying with the "you" and not the "dumber"). As the bus rolled on through Kansas, Nebraska, Oklahoma, and Nevada, under a million stars undimmed by city lights, Jeremy had his consciousness raised and therefore his life altered, by accident.

They walk across Santa Monica Boulevard and Jeremy explains the success of his business and how he is back in LA looking for a place to set up larger manufacturing quarters for Doggone Amplifiers. As he walks with her, he picks up her hand and says, "You look great; you really do look great."

This is what Lisa sees as she zeros in on them from fifty yards the other side of the Reynaldo Gallery: a man in a well-cut new suit holding Mirabelle's hand as they walk up Bedford Drive. And she assumes Jeremy is Mr. Ray Porter.

"Are you here alone?" Jeremy asks Mirabelle.

"I'm meeting a friend."

"Travel has left me friendless in LA," says Jeremy as he opens the door for her and escorts her in. Lisa slips in behind them and statistically becomes, at the already crowded party, the only woman there with a lavender-perfumed cunt.

Five o'clock is early for a party, but not in LA where the average wake-up call is 7:00 A.M. Dinners are normally at 7:30 on the dot, which is perfect for a jet-lagged New Yorker who arrives and is eating at 10:30 his time. So this party is just starting to fill up, and many of the familiar faces are there. Artist/Hero is there, with a date this time, but he remembers Mirabelle and calls her over. Jeremy separates from her and goes to the bar for a newly discovered favorite, soda water, cranberry juice, and vodka. Lisa views this as prime time and sidles next to him, overhears his order, and asks for the same thing. She waits till the drinks are delivered, then moves her aromatic twat within striking distance.

"Oh my God, I've never seen anyone else order one of these," says Lisa.

And she is off and running. She laughs at everything Jeremy says, which is difficult because Jeremy is not by nature a funny person. But Lisa knows that finding him funny is essential to her conquest of him, and she therefore finds herself chuckling even at his most innocuous utterances, including several observations about the current political scene. When she realizes these comments are serious, Lisa has to abort a grin midway and quickly twist her face into her version of profound concentration. Her assault continues, cajoling, poking him a couple of times, coyly dipping her tongue in her drink. Then she looks over at Mirabelle and says how insulting it must be for Jeremy to have her chatting up some other guy when the one she came in with is so attractive. "I have a secret," she says. "I know who you are. I'm Lisa, by the way."

Since we all live in our own worlds, Jeremy assumes that word of his exploits and success with amplifiers has reached the coast. He loves that an attractive redhead has been informed of his savvy entrepreneurship, so when she says do you wanna meet later for a drink, he glances over at Mirabelle—which reinforces Lisa's erroneous belief—feeling unexpected regret that it was not she who had done the asking. But he gives Lisa a fact-finding once-over, and says yes.

Lisa laughs and flirts with him for another half hour, then ups the stakes.

"Can you leave now?" she asks.

"Yeah, sure."

"What about Mirabelle?" says Lisa, feigning concern for another person.

"I do what I want," replies Jeremy, never thinking to mention that they are not a couple.

This comment releases a flood of estrogen into Lisa's bloodstream and has her dreaming of sex, babies, and a home in the valley.

Jeremy doesn't understand Lisa's aggressiveness but he doesn't need to. And neither does his recently elevated consciousness. There is no way the tranquil waters in which his brain floats so serenely can also calm two testicles of an unattached twenty-seven-year-old male.

"Let me say goodbye to her."

Lisa almost, but not quite, feels embarrassed. "Okay, but I'll wait outside."

At her apartment, which has been cleared of roommates by prearrangement, Jeremy gets the works from Lisa. He is shown the illustrated Kama Sutra of Lisa Cramer, cosmetics girl first class, with additional notes contributed by a dozen How to Fuck books, two radio psychologists, the gossip of two highly sexed girlfriends, articles in *Cosmo,* and an incredible instinct for arousing a man's superficial interest. He is slowly stripped and stripped for, he is levitated with oral hijinks, massaged and toyed with, rolled backward and masturbated, and finally finished off with a cosmic ejaculation while Lisa deep-breathes and chants. Afterward, Lisa's belief that she has just blasted the head off Ray Porter is reinforced when she asks if she is better than Mirabelle, and Jeremy, who has no idea that he is not Ray Porter, has no choice but to nod yes. After a customary but brief period of forced cuddling, Jeremy rolls out of her apartment with Lisa's last words being, "Call me."

While Lisa thinks she is giving him the works, Ray Porter arrives at the art party, scoops up Mirabelle, and takes her to dinner, where their familiar and bottomless lust asserts itself. Driving to his house, he reaches under the strap of her seat belt and glides his hand across her sweater, where he feels the spongy resilience of her breasts. At his house, they are destined to make love but a conversation starts instead. A deadly, hurtful conversation that begins by Ray Porter casually reasserting his independence, talking to her like a friend who is in the know, as if she were his partner in finding someone else.

"I was thinking of selling the house here, getting an apartment in New York. I love it there. Every time I land I get a rush. There's a four bedroom I like that a friend is selling, big enough in case I ever meet someone."

He says it, and there is a message in it, but its cruelty is not intended.

Mirabelle tires. The speech, delivered as though it were an aside, drains her of momentum. Her arms dangle to her sides, and she drops into a chair. She knows this, she knows everything already, she has heard this. Why does he have to reiterate? To remind her that this is nothing?

She looks up at him and asks him a horrible question. "So are you just biding your time with me?"

The answer is awful, and Ray doesn't say it. He doesn't say anything at all, just sits next to her. Mirabelle's mind blackens. The blackness is not a thought, but if it could be pressed into a thought, if a chemical from a dropper could be dripped onto it causing its color and essence to become visible, it would take the shape of this sentence: *Why does no one want me?*

He pulls her into him, her forehead on his shoulder. He knows that he loves her, but he cannot figure out in what way.

So she sits there, her short fingernails digging into him, trying to hold on to something that will keep her together, that will keep her from flying apart in all directions. As she clutches him, she feels herself sinking into a cold dark sea and there seems no way out of it, ever. The proximity of the man she has identified as her salvation makes it worse. He takes her to the bed and she lies face down on the covers and he rests his hand on the small of her back, occasionally stroking her. He tells her that she is beautiful, but Mirabelle cannot align this thought with his rejection of her.

The next morning, Lisa picks up the ringing phone.

"Hi. It's Jeremy."

"Who?" says Lisa.

"Jeremy."

"Do I know you?" says Lisa.

Jeremy jokes, "When do you really know someone." Getting no laugh, he continues, "Jeremy from last night."

Lisa goes through the list of men she spoke to last night. None is named Jeremy, though sometimes men will find her and call her because they think they've made eye contact with her when they really haven't.

"Refresh me," Lisa says.

Jeremy is dumbfounded at the possibility that all his exploits, all his catapulting, could be so quickly forgotten by morning. He continues, "Me, Jeremy. I was at your place last night. We did it."

Something all wrong dawns on Lisa. "Oh, Ray!"

When Jeremy hears "Oh, Ray," he presumes it is slang or pig Latin or some contemporary expression of elation that has gotten by him. So he says it back: "O, ray!"

"God, you were great last night," offers Lisa.

"O ray," says Jeremy.

"What?" says Lisa.

Jeremy, involved in a conversation he can't follow, finally asks, "Do you know who I am?"

"Sure, you're Ray Porter."

"Who?" says Jeremy.

"Ray Porter, from last night."

"Who's Ray Porter?"

"You are," then she adds, "aren't you?"

In the morning after the agony of the night, Ray drives Mirabelle to her car, in time for her to get to work by ten. He watches her walking stiffly away from him, overdressed for the morning, bearing her anguish so solitarily. He wonders if it will be the last time he will ever see her.

She puts on her driving glasses and starts up her new-for-her Explorer. She waves a small-fingered goodbye to Ray, and he notices her diligent concentration on driving as she pulls away.

She enters Neiman's, passes the disgraced Lisa, walks up four flights, and slides into her niche behind the counter. She stands there for the rest of the day, again stunned by an inexplicable world, her movements limited to those that her body has memorized.

Ray and Mirabelle's relationship does not collapse that day; it subtly dwindles over the next six months. There are fits and starts, but they can all be graphed on a downward slope. He takes her to dinners, drives her home, hugs her good night. Sex is over. Sometimes, she tells him he is wonderful and he presses her closer to him. She accepts a date with a sports equipment rep but she cannot offer him even the little bit required to keep him interested. Ray finally grasps that he is giving her nothing and that he has to think for the both of them and separate from her. He pulls back and she reflexively, protectively, does the same. For a while, Mirabelle believes there will be a moment when he will cave in and let himself love her, but eventually she lets the idea go. She hits bottom. She dwells in the muck for several months, not depressed exactly, but involved in a mourning that at first she thinks is for Ray but soon realizes is for the loss of her old self.

She is lying on her bed, day having passed into night without her ever getting up to turn on a lamp. She lights a candle in her darkened bedroom and is held in its tender illumination. Outside, sounds from surrounding apartments transition from dinnertime to TV time to quiet time. Her depression has consumed all of its fuel. She is exhausted from doing nothing to heal herself. As the darkness and solitude surround her, she drifts into communication with her smartest self. She admits that her college days are over, that her excursion into Los Angeles was transitional, and that Ray Porter is a lost cause.

It is morning, and Ray Porter's phone rings.

"Hi, it's me," says Mirabelle.

"Hang up, I'll call you back."

"No, that's okay," she says. "Guess what. I'm going to move." There is a lilt in her voice that Ray is not used to hearing.

"From your apartment?" says Ray.

"To San Francisco."

There is a short discussion about why she chose San Francisco, which is unrevealing, and there is no discussion about whether it's a wise move or not, as Mirabelle's determination is clear and strong. She makes one small request of Ray that he fulfills: She utilizes Ray's long chain of pull to land an interview with a gallery in San Francisco—not to be an artist with the gallery, but a receptionist. On Del Rey's ancient computer, she secures an apartment over the Internet and also makes contact with two potential roommates. Within three weeks she leaves Neiman's, whispers a goodbye to Los Angeles without looking back, and settles into a small flat in the Presidio district near the Golden Gate Bridge. Ray is surprised by her sudden movement, as she had seemed so frozen.

Mirabelle still faces difficulties, but Ray finances her move and eases a situation that even with his aid reduces her bank account to a long string of zeros, put the decimal anywhere. Her new job as receptionist re-creates the kind of tedium she endured at the glove counter, but at least she gets to be ambulatory. And the mean age of the customers is lower by twenty years.

Another plus: The San Francisco arts scene is livelier than the intermittent one in LA. Every third night there's something going on somewhere, which she can either attend or pass on and curl up in her own bed. The gallery action puts her in the center of a glut of testosterone. Mirabelle is a ripe, relative virgin, and her romantic life starts badly. At an art opening, she meets an artist named Carlo who courts her for a month, fucks her several times, and leaves her cruelly: She calls him on the phone, he says he is on the other line and that he will call her back, but he never does. Ever. She summarizes and explains this event to herself not by saying that she is yet again unwanted, but that she has learned something about her own decisions. She has learned that her body is precious and it mustn't be offered carelessly ever again, as it holds a direct connection to her heart. She sheathes herself in a protective envelope of caution and learns never to give away more than is being given to her. The mini-disaster of this brief romance accomplishes something else, too: Mirabelle is able to shift her anger from Ray to Carlo, and Ray is then able to become a friend.

While she adjusts to San Francisco, Mirabelle's spirits rise and fall, but she is determined to stay positive. Ray keeps in touch by phone and sends small checks her way when he reads the need in her voice. Mirabelle has long given up her instinct to refuse the aid, as she has no choice but to accept it, which she does with sincere humility and graciousness. She also pursues her art with a steady diligence, and her drawings are accepted in several group shows. The small drawing, not even eight inches square, of her lying nude floating in space is shown as being from the collection of Mr. Ray Porter.

In Mirabelle's new job, she meets artists and collectors. She is always careful not to promote herself through gallery contacts—her sense of correctness prevents it—but she now enjoys being a relevant person at the openings. She often calls Ray, who immediately calls her back according to plan. One afternoon she announces, "I'm going to an opening tonight and my goal is not to be a wallflower." Toward the end of each week, she has collected a few stories to report to him: her nights on the scene, who flirted with her, who slighted her. She also monitors the sporadic comings and goings of the vilified Carlo, who popped into one opening with a pregnant girlfriend on his arm, sending the fragile Mirabelle into an angry snit. She tried to get even with him through psychological warfare but couldn't, because he didn't care.

Mirabelle's stay in San Francisco stretches into several seasons. The frequency of her calls to Ray Porter diminish. She has a few flirtations, conversations really, that never amount to much. But one night, she takes the walk up the stairs of her new flat and notices on the doormat a small, oblong, clumsily wrapped box with an overly large Hallmark card taped to it. Once inside the apartment, she sets the box down on the kitchen table. She feeds the cats, then untapes the ends of the wrapping and inside finds a plain white box, and inside that, a rather cute Swatch watch. She opens the note and reads, "I would like to have dinner with you, Jeremy." And quickly scribbled below is the usually tacit implication, "My treat!"

Jeremy has been working around the West Coast for the last six months, during which time he's made an out-of-proportion six-year psychic leap by funneling the entire contents of the Bodhi Tree bookstore into his brain. He has been commuting to San Francisco ever since he hit the road and now, ready to settle down in LA and become a minor lord of amplifiers, he finds himself having to go to Oakland every week on business. Occasionally, Mirabelle's image floats into his consciousness and hangs there. The image he sees is not from his early pathetic dates with her but from his encounter with her in the parking lot on the night of the art party. Because not until then had he matured enough to recognize her as something beautiful and something worth holding as an object of real desire. He's found her by calling her old number, then looking up the new number in a reverse-directory on the Internet to find her address.

Mirabelle calls him at the number scrawled on Jeremy's note, her memories of the awkward night in her apartment also having been diluted by their short walk to the Reynaldo Gallery, now almost a year ago. A date is set several weeks in the future. When the day arrives, he shows up in a taxi, and from her window, Mirabelle sees him tip the driver several generous bucks. They walk to a local restaurant where, upon approaching the hostess, Jeremy announces, "Table for two, Mr. Kraft." Mirabelle has forgotten his name is Kraft but is aware that this is only the second man in her life who has taken her to a restaurant where a table has been reserved for them.

Mirabelle does most of the talking, and Jeremy listens intently without saying much. Later, Mirabelle will remember the dinner as the time she first found him to be very interesting.

On the walk home, as they warm up to each other and the night, Mirabelle recites the litany of reasons for her move, leaving out the most important one, and gets down to a final summation:

"I'm fixing myself."

"I'm fixing myself, too," says Jeremy.

And they know they will forever have something to talk about.

While Jeremy dates Mirabelle and makes tiny inroads into her, Ray continues to occasionally see her. In an act of self-preservation, she no longer makes love to him, and because he finally cares about her fully, he doesn't try.

Mirabelle takes months to accept Jeremy, and Jeremy patiently waits. And as he stands by, his feelings for Mirabelle grow. One night, she cries in his arms when a recollection of Ray flirts with her memory, and he holds her and doesn't say a word. Where his insight comes from as he courts her, even he doesn't know. It might have been that he was ready to grow up, and the knowledge was already in him, like a dormant gene. Whatever it is, she is the perfect recipient of his attention, and he is the perfect recipient of her tenderness. Unlike Ray Porter, his love is fearless and without reservation. As Jeremy offers her more of his heart, she offers equal parts of herself in return. One night, sooner than she would have liked, which made it irresistible, they make love for the second time in two years. But this time, Jeremy holds her for a long while, and they connect in a deep and profound way. At this point, Jeremy surpasses Mr. Ray Porter as a lover of Mirabelle, because as clumsy as he is, what he offers her is tender and true. That night, coming up for air from the unexpected love he is falling in, he gives some opinions on tweeter wholesaling that Mirabelle secretly calls "the second oration." After he nods off, she pokes her forefinger into his closed fist and falls asleep.

Their union is the kind of perfect mismatch that makes for long relationships. She is smarter than he is, but Jeremy is in love with his own bright ideas, and the enthusiasm he shows for them infects Mirabelle and pushes her forward into the world of drawing for money. She begins to enjoy tolerating his enthusiastic outbursts; this is her gift to him. Sometimes they lie in bed and Mirabelle relates the entire plot of a Victorian novel, and Jeremy is so captivated and engrossed that he believes the events in the story are happening right now, to him.

* * *

Mirabelle informs Ray that though she is cautious, perhaps she has met somebody. "I tell him about my medication and he doesn't care," she says. This is the moment Ray has always known is coming, when she succumbs to the unrestricted, unbounded, and free-flowing passion of someone who is her peer. In spite of its predictability, he still feels this moment as a loss, and a curious one: How is it possible to miss a woman whom you kept at a distance, so that when she was gone you would not miss her?

Ray also wonders why it is she and not he who has met someone accidentally in a Laundromat, someone who stumbles into your life and forever alters it. But just three months later, it happens to Ray—it isn't a Laundromat since he hasn't seen one in thirty years, but rather a dinner party—a forty-five-year-old woman, divorced with two children, touches his heart and then breaks it flat. It is then Ray's turn to experience Mirabelle's despair, to see its walls and colors. Only then does he realize what he has done to Mirabelle, how wanting a square inch of her and not all of her has damaged them both, and how he cannot justify his actions except that, well, it was life.

Jeremy and Mirabelle, who are not living together but are close to it, have shorter and shorter separations as he commutes south and north. Mirabelle and Ray continue to talk weekly or more, and they begin to be able to discuss the details of each other's romantic lives. On the phone, Mirabelle mentions that she wants to fly home to Vermont for a three-day weekend. She does not ask him for money—she never does—but Ray is always forthcoming when he senses her need. This time, however, he does not volunteer the dough and they chat on and hang up. He needs to sort something out.

As he stands on his balcony overlooking Los Angeles in the dusky orange sunset, Ray ponders his continuing concern for Mirabelle. If she is no longer seeing him, if she is now with someone new, wouldn't it be the new man's responsibility to pay for the odd necessity? Ray always had paid; he saw it as his gift to her, but now it is over. Yet he is still compelled to help her. Why?

He turns his powers of analysis away from the logic of symbols, and toward his churning subconscious. He strips his questions down to their barest form, and he finds the single unifying theme of his contradictory feelings. He suddenly knows why he feels the way he does about her, why she still touches him, and why, at irregular and unpredictable intervals, he wonders where she is and how she is doing: He has become her parent, and she his child. He sees, finally, that as much as he believed he was imposing his will on her, she was also imposing her need on him, and their two dispositions interlocked. And the consequence was a mutual education. He experienced a relationship in which he was the sole responsible party, and he notes its failures; she found someone to guide her through to the next level of her life. Mirabelle, standing on uneasy legs, now feeling the warmth of her first mature reciprocal love, has broken away from him. But he knows that like a parent, he will be there for her, ever.

Some nights, alone, he thinks of her, and some nights, alone, she thinks of him. Some nights these thoughts, separated by miles and time zones, occur at the same objective moment, and Ray and Mirabelle are connected without ever knowing it. One night, he will think of her as he looks into the eyes of someone new, searching for the two qualities that Mirabelle defined for him: loyalty and acceptance. Mirabelle, far away and in Jeremy's embrace, knows that what had been lost is now regained.

Months later, after the hard edges of their breakup had smoothed into forgetfulness, Mirabelle speaks with Ray Porter on the phone. She tells him about her new life, and he hears the fresh delight in her voice. She tells him, "I feel like I really belong here. For the first time, I feel like I really belong." She underplays Jeremy's place in her heart, as she thinks it might hurt Ray. She mentions that she continues to draw and sell, with a positive review in *Art News* to her credit. They reminisce about their affair and she tells him how he helped her and he tells her how she helped him, then he apologizes for the way he handled everything. "Oh, no . . . don't," she corrects him: "It's pain that changes our lives." And there is a pause, and neither speaks. Then Mirabelle says, "I took the gloves to Vermont and stored them in my memory box—my mother asked me what they were but I kept it to myself—and here in my bedroom, in my private drawer, I keep a photo of you."

ACKNOWLEDGMENTS

If writing is so solitary, why are there so many people to thank? First, Leigh Haber, who delicately edited the book without bruising my ego; Esther Newberg and Sam Cohn, who first uttered encouraging words; my friends April, Sarah, Victoria, Nora, Eric and Eric, Ellen, Mary, and Susan, who were all convinced that it was their idea to read and provide helpful comments on this book during its early stages. How can I thank them except to offer a twenty-five percent discount on bulk purchases when accompanied by a valid driver's license?

BAD NEIGHBOR SCHEDULE

6:30 A.M.: Let Tuffy out for barking epiphany.

7:30 A.M.: Test car alarm.

7:55 A.M.: Bring in Tuffy.

8:00 A.M.: Clean entire backyard, front porch, and driveway with leaf blower.

9:00 A.M.: One hour aerobics dance workout.

10:30 A.M.: Rev car engine for one hour.

12:00 P.M.: Tree trimming!

1:00 P.M.: Park car in front of neighbor's front path.

2:30 P.M.: Start inexplicable hammering on metal pipe.

3:30 P.M.: Rev car engine one more time.

4:00 P.M.: Tuffy needs to go out to communicate with other neighborhood dogs!

4:45 P.M.: Billy's bagpipe lesson.

5:00 P.M.: Bring in Tuffy.

5:15 P.M.: Host VFW motorcycle club tea.

6:00 P.M.: Vespers.

6:05 P.M.: Work out bugs in the new buzz saw.

7:00 P.M.: Whoo hoo! Chinese New Year!

9:00 P.M.: Poor Tuffy needs a bark 'n' pee!

11:00 P.M.: Madison's grad party with live backyard band.

3:30 A.M.: What's that sound? Oops, forgot to bring Tuffy in!

TAPING MY FRIENDS

JEROME

(friend, 22 years)

ME: Does your wife know?

JEROME: I hope she doesn't find out.

ME: Find out what?

JEROME: What I told you yesterday.

ME: Right. I remember what you told me yesterday, but the way you said it was so poignant. Would you say it?

JEROME: I just don't want her to find out about my having a drink with that waitress. I was so dumb.

ME: So you definitely had a drink with the waitress.

JEROME: [*Inaudible*]

ME: Sorry?

JEROME: Yes.

ME: Yes, what?

JEROME: I had a drink with the waitress.

ME: Whose name was?

JEROME: Dinah. Are you having memory problems?

ME: Yes. Could you recap?

JEROME: I had a drink with the waitress, Dinah.

ME: Let's keep this between us.

JEROME: Thanks, man.

VIRGINIA

(ex-girlfriend)

VIRGINIA: I'm feeling so guilty about what we did.

ME: Can you hang on a minute?

[*Sound of beep from tape recorder being turned on*]

VIRGINIA: What was that?

ME: What?

VIRGINIA: That beep.

ME: Federal Express truck backing up. You feel guilty about what?

VIRGINIA: You know, the other night. I'd feel terrible if Bob ever found out.

ME: How would he ever find out?

VIRGINIA: So you won't tell?

ME: I can't believe you're asking me that.

VIRGINIA: I'm sorry.

ME: Find out about what?

VIRGINIA: You know. The kiss and the . . . you know.

ME: It was beautiful. I'd love for you to describe it.

VIRGINIA: What a nice thing; you're so romantic now. When we were dating, I couldn't believe how cold you were, and how selfish...

[*Sound of tape recorder being turned off*]

[*Pause*]

[*Sound of tape recorder being turned back on*]

VIRGINIA:...ask for separate checks, you big loser. What was that beep?

ME: FedEx truck again, but get back to the kiss.

VIRGINIA: Well, we had just had lunch and you walked me back to my apartment and we kissed by the mailboxes, and you know.

ME: Who is we again?

VIRGINIA: We? You and I.

ME: And your name is?

VIRGINIA: Are you insane? I'm Virginia!

ME: I love it when you say your name....

WILHELMINA

(business acquaintance)

ME: It's nice walking along the lake, isn't it, Wilhelmina?

WILHELMINA: Oh yes, it's very nice. That sure is a nice flower on your lapel....

[Snifffff]

ME: Wilhelmina, I was wondering if you ever see, say, my ex-wife's new husband's tax return when you're working over there at the IRS?

WILHELMINA: Oh yes, I do, but I would never—

[Thud thud thud thud]

ME: I'm sorry, what was that?

WILHELMINA: I was saying that I would never reveal—

[Thud thud thud thud]

ME: Wilhelmina, please don't poke me on the lapel like that.

WILHELMINA: Sorry . . .

MOM

(mother)

ME: Mom, I'm really in a hurry, and I can't remember what you told me twelve years ago about how upset you were with Dad's false tax return.

MOM: Well, let me think. I think he had underreported some income on his night job . . . we were so desperate. Remember you needed that extra money for college?

ME: Oh yeah.

MOM: You needed money for . . . I can't remember.

ME: To buy SAT answers.

MOM: I can't hear you, son.

ME: I said—what was that beep?

MOM: FedEx truck backing up. You were saying?

ME: I needed cash to buy answers for my college entrance exam. But that's between us, Mom.

MOM: Of course, son. If you can't trust your mother, who can you trust?

THE NATURE OF MATTER AND ITS ANTECEDENTS

I was taking a meeting with my publicists last week, trying to figure out what to do next. Marty suggested that the audience wants a Steve Martin to be doing a comedy right now. Tony said that a Steve Martin should do a nice cameo in a drama, "kind of an award thing." Michelle's idea was different, "Jack has a Légion d'honneur; let's get you a Nobel. Why not make a profound scientific discovery and then write an essay about it? This is what the public wants right now from a Steve Martin." I had never thought of myself as a Steve Martin before, but I guess I was one, and frankly, it felt good.

"Go on," I implored.

"Well, maybe you could write something on matter, or the nature of matter. Cruise is doing something on reverse DNA. You could do something, too. Maybe better."

"The problem is it's not matter I'm interested in. It's prematter. The moment when it's 'not soup yet,' when it's neither nothing nor something."

"Steve, isn't that really just semantics?" said Michelle. "You're talking about something existing prior to existing." I looked at her and thought how stupid she was.

"Now you're talkin' like Bruce and Demi," I said. "Did you see their piece in *Actor/Scientist*? I would love to attack their semantics angle."

Michelle inched forward. "Why don't you, Steve?" I realized she had maneuvered me into acceptance.

I remembered when Stallone had turned in his first *Rambo* draft. Through all the rewrites, he was also quietly conducting experiments on the irregular movements of explosive sound. He conjectured that explosive sound will travel faster through air already jarred by another explosive sound, with the bizarre effect that between two simultaneous explosions, a perceiver will hear the farther explosion first. The studio head told me later that the studio wasn't too confident in the script at the time, but the scientific work was so fascinating, they decided to let Stallone keep writing. Sly asked for no public acknowledgment of his work but diligently spent hours editing to make sure the movie's sound corresponded to reality.

The next day, I had my noon shrink appointment, and luckily we got into Spago at a corner table. I talked openly about my fears of winning a Nobel, and I also admitted my concerns about getting airline reservations and decent hotel rooms in Stockholm during prize season. My shrink reminded me that there were personal rewards for writing a scientific essay: the satisfaction of doing something for no other reason than to do it well. My other shrink disagreed. I have a call into my third, "tiebreaker" shrink.

That night I was in a limo with Sharon Stone having sex and stopped for a minute with the question "Can something be in a state of becoming but not yet exist?" Sharon crossed her legs as only she can and said something so profound that everything in me tingled. "In Swahili, it can. Now, where were we?" In her words was my answer to Bruce and Demi: *Only in English and other Germanic derivatives must a thing exist prior to its existence.* Sharon's publicist leaned forward. "Go on, Sharon, I'm very curious about what you're meaning." Sharon explained further: "After all, you're not talking about a grape becoming a raisin; you're talking about the interstitial state between pure nothing and pure something." I looked down. I was still tumescent. Then she added, "Who made your sunglasses?" "They're Armanis. I saw them at his store in Boston, but they were on sale, so I waited and got them at Barneys at full price."

We finally arrived at the Ivy, where we were to meet Travolta, Goldie and Kurt, Tom and Nicole, and Sly for dinner. Our table wasn't ready, so we yanked some tourists off their table and took their food.

We talked through the evening. Sly astounded us by coming up with nine anagrams of the word *Rambo*, Travolta amused the table by turning our flat bottle Evian into gassy Perrier by simply adding saltpeter and rubber shavings. Kurt and Goldie discussed their cataloging of "every damn grasshopper in Colorado." Tom mentioned that he could cure the common cold in four seconds with a vacuum gun, except for the pesky weakness of the eardrums, which tended to dangle outside the ears after treatment. Our publicists stood behind us as we ate, and one of them wisely noted that it renews the soul to do something for yourself, something that you don't market in Asia, and we all acknowledged the truth of that. Of course, every time the waiter or a fan would approach the table, we quickly turned the topic of conversation to Prada leather pants, because for that night, anyway, we decided to keep our little secrets.

I drifted off for a few moments and thought about my paper. As much as I wanted to be known for my science writing and for it to be published under my own name, I also knew it might cost me the Nobel if I did. The committee would probably be disinclined to give an award to any man who has worn a dress to get a laugh from a monkey. I thought about publishing the essay under a pseudonym, like Stiv Morton or Steeve Maartin, in order to deceive the Nobel committee. My reverie was broken by Nicole, who asked the table, "Why do we do it, this science?" No one had an answer, until I stood up and said, "Isn't there money in a Nobel?"

THE SLEDGEHAMMER: HOW IT WORKS

Many of today's adults, who are otherwise capable of handling sophisticated modern devices, are united by a contemporary malady: sledgehammer anxiety. "I feel I'm going to break it"; "The old ways still work for me"; "This is where technology leaves me behind," are the most common chants of the sledgehammer-phobe. Much of this initial fear comes from a failure to understand just how it works. By attaching a "heavy weighted slug" to a truncated supercissoid, a disproportionate fulcrum is created. In other words, if you're a TV set showing Regis promoting a diet book, and you're in a room with an angry unpublished poet holding a sledgehammer, watch out.

The novice sledgehammerer (from the German *sledgehammeramalamadingdong*) must be familiar with a few terms:

- Thunk: the sound the "clanker" (street term for "heavy weighted slug") makes when wielded against the "stuff" (see next)

- Stuff: things that are to be wanged (see next)
- Wang: the impact of the clanker and the stuff
- Smithereens: the result of being wanged

Many people are surprised to find out that the sledgehammer has only one moving part: it. Yet "Should I buy now or wait for the new models?" is a refrain often heard from the panicky first-timer, who forgets that the number of sledgehammer innovations in the last three thousand years can be counted on one finger. There are currently only two types of sledgehammer on the market: the three-foot stick with a lead weight on the end, called the "normal," and a new model, currently being beta-tested, which is a three-foot stick with a lead weight in the middle, called the "below normal." But don't let market confusion keep you from getting your feet wet. The longer you wait, the fewer things you will demolish.

"There is a natural fear of sledgehammers," says the National Sledgehammer and Broken Toe Society, which, in response, has been charting the most common accidents and offers tips for the sledgehammer's safe use. The over-the-head position, for example, often leads to excruciating lower-body pain, caused when the sledgehammer wedges itself between the thighs at the end of the backswing. There is also the self-inflicted back-of-the-head knockout on lateral swings, which is very rare, and only afflicts—to use the researcher's lingo—"really dumb people." There are also cleaning accidents. A home hobbyist in Valdosta, Georgia, reported that while he was removing paint from his sledgehammer, it suddenly went out of control and destroyed his living room wall, even though he never let go of its handle.

Despite all these drawbacks, the world of the sledgehammer is rife with enthusiasts. "I find the sledgehammer very erotic," says Jane Parpadello, who is a stockbroker with Smith Barney and wants everyone to know her home phone number is listed. "I think it's because my father was shaped like a sledgehammer: the long wooden body and big metal head. Today when I see a man with that shape, I want to pick him up and swing him against an apartment wall."

The sledgehammer king, Marty Delafangio, whose net worth has been estimated at forty-two thousand dollars, was recently summoned before Congress to defend his reasons for attaching a mandatory web browser to his market-leading product. "I smelled money to be made," said Delafangio. "The combination of a web browser and a sledgehammer is a natural." Congress disagreed, and now the web browser can be sold only as an option, although, as a compromise, the powder-puff attachment remains.

Roustabouts have also noted a sharp increase in sledgehammer interest. "We used to raise a circus tent pretty much on our own," says Toby, a twenty-four-year veteran of Barnum & Bailey. "Now I have crazies every morning from the local sledgehammer club, watching me plug a spike; it's a disgusting, circuslike atmosphere. One of them interviewed me for his newsletter. I let him take a swing, too. He looked like Tinker Bell trying to lift a semi by its hood ornament. But it's not all bad; at least there's a never-ending supply of chicks. Although once some woman picked me up by the ankles and slammed me against an apartment wall."

In the last ten years, the sledgehammer has come into its own, finally recognized for what it is: a tool, a thing, and a heavy object. Hundreds of years from now, when technology has altered the sledgehammer's appearance into a sleek, digital, aerodynamic *über*machine, it will no doubt function as it does today, toppling the mighty and denting the hard.

THE PAPARAZZI OF PLATO

TABLOIDUS: Socrates, I wanted to show you my new Nikon FM2 with its six-hundred-millimeter lens.

SOCRATES: Thank you. It looks fine for taking pictures of ducks flying off in the distance.

MO-PED: That is a very fine purpose in combination with a speed bike and infrared night scope.

CLOOLUS: What else do you photograph, besides nature studies?

TABLOIDUS: I love to photograph children.

SOCRATES: That is a good and noble profession.

TABLOIDUS: There is nothing more beautiful to photograph than a mother breastfeeding her baby. Especially if it's Madonna.

CLOOLUS: You photographed Madonna breastfeeding her baby?

TABLOIDUS: Oh yes.

SOCRATES: What was she like in person?

TABLOIDUS: Well, I actually didn't meet her.

SOCRATES: Was she so full of herself that she wouldn't speak to you?

TABLOIDUS: Oh no. Because of the lens, I had to be three hundred yards away and shoot through her bedroom window.

CLOOLUS: It seems odd to me that Madonna would agree to have herself photographed this way.

TABLOIDUS: Her agreement was tacit.

CLOOLUS: But it seems to me you have invaded her privacy.

SOCRATES: Cloolus, what is privacy?

CLOOLUS: Privacy is the state of being secluded from the view of others.

SOCRATES: Are you private when you are alone in a crowded market?

CLOOLUS: Certainly not.

SOCRATES: Are you private when you're alone in a car?

CLOOLUS: More so, Socrates.

SOCRATES: Are you private when you're in a car with tinted windows?

CLOOLUS: That is starting to be private.

SOCRATES: Are you private when you're in your home?

CLOOLUS: Certainly.

SOCRATES: Is it not true that if you tint your windows or stay home, in some way you are protecting your privacy?

MO-PED: It cannot be otherwise.

CLOOLUS: But Madonna was in her home.

SOCRATES: Yes, but her windows were not tinted with UV 40 Reflecto-coat, nor was she alone.

MO-PED: She was with her baby!

SOCRATES: Therefore, she was not protecting her privacy, and how can one invade what is not protected?

CLOOLUS: I am confused.

SOCRATES: Can something be tinted and not tinted at the same time?

CLOOLUS: It would be impossible.

SOCRATES: Can something be private and public at the same time?

CLOOLUS: They are mutually exclusive.

SOCRATES: And is it not true that privacy and UV 40 Reflectocoat are one and the same?

MO-PED: He has proved it!

SOCRATES: Tabloidus, where were you when you took the picture?

TABLOIDUS: I was hiding on a rooftop. Further, I was wearing black clothing and a hood.

SOCRATES: So you were merely protecting your privacy, while Madonna invaded your camera lens?

TABLOIDUS: I cannot argue otherwise, Socrates.

CLOOLUS: But is it not wrong to spy on a woman breastfeeding her baby?

MO-PED: When you become a singing star, it is wrong to want your breastfeeding to be private.

CLOOLUS: But why?

TABLOIDUS: Because of the public's right to know.

SOCRATES: Is it not true, Cloolus, when the public is shopping in a supermarket, very often at the checkout point, it has an overwhelming desire to see Alec Baldwin's newborn or Frank Gifford having sex?

CLOOLUS: I cannot deny it.

SOCRATES: This desire, known in a democracy as "the checkout point of freedom," is important, because without it, Frank's children would never have known about his transgression.

CLOOLUS: Your argument is flawless. But why was there never a similar desire to see, say, Jimmy Stewart having sex?

SOCRATES: Because Jimmy Stewart didn't have "that special something."

TABLOIDUS: Alas, Cloolus, the public's taste in those days was not so sophisticated.

CLOOLUS: So I am living in a wonderful age.

MO-PED: There could not be one finer!

SOCRATES: Let us now try and get a snapshot of Plato and Aristotle cavorting on a nude beach. It might pay for lunch.

SIDE EFFECTS

Dosage: Take two tablets every six hours for joint pain.

Side Effects: This drug may cause joint pain, nausea, headache, or shortness of breath. You may also experience muscle aches, rapid heartbeat, or ringing in the ears. If you feel faint, call your doctor. Do not consume alcohol while taking this pill; likewise, avoid red meat, shellfish, and vegetables. Okay foods: flounder. Under no circumstances eat yak. Men can expect painful urination while sitting, especially if the penis is caught between the toilet seat and the bowl. Projectile vomiting is common in 30 percent of users—sorry: 50 percent. If you undergo disorienting nausea accompanied by migraine with audible raspy breathing, double the dosage. Leg cramps are to be expected; up to one knee-buckler per day is allowable. Bowel movements may become frequent, in fact every ten minutes. If bowel movements become greater than twelve per hour, consult your doctor, or in fact any doctor, or anyone who will speak to you. You may find yourself becoming lost or vague; this would be a good time to write a screenplay. Do not pilot a plane, unless you are in the 10 percent of users who experience "spontaneous test pilot knowledge." If your hair begins to smell like burning tires, move away from any buildings or populated areas and apply tincture of iodine to the head until you no longer hear what could be considered a "countdown." May cause stigmata in Mexicans. Do not sit on pointy conical objects. If a fungus starts to grow between your eyebrows, call the *Guinness Book of Records*. Do not operate heavy machinery, especially if you feel qualified for a desk job; that's good advice anytime. May cause famine and pustules. There may be a tendency to compulsively repeat the phrase "No can do." This drug may cause visions of the Virgin Mary to appear in treetops. If this happens, open a souvenir shop. There may be an overwhelming impulse to shout out during a Catholic mass, "I'm gonna wop you wid da ugly stick!" You may feel a powerful sense of impending doom; this is because you are about to die. Men may experience impotence, but only during intercourse. Otherwise, a powerful erection will accompany your daily "walking-around time." Do not take this product if you are uneasy with lockjaw. Do not be near a ringing telephone that works at 900 MHz, or you will be very dead, very fast. We are assuming you have had chicken pox. You also may experience a growing dissatisfaction with life, along with a deep sense of melancholy—join the club! Do not be concerned if you arouse a few ticks from a Geiger counter. You might want to get a one-month trial subscription to *Extreme Fidgeting.* The hook shape of the pill will often cause it to get caught on the larynx. To remove, jam a finger down your throat, while a friend holds your nose to prevent the pill from lodging in a nasal passage. Then throw yourself stomach-first on the back portion of a chair. The expulsion of air should eject the pill out of the mouth, unless it goes into a sinus cavity or the brain. WARNING: This drug may shorten your intestines by twenty-one feet. Has been known to cause birth defects in the user retroactively. Passing in front of a TV may cause the screen to moiré. While taking this drug, you might want to wear something lucky. Women often feel a loss of libido, including a two-octave lowering of the voice, an increase in ankle hair, and perhaps the lowering of a testicle. If this happens, women should write a detailed description of their last three sexual encounters and mail it to me, Bob, trailer 6, Fancyland Trailer Park, Encino, CA. Or e-mail me at "hotguy.com." Discontinue use immediately if you feel your teeth are receiving radio broadcasts. You may experience "lumpy back" syndrome, but we are actively seeking a cure. Bloated fingertips on the heart-side hand are common. Be sure to allow plenty of "quiet time" in order to retrain the eye to move off stationary objects. Flotation devices at sea will become pointless, as the user of this drug will develop a stonelike body density; therefore, if thrown overboard, contact your doctor. This product may contain one or more of the following: bungee cord, plankton, rubber, crack cocaine, pork bladders, aromatic oils, gum arabic—pardon me, an Arab's gums—gunpowder, corn husk, glue, bee pollen, English muffins, poached eggs, ham, hollandaise sauce, and crushed saxophone reeds. Sensations of levitation are illusory, as is the feeling of a "phantom third arm." User may experience certain inversions of language: Acceptable: "Hi, are how you?" Unacceptable: "The rain in Sprain slays blainly on the phsssst." Twenty minutes after taking the pills, you will experience an insatiable craving to take another dose. AVOID THIS WITH ALL YOUR POWER. It is advisable to have a friend handcuff you to a large kitchen appliance, ESPECIALLY ONE THAT WILL NOT FIT THROUGH THE

DOORWAY TO WHERE THE PILLS ARE. You should also be out of reach of any weaponlike utensil with which you could threaten friends or family, who should also be briefed to not give you the pills, no matter how much you sweet-talk them. *Notice:* This drug is legal in the United States only when the user is straddling a state line.

ARTIST LOST TO ZOLOFT

Performance artist Shelf Head 3 has decided to cancel his work *Frog Slave* and instead open a creperie in Brooklyn so he can live closer to his parents.

"This change is not related to my recent prescription for the mood-elevating drug Zoloft," said Shelf Head 3, who now prefers to be called Jeremy. "I find I can say things with a crepe that I just couldn't say through urine writing. The first day on the job, I created—and I say created because that's exactly what I did—a *croissant distant,* loosely translated as a 'faraway pie.' Because that's what we are, really, aren't we? At night, after dinner with the folks, I would listen to Yanni, but I stopped because, well, he's so *angry.*

"I'm also changing my mural in Bilbao. Murals don't really have to cover an entire wall. It's obtrusive to the weekend driver. Why not a picket-fence-high depiction that the eye can *choose* to see rather than be forced to see? Maybe with tips for the marooned motorist on how to change a tire; perhaps with line three having a satirical swipe at the current administration. I'd like that. *Touché!* In fact, why not an info-mural? A product tie-in would make a point.

"My early works *Parent Kill* and *Why Not Me, Mom?* have been criticized as 'juvenile, wasteful, boring, and why leave out disgusting?' Which was exactly the point, and subsequently, 'juvenile, wasteful, boring, and why leave out disgusting?' became the name of our movement. Let me remind you that at one time *impressionism* and *fauve* were derogatory terms. However, my new work, which I will do on Sundays, when the creperie is closed, makes the same point in a stronger way: I'm going to darn a hundred pair of socks while watching *The Brady Bunch*. The point is self-explanatory, which is part of its meaning. Obscurity used to turn me on, but I'm either through with that phase or high. I also won't be doing my performance piece *Ear Slice* anymore—I've done it once, and I would like to retain my remaining lobe, as I'm finding it useful for hearing orders at the creperie."

A WORRYING EFFECT

The use of Zoloft in the artistic community has a worrying effect on art dealers selling to the "anger market." "I can sell antiparent symbolist stuff all day," said an unidentified dealer, "but the artists aren't delivering it anymore. One artist, who used to give me birth canals with fangs, now sends me paintings of dogs playing poker. Who am I going to sell that to? English decorators who need fifty puppy pictures for a theme in the den, and that's all. The artist says his point is that although dogs playing poker has been painted many times before, it's usually bulldogs playing draw poker; there's still much to explore in lowball and stud. He also wonders why there's never been a wiener dog in these paintings. I just stare at him. I hate to think what would have happened to Jackson Pollock when the Zoloft kicked in. We may have to divide downtown galleries into zones, so that the collectors on Prozac can easily find the galleries on Prozac, and the ones on Zoloft don't accidentally wander into a Valium gallery. I used to worry about these issues, until I started on Zoloft myself so I could understand just what exactly my artists were painting.

"I have actually resorted to breaking into my artists' medicine cabinets and substituting their Zoloft with placebos, just enough for a week or two," continued the dealer. "This sudden withdrawal sends them on a wild emotional ride. Then I call Ernie's Artistic Supplies and have them deliver canvas, paints, and palette knives while the artists are still bouncing off the walls. Two weeks later, I get half a dozen canvases that are at least salable. Then the artists get back on the real pills, not knowing what hit them, and I start getting the Lassie-at-the-card-club stuff. I ship them off to Asia and tell the artists they were sold, crossing my fingers that they never go shopping at the Thailand airport mall."

The artist Screaming Mimi, now Kathy, has summed up this problem nicely in her recent work *I Enjoy Being a Girl*. The work consists of a lovely moonscape, with an accompanying explanatory note that hangs beside it. It should be noted that the effect of the Zoloft was wearing off as the painter reached midsentence:

> I hope you all enjoy this painting, where the moon symbolizes the light of mystery, the misty damp air recalls the fog of ignorance, and the sea below it represents my desire to put you on a plate and eat you with a power tool.

HOW I JOINED MENSA

I started with the phone book. Looking up Mensa was not going to be easy, what with having to follow the strict alphabetizing rules that are so common nowadays. I prefer a softer, more *fuzzy* alphabetizing scheme, one that allows the mind to float free and "happen" upon the word. There is pride in that. The dictionary is a perfect example of overalphabetization, with its harsh rules and every little word neatly in place. It almost makes me want to go on a diet of grapes and waste away to nothing.

Being a member of Mensa means that you are a genius, with an IQ of at least 132. This enables you to meet other members, who will understand what the hell you are talking about when you say, for example, "That lamppost is tawdry." That's the kind of person they're after. Joining Mensa instills in you a courtly benevolence toward nonmembers who would pretend to know what you know, think what you think, and stultify what you perambulate.

I worried that the 132 cutoff point might be arbitrary until I met someone with an IQ of 131, and honestly, he was a bit slow on the uptake. If you have a dinner party of 132s and there's a 131 attending, you can actually feel the 131er hit the wall of stupidity. He acquires that dog look—the one with the wide eyes and the cocked head and the big grin—which tells you he's just not getting it. But unlike a dog, your guest cannot be put out in the yard to play with a ball, unless it has been agreed on beforehand.

I gave up on the phone book, which led me astray time and again with its complex passages, and then tried blind calling, with no success. Next, 1-800-MENSA, which weirdly brought dead silence on the other end of the phone. A week later, while *volksvalking*, I realized that MENSA didn't contain enough numerals to be a phone number and knew it must be some kind of test: Any future member should be able to figure out the next two digits in the sequence. I tried dialing MENSANE, MENSAIL, MENSAFE, and MENSAPS, but I got three rebuffs and a fax tone.

So it was a complete accident that I stumbled into a party in my building, having inverted my floor number and gotten off at 21 instead of 12. Slipping past the first bloc of chatterers and avoiding the host, whom I identified through deduction, I flipped back the Oushak rug and counted the knots per square inch. These people had money. I heard snippets of conversation; words like *feldspar* and *eponym* filled the air. In the corner, a lone piper played a dirge. I knew where I was. This was a Mensa party.

That's when I saw Lola. She had hair the color of rust and a body the shape of a Doric column, the earlier ones, preinvasion. She walked across the room carrying one of those rum drinks and endearingly poked herself in the face with her straw as she slid herself onto the blue velveteen sofa. If she truly was Mensa, she would have no problem with my introduction. "Please don't relegate me to a faraway lea," I ventured.

"I can see you've read Goethe, the Snooky Lanson translations," she countered. "Lozenge?"

I was pegging her around 140. Her look told me she had put me in the low 120s. My goal was to elevate her assessment and wangle a Mensa membership form out of her. Taking a hint from soap operas, I talked to her with my back turned while staring out a window. "Wouldn't you rather parse than do anything?" I queried. "Hail Xiaoping, the Chinese goddess of song," she rejoined.

Lola then engaged in some verbal sparring that left me reeling. "This is quite an impressive apartment," she offered.

I saw a dictionary on its stand. Oh, how I longed to run to it and look up *impressive*! How I wanted to retort in Mensa-ese! I felt the dog look creeping over my face, but it was my turn, and I spoke: "I'm not sure if that's a compliment or an insult." I threw my head back, laughing, coughed out my lozenge, and watched it nestle into the Oushak. She asked me my name. "Call me Dor." Later, I realized I meant "Rod."

Lola and I sat and talked through the night. After the party, I held her and whispered, "I love that you're in Mensa." She whispered back, "I love that you're in Mensa, too." My temperature dropped to arctic. She told me her phone number, but since it was all sevens, I couldn't remember it. Then she walked to the elevator, turned back toward me, and said, "We have to stop meeting like this." Those words hit me like tiny arrows in the heart. That night, I cried and cried into my pillow. Eight months later, it was explained to me that it had been a joke.

Most things one wants in life come when they are no longer needed. My membership was awarded exactly one year later, when I applied and became an honorary Mensa "plaything." Answering a brochure ad that came with my introductory packet, I went on a Mensa love boat trip to Bermuda. Embarking, I saw a woman standing aft, her back to me, bent slightly over the railing, looking very much the way a Doric column would look if it were bent over a railing. She turned and saw me, and I again saw my Lola. It was as though nothing had changed in a year, because we were both wearing the same thing we wore on that first night, still unwashed. She spoke: "Long time no see, Dor."

I corrected her, gaining the upper hand: "My name's not Dor."

"What is it?" she asked.

"It will come to me."

"Would you like to take a walk on the boat deck?" she asked.

Boat deck? Where is the damn dictionary when you need it?

She spoke: "I have only two years to live. Let's enjoy them while we slaver."

"Then slaver we shall, slaver we shall." I took her hand and we turned eastward, toward the setting sun. "And by the way, I think my name is Rod."

BAD DOG

"You're a bad dog, a very bad dog!" shouts Dr. Fogel.

I'll show you what a bad dog is, thinks Jasper, padding down the hallway to his dog bowl, where he can think.

Sulking next to his dish, Jasper tries to sort everything out. The FedEx man is supposed to be barked at, dammit. When he is outside the gate, he is outside the threshold of recognition. As he nears, he comes inside the threshold of recognition. Of course I'm going to bark at him, even if I know who he is. The plumber is even lower than the FedEx man. I'm just saying, Watch out, he's got a wrench. Is that so terrible?

The cat slinks by. Jasper thinks the one epithet he could never say: Fraidy.

In the next room, Dr. Fogel is on the phone. "Well, I need that package today, doggone it." Jasper shudders. I hate it when he uses that word. Does he know how it hurts me? Does he know what he's saying? Why can't he say Goddammit, like everyone else? Goddammit is a decent, benign swear word, no matter how you look at it. Even backward, it's . . . it's . . . oh my dog!

The doorbell rings. Jasper's up and running to the front door, barking. Master and dog arrive at the same time. "Quiet, Jasper!

Quiet!" says Dr. Fogel, but Jasper can't keep quiet. The door opens. It's the FedEx man.

Oops, thinks Jasper. He immediately puts his nose between the deliveryman's legs. They love this; this will be my salvation, he calculates.

But from above he hears, "Bad dog! Bad, bad dog."

What? Bad dog? Jasper keeps on the happy face but is killed inside. He watches the exchange of signature and receipt, then follows Him, hoping for a pat or a word of understanding or just anything. It does not come.

Jasper dips into his bowl of water, hiding his big sad eyes. This is a major, major problem, he thinks. That night, lying on his sawdust-filled bed, Jasper realizes that there's something in his brain telling him to distinguish between the Federal Express man, who must be barked at in all circumstances, and Granny Fogel, for whom he demonstrates his admiration by rolling over and showing his genitals. But how can I stop myself from doing what I want to do—nay, what I must do? This urge is so strong, based on so many factors, so many subtle discernments. He decides that he lacks some key piece of information, some general rule of understanding that would put him on the clear path. He resolves to search for that knowledge by taking a trip around the world. For Jasper, the world is defined by a five-foot fence that surrounds his yard, the house, and all its contents.

The next morning, Jasper is out early. He sidles along the fence, hugging the wall, nose lowered into the grass. After an hour, he realizes that what he's doing is pointless, except for the pure fun of it all. He hangs around the kitchen for a while, doing the big-eyes thing, but gets nothing. Unrewarded, he moves to his bed for a snooze. Jasper puts his nose next to his last saved biscuit and nuzzles it. He thinks, Questing is hard, and he rolls over on his back, sticks his legs in the air, and falls asleep.

Falling hard into a dream, Jasper imagines himself paddling through the air in a vast gallery of paintings. Although he's never actually been to a museum, he once guided himself accidentally through London's Tate Gallery Internet site (the letters *T-A-T-E* are all left-handers on a keyboard, and one lucky paw slap sent Jasper spiraling into cyberspace). Now, in his dream, he is able to whirl and twist in the air, viewing the pictures up close and reading their museum labels. His dream, swirling up from his simple unconscious, changes each painter's bio: "Johann Fuseli, Swiss painter and former dog." "Giovanni Battista Tiepolo, Italian painter and former dog." Jasper sees that these artists have transformed the canine within themselves into wonderful works of art.

The doorbell jars Jasper out of his sleep. Consciousness takes over, and the beautiful dream fades back into his thin cortex. Rising, he looks through a series of windows, from the bedroom to the kitchen, and beyond the kitchen to the street. He sees the white rectangle of the FedEx truck. Impulsively, he runs toward the front door.

Charging down the hall, he can feel the bark welling up inside him. He is like a boxer with a coiled left hook about to be thrown, like the clapper of an alarm, already in motion toward its bell. He knows what he is facing: the cold censure of his master, balanced by the deliciously frightened face of the FedEx man. The bark churns deep within him. He feels it in his belly, moving up through his lungs. His body chemistry pumps him forward like a jockey's whip, and he turns the corner to the foyer. There in gleaming white is the target, handing over the trim FedEx box to Jasper's beloved and vulnerable master. As he slows, the fleshy part of his paws struggling against the hardwood floor, Jasper's locomotion compresses his energy, forcing the bark into his throat. With his master looking on, he opens his mouth; the bark now lies just behind his tongue. As it rolls over the damp, spongy, pink surface, the miracle that is Art rises from his shallow unconscious and transforms the sound waves, curving the pointy spikes of the highs and rounding the crevices of the jagged lows. Jasper looks up at his master, and out comes, in a lovely baritone:

We're having a heat wave
A tropical heat wave...

Now there is not a sound. A performer's eon passes: the time between the final note of the aria and the whooshing, enveloping applause of the audience. Finally, into the silent ethereal mist that swarms in Jasper's head, comes his master's voice: "Good boy—you're a good, good boy."

Jasper turns, feeling the euphoric relief of an adrenaline shutdown. He moves away from the door. The cat walks by. There but for the grace of God go I, thinks Jasper. He walks into the kitchen, laps some water, looks back at the startled tableau by the front door, and goes outside to lie in the sun.

AN AUTHOR RESPONDS

In Eric Mendelssohn's review in this journal of my book, *Europe, a Nation Asunder,* he is critical of my thesis, facts, usage, and punctuation. I doubt that Dr. Mendelssohn read my book all the way through since he said, "The title page was the book's last moment of excitement and coherency." I am writing this letter to the *London Review of Books* because, so far, Dr. Mendelssohn has not responded to my hourly emails, threats, keying of his car, or notes tied to rocks.

Dr. Mendelssohn may have a point that Europe, strictly speaking, is not a "nation." It is true, upon further research, that Kukla was not an emperor of Germany, but a puppet. And perhaps the phrase "Whoa, Nelly" doesn't belong in a modern history. Yes, perhaps I was wrong to include four hundred pages on Iceland, which the picky Mendelssohn correctly points out is only near Europe, not in it. But following his argument, should I have excluded Greenland on the same grounds?

Mendelssohn continually cites conventional, established reference works on Europe to contradict assertions made in my book. However, my bibliographic citations are also accepted among scholars, and all are named in the appendix. They are too numerous to list so I will name only a few: *The Golden Treasury of Europe, The Big Book of Europe, Yur-hup, Y'all Come!*, and "Amsterdam, You Name It, It Will Be in Your Hotel."

Mendelssohn gets overly indignant about the usual factual errors common to any extensive work, but I am happy to correct them in this journal. Gaudi's Sagrada de Familia in Barcelona is not "like, a mile high"; it is only three hundred feet in elevation. The Swiss live in Switzerland, not Sweden; the Eiffel Tower is not a tugboat, but a vertical edifice. An eggplant is a vegetable, not part of a dairy. The river that flows through Paris is the Seine, not the Swannee (and I can't forgive Mendelssohn for jumping on this common misconception). And it is not true that the Black Forest is pumping twenty-seven trillion tons of methane into the atmosphere; I meant to say oxygen.

Despite, however, the "noted scholar, author, linguist, philosopher, and Nobel Prize winner's" criticism, he makes a final statement I find very complimentary: My book belongs in a literary cannon.

THE PLEASURE OF MY COMPANY

A NOVEL

To my mother and father

If I can get from here to the pillar box
If I can get from here to the lamp-post
If I can get from here to the front gate
before a car comes round the corner . . .
Carolyn Murray will come to tea
Carolyn Murray will love me too
Carolyn Murray will marry me
But only if I get from here
to there before a car comes round the corner . . .

—MICK GOWAR, FROM *OXFORD'S ONE HUNDRED YEARS OF POETRY FOR CHILDREN*

This all started because of a clerical error.

Without the clerical error, I wouldn't have been thinking this way at all; I wouldn't have had time. I would have been too preoccupied with the new friends I was planning to make at Mensa, the international society of geniuses. I'd taken their IQ test, but my score came back missing a digit. Where was the 1 that should have been in front of the 90? I fell short of genius category by a full fifty points, barely enough to qualify me to sharpen their pencils. Thus I was rejected from membership and facing a hopeless pile of red tape to correct the mistake.

This clerical error changed my plans for a while and left me with a few idle hours I hadn't counted on. My window to the street consumed a lot of them. Nice view: I can see the Pacific Ocean, though I have to lean out pretty far, almost to my heels. Across the street is a row of exotically named apartment buildings, which provide me with an unending parade of human vignettes. My building, the Chrysanthemum, houses mostly young people, who don't appear to be out of work but are. People in their forties seem to prefer the Rose Crest. Couples whose children are grown gravitate toward the Tudor Gardens, and the elderly flock to the Ocean Point. In other words, a person can live his entire life here and never move from the block.

I saw Elizabeth the other day. What a pleasure! She didn't see me, though; she doesn't know me. But there was a time when Liz Taylor and Richard Burton had never met, yet it doesn't mean they weren't, in some metaphysical place, already in love. Elizabeth was pounding a FOR LEASE sign into the flower bed of the Rose Crest. Her phone number was written right below her name, Elizabeth Warner. I copied it down and went to the gas station to call her, but the recorded voice told me to push so many buttons I just gave up. Not that I couldn't have done it, it was just a complication I didn't need. I waved to Elizabeth once from my window, but maybe there was a reflection or something, because she didn't respond. I went out the next day at the same hour and looked at my apartment, and sure enough, I couldn't see a thing inside, even though I had dressed a standing lamp in one of my shirts and posed it in front of the window.

I was able to cross the street because just a few yards down from my apartment, two scooped-out driveways sit opposite each other. I find it difficult—okay, impossible—to cross the street at the corners. The symmetry of two scooped-out driveways facing each other makes a lot of sense to me. I see other people crossing the street at the curb and I don't know how they can do it. Isn't a curb forbidding? An illogical elevation imposing itself between the street and the sidewalk? Crosswalks make so much sense, but laid between two ominous curbs they might as well be at the bottom of the Mariana Trench. Who designed this? Daffy Duck?

You are now thinking I'm either brilliant or a murder suspect. Why not both? I'm teasing you. I am a murder suspect, but in a very relaxed way and definitely not guilty. I was cleared way early, but I'm still a suspect. Head spinning? Let me explain. Eight months ago a neighbor downstairs, Bob the appliance repairman, was knifed dead. Police came to interview me—it was just routine—and Officer Ken saw a bloodstained parka on my coatrack. Subsequently the lab found fibers from my parka on the corpse. Can you figure out my alibi? Take a minute.

Here it is: One night a naked woman burst out of Bob the appliance repairman's apartment, hysterical. I grabbed my parka and threw it around her. Bob came and got her, but he was so polite he made me suspicious. Too bad I didn't get fully suspicious until a week later, just after the naked woman had penetrated his liver with a kitchen knife. One day, the naked woman, now dressed, returned my parka, unaware that blood and other damning evidence stained the backside. I was unaware too until the savvy cop spotted the bloodstain when the parka was hanging on a coat hook near the kitchen. The cops checked out my story and it made sense; Amanda, hysterical woman, was arrested. End of story.

Almost. I'm still a suspect, though not in the conventional sense. My few moments of infamy are currently being reenacted because the producers of *Crime Show*, a TV documentary program that re-creates actual murders, love the bloodstained parka angle, so I'm being thrown in as a red herring. They told me to just "act like myself." When I said, "How do I do that?" they said to just have fun with it, but I'm not sure what they meant.

I'm hoping that my status as a murder suspect will enhance my first meeting with Elizabeth. It could jazz things up a bit. Of course, in the same breath I will tell her that I was cleared long ago, but I'll wait just that extra second before I do in order to make sure I've enchanted her.

The larger issue, the one that sends me to the dictionary of philosophy, if I had one, is the idea of acting like myself. Where do my hands go when I'm myself? Are they in my pockets? I frankly can't remember. I have a tough time just *being* myself, you know, at parties and such. I start talking to someone and suddenly I know I am no longer myself, that some other self has taken over.

The less active the body, the more active the mind. I had been sitting for days, and my mind made this curious excursion into a tangential problem: Let's say my shopping list consists of two items: soy sauce and talcum powder. Soy sauce and talcum powder could not be more dissimilar. Soy: tart and salty. Talc: smooth and silky. Yet soy sauce and talcum powder are both available at the same store, the grocery store. Airplanes and automobiles, however, are similar. Yet if you went to a car lot and said, "These are nice, but do you have any airplanes?" they would look at you like you're crazy.

So here's my point. This question I'm flipping around—what it means to act like myself—is related to the soy sauce issue. Soy and talc are mutually exclusive. Soy is not talc and vice versa. I am not someone else, someone else is not me. Yet we're available in the same store. The store of Existence. This is how I think, which vividly illustrates Mensa's loss.

Thinking too much also creates the illusion of causal connections between unrelated events. Like the morning the toaster popped up just as a car drove by with Arizona plates.

Connection? Or coincidence? Must the toaster be engaged in order for a car with Arizona plates to come by? The problem, of course, is that I tend to behave as if these connections were real, and if a car drives by with plates from, say, Nebraska, I immediately eyeball the refrigerator to see if its door has swung open.

I stay home a lot because I'm flush with cash right now ($600 in the bank, next month's rent already paid), so there's no real need to seek work. Anyway, seeking work is a tad difficult given the poor design of the streets with their prohibitive curbs and driveways that don't quite line up. To get to the Rite Aid, the impressively well-stocked drugstore that is an arsenal of everything from candies to camping tents, I must walk a circuitous maze discovered one summer after several weeks of trial and error. More about the Rite Aid later (Oh God, Zandy—so cute! And what a pharmacist!).

My grandmother (my angel and savior) sends me envelopes periodically from her homestead with cash or cash equivalents that make my life possible. And quite a homestead she has. Think *Tara* squashed and elongated and dipped in adobe. I would love to see her, but a trip to Helmut, Texas, would require me to travel by mass transportation, which is on my list of no-no's. Crowds of four or more are just not manageable for me, unless I can create a matrix that links one individual to another by connecting similar shirt patterns. And airplanes, trains, buses, and cars . . . well, please. I arrived in California twelve years ago when my travel options were still open, but they were quickly closed down due to a series of personal discoveries about enclosed spaces, rubber wheels, and the logic of packing, and there was just no damn way for me to get back home.

You might think not going out would make me lonely, but it doesn't. The natural disorder of an apartment building means that sooner or later everyone, guided by principles of entropy, will inadvertently knock on everyone else's door. Which is how I became the Wheatgrass guy. After the murder, gossip whipped through our hallways like a Fury, and pretty soon everyone was talking to everyone else. Philipa, the smart and perky actress who lives one flight up, gabbed with me while I was half in and half out of my open doorway (she was a suspect too for about a split second because the soon-to-be-dead guy had once offended her in a three-second unwelcome embrace by letting his hand slip lower than it properly should have, and she let everyone know she was upset about it). Philipa told me she was nervous about an upcoming TV audition. I said let me make you a wheatgrass juice. I wanted to calm her down so she could do her best. She came into my apartment and I blended a few herbs in a tall glass. Then, as a helpful afterthought, I broke an Inderal in half, which I carried in my pocket pillbox, and mixed it into the drink. Inderal is a heart medication, intended to straighten out harmless arrhythmias, which I sometimes get, but has a side effect of leveling out stage fright, too well, Philipa reported later that she gave the best audition of her life and got two callbacks. Probably no connection to the Inderal-laced drink, but maybe. The point is she wanted to believe in the wheatgrass juice, and she started coming back for more at regular intervals. She would stop by and take a swig, sit awhile and talk about her actress-y things, and then leave for her next audition with a tiny dose of a drug that was blocking her betas.

If the moon is out of orbit one inch a year, eventually, somewhere in a future too distant to imagine, it will spin out of control and smash into, say, India. So comparatively speaking, a half an Inderal in a wheatgrass juice once or twice a week for Philipa is not really a problem, but if I'm to stay in orbit with Philipa, my own prescription count needs to be upped. Easy for me, as all I have to do is exaggerate my condition to the doctor at the Free Clinic and more pills are on the way. My real dilemma began one afternoon when Philipa complained that she was not sleeping well. Did I have a juice drink that might help? she asked. I couldn't say no to her because she had grown on me. Not in the way of Elizabeth the Realtor, who had become an object of desire, but in the way of a nice girl up the stairs whose adventures kept me tuned in like a soap opera.

Philipa couldn't see that she was in the charmed part of her life when hope woke her up every day and put her feet into her shoes. She lived with a solid, but in my view, dimwit guy, who would no doubt soon disappear and be replaced by a sharper banana. I went to the kitchen and blended some orange juice, protein powder, a plum, and a squirt of liquid St. John's Wort from the Rite Aid, and then, confidently motivated by poor judgment, I dropped in one-quarter of a quaalude.

These quaaludes were left over from a college party and had hung out in my kitchen drawer ever since, still in their original package. I didn't even know if they were still potent, but they seemed to work for Philipa, because about ten minutes after she drank my elixir, a dreamy smile came over her face and she relaxed into my easy chair and told me her entire history with the current boyfriend, whose name was Brian. She commented on his hulking, glorious penis, which was at first phrased as "great dick"—Philipa had begun to slur—and then later, when she began to slur more poetically, was described as a "uniform shaft with a slight parenthetical bend." Evidently it had captivated her for months until one day it stopped captivating her. Brian still assumed it was the center of their relationship, and Philipa felt obligated to continue with him because her fixation on his fail-safe penis had drawn him into her nest in the first place. But now this weighty thing remained to be dealt with, though Philipa's interest had begun to flag.

The quaalude drink became first a monthly ritual, then biweekly, then bidiurnal, and then I started hiding every night around 11:00 P.M. when she would knock on my door. My supply of the secret ingredient was getting low, and I was glad, because I was beginning to doubt the morality of the whole enterprise. She did say one night, as she waited for the plum/orange elixir to take effect, that the drink had rekindled her interest in Brian's thing and that she loved to lie there while he did things to her. In fact, that's the way she liked it now, her eyelids at half-mast and Brian at full. When I started to cut back on the amount of the drug, for reasons of conscience as well as supply, her interest in him waned and I could tell that Brian was on his way out again. For a while, by varying the dose, I could orchestrate their relationship like a conductor, but when I finally felt bad enough, I cut her off without her ever knowing she'd been on it and seemingly with no deleterious effects. Somehow, their relationship hung together.

Santa Monica, California, where I live, is a perfect town for invalids, homosexuals, show people, and all other formerly peripheral members of society. Average is not the norm here. Here, if you're visiting from Omaha, you stick out like a senorita's ass at the Puerto Rican day parade. That's why, when I saw a contest at the Rite Aid drugstore (eight blocks from my house, takes me forty-seven minutes to get there) asking for a two-page essay on why I am the most average American, I marveled that the promoters actually thought that they might find an average American at this nuthouse by the beach. This cardboard stand carried an ad by its sponsor, Tepperton's Frozen Apple Pies. I grabbed an entry form, and as I hurried home (thirty-five minutes: a record), began composing the essay in my head.

The challenge was not how to present myself as average, but how to make myself likable without lying. I think I'm pretty appealing, but likability in an essay is very different from likability in life. See, I tend to grow on people, and five hundred words is just not enough to get someone to like me. I need several years and a ream or two of paper. I knew I had to flatter, overdo, and lay it on thick in order to speed up my likability time frame. So I would not like the sniveling, patriotic me who wrote my five hundred words. I would like a girl with dark roots peeking out through the peroxide who was laughing so hard that Coca-Cola was coming out of her nose. And I guess you would, too. But Miss Coca-Cola Nose wouldn't be writing this essay in her Coca-Cola persona. She would straighten up, fix her hair, snap her panties out of her ass, and start typing.

"I am average because," I wrote, "I stand on the seashore here in Santa Monica and I let the Pacific Ocean touch my toes, and I know I am at the most western edge of our nation, and that I am a descendant of the settlers who came to California as pioneers. And is not every American a pioneer? Does this spirit not reside in each one of us, in every city, in every heart on every rural road, in every traveler in every Winnebago, in every American living in every mansion or slum? I am average," I wrote, "because the cry of individuality flows confidently through my blood, with little attention drawn to itself, like the still power of an apple pie sitting in an open window to cool."

I hope the Mensa people never see this essay, not because it reeks of my manipulation of a poor company just trying to sell pies, but because, during the twenty-four hours it took me to write it, I believed so fervently in its every word.

Tuesdays and Fridays are big days for me. At least at 2:00 P.M. At 2:00 P.M. Clarissa comes. She talks to me for exactly forty-five minutes, but she's not a full shrink; she's a student shrink. So officially she's a visitor and her eyes are green. She brings a little gift bag each time, sometimes with packaged muffins, or phone cards, all of which I assume are donated. She asks me how I am, and she always remembers something from last time that she can follow up on this time. If I told her that I planned to call my mother with the new phone card, she remembers to ask how the call went. Problematic for me, because when I say I'm going to call my mother I am lying, as my mother has been dead—is it six years now? Problematic for her, because Clarissa knows my mother is dead and feels she has to humor me. I know I'm lying and not fooling her, and she thinks I'm crazy and fooling myself. I like this little fib because it connects us at a much deeper level than hello.

Clarissa makes several other stops on Tuesdays and Fridays to other psychiatric charity cases, which I'm sure have earned her several school credits. I was, it seems, one of the low men on the totem pole of insanity and therefore the recipient of treatment from a beginner. This I have scoped out one data bit at a time. When someone doesn't want to give you information about themselves, the only way to acquire it is by reverse inquiry. Ask the questions you don't want answered and start paring away to the truth. My conclusion about her was hard to reach because she's *at least* thirty-three. And still a student? Where were the missing years?

She's probably reporting on me to a professor or writing about me in a journal. I like to think of her scrawling my name in pencil at the end of our sessions—I mean visits—but really, I'm probably a keyboard macro by now. She types *D* and hits control / space bar and Daniel Pecan Cambridge appears. When she looks me in the face on Tuesdays and Fridays she probably thinks of me not as Daniel Pecan Cambridge but as D-control / space bar. I, however, think of her only as Clarissa because her movements, gestures, and expressions translate only into the single word of her name.

Last Tuesday: Clarissa arrived in her frisky lip-gloss-pink Dodge Neon. She parked on the street, and lucky for both of us, there's a two-hour parking zone extending for several blocks in front of my apartment. So of course she's never gotten a ticket. From my window I saw her waiting by her car talking on the cell phone; I watched her halt mid-street for a car to pass, and I saw its hotshot driver craning his neck to see her in his rearview mirror. She was wearing a knee-length skirt that moved like a bell when she walked. Clarissa has a student quality that I suspect she'll have her whole life. She's definitely the cutest girl in class, and any romantically inclined guy looking for an experiment in cleanliness would zero in on her. Her hair is auburn—do we still use that word?—it looks dark blond in the Santa Monica sun, but it flickers between red and brown once she's in the apartment. And as Clarissa's hair color is on a sliding scale depending on light and time of day, so is her beauty, which slides on a gradient between normal and ethereal.

She was already focused on me and she set her things down without even looking where she was dumping them. "Sorry I'm late," she said. I said, "You're not." "Well, almost," she added.

I didn't say anything about her apologizing for being *almost* late. I couldn't quite wrap my head around the concept even. If you're almost late, it means you're not late, so what are we talking about?

The thing I like about Clarissa is that she starts talking immediately, which gives me the opportunity to watch her without saying anything.

"You won't believe what happened to me. Yesterday, I had a return flight from San Francisco. I really wanted to leave at eight but could only get the reduced fare on the five o'clock. I get to the airport and the five o'clock is canceled, and they've put us on the eight o'clock flight and charged us the full fare! But now my car's parked at Burbank and the eight o'clock goes to LAX, so now I have to pay for a taxi to get me to my car. AND I lost three extra hours in San Francisco."

It seems as though little ills like this are always befalling Clarissa, which makes her seem younger than she actually is. Once she lost her passport right before a trip to Mexico. Once her cell phone battery went dead at the same time as her car battery. But if Clarissa is hapless, it is not the definition of her. Because I see something that describes her more clearly. It occurs in the pauses in her speech when her eyes fix on an air spot roughly waist-high and she seems to be in a trance. And then suddenly it's as if her mind races, trying to catch up to real time, and she continues right where she left off.

If you saw her in these moments, you might think she was collecting her thoughts in order to go forward. But I see it another way: Her mind is being overwhelmed by two processes that must simultaneously proceed at full steam. One is to deal with and live in the present world. The other is to reexperience and mourn something that happened long ago. It is as though her lightness pulls her toward heaven, but the extra gravity around her keeps her earthbound.

Or is it that I think too much?

My redress with the Mensa people is going well. Here's the progress so far: I am thinking of writing a letter asking them to rescore my test. My potential inquiry could be embarrassing for them. They would be compelled to look harder at my results and install me as a full Mensa member, with apologia, if there is such a category. Right now, there's not much more I can do other than wait for me to write the letter.

I don't know if I want to approach Elizabeth the Realtor until the Mensa thing is worked out. My membership would be nice to drop over drinks on our third date. If I get the feeling there might not be a third date, I have no qualms about moving it up to our second date, or even blurting it out on our first date right after "Hello." I am thinking about her because I spotted her twice today, once going and once coming. The apartments across the street are not easy to rent, lucky for me, and therefore numerous showings are required in order to find the one customer who is willing to pay top dollar for the mediocre. When she pulled up in front of the Rose Crest, every one of my senses went on alert. I slid open the window, and I swear the scent of lilac or lavender wafted toward me even though she was at least a hundred feet away. The aroma was so heavy I tasted it on my tongue. I gripped the windowsill, burying my fingers in the aluminum groove. I saw her angle herself out of her diesel Mercedes with the practiced perfection of a beauty queen. I heard her shoes hit the asphalt with a clap.

She went into the building, never moving her cell phone from her ear, and twenty minutes later I saw a couple in their thirties, Porsche-equipped, pull up and park half in the red zone. Oh, I can read them like a book: too much money in the Porsche, not enough left over for the rent. This is a young hotshot three years into his first good job, and the one thing he wants is a Porsche. Sort of the boyhood dream thing. Finally, he gets the car and has a strong attachment to it. The wife came later, but dang, he still loves his Porsche. So they think they have plenty of money for rent until they start checking into prices and find that their affordable number of bedrooms has shrunk by 1.5.

I could imagine myself living with Elizabeth. Pantyhose at breakfast, high heels before lunch. I wonder if the age difference is a problem? She must be forty-two. I must be, say, thirty-five. (Of course, I know my own age, and I have no qualms about mentioning it. It's just that I would act older than I am if I were with Elizabeth, and I would act younger than I am if I were with Zandy the pharmacist.) I doubt that Elizabeth would want to live here in my place. I assume she lives in some fine rental property, the choicest out of the hundreds she must handle daily, and gotten at a bargain price. So obviously *I* would be moving in with *her*. But would she be tolerant when I started listing my peculiarities? Would she understand my need for the apartment's light bulbs to total exactly 1,125 watts when lit?

I sat waiting at my window for Elizabeth to reemerge, my eyes shifting from her car to the apartment's security gate and back again. The thing about a new romance like this is that previously explainable things become inexplicable when juiced with the fury of love. Which led me to believe, when I saw the trunk of her car mysteriously unlatch and the lid slowly yawn open, that it was caused by the magnetic forces of our attraction to each other. Now, looking back, I realize it was a radar feature on her car key that enabled her to open the trunk from forty feet, when she was just out of my sight line. When she got to her car, she reached in the trunk and handed her clients two brochures that I suppose were neatly stacked next to the spare tire.

They stood and chatted curbside, and I saw that this wasn't a perfunctory handshake and goodbye; she was still pitching and discussing the apartment. This was my opportunity to meet my *objet d'amour*. Or at least give her the chance to see me, to get used to me. My plan was to walk by on my side of the street and not look over her way. This, I felt, was a very clever masculine move: to meet and ultimately seduce through *no contact at all*. She would be made aware of me as a mysterious figure, someone with no need of her whatsoever. This is compelling to a woman.

When I hit the street, I encountered a problem. I had forgotten to wear sunglasses. So as I walked by her, facing west into the sun, while I may have been an aloof figure, I was an aloof figure who squinted. One half of my face was shut like a salted snail, while the other half was held open in an attempt to see. Just at the moment Elizabeth looked over (I intentionally scuffled my foot, an impetuous betrayal of my own plan to let her notice me on her own), I was half puckered and probably dangerous-looking. My plan required me to keep walking at least around the corner so that she wouldn't find out I had no actual destination. I continued around the block, and with my back now to the sun, I was able to swagger confidently, even though it was pointless, as I was well out of her sight. Ten minutes later, I came round again. To my dismay, Elizabeth and her clients were still there, and I would again be walking into the 4:00 P.M. direct sun. This time, I forced both my eyes open, which caused them to burn and water. The will required to do this undermined my outward pose of confidence. My walk conveyed the demeanor of a gentleman musketeer, but my face expressed a lifetime of constipation.

Still, as freakish as I may have appeared, I had established contact. And I doubt that her brief distorted impression of me was so indelible that it could not, at some point, be erased and replaced with a better me.

Which leads me to the subject of charisma. Wouldn't we all like to know the extent of our own magnetism? I can't say my charm was at full throttle when I strolled by Elizabeth, but had she been at the other end of the street, so that I was walking eastward with the sun behind me, squintless and relaxed and perhaps in dusky silhouette, my own charisma would have swirled out of me like smoke from a hookah. And Elizabeth, the enthralling Elizabeth, would already be snared and corralled.

But my charisma has yet to fully bloom. It's as though something is keeping me back from it. Perhaps fear: What would happen to me and to those around me if my power became uncontained? If I were suddenly just too sensational to be managed? Maybe my obsessions are there to keep me from being too powerfully alluring, to keep my would-be lovers and adventures in check. After all, I can't be too seductive if I have to spend a half hour on the big night calculating and adjusting the aggregate bulb wattage in a woman's apartment while she sits on the edge of the bed checking her watch.

Around this time, the *Crime Show* called, wanting to tape more footage for their show. They needed to get a long shot of me acting suspicious while I was being interrogated by two policemen who were in fact actors. I asked them what I should say, and they said it didn't matter, as the camera would be so far away we would only have to move our mouths to make it look like we're talking. I said okay, because as nervous as it made me, the taping gave the coming week a highlight. The idleness of my life at that time, the unintended vacation I was on, made the days long and the nights extended, though it was easy for me to fill the warm California hours by sitting at the window, adjusting the breeze by using the sliding glass as a louver and watching the traffic roll by.

Eight days after my last sighting of her, I again saw Elizabeth standing across the street, this time with a different couple but doing the same routine. She stood at the car, handing over the brochures, and then dallied as she made her final sales pitch. I decided to take my walk again, this time wearing my sunglasses to avoid the prune look. I outdid myself in the clothes department, too. I put on my best outfit, only realizing later that Elizabeth had no way of knowing that it was my best outfit. She could have thought it was my third- or fourth-best outfit, or that I have a closet full of better outfits of which this was the worst. So although I was actually trying very hard, Elizabeth would have to scour my closet, comparing one outfit against another, in order to realize it. This outfit, so you know, consisted of khaki slacks and a fashionably frayed white dress shirt. I topped it off with some very nice brown loafers and matching socks. This is the perfect ensemble for my neighborhood, by the way. I looked like a Californian, a Santa Monican, a man of leisure.

I attained the sidewalk. I decided this time not to look like someone with a destination but to go for the look of "a man taking his dog for a walk." Though I had no dog. But I imagined a leash in my hand; this was so vivid to me I paused a few times to let the invisible dog sniff the occasional visible bush. Such was the depth of my immersion in my "walking man" character. This time, full eye contact was made with Elizabeth, but it was the kind where even though her eyes strayed over toward me, she kept on talking to her clients, in much the same way one would glance over to someone wearing a giant spongy orange fish hat: You want to look, but you don't want to engage.

A plan began to form. As I passed her, I noticed the two opposing driveways coming up, which meant I could cross the street if I wanted and end up on her block. In order to walk near Elizabeth, I would have to reverse my direction once I had crossed the street. But it seemed perfectly natural to me that a man would walk down the street, decide to cross it, then go back and read the realtor sign before going on. This required a little acting on my part. I came to the low scoop of the driveway and even walked a little past it. I paused, I deliberated, I turned and looked back at the sign, which was about a dozen feet from where Elizabeth was standing. I squinted at it, as if it were too far away to see, and proceeded to cross the street and head in Elizabeth's direction.

She was facing away from me; the sign was behind her and stuck into the flower bed, which was really more of a fern bed. She was wearing a tight beige-and-white paisley skirt, and a short-sleeve brown blouse that was bursting from within because of her cannonball breasts. Her hair was combed back over her head and held in place by a black velour hair clamp, which fit like headphones. Her feet were plugged into two open-toed patent leather heels and were reflected in the chrome of her Mercedes's bumper. I couldn't imagine any man to whom this package would not appeal.

As I approached her, I felt a twinge where it matters. And if my theory is correct, that sexual attraction is usually mutual—an evolutionary necessity; otherwise, nobody would be doing it with anybody—then Elizabeth must have been feeling something, too. That is, if she ever looked over at me. I came to the sign, leaned over, and pretended to read the description of the apartment, which was reduced to such extreme abbreviations as to be indecipherable. What's a *rfna*? I had to do mental somersaults to align the fact that while I was reading Elizabeth's name, her actual person was by now two steps behind me.

I stepped backward as if to get a better view of the sign and, I swear this was an accident, bumped right into Elizabeth, glute to glute. She turned her head and said airily, "I'm sorry," even though it was I who had bumped into her. "Oh, excuse me," I said, taking all the blame.

"Are you the realtor?" I asked.

"Yes, I am," she said and she browsed inside her purse without ever losing eye contact with me.

"How many apartments are there for rent in the entire complex of apartments?" I said, using too many words.

"Just three. Would you like a card?"

Oh yes, I wanted a card. I took it, palming it like an ace of spades, knowing it was a memento that I would pin up on my bulletin board. In fact, this would be the first item on the board that could even come close to being called a bulletin. "That's you," I said, indicating with a gesture that the name on the card and the name on the sign were one and the same.

"Are you looking for an apartment?" she asked.

I said something exquisite: "I'm always looking to upgrade." I muttered this casually as I sauntered off. The wrong way, I might add. The next opposing scooped-out driveways were so far out of my way that I didn't get home for twenty-five minutes, and while I walked I kept looking back over my shoulder at my apartment, which had begun to recede into a pinpoint.

Once home, I reflected on the encounter, and two moments in particular stood out. One was Elizabeth's response to my inquiry about the number of apartments for rent. "Just three." It was the "just" I admired. "Just a few left," "Only three and they're going fast" was the implication. Elizabeth was obviously a clever saleswoman. I figured that three were a lot of empty apartments for this building, and that the pressure was on from the owners to get them rented fast. I'll bet they knew what they had in Elizabeth: the very, very best.

The second moment—contact between me and Elizabeth—was harder to relive because it had occurred out of my sight, actually behind my back. So I had to picture the unseen. Our—pardon my language—butts had backed right into each other like two marshmallows coming together in a sudden splat. Boing. If I had intended this sort of physical encounter, I would be a different kind of person. The kind I am actually not. I would never do such a thing intentionally, like a subway creep. But I had literally impressed myself upon Elizabeth, and at our next meeting we would be further along than I ever could have imagined, now that she and I had had intimate contact. My hip had touched hers and hers had touched mine. That's probably more than a lot of men have done who have known her a lot longer.

My third contact with Elizabeth, which occurred one week later, was a total failure, with an explanation. I was coincidentally on the street when Elizabeth pulled up and got out of her car. Nothing could have seemed more casual, more unplanned, than my presence in front of the Rose Crest. She unfolded herself from the Mercedes, all legs and stockings, and gave me a jaunty wave. I think she was even about to speak to me. The problem was, I was taping my long shot for the *Crime Show*, in which I was supposedly being interrogated by two cops on the street.

So when Elizabeth waved, I was approached by two "policemen" who seriously overacted in their efforts to make me look guilty by snarling and poking at me. Luckily, it was a long shot, so their hambone performances couldn't be seen on camera. No Emmy for them. I thought I was pretty good. We were given no dialogue to say, but we had been asked to spout gibberish while a narrator talked over us. They weren't recording us, they just wanted our mouths to be moving to make it look like we were talking. One "policeman" was saying, "I'm talking, I'm talking, I'm moving my mouth, it looks like I'm talking." And then the other one would say, "Now I'm talking, I'm moving my mouth like I'm talking." Then they would say to me, "Now you talk, just move your mouth." So I would say, "I'm talking, I'm talking, I'm talking back to you," and so on. I couldn't wave to Elizabeth, even though she'd waved at me, as it would have spoiled the scene. I must have looked strange, because even though it was eighty-five-degree weather, I was wearing the blue parka with the bloodstain to look even more suspicious for the camera. This couldn't have made Elizabeth too comfortable, particularly if she'd had any inclination toward viewing me as her next husband.

I am always amazed by what lies buried in the mind until one day for no particular reason it rises up and makes itself known. That night in bed, a vision of Elizabeth's face entered my consciousness, and I saw clearly that she had gray-green eyes. It was a small fact I hadn't realized I knew.

On Sunday, I decided to distract myself by going down to the Rite Aid and taking a look at Zandy. This was no ordinary girl-watching. Zandy works at the pharmacy, behind an elevated counter. She's visible only from the neck up as she sails from one end to the other. If I visit the pay phone / Coke machine alcove, I can get an employee's view of Zandy's pharmacy-white outfit against her pharmacy-white skin. She's a natural California girl, except her face has never been touched by makeup or sun, only by the fluorescent rays of the ceiling lights. Her hair is almost unkempt, with so many dangling swoops and curls that I long for a tiny surfboard so I can go swishing amid the tresses. I have no designs on Zandy because the rejection would be overwhelming for me. Plus, she's a genuine blonde, and I prefer Elizabeth's dyed look.

The Rite Aid is splendidly antiseptic. I'll bet the floors are hosed down every night with isopropyl alcohol. The Rite Aid is the axle around which my squeaky world turns, and I find myself there two or three days a week seeking out the rare household item such as cheesecloth. Like every other drugstore on earth, it is filled with quack products that remind me of nineteenth-century ads for hair restorers and innervating elixirs. These days there is a solid percentage of products in the stores which actually work, but they're on display next to liquid-filled shoe inserts that claim to prevent varicose veins.

I pretended to stop for a Coke 'n' phone—even though my phone card was on empty—and saw Zandy gliding behind the counter, as though she were on skates. I moved to the end of the displays, pretending to read the instructions for the Coke machine, and good news, the wonderful minds at the Rite Aid had decided to move the Tepperton's Apple Pie Most Average American essay contest placard next to the Coke machine, where I could tear off an entry form and, for the next few minutes, write another five hundred words while Zandy, delicious as a meringue, went about her work in full view. I did not really want to write another five hundred words or even two hundred words, but it was easy enough considering the trade-off. There were several dull pencils in a box on the display, so dull that when I wrote with them the wood scraped against the paper, but I buckled down and began my second patriotic essay in two weeks, after a lifetime of none.

America lets me choose not to be a pioneer. I am uplifted by doing ordinary work. The work of society, the common work of the world . . .

And so it went. I was impressed with myself because this essay expressed the exact opposite idea of my first essay—one week I said I had the pioneer spirit and the next week I didn't—and I wrote both opinions with such ease that I believed I could take any subject and effectively argue either side. This skill would be valuable in dating. Just think, I could switch positions midstream if I sensed my date reacting badly.

While I was writing, I barely looked up at Zandy, since I'd realized what a foolish enterprise this was anyway. There is no pleasure in staking out a woman and eyeing her endlessly. I get no more joy from looking at a Monet for twenty minutes than I do after five. A glimpse of Zandy was all that was necessary, and perhaps I used her as an excuse to get out of the house. I signed this second essay using a pseudonym—Lenny Burns—and dropped it in the bin. I bought some foam earplugs (not that I needed them, but at two dollars a dozen, they were too cheap to pass up) and went home.

My ceiling is not conducive to counting. Its texture is created by pulling the trowel flatly away from the wet plaster, leaving a rippled surface, as though a baker had come in and spread around vanilla icing with a spatula. Counting prefers symmetry of some kind, though at my level of sophistication I can get around most obstacles. The least interesting ceiling for me now is one that is practically counted out already: squared-off acoustical tiles with regular punctures that simply require a little multiplication on my part. Each tile has sixty-four sound-absorbing holes times the easily calculated number of tiles in the ceiling. Ugh.

But my irregular ceiling—no tiles, no quadrants, no recurring punctures—takes a little thought on my part to slice up, count, and quantify. Like an ocean, its surface is irregular, but also like an ocean it's easy to imagine an unbroken plane just below the surface of the undulating waves. Once I can imagine an unbroken plane, the bisecting and trisecting of my fairly square ceiling becomes much easier. Triangles, rectangles, and interlocking parallelograms are all superimposed over the ceiling, and in my mind they meld into the birthday-cake frosting of the plaster.

The problem with counting is that anything, any plane, any object, can be divided infinitely, like the distance covered by Zeno's tortoise heading for the finish line. So it's a problem knowing when to stop. If I've divided my ceiling into sixty-four sections (sometimes irregular sections just to annoy myself), I wonder whether to halve it again and again and again. But that's not all. The sections must be sliced up in three-dimensional space, too, so the numbers become unmanageable very quickly. But that's the thing about a brain: plenty of room for large numbers.

Sure, I've gotten some disbelieving stares when I've tried to explain this little habit of mine to, say, a bus seatmate. I've watched a guy adjust his posture, or get up and move back several rows, even if it meant he now sat next to someone else who was clearly on the verge of some other kind of insanity. You should know, however, that my habit of counting began early—I can't remember if I was a teen or bubbling under at age twelve. My mother was driving up Lone Star Avenue and I was in the back seat. A gasoline truck pulled up next to us at a stoplight and I became fixated on its giant tires. I noticed that even though the tires were round, they still had four points: north, south, east, and west. And when the light changed and the truck started rolling, the north, south, east, and west points of the tire remained constant, that the tire essentially rolled right through them. This gave me immeasurable satisfaction. When the next truck came by, I watched the tires rotate while its polar quadrants remained fixed. Soon, this tendency became a habit, then a compulsion. Eventually, the habit compounded and not only tires, but vases, plates, lawns, and living rooms were dissected and strung with imaginary grids.

I can remember only one incident of this habit prior to my teen years. Eight years old, I sat with my parents in our darkened living room watching TV. My father muttered something to me, and my response was slow. Perhaps intentionally slow. I replied disinterestedly, "Huh?" with hardly enough breath to make it audible. My father's fist uppercut the underside of his dinner tray, sending it flying, and he rose and turned toward me, whipping his belt from his waist. My mind froze him in action and I saw, like ice cracking, a bifurcating line run from his head to his feet. Next, a horizontal line split him at midpoint, then the rest of the lines appeared, dividing him into eighths, sixteenths, thirty-seconds, and so on. I don't remember what happened next.

My counting habit continued into college, where its real import, purpose, and power were revealed to me. The class assignments seemed trifling, but the irresistible counting work seemed vital not only to my well-being but to the world's. I added textbook page numbers together, divided them by the total page numbers, and, using my own formulas, redistributed them more appropriately. Page 262 of *Science and Environment* could become a more natural page 118, and I would razor-cut the leaves from their binding and rearrange them to suit my calculations. I had to read them in their new order, too, which made study difficult, and then finally, as I added new rules and limitations to my study habits, impossible. Eventually, my quirks were picked up by various professors and savvy teaching assistants, and they, essentially, "sent me to the nurse." After a few days of testing, I was urged out of school. I then went to Hewlett-Packard, where I landed a job as a business communiqué encoder.

One time, when I was working at Hewlett-Packard, I tried medication, but it made me uneasy. It was as though the drug were keeping me from the true purpose of each day, which was to count loci and accommodate variables. I slowly took myself off the pills and eventually I left my encoding job. Or maybe it left me. When the chemicals let go of my mind, I could no longer allow myself to create a code when I knew all along that its ultimate end was to be decoded. But that's what the job was, and I couldn't get the bosses to see it my way. Finally, the government began providing me with free services and one of them was Clarissa.

Clarissa the shrink-in-training clinked three times on my door with her Coke can. The knock of someone whose hands are full. The door opened on its own, and I remembered not hearing it latch when I entered earlier with my small sack of earplugs. Clarissa, balancing a cell phone, briefcase, sweater (pointless in today's weather), Palm Pilot, soda can, and wrapped baby gift (she hadn't wanted to leave it in the car), closed the door and made a purse-induced leathery squeak as she crossed the room. I liked her outfit: a maroon skirt topped by a white blouse with a stiffly starched front piece that was vaguely heart-shaped, giving her the appearance of an Armani-clad nurse. (Oh yes, I keep up with the fashions. I noted how close her outfit was to my own favorite: light cotton pants with a finely pressed white dress shirt. No problem, as I love to iron. Once I ironed a pillow almost perfectly flat.) "Hi," she said, and "Hi," I said back. "Oh," she said, "sorry I'm late." Of course she wasn't. She just assumed she was late because the traffic had been murder. "Are you having a good week?" she asked.

I was having a good week, though I couldn't really tell her why. At least, not without her thinking I was obsessed with women. I didn't tell her about my three encounters with Elizabeth, or about eyeballing Zandy at the pharmacy. So I lied and said . . . well, I don't remember what I said. But I do remember a particular moment when, after I'd asked her how she was, she paused that extra second before she said the perfunctory "Fine." She wasn't fine, and I could tell. I could tell because my mind has the ability to break down moments the way it can break down ceiling tiles. I can cut a moment into quarters, then eighths, then et cetera, and I am able to analyze whether one bit of behavior truly follows another, which it seldom does when a person is disturbed or influenced by a hidden psychic flow.

I couldn't make out what was troubling Clarissa because she's adept at being sunny. I'm going to tell you one of the joys of being Clarissa's "patient." While she is analyzing me, I am analyzing her. What makes it fun is that we're both completely unskilled at it. Our conversation that day went like this:

"Did you find a parking space okay?" I asked.

"Oh yes."

I said they've been hard to find because of the beachy weather.

"Did you go out this week?" she asked.

"Several walks and a few trips to the Rite Aid."

"You were fine with it?" she said.

"Yeah. The rules are so easy to follow. Don't you think?"

"I'm not sure what your rules are."

"I'll bet more people have rules like mine than you think." I asked, "What are your rules?" (I wondered if she'd fall for this.)

"Let's stick to you," she said.

Outwitted!

The conversation went on, with both of us parrying and thrusting. I urged myself to never get well because that would be the end of Clarissa's visits . . . wouldn't it? Though she would probably have to stop one day when she graduates or when her course—meaning me—is over. One of us is getting screwed: Either she's a professional and I should be paying her, or she's an intern and I'm a guinea pig.

Then something exciting happened. Her cell phone rang. It was exciting because what crossed her face ranged wildly on the map of human emotion. And oh, did I divide that moment up into millionths:

The phone rang.

She decided to ignore it.

She decided to answer it.

She decided to ignore it.

She decided to check caller ID.

She looked at the phone display.

She turned off the phone and continued speaking.

But the moment before turning off the phone broke down further into submoments:

She worried that it might be a specific person.

She saw that it was.

She turned off the phone with an angry snap.

But this submoment broke down into even more subsubmoments:

She grieved.

Pain shot through her like a lightning strike.

So, Clarissa had an ex she was still connected to. I said, "Clarissa, you're a desirable girl; just sit quietly and you will resurrect." But wait, I didn't say it. I only thought it.

I stayed in my apartment for the next three days. A couple of times, Philipa stopped by hoping for more joy juice. I was starting to feel like a pusher and regretted giving her the Mickeys in the first place. But I eased the guilt by reminding myself that the drugs were legal or, in the case of quaaludes, had at one time been legal. I gave her the plain Jane concoctions of apple and banana, though I wrestled with just telling her the truth and letting her get the drugs herself. But I didn't, because I still enjoyed her stopping by, because I liked her—or is it that I liked her dog? "Here, Tiger." When Philipa walked up or down the stairway, so did her dog, and I could hear his four paws ticking and clicking behind her. She'd talk to him as if he were a person, a person who could talk back. Often when she said, "Here, Tiger," I would say to myself, "No, *here*, Tiger," hoping doggy ESP would draw him toward my door, because I liked to look into his cartoon face. Tiger was a perfectly assembled mutt, possessing a vocabulary of two dozen words. He had a heart of gold and was keenly alert. He had a variety of quirky mannerisms that could charm a room, such as sleeping on his back while one active hind leg pedaled an invisible bicycle. But his crowning feature was his exceedingly dumb Bozo face, a kind of triangle with eyes, which meant his every act of intelligence was greeted with cheers and praise because one didn't expect such a dimwit to be able to retrieve, and then sort, a bone, a tennis ball, and a rubber dinosaur on verbal commands only. Philipa demonstrated his talent on the lawn one day last summer when she made Tiger go up to apartment 9 and bring down all his belongings and place them in a rubber ring. Philipa's boyfriend, Brian, stood by on the sidelines drinking a Red Bull while shouting, "Dawg, dawg!" And I bet he was also secretly using the dog as a spellchecker.

The view from my window was quite static that weekend. Unfortunately, the Sunday *Times* crossword was a snap (probably to atone for last Sunday's puzzle, which would have stumped the Sphinx), and I finished it in forty-five minutes, including the cryptic, with no mistakes and no erasures. This disrupted my time budget. A couple of cars slowed in front of Elizabeth's realty sign, indicating that she might be showing up later in the week. But the weather was cool and there were no bicyclists, few joggers, no families pouring out of their SUVs and hauling the entire inventory of the Hammacher Schlemmer beach catalog down to the ocean, so I had no tableaux to write captions for. This slowness made every hour seem like two, which made my idle time problem even worse. I vacuumed, scrubbed the bathroom, cleaned the kitchen. Ironed, ironed, ironed. What did I iron? My shirt, shirt, shirt. At one point I was so bored I reattached my cable to the TV and watched eight minutes of a Santa Monica city government hearing on mall pavement.

Then it was evening. For a while, everything was the same, except now it was dark. Then I heard Brian come down the stairs, presumably in a huff. His walk was an exaggerated stomp meant to send angry messages like African drums. Every footstep boasted, "I don't need her." No doubt later, in the sports bar, other like-minded guys would agree that Brian was not pussy-whipped, affirmed by the fact that Brian was in the bar watching a game and not outside Philipa's apartment sailing paper airplanes through her window with I LOVE YOU written on them.

Brian strode with a gladiator's pride to his primered '92 Lincoln and split with a gas pedal roar. I then heard someone descending the stairs, who was undoubtedly Philipa. But her pace was not that of a woman in pursuit of her fleeing boyfriend. She was slow-walking in my direction and I could hear the gritty slide of each deliberate footstep. She stopped just outside and lingered an unnaturally long time. Then she rang my doorbell, holding the button down so I heard the *ding*, but not the *dong*.

I pretended to be just waking as I opened the door. Philipa released the doorbell as she swung inside. "You up?" she asked. "I'm way up," I said, dropping my charade of sleep, which I realized was a lie with no purpose. I moved to my armchair (a gift from Granny) and nestled in. Philipa's center-parted hair, long and ash brown, fell straight to her shoulders and framed her pale unmade-up face, and for the first time I could see that this was a pretty girl in the wrong business. She was pretty enough for one man, not for the wide world that show business required. She looked sharp, too; they must have come from an event, had a spat, and now here she was with something on her mind. She sat down on the sofa, stiffened her arms against the armrests, and surprised me by skipping the Brian topic. Instead, her eyes watered up and she said, "I can't get a job."

She definitely had had a few drinks. I wondered if she wanted something chemical from me, which I wasn't about to give her, and which I didn't have. "I thought you just finished a job, that show *The Lawyers*."

"I did," she said. "I played a sandwich girl, delivering lunches to the law office. I was happy to get it. I poured my heart into it. I tried to be a sexy sandwich girl, a memorable sandwich girl, but they asked me to tone it down. So I was just a delivery girl. My line was 'Mr. Anderson, same as yesterday?' I did it perfectly, too, in one take, and then it was over. I look at the star, Cathy Merlot—can you believe how stupid that name is? Merlot? Why not Susie Cabernet?—and I know I'm as good as she is, but she's the center of attention, she's the one getting fluffed and powder-puffed and . . ."

Philipa kept talking but I stopped listening. By now her body was folded in the chair like an origami stork, her elbows, forearms, calves, and thighs going every which-a-way. She didn't even finish her last sentence; it just trailed off. I think the subject had changed in her head while her mouth had continued on the old topic, not realizing it was out of supplies. She asked me how old I was.

"Thirty-three," I said. "I thought you were late twenties," she said. I explained, "I never go out in the sun." She said, "Must be hard to avoid." I thought, Oh goody, repartee. But Philipa quieted. It seemed—oddly—that she had become distracted by my presence, the very person she was talking to. Her eyes, previously darting and straying, fell on me and held. She adjusted her body in the sofa and turned her knees squarely toward me, foreshortening her thighs, which disappeared into the shadows of her skirt. This made me uncomfortable and at the same time gave me a hint of an erection.

"When's your birthday?" she asked.

"January twenty-third."

"You're an Aquarius," she said.

"I guess. What's yours?" I asked.

"Scorpio."

"I mean your birth date."

"November fifteenth."

I said, "What year?"

She said, "Nineteen seventy-four."

"A Friday," I said.

"Yes," she said, not recognizing my sleight of hand. "Do you date anyone?"

"Oh yeah," I said. "I'm dating a realtor."

"Are you exclusive?"

"No," I said. "But she wants me to be."

Then she paused. Cocked her head like Tiger. "Wait a minute. How did you know it was a Friday?" she finally asked.

How do I explain to her what I can't explain to myself? "It's something I can do," I said.

"What do you mean?"

"I mean I don't know, I can just do it."

"What's April 8, 1978?"

"It's a Saturday," I said.

"Jeez, that's freaky. You're right; it's my brother's birthday; he was born on Saturday. What's January 6, 1280?"

"Saturday," I said.

"Are you lying?" she asked.

"No."

"What do you do for a living, and do you have any wine?"

"No wine," I said, answering one question and skirting the other.

"So you want some wine? I've got some upstairs," she said. Open, I'll bet, too, I thought. "Okay," I said, knowing I wasn't going to have any. Philipa excused herself and ran up to her apartment with a "be right back." I stayed in my chair, scratching around the outline of its paisley pattern with my fingernail. Soon she was back with a bottle of red wine. "Fuck," she said. "All I had was Merlot."

Philipa poured herself a tankard full and slewed around toward me, saying, "So what did you say you do?"

I wanted to seem as if I were currently employed, so I had to change a few tenses. Mostly "was" to "am." "I encode corporate messages. Important messages are too easily hacked if sent by computer. So they were looking for low-tech guys to come up with handwritten systems. I developed a system based on the word 'floccinaucinihilipilification.' " I had lost Philipa. Proof of how boring the truth is. She had bottomed-up the tankard, and I know what wine does. Right now I was probably looking to her like Pierce Brosnan. She stood up and walked toward me, putting both hands on my chair and leaning in. I kept talking about codes. She brushed my cheek with her lips.

I knew what I was to Philipa. A moment. And she was attached to Brian, in spite of the recent storm clouds. And I was attached to Elizabeth even though she didn't know my name. And I knew that if Philipa and I were to seize this moment, the hallway would be forever changed. Every footstep would mean something else. Would she avoid me? Should I avoid her? What would happen if she met Elizabeth? Would Elizabeth know? Women are mind readers in the worst way. But on the other hand, I knew that if I dabbled with Philipa that night, I could be entering the pantheon of historical and notable affairs. There is a grand tradition involving the clandestine. The more I thought about it, the less this seemed like a drunken one-off and more like the stuff of novels. And this perhaps would be my only opportunity to engage in it.

By now, Philipa's eyelashes were brushing my cheek and her breath was on my mouth. With both hands, I clutched the arms of my chair as if I were on a thrill ride. I pooched out my lower lip, and that was all the seduction she needed. She took my hand and led me into my own bedroom. I'm sure that Philipa was lured on by my best asset, which is my Sure-cuts hairdo. I'm lanky like a baseball pitcher, and the Sure-cut people know how to give me the floppy forehead at a nominal price. So without bragging, I'm letting you know that I can be physically appealing. Plus I'm clean. Clean like I've just been car-washed and then scrubbed with a scouring pad and then wrapped in palm fronds infused with ginger. My excellent personal hygiene, in combination with the floppy casual forehead, once resulted in a provocative note being sent to me from my former mailwoman. Philipa never saw females going in and out, so she knew I wasn't a lothario, and I had come to suspect that she regarded me as a standby if she ever needed to get even with Brian the wide receiver.

I never have interfered with a relationship, out of respect for the guy as much as for myself, but Brian is a dope and Philipa is a sylph and I am a man, even if that description of myself is qualified by my failure to be able to cross the street at the curb.

The bedroom was a little too bright for Philipa. She wanted to lower the lights, so I turned out three sixty-watt bulbs but had to go to the kitchen to turn on a one-hundred-watt bulb and a fifty-watt bulb and two fifteens, in order to maintain equity. It is very hard to get thirty-watt bulbs, so when I find them I hoard them.

She still didn't like the ambience. The overhead lights disturbed her. I turned them off and compensated by turning on the overheads in the living room. But the light spilling into the bedroom was just too much; she wanted it dim and sexy. She went over and closed the door. Oh no, the door can't be closed; not without elaborate preparations. Because if the door is closed, the light in the bedroom is cut off from the light in the living room. Rather than having one grand sum of 1,125 watts, there would be two discrete calculations that would break the continuity. I explained this to Philipa, even though I had to go through it several times. To her credit, she didn't run, she just got tired, and a little too drunk to move. Our erotic moment had fallen flat, so I walked her to the door. I hadn't succeeded with Philipa, but at least I could still look Elizabeth straight in the eye.

After Philipa left, I lay in the center of the bed with the blanket neatly tucked around me; how Philipa and I would have mussed it! Inserted so neatly between the bed and the sheets, I thought how much I must look like a pocket pencil. My body was so present. I was aware of my toes, my arms, my weight on the bed. There was just me in a void, wrapped in the low hum of existence. The night of Philipa had led me to a quiet, aesthetic stillness. You might think it odd to call a moment of utter motionlessness life, but it was life without interaction, and I felt joy roll over me in a silent wave.

As long as I remained in bed, my relationship to Elizabeth was flawless. I was able to provide for her, to tease out a smile from her, and to keep her supplied with Versace stretch pants. But I knew that during the day, in life, I could not even cross the street to her without a complicated alignment of permitting circumstances. The truth was—and in my sensory deprivation I was unable to ignore it—I didn't have much to offer Elizabeth. Or for that matter, Philipa (if that were to happen) or Zandy (if she were to ever look at me).

I guessed that one day the restrictions I imposed on myself would end. But first, it seemed that my range of possible activities would have to iris down to zero before I could turn myself around. Then, when I was finally static and immobile, I could weigh and measure every exterior force and, slowly and incrementally, once again allow the outside in. And that would be my life.

The next morning, I decided to touch every corner of every copying machine at Kinko's. Outside the apartment I ran into Brian, who was lumbering toward Philipa's, wearing what I suspect were the same clothes he had on yesterday. He had the greasy look of someone who had been out all night. Plus he held his cell phone in his hand, which told me he was staying closely connected to Philipa's whereabouts. His size touched me, this hulk. And after last evening, with my canny near-seduction of his girlfriend, I felt I was Bugs Bunny and Mercury to his Elmer Fudd and Thor.

I decided to pump Brian to find out how much he knew about my night with Philipa. I trudged out my technique of oblique questioning: I would ask Brian mundane questions and observe his response.

"I'm Daniel. I see you sometimes around the building. You an actor, like Philipa?"

Now if Brian cocked his head and glared at me through squinted eyes, I could gather that he was aware of my escapade with his girlfriend. But he didn't. He said, "I'm a painter," and like a person with an unusual name who must immediately spell it out, he added, "a house painter." Then he looked at me as if to say, "Whadya think about that?"

His demeanor was so flat that not only did he not suspect me, but this guy wouldn't have suspected a horned man-goat leaving Philipa's apartment at midnight while zipping up his pants. He didn't seem to have a suspicious bone in him. Then he rattled on about a sports bar and a football game. Staring dumbly into his face to indicate my interest, I realized Brian would not have been a cuckold in the grand literary tradition. In fact, he was more like a mushroom.

I had felt very manly when I first approached Brian, having just had a one-nighter with his girl, but now I felt very sheepish.

This harmless fungus was innocent and charmless, but mostly he was vulnerable, and I wondered if I was just too smooth to be spreading my panache around his world. "Hey, well, best of luck," I said and gave him a wave, not knowing if my comment was responsive to what he had been talking about. Then he said, "See ya, Slick." And I thought, Slick? Maybe he is onto me after all.

My Kinko's task was still before me, so I turned west and headed toward Seventh Street, drawing on all my navigational skills. Moving effortlessly from one scooped-out driveway to the next, I had achieved Sixth Street in a matter of minutes when I confronted an obstacle of unimaginable proportions. At my final matched set of scooped-out driveways, which would have served as my gateway to Kinko's, someone, some lad, some fellow, had, in a careless parking free-for-all, irresponsibly parked his '99 Land Cruiser or some such gigantic turd so that it edged several feet into my last driveway. This was as effective an obstacle for me as an eight-foot concrete wall. What good are the beautiful planes that connect driveway to driveway if a chrome-plated two-hundred-pound fender intersects their symmetry? Yeah, the driver of this tank is a crosswalk guy, so he doesn't care. I stood there knowing that the copiers at Kinko's needed to be touched and soon, too, or else panic, so I decided to proceed in spite of the offending car.

I stood on the sidewalk facing the street with Kinko's directly opposite me. The Land Cruiser was on my right, so I hung to the left side of the driveway. There was no way to justify the presence of that bumper. No, if I crossed a driveway while a foreign object jutted into it, I would be committing a violation of logic.

But, simultaneously driven forward and backward, I angled the Land Cruiser out of my peripheral vision and made it to the curb. Alas. My foot stepped toward the street, but I couldn't quite put it down. Was that a pain I felt in my left arm? My hands became cold and moist, and my heart squeezed like a fist. I just couldn't dismiss the presence of that fender. My toe touched the asphalt for support, which was an unfortunate maneuver because I was now standing with my left foot fully flat in the driveway and my right foot on point in the street. With my heart rapidly accelerating and my brain aware of impending death, my saliva was drying out so rapidly that I couldn't remove my tongue from the roof of my mouth. But I did not scream out. Why? For propriety. Inside me the fires of hell were churning and stirring; but outwardly I was as still as a Rodin.

I pulled my foot back to safety. But I had leaned too far out; my toes were at the edge of the driveway and my body was tilting over my gravitational center. In other words, I was about to fall into the street. I windmilled both of my arms in giant circles hoping for some reverse thrust, and there was a moment, eons long, when all 180 pounds of me were balanced on the head of a pin while my arms spun backward at tornado speed. But then an angel must have breathed on me, because I felt an infinitesimal nudge, which caused me to rock back on my heels, and I was able to step back onto the sidewalk. I looked across the street to Kinko's, where it sparkled in the sun like Shangri-la, but I was separated from it by a treacherous abyss. Kinko's would have to wait, but the terror would not leave. I decided to head toward home, where I could make a magic square.

Making a magic square would alphabetize my brain. "Alphabetize" is my slang for "alpha-beta-ize," meaning, raise my alphas and lower my betas. Staring into a square that has been divided into 256 smaller squares, all empty, all needing unique numbers, numbers that will produce the identical sum whether they're read vertically or horizontally, focuses the mind. During moments of crisis, I've created magic squares composed of sixteen, forty-nine, even sixty-four boxes, and never once has it failed to level me out. Here's last year's, after two seventy-five-watt bulbs blew out on a Sunday and I had no replacements:

52	61	4	20	29	13	36	45	=260
14	3	62	46	35	51	30	19	=260
53	60	5	12	28	12	37	44	=260
11	6	59	43	38	54	27	22	=260
55	58	7	23	26	10	39	42	=260
9	8	57	41	40	56	25	24	=260
50	63	2	18	31	15	34	47	=260
16	1	64	48	33	49	32	17	=260
=260	=260	=260	=260	=260	=260	=260	=260	

Each column and row adds up to 260. But this is a lousy 8 × 8 square. Making a 16 × 16 square would soothe even the edgiest neurotic. Benjamin Franklin—who as far as I know was not an edgy neurotic—was a magic square enthusiast. I assume he tackled them when he was not preoccupied with boffing a Parisian beauty, a distraction I do not have. His most famous square was a king-size brainteaser that did not sum correctly at the diagonals, unless the diagonals were bent like boomerangs. Now that's flair, plus he dodged electrocution by kite. Albrecht Dürer played with them, too, which is good enough for me.

I pulled my leaden feet to the art supply store and purchased a three-foot-by-three-foot white poster board. If I was going to make a 256-box square, I wanted it to be big enough so I didn't have to write the numbers microscopically. I was, after the Kinko's incident, walking in a self-imposed narrow corridor of behavioral possibilities, meaning there were very few moves I could make or thoughts I could think that weren't verboten. So the purchase didn't go well. I required myself to keep both hands in my pockets. In order to pay, I had to shove all ten fingers deep in my pants and flip cash onto the counter with my hyperactive thumbs. I got a few impatient stares, too, and then a little help was sympathetically offered from a well-dressed businessman who plucked a few singles from the wadded-up bills that peeked out from my pockets and gave them to the clerk. If this makes me sound helpless, I feel you should know that I don't enter this state very often and it is something I could snap out of, it's just that I don't want to.

Once home, I laid the poster board on my kitchen table and, with a Magic Marker and T square, quickly outlined a box. I drew more lines, creating 256 empty spaces. I then sat in front of it as though it were an altar and meditated on its holiness. Fixing my eyes on row 1, column 1, a number appeared in my mind, the number 47,800. I entered it into the square. I focused on another position. Eventually, I wrote a number in it: 30,831. As soon as I wrote 30,831, I felt my anxiety lessen. Which makes sense: The intuiting of the second number necessarily implied all the other numbers in the grid, numbers that were not yet known to me but that existed somewhere in my mind. I felt like a lover who knows there is someone out there for him, but it is someone he has not yet met.

I filled in a few other numbers, pausing to let the image of the square hover in my black mental space. Its grids were like a skeleton through which I could see the rest of the uncommitted mathematical universe. Occasionally, a number appeared in the imaginary square and I would write it down in the corresponding space of my cardboard version. The making of the square gave me the feeling that I was participating in the world, that the rational universe had given me something that was mine and only mine, because you see, there are more possible magic square solutions than there are nanoseconds since the Big Bang.

The square was not so much created as transcribed. Hours later, when I wrote the final number in the final box and every sum of every column and row totaled 491,384, I noted that my earlier curbside collapse had been ameliorated. I had eased up on my psychic accelerator, and now I wished I had someone to talk to. Philipa maybe, even Brian (anagram for "brain"—ha!), who I now considered as my closest link to normalcy. After all, when Brian ached over Philipa, he could still climb two flights up and weep, repent, seduce her, or buy her something. But my salvation, the making of the square, was so pointless; there was no person attached to it, no person to shut me out or take me in. This healing was symptomatic only, so I tacked the cardboard to a wall over Granny's chair in the living room in hopes that viewing it would counter my next bout of anxiety the way two aspirin counter a headache.

* * *

47,800	51,863	55,448	59,511	1,912	5,975	9,560	13,623	17,208	21,271	24,856	28,919	32,504	36,567	40,152	44,215	= 491,384
13,862	9,321	6,214	1,673	59,750	55,209	52,102	47,561	44,454	39,913	36,806	32,265	29,158	24,617	21,510	16,969	= 491,384
47,322	52,341	54,970	59,989	1,434	6,453	9,082	14,101	16,730	21,749	24,378	29,397	32,026	37,045	39,674	44,693	= 491,384
14,340	8,843	6,692	1,195	60,228	54,731	52,580	47,083	44,932	39,435	37,284	31,787	29,636	24,139	21,988	16,491	= 491,384
48,039	51,624	55,687	59,272	2,151	5,736	9,799	13,384	17,447	21,032	25,095	28,680	32,743	36,328	40,391	43,976	= 491,384
13,145	10,038	5,497	2,390	59,033	55,926	51,385	48,278	43,737	40,630	36,089	32,982	28,441	25,334	20,793	17,686	= 491,384
48,517	51,146	56,165	58,794	2,629	5,258	10,277	12,906	17,925	20,554	25,573	28,202	33,221	35,850	40,869	43,498	= 491,384
12,667	10,516	5,019	2,868	58,555	56,404	50,907	48,756	43,259	41,108	35,611	33,460	27,963	25,812	20,315	18,164	= 491,384
48,995	50,668	56,643	58,316	3,107	4,780	10,755	12,428	18,403	20,076	26,051	27,724	33,699	35,372	41,347	43,020	= 491,384
12,189	10,994	4,541	3,346	58,077	56,882	50,429	49,234	42,781	41,586	35,133	33,938	27,485	26,290	19,837	18,642	= 491,384
49,473	50,190	57,121	57,838	3,585	4,302	11,233	11,950	18,881	19,598	26,529	27,246	34,177	34,894	41,825	42,542	= 491,384
11,711	11,472	4,063	3,824	57,599	57,360	49,951	49,712	42,303	42,064	34,655	34,416	27,007	26,768	19,359	19,120	= 491,384
46,844	52,819	54,492	60,467	956	6,931	8,604	14,579	16,252	22,227	23,900	29,875	31,548	37,523	39,196	45,171	= 491,384
14,818	8,365	7,170	717	60,706	54,253	53,058	46,605	45,410	38,957	37,762	31,309	30,114	23,661	22,466	16,013	= 491,384
46,366	53,297	54,014	60,945	478	7,409	8,126	15,057	15,774	22,705	23,422	30,353	31,070	38,001	38,718	45,649	= 491,384
15,296	7,887	7,648	239	61,184	53,775	53,536	46,127	45,888	38,479	38,240	30,831	30,592	23,183	22,944	15,535	= 491,384
= 491,384	= 491,384	= 491,384	= 491,384	= 491,384	= 491,384	= 491,384	= 491,384	= 491,384	= 491,384	= 491,384	= 491,384	= 491,384	= 491,384	= 491,384	= 491,384	

Clarissa burst through the door clutching a stack of books and folders in front of her as though she were plowing through to the end zone. She wasn't, though; she was just keeping her Tuesday appointment with me. She had brought me a few things, probably donations from a charitable organization that likes to help half-wits. A box of pens, which I could use, some cans of soup, and a soccer ball. These offerings only added to my confusion about what Clarissa's relationship to me actually is. A real shrink wouldn't give gifts, and a real social worker wouldn't shrink me. Clarissa does both. It could be, though, that she's not shrinking me at all, that she's just asking me questions out of concern, which would be highly unprofessional.

"How . . . uh . . ." Clarissa stopped mid-sentence to regroup. She laid down her things. "How have you been?" she finally asked, her standard opener.

I couldn't tell her about the only two things that had happened to me since last Friday. You see, if I told her about my relationship with Elizabeth and of my misadventures with Philipa, I would seem like a two-timer. I didn't want to tell her about Kinko's, because why embarrass myself? But while I was trying to come up with something I could tell her, I had this continuing tangential thought: Clarissa is distracted. This is a woman who could talk nonstop, but she was beginning to halt and stammer. I could only watch and wonder.

"Ohmigod," she said, "did you make this?" and she picked up some half-baked pun-intended ceramic object from my so-called coffee table, and I said yes, even though it had a factory stamp on the bottom and she knew I was lying, but I loved to watch her accommodate me. Then she halted, threw the back of her hand to her forehead, murmured several "Uhs," and got on the subject of her uncle who collected ceramics, and I knew that Clarissa had forgotten that she was supposed to ask me questions and I was supposed to talk. But here's the next thing I noticed. While she spun out this tale of her uncle, something was going on in the street that took her attention. Her head turned, her words slowed and lengthened, and her eyes followed something or someone moving at a walking pace. The whole episode lasted just seconds and ended when she turned to me and said, "Do you ever think you'd like to make more ceramics?"

Yipes. Is that what she thinks of me? That I'm far gone enough to be put in a straitjacket in front of a potter's wheel where I can sculpt vases with my one free nose? I have some image work to do, because if one person is thinking it then others are, too.

By now the view out the window had become more interesting, because what had so transfixed Clarissa had wandered into my field of vision. I saw on the sidewalk a woman with raven hair, probably in her early forties. She was bent down as she walked, holding the hand of a one-year-old boy who toddled along beside her like a starfish. I had looked out this window for years and knew its every traveler, could cull tourists from locals, could discern guests from relatives, and I had never seen this raven-haired woman nor this one-year-old child. But Clarissa spotted them and was either curious or knew something about them that I didn't know.

Then Clarissa broke the spell. "What's this?" she asked.

"Oh," I said. "It's a magic square."

Clarissa arched her body back while she studied my proudest 256 boxes.

"Every column and row adds up to four hundred ninety-one thousand, three hundred eighty-four," I said.

"You made this?"

"Last night. Do you know Albrecht Dürer?" I asked. Clarissa nodded. I crouched down to my bookshelf, crawling along the floor and reading the titles sideways. I retrieved one of my few art books. (Most of my books are about barbed wire. Barbed wire is a collectible where I come from. I admired these books once at Granny's house and she sent them to me after Granddaddy died.) My book on Dürer was a real bargain-basement edition with color plates so out of register they looked like Dürer had painted with sludge. But it did have a reproduction of his etching *Melancholy*, in which he incorporated a magic square. He even worked in the numbers 15 and 14, which is the year the print was made, 1514. I showed the etching to Clarissa and she seemed spellbound; she touched the page, lightly moving her fingers across it as if she were reading Braille. While her hand remained in place, she raised her eyes to the wall where I had tacked up my square. She then went to her Filofax and pulled out a Palm Pilot, tapping in the numbers, checking my math. I knew that magic squares were not to be grasped with calculators; it is their mystery and symmetry that thrill. But I didn't say anything, choosing to let her remain in the mathematical world. Satisfied that it all worked out, she stuck the instrument back into its leatherette case and turned to me.

"Is this something you do?" she said.

"Yes."

"Do you use a formula to make them?" Something about my ability to construct the square piqued Clarissa's interest; perhaps it would be the subject of a term paper she would write on me, perhaps she saw it as a way to finally categorize me as a freak.

"There are formulas," I said, "but they rob me of the pleasure."

I could tell Clarissa was dying to write this down because she glanced at her notepad with longing, but we both knew it would be too clinical to actually make notes in front of me. So I pretended that she didn't look at the notepad and she pretended that she was looking past it. Problem was, there was nothing past it, just wall.

Then Clarissa said, "Have you ever thought of using this . . . ability, like in a job?"

"I have, but haven't come up with anything yet, Clarissa." I had rarely, if ever, called Clarissa by name, and as I said it I knew why: It was too intimate and I felt myself squirm.

"If you were using your talents in a job, do you think it might make going to work less stressful?"

"Sure," I said, not meaning it. And here's why. I know that I have eighteenth-century talents in a twenty-first-century world. The brain is so low-tech. Any boy with a Pentium chip can do what I do. I could, however, be a marvel at the Rite Aid, making change without a register.

"Daniel, do you have any male friends?" she asked.

"Sure," I said. "Brian, upstairs."

"It's good for you to have a male friend. What do you two do?"

"Jog. You know, work out."

This was, of course, a lie, but it was the kind of lie that could become true at any moment, as I potentially could work out or jog if I chose. I'm not sure if Clarissa had ever seen this masculine side of me before, which must have sent a chill through her. Then her focus was torn away from me by an internal alarm that she couldn't ignore. She quickly checked her watch and wrapped things up with a few absent-minded and irrelevant homilies that I took to heart, then forgot immediately. She collected her things and went out the door with a worried look, which I could tell was unrelated to our session.

The next morning, I woke up to the sound of Philipa's stereo. I can never make out actual songs; I can only hear a thumping bass line that is delivered through my pillows, which seem to act like speakers. I got up but stayed in my pajamas and swept the kitchen floor, when there was a knock on the door. It was Brian. Uh-oh. What does he know? Maybe Philipa broke down last night and confessed to our indiscretion and now he was going to bust me open. I sifted through a dozen bon mots that I could utter just before he punched me, hoping that someone nearby would hear one and deliciously repeat it to my posthumous biographer. But Brian surprised me: "Wanna go jogging?" "Sure," I said. "Around the block?" he said. "I can't go off the block," I added.

"Okle-dokle," he said. "You change, I'll be downstairs."

I was stunned that after my lie to Clarissa about my passion for jogging, a redemption should materialize so suddenly and so soon. The moral imperative to turn this lie into a truth was so strong in me that I said yes even though I have never jogged, don't get jogging, don't want to jog, especially with The Brian. I might jog with a girl. But I saw this as a way to straighten things out in heaven with my therapist / social worker. I went to my bedroom and put on the only clothes I had that could approximate a jogging outfit. Brown leather loafers, khaki pants with a black belt, an old white dress shirt, and a baseball cap. When Brian saw me in this outfit, his face turned into a momentary question mark, then he relaxed, deciding not to get into it. "To the beach and back," he said. "Oh no, just around the block," I said, trying to thwart him. How do I explain my conditions to him? This lug. "Okay, around the block," he said and started off.

Brian, in jogging shorts, ventilated T-shirt, and headband, looked like an athlete. I looked like I was going off to my first day of high school. Brian was disappearing into the distance and I dutifully tried to follow, but instead stepped out of my left shoe. I continued to hop in place while I slipped it back on and began my initial, first-ever, run around any block since graduation. Brian took it easy on me, though, and I was able to close the distance between us. I wished Elizabeth were finalizing a deal on the sidewalk as we whizzed past so heroically. We went around the block once, pausing only while a family unloaded kiddy transportation from a station wagon. Brian jogged in place; I breathed like a bellows. When we started up again, Brian ran across the short end of the block and I followed. But Brian came to the corner and, instead of turning, dashed across the street. I couldn't follow. I stayed on my block and ran parallel to him with the street between us. Brian seemed not to care that he was violating my aside to him, which obviously he had not understood to be binding. Brian seemed to think that this is what guys do; they jog parallel up the street. Then he suddenly dashed across the street again, joining me on my block as if nothing had happened. The two jogging guys were together again. I sensed that Brian's betrayal of our pact was done with the same thoughtless exuberance of a dolphin leaping out of the water: It was done for fun.

Even though Brian was moderating the pace for me, I still felt a euphoric wave of my favorite feeling: symmetry. Though he was yards ahead of me, we were step for step and stride for stride. My energy was coming from Brian by way of induction. I was swept along in his tailwind. I was an eagle, or at least a pigeon. But then I saw where Brian was going. He was heading straight, straight across the street. I already knew that Brian did not see my request to stay on one block as an edict; he saw it as a whim, a whim that could be un-whimmed in the heat of athletic enterprise. There before me was the curb, coming up on Brian and hence me. This time, though, I felt my pace slowing but oddly not my sense of elation. I saw Brian leap over the curb in a perfect arc. Oh yes, this made sense to me. The arc bridged this mini-hurdle. If I could arc, I could fly over it, too. The curb could be vanquished with one soaring leap. I was ten paces away and I started timing my steps. Six, five, four, three, two, and my right foot lifted off the ground and I sailed over the impossible, the illogical. The opposing curb timed out perfectly. I didn't have to adjust my step in the street before I flew over it, too, and inertia propelled me into the grass, where I collapsed with exhaustion, gasping for air as if I were in a bell jar. Brian turned around, still jogging in place. "Had it? That's enough for today. Good hustle. Good hustle."

My legs were shaking uncontrollably and I was thankful that I was wearing ankle-length khaki pants where my limbs could vibrate in private. Even though I walked back the long way, across three sets of scooped-out driveways, I now knew that I could run across the street at the curb. I could jog over them, fly over them. Brian had liberated me, had shone a spotlight on the wherewithal that had always been inside me, but needed to be coaxed out by human contact.

The next morning, I sprang out of bed and promptly fell over. Overnight my muscles had tightened around my bones like O-rings. I would have screamed in pain but it seemed inadequate. I lifted myself back into bed while my mind scanned the medicine cabinet. Nose drops. Tums. Aspirin . . . yes! I could legitimately take four. Off I went to the bathroom, which gave me the opportunity to take measure of exactly where I was hurting: everything below the beltline, every connective tissue, every lateral muscle. They hurt not only in use, but to the touch. Next to the aspirin was something in a blue jar called Mineral Ice. The bottle was so old it was a collectible. But it said analgesic on it and I had a vague recollection of using it in college. So I swallowed the aspirin and took the Mineral Ice back with me to the bed and began applying the menthol gel to my legs, my thighs, my buttocks. After a few moments it began to tingle, which I assumed was evidence of its pain-relieving properties.

But oily gels don't stay where you apply them. They ooze. They creep like vines and spread themselves to places they're not supposed to go. Like testicles. Mine had somehow come in contact with the stinging concoction, which was now migrating over the eyelid-thin skin of my genitals like flames consuming a field of bluegrass. And there is no washing this stuff off. In fact, the more soap and water are applied, the worse it gets. Soap seemed to act like an agent, enabling it to transpire deeper into every pore. All I could do was lie there and wait for it to peak. And peak it did. Alps. Matterhorn. I would have cursed the Virgin Mary but I knew it was not her fault, so I cursed Brian, whose fault it most directly was. Forty-five minutes later, the throbbing subsided, but there was still the suggestion of an icy breeze wafting around my testicles until way after lunch. Which reminds me that the taste of menthol somehow infected my tuna sandwich, even though I was careful not to handle it without the waxed paper.

That afternoon, Brian knocked on my door and I knelt down in the kitchen and hid. I was just making doubly sure that there would not be a second invite to go racing around the block at blinding jock speed.

By the second day, my hard line toward Brian began to soften. I stopped thinking he'd done it to get even with me. After all, he had provided me with an astounding moment of conquest, the recollection of which would momentarily numb my tendons.

Not until the third day did I begin to emerge from my invalid state. My muscles began to return to normal and I assumed they were better for it; yes, I was now in tip-top shape. My mind had sharpened, too, because a plan had begun to form that would impress Elizabeth with my newly found machismo. I would wait until she was showing apartments at the Rose Crest and then jog by at a nice casual speed. This would possibly erase and replace her previously formed image of me as a person to be avoided. The occasion presented itself the next weekend. Saturday was becoming *the* busy realtor day at the Rose Crest, and Elizabeth was in and out hourly with lots of street time spent in front of the potential renters' automobiles for the final sales chat. I was ready to go in my jogging outfit, same brown loafers (with thick socks this time to prevent them from falling off), same khaki pants, and same white shirt, and all had been cleaned and ironed (except for the shoes, though I had thought about it). It was not so much the jogging part that I thought would turn Elizabeth's head but the leap over the curb that I knew would hold the magic. I'm smart enough to know that Elizabeth had no doubt seen dozens of men leap over curbs without her falling in love with the leaper, but I do believe this: When an endeavor is special in a person's life, others discern it intuitively and appreciate it more, like the praise a child receives for a lumpy clay sculpture. And as ordinary as such an event might be, it can be instilled with uncommon power. So I reasoned that my leap, my soaring, arcing flight, would have a hero's impact upon her and would neutralize my earlier flubs.

It was not until 2:00 P.M. that Elizabeth became engaged in a street conversation that seemed it would last long enough for me to parade my newly cultivated right stuff. There was no time for me to delay, think twice, or balk. I had to do it now. I ran down my apartment steps, took the walkway, cut the corner of the grass, and was heading to the end of the block with effortless but mighty strides. My sudden appearance caused Elizabeth and her clients to look toward me. I liked my pace. Easy, confident. Soon the curb was nigh. I checked traffic out of the corner of my eye. No cars. I began to adjust my step—so many details of the week's earlier triumph were coming back to me! I pictured myself airborne while Elizabeth took it all in. But I was not twenty feet away when a squeezing sensation took hold in my chest. This was the familiar ring of panic. The curb suddenly did not make sense, nor did my impending leap over it. I was rapidly collapsing in on myself, and the curb seemed to have reacquired all of its old daunting properties of impossibility. However, I was still shooting forward like a cannonball when, just this side of the point of no return, I put on the brakes and urked to a cartoon halt, and for a second I was the Road Runner and the curb was the Grand Canyon. I was back where I'd been four days ago, only this time the love of my life, and her clients, were watching. Even as I stood there, barely balanced, drenched in humiliation, leaning over the precipice trying to regain my center of gravity, my mind pumped out one clear thought. It was not the idea of the soaring arc that had liberated me, nor was it the thrill of the pace. It had been the presence of Brian, the person who had so confidently led me, who had made my successful leap so possible. He had allowed me to put one foot in the conventional world, and I was about to place down the other. But my conventions, it turned out, could not be broken overnight, because they had been forged in my brain like steel, and nothing so simple as longing could dislodge them. By now I was flushed with embarrassment and hoped that Elizabeth had not registered my failure.

Let me tell you about my mailbox. It is one of twelve eroded brassy slots at the front entrance of my building. It is also my Ellis Island, because, as I don't have a phone or a computer, and I disconnected my TV, everything alien that comes to me comes through it first. The Monday after my dismal showing with Elizabeth, I went to the mailbox and retrieved six pieces of mail, took them to my kitchen table, and began sorting them into three piles. Into the Highly Relevant pile went two personal letters, one hand-addressed. In the Relevant pile, I put the mail that wasn't personal even though it was addressed to me—ads, announcements, and so on, because anything with my name on it I consider relevant. Third were the letters addressed to "resident" and "occupant." The Irrelevant pile. I had considered a fourth pile, because to me, "resident" is quite different from "occupant," and I have struggled and succeeded in coming up with a practical usage guide. Yes, I'm a resident and occupant of the Chrysanthemum Apartments, but if I went out on the sidewalk and put a large cardboard box over me and sat on the lawn, it could be said that I was an occupant of the cardboard box but not a resident of it. So "resident" letters could be sent only to my apartment, but "occupant" letters could be sent to cardboard boxes, junked cars, and large paint cans that I could stick my feet in. "Occupant" letters could legitimately be considered Very Highly Irrelevant.

The two letters that arrived that day were not insignificant. The first was from the *Crime Show,* informing me that the taping was completed on my episode and thanking me for my participation. Enclosed was a copy of the waiver I had signed that exempted the producers from all responsibility and made me liable for any lawsuits resulting from my appearance. It was probably not clever of me to sign it, but I wanted to be on TV. Plus, it seemed like it would be the nice thing to do. The letter also informed me that the show would be on several weeks from now and to keep checking my local listings for the exact date and time.

The second letter was an airy breeze of a handwritten note from Granny. I always delay opening her letters in the same spirit as saving the center of the Oreo for last. Granny lives on her pecan plantation in southern Texas (hence, my middle name, Daniel Pecan Cambridge). She is the one family member who understands that my insanity is benign and that my failure to hold a job is not due to laziness. The letter sang with phrases that I swear lifted me like a tonic: "Life is a thornbush from which roses spring; all the hearts in Texas are wishing for you; I smother you with the kisses that are in this letter." And then a check for twenty-five hundred dollars fell out of the envelope. The irony is that the one person who gives me money is the one person I wish I could hand the check back to and say no, only joy can pass between you and me. I found it difficult to write back. But I did, stingy with loving words because they don't come out of me easily. I hoped she could read between the lines; I hoped that the presence of the letter in my own hand, the texture of it, the wear and tear it had received on its trip across five states revealed my heart to her. I can't explain why it's easy to tell you and not her how she smooths the way for me, how her letters are the only true things in my life, how touching them connects me to the world. If only Tepperton's Pies had a Most-Loved Granny essay contest, I'd enter and my fervor would translate into an easy win. I could forward her the published piece in Tepperton's in-house journal and she could read it knowing it was an ode to her.

The week had been one of successes and setbacks. There was the triumph of my run with Brian and the failure of my peacocking for Elizabeth. There was my excitement at receiving Granny's letter but then the reminder of my own needy status when the check fell onto the kitchen table. But overall, there was an uptick in my disposition and I thought this might be the week for me to find the elusive Northwest Passage to the Third Street Mall.

The Third Street Mall is in the heart of Santa Monica on a street closed to traffic and has hundreds of useful shops with merchandise at both bargain and inflated prices. But it also has a Pavilions supermarket. I have been suffering along with the limited selection of groceries at the Rite Aid because it's the only place to which I'd mapped out a convenient route. If I could manage to get to the Pavilions, well, it would be like moving from Iraq to Hawaii. From barren canned goods and dried fruit to the Garden of Eden. Also, coffee. Jeez, the Coffee Bean, Starbucks. I might not seem like the type who could sit at an outdoor café drinking a latte, but I am. Why? No motion required. It's just sitting. Sitting and sipping. I can't imagine a neurosis that would prevent one from raising one's arm to one's mouth while holding a cup, though given time, I'm sure I could come up with one. I also like the idea of saying "java." That is, saying it with an actual intent of getting some and not as a delightful sound to utter around my apartment.

I had tried and failed in this quest for Pavilions before, and I know why: cowardice and lack of will. This time, I was determined to be determined, but there would be trials. My initial excursions hadn't allowed for anything less than perfection. The route had to make absolute logical sense: no double backs or figure eights, and the driveways had to be perfectly opposing each other. But if I thought the way an explorer would—yes, there would be rapids, there would be setbacks—perhaps I could eventually find the right path.

Maps, of course, are of no assistance except in the most general way. Maps show streets, but not obstacles. If only city maps could be made by people like me. They wouldn't show streets at all; they would show the heights of curbs, the whereabouts of driveways and crosswalks, and the locations of Kinko's. What about all those drivers who can't make left turns? Why aren't there maps for them? No, I was forced to discover my route by trial and error. But because I now had a catalog of opposing driveways and their locations in my head, noted from various other attempts to find various other locations through the years, I was able to put together a possible route before I even started. With a few corrections made spontaneously, on my third attempt I finally established a pathway to the mall, and for three evenings afterward I fell asleep wrapped in the glow of enormous pride.

Having a route to the Third Street Mall meant that I was out in public more, so I had to come up with some new rules to make my forays outside my apartment more tolerable. When I was relaxing at the Coffee Bean having a java, for example, I drew invisible lines from customer to customer connecting plaids with plaids, solids with solids, and T-shirts with T-shirts. Once done, it allowed my anxiety meter to flatline. I got a kick out of the occasional conversation that arose with a "dude." One time, while enjoying my coffee, a particular tune was playing somewhere in the background. The melody was so cheerful that everyone in the place became a percussionist one way or another and with varying intensity. For some it was finger-drumming and for others it was foot-tapping. I was inspired to blow on my hot coffee in three-quarter time. But the oddest thing of all was that I knew this song. It was a current pop hit, but how had I come to know it? How had this tune gotten to me, through the mail? Somehow it had reproduced, spread, and landed in my mental rhythm section. While it played, I and everybody else in the Coffee Bean had become as one. I was in the here and now, infected with a popular song that I had never heard, sitting among "buddies." And there was, for three long minutes, no difference between me and them.

The chairs and tables of the Coffee Bean spilled onto the mall like an alluvial fan. I grabbed a seat that was practically in the street because I could see at least a full block in either direction. No need, though. Because what went on within the perimeter of the sidewalk café was enough for an afternoon's entertainment. People, I thought. These are people. Their general uniformity was interrupted only by their individual variety. My eyes roved around like a security camera. Then I was startled out of my reverie by the sight of the one-year-old who had passed by my window last week. His hand was held tightly by the same raven-haired woman, and he leaned in toward the doorway of a bookstore, straining like a dog on a leash. In answer to a voice from inside, the woman turned toward the door and let the child's hand loose. The boy careened the few steps inside and I saw him lifted into the air by two arms behind the glass storefront. Everything else in the window was obscured by a reflection from the street. The raven-haired woman was not the mother; this I had gathered. The raven-haired woman I assumed to be a sitter or friend. The child clung to the woman behind the glass, and when I saw that it was Clarissa who emerged from the shop, holding this child, so much of her behavior the previous week suddenly made sense.

On the way home, I mentally constructed another magic square, but one of a different order; this square fell under the heading of "Life":

Granny	Philipa	Brian
Kinko's	?	Rite Aid
Elizabeth	Zandy	Clarissa

I tried a few things in the empty center square, but nothing stuck; anything I wrote in it seemed to fall out. As I studied the image, this graphic of my life, I realized it added up to nothing.

As I walked home, the day was still sunny and bright. Something bothered me, though: the sight of a mailman coming off my block at two-thirty in the afternoon. The mailman was never in my neighborhood later than ten, and this meant there could be a logjam in my planned events of the day. Earlier, when I trotted down with an elaborately planned haphazard flair to check the mail—jeez, I think I remember whistling—the slot had been empty and I assumed there was no mail to sort, so I foolishly changed my schedule. Oh well, the day had already convoluted itself when I sighted Clarissa on the street, and now I was going to sort mail in the afternoon. Sometimes I just resign myself to disaster.

Most favorite mail: Granny's scented envelopes from Texas (without a check). Least favorite: official-looking translucent-windowed envelope with five-digit box number for a return address. But today, at the godforsaken hour of two-thirty in the afternoon, an envelope arrived that was set dead even between most favorite and least favorite. It was plain white and addressed to Lenny Burns. No return address on the front of the envelope, and I couldn't turn it over until I analyzed all my potential responses to whatever address could be on the back. Which I won't go into.

The name Lenny Burns rattled around in my head like a marble in a tin can. There was no one in my building named Lenny Burns, and the address specifically noted my apartment number. The previous tenant hadn't been anyone named Lenny Burns; it had been a Miss Rogers, an astrologer with a huge pair of knockers. And evidently there was some doubt about whether she earned her living exclusively from astrology. The name Lenny Burns was so familiar that I paused, tapping the letter on the kitchen table like a playing card, while I tried to come up with a matching face. Nothing popped. Finally, I flipped over the envelope and saw the return address, and I wonder if what I saw will send a shiver of horror through you like it did me.

Tepperton's Pies. Like Mom never made.

Oops. I suddenly remembered that Lenny Burns was the pseudonym I had used on my second essay in the Most Average American contest, written almost automatically while I ogled Zandy. While I didn't imagine that the contents of the envelope held good news, I also didn't think that it held actual bad news, either. The letter informed me that not only was Lenny Burns one of five finalists in the Most Average American contest, but so was Daniel Pecan Cambridge. And both of them are me.

So the real me and a false me were competing with each other to win what? Five thousand dollars, that's what. And the competition would involve the finalists reading their essays aloud at a ceremony at Freedom College in Anaheim, California. This meant that my two distinct and separate identities were to show up at the same place and time. This is like asking Superman and Clark Kent to appear at Perry White's birthday lunch. The other competitors, the letter informed me, were Kevin Chen, who was, evidently, Asian American; Danny Pepelow, redhead-sounding; and Sue Dowd, whom I could not form a picture of. I wondered what the legal consequences of my deception would be; I wondered if I would have to blurt out in a packed courtroom that I had been swooning in a lovesick haze over Zandy the pharmacist and therefore this was a crime passionel. I calmed down after telling myself that any action taken against me would probably be civil and not criminal, and if they did levy a suit against me, it would be very easy to choke on a Tepperton pie, cough up a mouse, and start negotiating.

The next day, I was nervous about the inevitable arrival of the second pie letter, the one that would be addressed to the real me. This led me to an alternative fixation. I should capitalize it because Alternative Fixation is a technique I use to trick myself out of anxiety. It works by changing the subject. I simply focus on something that produces even greater anxiety. In this case, I chose to plan a face-to-face encounter with Elizabeth the Realtor. I had on one occasion written her a "get to know me" letter that I never sent because no matter how much I approached it, how I rewrote it, I always sounded like a stalker. "I have observed you from my window . . ." "Your license plate, REALTR, amused me . . ." It all sounded too observant and creepy. Which made me ask myself whether I actually was too observant and creepy, but the answer came up no, because I know my own heart.

I had to admit that my previous plans to impress her had backfired like a motorcycle. It was time to do the manly thing: to meet her without deception, without forethought. I decided to present myself as an interested renter, one who is looking to move up to a two-bedroom to make room for an office, in which I would be working with the renowned writer Sue Dowd on a biography of Mao. This seemed to be the honest thing to do.

I called the number on the rental sign, expecting to get, and prepared to deftly handle, the instructions that would take me through the telephonic maze that would finally connect me to her voicemail. But a miracle happened. She answered. *Crackle pop,* she was on a cell phone in her car. I explained who I was, Daniel Cambridge (a swell-sounding name when I leave out the Pecan), that I live near the Rose Crest, and that I was looking to move up. I left out the part about the Mao bio because, jeez, she's not an idiot.

She told me she was between appointments, had twenty minutes free, and could meet me there in ten. I hardly had time to bathe. Well, okay, I said. I could postpone my conference call, I said. I hung up and cranked on my shower with stunning accuracy. Perfect temperature with one swing of the wrist. I stepped in, knowing I was on the clock, and yet I still experienced one recurring sensation intractably linked to my morning shower. The flowing, ropey hot water sent me back in time to home, to Texas, to the early hours of the morning. To save money, my mother had always turned off the heat at night, which made our house into an ice hotel. Every wintry morning, as a frosted-over adolescent, I made the chilly jaunt from bedroom to spare bathroom. Stepping into the steamy shower was the equivalent of being cuddled in a warm towel by a loving aunt, and now I'm sometimes rendered immobile by an eerie nostalgia in the first few moments of even a quick rinse. This sensation slowed me down like an atom at absolute zero, even though Elizabeth was at this very moment probably running yellow lights to fit me in.

I was toweling off at the window when Elizabeth the Realtor pulled up in front of the Rose Crest. She remained in the car for several minutes talking to herself. I realized she was probably using the hands-free car phone, at least I hoped she was, as one nut in the family would be enough. I threw on some clothes and scampered down the stairs, skipping across the street at the driveways. I was overcome with an impression of myself as an English schoolboy. I might as well have been wearing a beanie and short pants. As Elizabeth got out of her car, I appeared from behind her and greeted her with a "Hello, y'all, I'm Daniel Cambridge." I had not intended the slight country twang that affected my speech. And I do not know, if I perceived myself as an English schoolboy, why my greeting came out as though it were spoken by the cook on a wagon train. I suppose I was confused about just who I actually was at that moment. I had now committed myself to a drawl, and I was rapidly trying to uncommit. So over the next few sentences I fell into a brogue, then a kind of high nasal English thing, then migrated through the Bronx, searching until I found my own voice. I finally did, but not before Elizabeth had asked, "Where are you from?" to which I saved myself with, "I'm an army brat."

I followed Elizabeth up one flight of stairs. She reached into her purse, producing a daunting ring of apartment keys that jangled like a tambourine. There was a delay while she flipped and sorted the keys on the ring, and she managed to open the door on the sixth try. There were three odors inside. One was mildew, one was tangerine, both emanating from the same source: a bowl of fruit rotting in the center of the kitchen table. The third aroma was from Elizabeth, a familiar lilac scent that made itself quite known now that she was contained within the four walls of the sealed apartment. This scent thickened and intensified as though it were pumped into the room by a compressor.

Elizabeth swept the pungent tangerines into a paper bag and stuck them in the waste can under the sink, all the while talking up the glories of apartment 214. She wore a tight brown linen skirt that stopped about three inches above her knees, a matching jacket, and a cream silk blouse with a cream silk cravat. She turned on the air conditioner to max, which intensified the moldy smell, causing us both to sneeze. She flipped on the built-in kitchen television to make the place seem lively and swung open the refrigerator to show me its massive cubic feet interior. Price seventeen hundred a month, she said, first and last, plus a security deposit.

"This is a great building," she said. "Usually they want references, but I can get you around it."

"Don't worry, I have references," I said, wondering who I meant.

This was the first time I'd had a chance to really see Elizabeth. She had always been either too far away or too close up. Now I could frame her like a three-quarter portrait and see all her details. She was tan. Probably not from the sun, I guessed. She wore several gold rings studded with gems; none was on her wedding finger. She had a gold chain around her neck, at the end of which was a pair of rhinestone-encrusted reading glasses. Her eyes were blue. Not her irises, but her lids, which had been faintly daubed with eye shadow. Her skin had a hint of orange; her hair was a metallic gold, which darkened as it neared the roots. She was a collection of human colors that had been lightly tweaked and adjusted. Her efforts in the area of presentation made me admire her more.

Elizabeth was a prize object. She had picked up beauty tricks from everywhere; she had assembled herself from the best cosmetics had to offer. Any man she chose to be with would be envied, and made complete by her. A man who built an empire would certainly need Elizabeth by his side; he would need her and he would deserve her. I knew now that no matter how much I lied to her, the truth would come out about who and what I was, but I just stood there anyway, continuing my dumb charade while she radiated perfection.

She asked if I also wanted to see a three-bedroom down the hall that had just come up. I must have said yes, because the next thing I knew I was in the apartment next door, being shown each closet and bathroom. This place was unfurnished, and Elizabeth's high heels clacked on the bare floor with such snap that it was like being led around by a flamenco dancer. I looked at the apartment with longing, as it was roomy, filled with light, and freshly painted. No tangerine rot here, and I told Elizabeth, who by now was calling me Daniel, that I would check with my co-biographer Sue Dowd to make sure the size of the place wouldn't intimidate her and thus hinder her writing.

After the ritualized locking of both apartments, Elizabeth led the way back down the stairs and onto the street. She sprung her car trunk from forty feet, reached in it, and handed me a brochure. She stood there on the sidewalk just as I had seen her do so many times from my window. Only now it was me to whom she was saying, "This is a very desirable area," and "Each apartment has two parking spaces underground." I was in on it. I was in on the conversations I had only imagined. Even after these few minutes of talking with her, spending time with her, trying to see her as fallible, Elizabeth lived on in my psyche as unattainable and ideal, and I was still the guy across the street dreaming beyond his means.

"What is your current apartment like?" she asked.

"It's a one-bedroom. But I'm starting to feel cramped," I said.

"Is it in this area?"

"Yes," I said.

"Perhaps I should look at it. I can do swaps, deals, all kinds of things," she said.

I nodded happily, indicating that I appreciated her can-do, full-service attitude. The thought of Elizabeth in my apartment delighted me; it would be a small tryout of our cohabitation. But I wasn't about to take her on my crazy-eights route to a destination only a few linear steps away. She might look at me askance.

"I could come by tomorrow, or next week," she said.

"Next week is good."

"What's your phone number?"

"I'm changing it in two days and don't have the new one yet. We could make an appointment now."

"You want to give me directions?"

I said sure. "You come down Seventh Street toward the ocean." She began to write in a spiral notepad. "Make a right on Lincoln, left on Fourth, right on Evans, left on Acacia. I'm at 4384."

Elizabeth looked at me askance. It didn't take her realtor's mind long to compute that my apartment was right across the street. It seemed absurd not to take her over there now, let alone to have given her directions to a location within skipping distance. She didn't call me on it because I guess she'd seen stranger things, and we made arrangements to meet next Friday, right after Clarissa's visit.

Elizabeth drove off while I pretended to be about to step off the curb. My stall involved bending over and acting as if I had found something urgently wrong with the tip of my shoe. Once she rounded the corner, I took my regular paper-clip-shaped route home, checking the mailbox and retrieving what I already knew would be there, the second letter from Tepperton's Pies telling me that Daniel Pecan Cambridge was in competition with Lenny Burns, Sue Dowd (who, if she turned out to be Elizabeth's half sister, would be bad luck for me), Danny Pepelow, and Kevin Chen.

It was inconceivable that Clarissa hadn't shown for her Friday appointment. I confess that disappointment rang through me, not only because our sessions were the cornerstone of my week but also because I couldn't wait to observe her from my new perspective of secret knowledge. Something else besides disappointment went through me, too; it was concern. For Clarissa not to show meant that something was seriously wrong; she didn't even know how to be late. Her earnestness included fulfilling her obligations, and I guessed she would have called if I had had a phone. I used the hour constructively. I imagined Clarissa's life as a jigsaw puzzle. The individual pieces hovered around Clarissa every time I saw her or thought about her, which now included a small male child, a raven-haired woman, her pink Dodge, her ringless fingers, her stack of books and notepads, her implied rather than overt sexuality. I stood her next to Elizabeth, her opposite. What I saw was Elizabeth as woman and Clarissa as girl. But something was confusing. It was Clarissa who had a child, and Elizabeth who was trolling for a husband. Clarissa, girl-like, had done womanly things, and Elizabeth, womanlike, was doing girly things. It was Clarissa who was being tugged at the ankles by a one-year-old, her schedule dictated by babysitters and playdates, and it was Elizabeth who made herself up every day, whose life was governed by the cell and the cordless. In my mind, Elizabeth was all browns and golds; Clarissa was pastels and whites. And although Elizabeth was adult and smart and savvy and Clarissa was scattered and struggling and a student, it was Clarissa who had every adult responsibility and Elizabeth who remained the sorority deb.

I put this information on hold. I turned my focus to the Clarissa rebus I had laid out in airspace above the kitchen table. One piece missing: Where was Clarissa's man? Her impregnator. I assumed he was already gone or in the process of being gone, that he was the source or subject of the distressed phone calls. He had been replaced by Raven-Haired Woman, who, I assumed, was a friend filling in for babysitters. Raven-Haired Woman was now demystified into Betty or Susie. Clarissa was living advanced juggling and was probably in a mess. Oddly, I now knew more about my shrink than my shrink knew about me, since I had never allowed her to penetrate beyond my habits, which of course is the point of their existence.

I anticipated my next session with Clarissa because I would see what form her apology would take. Or at least the extent of the apology. If she explained too much, she would reveal too much ("My husband is gone and I'm on my own and couldn't find someone to take care of my one-year-old"), and she'd risk violating what I suppose is a shrink tenet. On the other hand, if she under-explained, she might seem callous. She'd found herself in a spot, all right, and I was going to enjoy watching her wriggle free, because how she handled it would reveal how she felt about me.

Forty minutes later, Elizabeth, former woman-of-the-world turned sorority deb, showed up at my place on her tour through the available apartments of Santa Monica. She mistakenly knocked on Philipa's door, which set Tiger barking. I called up the landing to her and her voice, like a melodeon, greeted me with an "Oh," and she turned her scrap of paper right-side up, causing the 9 to be a 6. She came down the steps at a bent angle, her torso twisted from trying to see the steps from around her breasts.

I tried to appear richer than I was, but it was hard, as I didn't have much to work with. Mostly I had put things away that would indicate poverty, like opened bags of Cheetos with their contents spilling onto the Formica. I did set out a packet of plastic trash liners because I thought they were a luxury item. She came in and stood stock-still in the middle of the living room. As she surveyed the place, wearing a tawny outfit with her knees thrust a bit forward from the cant of her high heels, she gave the impression of a colt rearing up. Nothing much seemed to impress her, though, as she only seemed to notice the details of my apartment as they would appear on a stat sheet: number of bedrooms, or should I say number of bedroom, kitchenette, cable TV, which she flipped on (though it's not really cable, just an ancient outlet to the roof antenna), AC, which she tested, number of bathrooms (she turned on the tap, I presume to see if rusty water would come out). I loved it when she looked at my bedroom and declared, "This must be the master." Calling my dreary bedroom a master was like elevating Gomer Pyle to major general.

She sat in the living room, jotted efficiently on her clipboard, and asked me how I was feeling about the apartment across the street. Had I decided? I went into a rhapsody about the complications of my decision, about the necessity of contacting my nonexistent writing partner. I had been talking for a minute or so when I noticed a rictus forming on Elizabeth's face. She was looking past me at waist level with her mouth dropped open and her writing hand frozen. I turned my head and looked at the TV, and my mouth went open, and if I had been writing, my hand would have frozen, too. There I was on TV, being shuffled along in mock arrest on the *Crime Show*. There was a long moment before I came out with "My God, that fellow looks like me." What filled the long moment was my shock, not at the bad luck of the show's air date and time slot, but at how I looked on TV. The blue parka made me look fat, which I'm not. It made me look like a criminal, and I'm not. The show then jumped to the long shot of me talking to the two policemen. Now we could see my apartment in the background, so there was no use denying the obvious. "Oh right, it is me," I ventured. "I made a bundle off this," and I nodded up and down as if to verify my own lie. Then I turned to Elizabeth and said, "All I'm saying there is 'I'm talking, I'm talking, I'm trying to look like I'm talking.' " She looked over at me, then back to the TV, and I knew that she had identified me as someone dangerous.

This moment was like a pivot. Everything in my little universe swung on its axis and reordered itself. Here's why: Elizabeth, whom I had previously seen only on her turf, or through a window, or in my head, was, now that she had crossed the threshold of my apartment, an actual being who would demand closet space. I didn't even have enough closet space for the clothes she was currently wearing. I knew that I could not share a bathroom with eighteen gallons of hair stiffener, and I began to see how clearly she misfit my life. At the same time, when she saw me on TV, her face hid a well-tempered revulsion. In these few elongated seconds, our magnetic poles flopped as she became ordinary and I became notorious.

Elizabeth must have now viewed my apartment as a halfway house, since she asked me if addicts lived in the building. I said no and did a pretty good job of explaining the TV show, though when I began to explain about the murder downstairs she got the hiccups and asked for water. I felt a small surge of pride because the water from the kitchen tap was not murky or even slightly brown. Her cell phone rang and she spoke into it, saying "Yeah" three times and hanging up. Her tone was as if the person on the other end of the line had heard stress in her voice and was trying to suss out her predicament with questions like, "Are you all right?" "Are you in danger?" and "Do you want me to come get you?" She was out the door, and I looked at her from my spot by the window and felt a twinge of the old longing, no doubt brought on by placing myself in the old circumstances.

After seeing the two women side by side, Elizabeth actually before me and Clarissa in my mind, a thought came into my head that jarred me: Would it be possible to scoop up my love for Elizabeth and steam-shovel it over onto Clarissa? This thought disturbed me because it suggested that the personalities of the two women had nothing whatever to do with the knot of love inside me. It implied that, if I chose, I could transfer my adoration onto anyone or thing that tweaked my fancy. But my next thought set me straight. I knew that once love is in place, it does not unstick without enormous upheaval, without horrible images of betrayal flashing uncontrollably through the mind, without visions of a bleak and inconsolable self, a self that is a captive of grief, which lingers viscously in the heart.

But Clarissa was making the decision easy for me. She reflected light; Elizabeth sucked it up. Clarissa was a sunburst; Elizabeth was a moon pie. So now my preoccupation with Elizabeth became a post-occupation as I turned my Cyclops eye onto Clarissa. Yes, I would always love Elizabeth in some way, and one day we would be able to see each other again. But it was too soon right now. Better to let her handle her own pain, with her own friends, in her own way. But Elizabeth was at fault here. She had destroyed whatever was between us by making a profound gaffe: She met me.

Long after the sun had set, my thoughts continued to accumulate, spread, and divide. What were my chances with Clarissa? None. Clearly, none. In nine months of twice-weekly visits, she had not placed on my tongue one sacrament of romantic interest. And not only that, she spoke to me in the tone one uses with a mental patient: "And how are we today?" meaning, "How are you and all those nuts living inside you?" At least Clarissa knows I'm benign. But that is not an adjective one wants to throw around about one's spouse: "This is my husband. He's benign."

In spite of the gleaming bursts of well-being that were generated by the idea of loving Clarissa instead of Elizabeth, in the deeper hours of the night I began to look at myself, to consider myself and my condition, to measure the life I'd led so far. I did not know what made me this way. I did not know of any other way I could be. I did not know what was inside me or how I could redeem what was hidden there. There must be a key or person or thing, or song or poem or belief, or old saw that could access it, but they all seemed so far away, and after I drifted further and further into self-absorption, I closed the evening with this desolate thought: There are few takers for the quiet heart.

In the middle of the night, I woke spooked and perspiring. I clutched the blanket, drawing it up to my mouth as protection against the murderous creature that no doubt was lurking in the room. I lay still in case it did not yet know I was there. I held my breath for silence, then slowly let it out without moving my chest. Eventually, this technique caught up with me and I had to occasionally gasp for air. But no one killed me that night, no knife penetrated the blanket, no hand grabbed at my throat. Looking back, I can identify the cause of my panic. It was that my earlier Socratic dialogue with myself about the nature of love had no Socrates to keep me logical. There was just me, seesawing between the poles. There was no one to correct me and consequently no thought necessarily implied the next, in fact, a thought would often contradict its predecessor. I had tried to force clarity on my confused logic, and this disturbed my demanding sense of order.

Two days later, I saw a man in a suit and tie standing on the sidewalk in front of the apartment next door. He was rail thin and for a moment I could have been in Sleepy Hollow except this man had a head and no horse. He swayed from left to right, scanning up and down the block for street numbers. He was all angles as he craned sideways and looked up, twisting at the waist to check an address he held in his hand. This one-man menagerie crabbed along the sidewalk, with his neck moving owllike as he looked far and close.

When he saw the address above the stairs of my building, it seemed he'd found what he was looking for. He collected himself and came up the steps and knocked at my door.

"Daniel Cambridge?" he called out.

I counted to three, then opened the door.

"Yes?" I said.

"Gunther Frisk from Tepperton's Pies," he said.

We sat chair and sofa; this time with the TV off, as I didn't want an errant *Crime Show* to leak into my living room. He asked whether I would be available on March 4 to read my essay at Freedom College in the event I won. "I would check my schedule," I said, "but I can always move things around."

"I have to ask you a few questions. Your age?"

"Twenty-nine."

"Married?"

"Engaged."

"Where do you work?"

"I train boxers."

He chuckled. "The fighters or the dogs?"

I made a choice. "The dogs."

"Ever been in trouble with the law?"

"No."

I wondered when he was going to ask me a question to which I wasn't going to lie.

"Are you the exclusive author of your essay?"

"Yes." I marveled at my ability to answer truthfully with the same barefaced sincerity as I'd displayed on my five previous whoppers.

He explained the judging process to me, made me sign a document promising not to sue, gave me a coupon for a frozen pie, and left. I watched from the window as he walked back to his car, got in it, and sat. He picked up a clipboard from the passenger's seat, gave it a befuddled examination, and then again elongated his neck as he looked out the windshield toward my apartment and back to the clipboard. I'd only seen comedians do double takes, but here was one occurring in real life. He got out of his car, once again checking the clipboard against the street numbers. He came up my steps, shuffled in front of my apartment, and rapped a couple of times. I opened the door and saw on his face an expression of bewilderment, as though he had stepped into his shoes in the morning and they were size seventeen.

"I'm sorry," he said, checking his clipboard. "I . . . I . . . Does Lenny Burns live here?"

We just hung there staring at each other. Thank God my eventual response justified the eternity that elapsed before I spoke.

"Dead," I said. "Dead!" My voiced raised. "Dead at twenty-eight!" I cracked out a half sob, drawing on the same intensity of belief I had employed when I wrote the name *Lenny Burns* on the essay. For dramatic effect, I reeled backward onto the sofa. Could my experience with the *Crime Show,* I thought, have given me the skills of Pacino?

Gunther stood in the doorway. "Oh, I'm sorry," he said. "Mr. Burns lived here?"

"He was a cousin; my third cousin removed from my step-mother's side, but we were like *this*. You can't imagine how sudden . . . everybody in the building loved him." My sincere belief in what I was saying made me choke up.

"He was a finalist, too . . . just like you," said Gunther.

"Oh my God, the irony!" I cried. "We entered together. Lenny loved the idea that he might be typical, and once he got that into his head, he wanted to be the *most* typical. He would have loved to have been a finalist. Why couldn't you have come yesterday, before he passed?"

In the hallway Philipa came by and heard me keening inside. She saw the door wide open and the distressed posture of Gunther Frisk.

She called in to us, "What's the matter?"

"It's Lenny," said Gunther, trying to be helpful. "Lenny died."

Philipa's face was so blank, so unresponsive, that it was possible to interpret her expression as sudden, catastrophic, morbid shock. I rose and pulled her in, holding her face against my shoulder in comfort. Also so she couldn't talk. I said to Gunther, "Could you excuse us?" He muttered an apology, acknowledging that he might have just blurted out private information that would have been better delivered by a priest. "I will contact you," he said as he backpedaled out of my apartment.

It was a shimmering Southern California day, and the light poured into the Rite Aid through its plate glass windows the size of panel trucks. The merchandise inside broke the light like a million prisms. Candy bars, laid out like organ keys, glistened in their foil wrappers. Tiers of detergent boxes bore concentric circles of vibrating color. The tiny selection of pots and pans reflected elongated sideshow images. Green rubber gloves dangled from metal racks like a Duchamp, and behind it all was Zandy's yellow hair, which moved like a sun, rising and setting over the horizon of ointments and salves.

I had actual purchases to make at the pharmacy and it was just luck that I fell into the correct rotation that allowed Zandy to wait on me. I was buying sixteen ChapSticks. This was not a compulsion; this was practical. Ten go in a drawer, and I place the other six around the apartment for handy access. I handed her the cash and she might as well have called me by name, as she referenced every prescription drug I ever took.

"Still taking the Inderal?" she asked.

I had tried Inderal for a while to keep my heart from racing; I was off it now. "Not much," I said.

"How'd you like Valium?"

"Left me kind of groggy."

"You stopped your Prozac."

"Don't need it anymore."

"Got a thing for ChapStick, huh?"

She could have been on a data-gathering mission, or she could have been flirting with me. I couldn't tell which. But it was profoundly intimate for her to know what drugs were flowing through my own personal veins. If a waitress were asking me these questions I would definitely consider it a come-on.

Up close, Zandy failed in the perfection department, which made me like her more. The button of her nose was askew, as though someone had dialed it to three. Her skin, though, was so dewy and fresh I couldn't quite turn to go. I picked up my sack of ChapSticks, and she said, "Don't forget your change," and then she added a wonderful thing: She said, "See ya." I had to stay there a second and take her in before I was able to unstick my gummy feet from the floor.

It was nearing two and I wondered if Clarissa was going to show up this time. There was no reason to think that she wouldn't, as she had slipped a handwritten note under the door earlier in the week with a sincere but formal apology, promising we would resume the following week at our usual time. I assumed that this was the standard apology that one learns in chapter 15 of the therapist's handbook: Don't give out too much personal information. But the idea of the dispassionate shrink slinking up the patient's stairs and secreting a note under the doorjamb probably wouldn't go down well with whatever board would review such things. Still, Clarissa was only a student and allowed to act like one.

Friday at two o'clock—precisely when the second hand fell on neither side of twelve—Clarissa knocked, pushing open the door that I had purposely left ajar. She said, "I'm so sorry." Clarissa was an apology champion. "Are you all right?" I asked, probing for information I already knew but wanted her to tell me. "Oh yes," she said, "I couldn't get a—" She was about to say *babysitter* and then realized it would reveal too much and she changed mid-sentence to "I got tied up and there was no way to reach you."

"Would you like something to drink?" I offered.

"Do you have a Red Bull?"

Red Bull is a potent caffeine-infused soft drink that turns grown men into resonating vibraphones. Drinking a Red Bull is more impressive to me than drinking a bottle of scotch. Several years ago after my first Red Bull—which was also my last—I got in marksman position on the living room floor, opened a pack of playing cards, and repeatedly dealt myself poker hands. I computed that good hands came in bunches; that one full house in a shuffle implies a possibility of more full houses. And lousy hands in a shuffle only create the possibility of more lousy hands. So Red Bull was not allowed in my house, only because this little episode lasted nine hours. Clarissa's request for the caffeine recharge indicated to me that she was going to have to be bucked up if she was going to make it through my session.

"I don't have any Red Bull but I know who might," I said.

I excused myself to go to Brian and Philipa's amid protestations of "You don't have to" from Clarissa. I peered into her apartment and saw Brian flaked out on the sofa, his jaw hanging open like a drawbridge. I didn't have the heart to wake him. I came back to see that Clarissa had settled into the easy chair and was staring at the floor. She was wearing a prim pink blouse that made her look so wholesome it was as if Norman Rockwell had painted a pinup. She had a bloom on her cheeks that lied about her real age. Her face had gentle angles, one rosy thing sloping into the next, and it suggested none of the hardness she must have experienced. It seemed as though she were determined to stay innocent, to hang back even though life was dragging her painfully forward. And all my conjecture bore out because she looked up at me and tried to say, "And how are you?" She choked it out but couldn't continue. She looked down again and I was stymied. I sat. Oh, this was enough to make me love her, because I was right with her, understanding every second and longing to step in. I didn't even need to know the specific that was troubling her, because to me her halting voice easily stood for the general woe that hangs in the air, even on life's happiest days.

Clarissa didn't apologize for her broken voice, which meant that she was, in these few moments, being personal with me. Her apologies were a way of maintaining distance and formality. She turned toward the window and braced herself up a few inches to see the sidewalk. I knew that soon I would maneuver myself into position to see what she was looking at. Everything seemed to be okay and she turned back to me with an empty sigh. "Sometimes," she said, "I feel like I've been to heaven and been brought back to earth. I've seen how things should be and now I'm here seeing how things really are." Her head glanced around again.

I got up, folded my hands across my chest, and leaned against the wall. I could see the raven-haired woman on the street, hand in hand with the boy—the same boy I had seen her with at the mall—and I wondered why Clarissa, if she had someone to watch her child, would have them tag along on her work rounds. As I listened to Clarissa and watched the plotless drama on the street, I noted a black Mercedes turn the corner and cruise by. I noted it because it was the second time I had seen it in less than a minute and it was significantly under speed. This second time it passed, the raven-haired woman saw it and took a few steps back. The car slowed to a stop, then reversed itself. Clarissa saw me looking out the window and she rose and turned to me, scared. The car was now stopped in the street, carelessly angled. The driver got out of the car and left the door open, approaching the woman and child. He was groomed like a freshly cut lawn. A trim beard framed his face; close-cut gray sideburns fringed his bald head. His suit was well cut and dark and set off by a stark white shirt. I could hear him yelling and cursing. He was wound tight and unwinding rapidly in front of us.

A horrible chain reaction occurred. The man, who looked like an Armani-clad Mussolini, increased his screaming and made his hand into a beak and began poking at the woman like an angry swan. She was knocked unsteady with each jab but defended herself with angry, equal shouts. But the man lost control and pushed her too hard. She lurched back, tripping. But she was holding the hand of the boy and as she fell, he fell with her. With this blow the chain reaction became uncontained, entering my apartment. I felt the shove that drove the boy to the ground and experienced his terror at the noise and violence. I was down the steps running toward the scene, hearing Clarissa screaming and running behind me, hearing Tiger barking from Philipa's window. I took the steps in threes as the legendary slow motion of panic set in and turned seconds into minutes. I wondered, in these moments while time stretched itself, why I could not step off a curb but stairs did not present a problem. Why could I not rename the curb to stair step and be on my way? Why do I see the light from a lamp as a quantity and not as a degree? Because it was written on the bulb, that's why. I suddenly knew what my enabler was: language. It was my enemy. Language allowed me to package similar entities in different boxes, separate them out, and assign my taboos. I was at the bottom of the stairs when time caught up to itself. A child's scream broke my thoughts; chaotic and angry voices jarred me. I heard my breath gasp and heave as I turned and headed toward the lawn.

The attacker pushed his voice to a rasp and I heard him yelling cunt, cunt, you cunt. I was barreling across the grass when he turned and grabbed the child's arm, trying to pull him up, but I threw myself between them and covered the boy like a tarpaulin.

The man tried to pull me off, but I had clenched my fist around a countersunk lawn sprinkler and I was impossible to move. He began to kick my ribs. Fuck you fuck he said.

He tore at my shirt trying to lift me off the boy, whose shrieks had intensified, had penetrated Philipa's apartment, and had roused an angry superman. For the next thing I knew, the bearded man had been lifted off me and thrown against his car. And I saw Brian holding him there, standing between me and him, while Tiger gnarled a few feet away. The man was foaming and spitting and he swore at Clarissa and jerked himself away from Brian, who was twice his size and a hundred times more a man, and who continued to menace him, forcing him back to his car. Before he peeled away, Brian took his foot and kicked the Mercedes door, which I realized later had probably created a three-thousand-dollar dent.

Clarissa swept up her boy, who was wailing like a siren. She held the back of his head against her and he slowly calmed. The scene quieted, and we stood there in silent tableau, but anyone coming upon us would have known that something awful had just happened. Clarissa approached where I lay in a clump on the ground and asked was I all right. I said yes. She pointed to the raven-haired woman and said this is my sister Lorraine, and I said that's Brian. And Brian stood there like Rodin's *Balzac*. He looked around. "Everybody okay?" Yeah, we all said. Then Clarissa urged the child forward and said, "This is Teddy." Teddy held up his arm, spreading his fingers and showing me a grass-stained hand. My shirt was torn open and Clarissa touched my exposed ribs. "Ouch," I said. And I was pleased that I had chosen the perfect word for the occasion.

After making sure that Mussolini was gone and couldn't see our destination, we five soldiers marched up to my apartment. Brian took charge and I asked if he had a Red Bull and yes, he did. Then I wondered if I had made a mistake; I worried that it might be dangerous for Clarissa to have a Red Bull now, when she was most inclined to load a gun and mow down her child's attacker. I decided to put her on crime watch. If ever there was a moment for my quaalude-laced wheatgrass drink, it was now, but I had long since decided that spiking punch was a bad idea, bordering on the immoral. Anyway, I was nervous about the chemical collision of an upper and a downer, and wondered if the combination could create a small explosion right in the can.

Teddy scrambled around my apartment on hands and knees, occasionally rising on two feet and moving hand over hand along the windowsill. Brian stood like a sentry and was asking questions like "Who was that guy?" that never quite got answered. But I did know what he was: an angry, unmanageable tyrant, haunted by imagined slights, determiner of everything, father of Teddy, ex-husband of Clarissa. This marriage couldn't have lasted long, as she's young, the boy's an infant, and the husband's too violent to have been with her a long time. I assumed that Clarissa would have left when his monstrous streak first appeared and that he had no reason to hide it once he was in possession of her.

Clarissa's sister, who evidently had flown in from somewhere to stand sentry over Teddy until the crisis passed, was the most upset at Mussolini and also was the most lucid, rattling off all his worst qualities to Clarissa and listing all the legal and practical ways to intimidate him. "Clarissa, I know you can't hate him because he's the father of your child, so I'll hate him for you," she said.

Clarissa quaked imperceptibly, and I watched her contain herself. She pulled herself inward, doing what she had to do as a mother: think how she could protect Teddy. She looked around the room as she thought, holding each position for an instant before shifting her head or body. As ideas occurred through her, she would respond to them physically. She shook her head; she would express dismay; her lips would tighten. Finally, she whispered, "I can't go home. Where can I go?"

Lorraine said, "You can stay with me."

"No, no," said Clarissa. "He knows where your hotel is."

I said, "You could stay here for the night. All of you." They all looked at one another and knew it was a good idea.

A few hours passed. Brian had secreted Clarissa's car behind the building and parked it in Philipa's space; if Mussolini drove by later and saw her car in the street, he would bang down every door in the neighborhood trying to find her. Lorraine and Clarissa were going to sleep in my bed with Teddy between them. I would sleep on the sofa. Philipa brought in a sack of fried chicken, a donation. Tiger smelled it and gave me an imbecilic grin of anticipation. I offered him a leg and tried to switch it at the last second with a palmed dog biscuit, but he wasn't fooled, even after I had smeared it with chicken grease. I made the sofa into a bed with a blanket I borrowed from Tiger, which was covered with a wide swath of dog hair.

As night began to fall, I started to worry. When Clarissa went to sleep, she would naturally turn out the lights in my bedroom, which would prevent me from turning out the lights in the living room, which meant I would be sleeping under 1,125 watts of power. Later in the evening, I noticed she had left a night-light on, which meant I could kick off the fifteen-watt range light. But that was it. I was attempting sleep in the land of the midnight sun. I turned face down and buried my head in the cushions. After a restless twenty minutes of pretending, I heard a door creak and then footsteps headed my way. Clarissa's hand touched my shoulder and I turned.

"I just wanted to say thank you."

"Oh," I said. "I didn't do anything."

"Daniel, I was lying in bed thinking about all this and I realized I won't be able to treat you anymore. It's not proper for you to know all this about me. I'll have to ask them to refer you to someone else."

"Do the same rules apply even if you're only an intern?" I asked hopefully.

"Even more so. I have to show respect for how things are done," she said. "It would be serious for me not to report this."

Clarissa was Mother Teresa to my leprosy. She leaned in toward me. I watched her lips part and close; I heard her breath between the words. In close, her voice changed. Lower, more resonant, like wind across a bottle top. In close, her beauty trebled. Her hair fell forward and scattered the hard light on her face into softer shadows. Her hand rested languidly on the sofa, palm up, almost like it wasn't part of her, and the pale side of her wrist was lost and wan, longing for sun.

"Thank you for letting us stay here. We'll look for somewhere else tomorrow."

"You can stay here as long as you need to," I said.

"We might need to stay here tomorrow. I called his sister. She told me he's got to be back in Boston on Saturday. If he goes, we'll be all right."

Clarissa squeezed my elbow and then stood up. "Do you want me to turn out the lights?" she asked.

"No," I said, "I want to read." There wasn't a book nearby and I had never told her of my wattage requirements, so she looked around, momentarily puzzled. But this was such a tiny bewilderment at the end of doomsday it hardly mattered. She retreated into the bedroom, leaving the door cracked open.

As midnight closed in on us, the extraneous sounds of televisions and cars, footsteps and distant voices unwove themselves from the night. I closed my eyes. The light no longer bothered me. I thought of the two women in my bed and the protective sandwich they made that held Teddy in place. My body curled and tightened as if being pulled by a drawstring. I gasped for breath. I pictured myself spread over Teddy like a blanket, but I was watching from above, just as Clarissa watched herself from heaven. The kicks intended for Teddy were taken and absorbed by my body. There was something about having intervened at the exact moment of heartbreak that evoked a deepening melancholy, and I hiccupped a few sobs. I then saw myself as the boy, hearing and sensing the blows from overhead, and why did I, rolled up on the sofa clutching a pillow, say out loud, "I'm sorry, I'm sorry"?

I heard a few small *wahs* during the night, a few footsteps pattering around, and I think we all had a fitful sleep. By 5:00 A.M., however, nothing stirred except my eyeballs, which delighted in having a fresh ceiling to dissect. Silence had finally struck Santa Monica, which put my mind in the opposite of a Zen state. Rather than my head being empty of thought, every crevice was bursting with facts, numbers, revelations, connections, and products. After I had deduced, or more properly, induced how Aquafresh striped toothpaste is coaxed into the tube back at the factory, I created a new magic square:

Granny	Philipa	Brian
Lorraine	?	Rite Aid
Teddy	Zandy	Clarissa

I was lost in the vision of the square, this graphic of my current life, when one of its components, Teddy, creaked open my bedroom door and crawled a few feet into the living room, pausing on all fours. The component looked over at me and grinned. He then made a surprising feint right but went left, then pulled himself up and leaned against the wall, moving his eyes off me only for necessary seconds. He turned and pressed his palms against the wall and then circumnavigated the room until he had gotten to the sofa where I was trying so hard to sleep. He plopped back on his rear end and extended his arms toward me, which I supposed to be some sort of cue for me to pick him up, and I did. I placed him on my chest, where he sat contentedly for about a minute, and I said something that had an intentional abundance of the letter *b* in it, as I thought the letter *b* might be amusing to a one-year-old. I started with actual words—baby, booby, bimbo—then degenerated into nonsense sounds: bobo, boobah, beebow. His expressions ranged from concentration, to displeasure, to happiness, to confusion, to distress, though as far as I could tell, there was absolutely nothing to feel displeasure, happiness, confusion, or distress about. Except for the letter *b*.

I put my hand on his stomach to tickle him and found that my palm extended over his entire rib cage. I picked him up and hoisted him above my head, balancing him in the air on my stiff right arm, which he seemed to relish. I twisted him from side to side and he spread his arms, and for a few moments he was like an airplane on a stick. This simulation of flight seemed to please him inordinately, and his mother, who must have sensed that her boy had gone missing, said from over my shoulder, "Are you flying, Teddy? Are you flying in the air?"

In the morning, they slipped away like a caravan leaving an oasis, and the return to quiet unnerved me.

The next few days were stagnant. I was distressed to think that my regular visits from Clarissa were over. I wondered how I was going to fill those two hours that had become the binary stars around which my week revolved. I was also concerned for Clarissa, who had not contacted me in several days. I wondered if I had been ostracized from the group because I represented a horrible memory. But on the day and almost the hour of my regular visit, I saw Clarissa crossing the street with Teddy, carrying him under her arm like a gunnysack full of manure. Her other arm toted a cloth bag stuffed with baby supplies that bloomed and poked out of its top.

I opened the door and started to say the *h* in hello, but she cut me off with, "Could I ask you a favor?" The request held such exasperation that I worried she had used up all the reserve exasperation she might need on some other occasion. "Could you watch Teddy for a couple of hours?" Without saying anything, I came down the stairs and relieved her of the boy. I then understood why she had carried him like a sack of manure. "He needs changing," she said. *And how,* I thought. Going in my apartment, Clarissa added, "I'll change him now and that should hold him." Clarissa, who was clearly on the clock, rushed the diaper change, pointed to a few toys to waggle in front of him, gave me a bottle of apple juice, wrote down her cell phone number, tried to explain her emergency, said she would be back in two hours, added that Lorraine had gone back to Toronto, kissed Teddy goodbye, hugged me goodbye, and left.

Thus I went from being Clarissa's patient to becoming her son's babysitter.

Teddy and I sat on the floor and I poured out the contents of the bag, which included a twelve-letter set of wooden blocks. These blocks were the perfect amusement for us, because while Teddy was fascinated with their shape, weight, and sound as they knocked together, I was fascinated with the vowels and consonants etched in relief on their faces. It was not easy to make words with this selection. Too many *C*s, *B*s, *G*s, *X*s, and *Y*s, and not enough *As*, *Es*, and *Is*. So while he struggled to build them up, I struggled to arrange them coherently. Whatever I did, Teddy undid; when he toppled them, I rebuilt them, and when he stacked them haphazardly, I rearranged them logically. Two hours went by and when Clarissa returned, she found us in the middle of the floor, transfixed.

Two days later, I agreed to watch Teddy from four to six and she offered to pay me five dollars an hour, which I refused.

Occasionally, I amuse myself by imagining headlines that would trumpet the ordinary events of my day. "Daniel Pecan Cambridge Buys Best-Quality Pocket Comb." "Santa Monica Man Reties Shoe in Midafternoon." I imagine these headlines are two inches high and I picture citizens standing on street corners reading them with a puzzled expression. But the headline that was now in my mind was prompted by a letter from Tepperton's Pies, which I pinched between my stunned thumb and bewildered forefinger: "Insane Man Chosen as Most Average American." The letter began with "Congratulations!" and it told me that I had won the Tepperton's Pies essay contest. It went on to describe my duties as the happy winner. I was to walk alongside the runners-up in a small parade down Freedom Lane on the campus of Freedom College. We would then enter Freedom Hall, walk on the stage, and read our essays aloud, after which I would be presented with a check for five thousand dollars.

I was getting a little nervous about the letter's frequent repetition of the word *Freedom*. It could be an example of a small truth I had uncovered in my scant thirty-five years of life: that the more a word is repeated, the less likely it is that the word applies.

Bargain, only, fairness, are just a few, but here the word *Freedom* began to smell like Teddy's underpants. But what difference did it make? I am not a political person—in college I voted for president of the United States. He promptly lost and I never wanted to jinx my candidate again by voting for him. But whatever was the political underbelly of Freedom College, I was going to make five thousand dollars for reading an essay aloud.

That week, I practiced reading my essay by enlisting Philipa to listen to a few dry runs and coach me. Her contribution turned out to be so much more than just a few pointers. Philipa saw it as an opportunity to express to someone, anyone, just how complicated the simplest performance can be. She told anecdotes, got mad, complimented me, sulked, screamed "Yes!" and generally took it all way too far. Her goal was to impress upon someone, anyone, mainly herself, just how difficult her work was, that a nobody like me needed professional guidance. She almost had me convinced, too, until I realized I was much better when she wasn't in the room.

Friday came and Clarissa dropped off Teddy with a warm thank-you and a bundle of goodies. She gave me a hug that I had trouble interpreting. It could have been, at its highest level, a symbolic act indicating her deepening love for me; at its worst, well, there was no worst, because at its lowest level, it was symbolic of the trust she'd bestowed on me as the temporary guardian of her child. When she left, Teddy burst into tears and I held him up at the window so he could see her. I'm not sure if it was a good idea, because no matter what spin I tried to put on it, he was still looking at his mother leaving. Left alone with Teddy, I then began the game of Distraction and Focus. The object of the game was to Focus Teddy on something he liked and to Distract him from something he didn't. That afternoon I discovered a law that states that for every Focus there is an equal and opposite Distraction and that they parse into units of equal time. Five minutes of Focus meant that somewhere down the line waited five minutes of Distraction.

Within the first hour, I had exhausted my repertoire of funny faces and their accompanying nonsensical sounds. I had held up every unique object in my apartment. I had taken him on my forearm seat and marched him around to every closet, window cord, and cabinet pull. We had stacked and restacked the wretched wooden blocks. In a desperate move, I decided to take him down to the Rite Aid, which I remembered had a small selection of children's toys, and I was hoping that Teddy, the man himself, would indicate exactly which of them would put an end to his frustration.

There was about an hour of daylight left and I toddled him down my street to the first opposing driveways of my regular route. I had a moment of concern about crossing with him in the middle of the street but decided that extra care in looking both ways would ease my mental gnaw. And so Teddy became the first human ever to accompany me on my tack to the Rite Aid. He, of course, had no questions, no quizzical looks, no backsteps indicating he thought I was nuts, and I felt almost as if I were cheating: It seemed to me that if one is crazy, it's unfair to involve someone who doesn't understand the concept. If, as the books say, my habits exist to keep demons at bay, what was the point of exhibiting them in front of someone who was so clearly not a demon? Who, in fact, was so clearly a demon's opposite?

It was dusk, and the interior of the Rite Aid was bathed in its own splendid white light, which democratically saturated every corner of the store. The light was reflected from the polished floors and sho-cards so evenly that nothing had a shadow. I held Teddy's hand as I led him down the aisles, heading for the toy section. We passed a display of crackers that held him enthralled, and it took some doing to lure him away from those elephantine red boxes spotted with orange circles and blue borders. As I cajoled him with head nods and high-pitched promises of the delights that awaited us just around the aisle, I noticed Zandy looking directly at us from her high perch in Pharmacy. She didn't do anything, including looking away. A customer intervened with a question. She turned toward him, and in the second it took to shift her attention, she turned her face back to me and emitted one silent, happy laugh.

I now had Teddy moored in front of a hanging display of games and toys, and not only did I show him everything, I presented each prospect as though it were a tiara on a velvet pillow. And he, like a potentate reviewing yet another slave girl, rejected everything. He kept looking back and mewing and, unable to point, threw open his palm with five fingers indicating five different directions. Somehow, and I'm not sure telepathy was not involved, he navigated us back to crackers. This was his choice, and I saw that it was a good one, because what was inside was textural, crushable, and finally, edible.

It was night by the time we left the drugstore. Teddy and I played motorboat and moved into the darkness. The gaily lit Rite Aid receded behind us like a lakeshore restaurant. We walked along the sidewalks and driveways, passing the apartments and parked cars, hearing the occasional helicopter. I held Teddy in one arm and the crackers in another. We came alongside a high hedge bearing waxy green leaves and extending the full length of a corner lot. It was a dewy night but not cold, and there was a silence that walked with us. Teddy held out one arm so that his hand could graze the hedge. He let the leaves brush his palm. He watched and listened, and would sometimes grab and hold a twig to feel it tugged out of his hand as I moved him forward. Soon he established a sequence of feeling, grabbing, and then losing the leaf. I reseated him on my arm so he could lean out farther, and then slowed my walk to accommodate his game and extend the rapture. I came to the end of the block and it was like coming out of a dream.

Clarissa arrived promptly at six to find Teddy and me at the kitchen table in front of two dozen dismembered saltines. The box was torn and bent, and the wrappers were strewn across table and floor. This would have been a mess of the highest order except that nothing wet was involved. We made the transfer and she offered to help me clean up, but I shooed her out, knowing she had better things to do. At the door she said, "By the way, he's back in Boston and calmed down. He even sent me a support check." This small comment made me think all night about atonement, about what could be made up for, what could be forgiven, about whether Mussolini's obligatory check meant I should forget about the clobbering I'd received. I decided that the answer would be known only when I saw him again and would be able to witness my own reaction to an offer of contrition.

Speech day at Freedom College was drawing menacingly close and Philipa continued to rehearse me even though I did everything

I could to indicate to her that I was sick of the sound of my own voice and weary of her relentless fine-tuning of me. I performed once for Brian—the first outsider to hear me—and he complimented me so profusely that I felt like a three-year-old who had just had his first drawing taped to the refrigerator. Brian then offered to drive me to Anaheim on the day of the award, and I accepted, happy to know I would have a familiar face in the audience. Later I realized I had made no plans to get to the event and Brian was my only real possibility. We would leave at 8:30 A.M., he said. It would take an hour and a half to get to Anaheim. The Freedom Walk begins at eleven, and the speeches start at noon, to be over by one. Brian had gotten all this information off the Internet and printed it out for me, which he proudly cited as a demonstration of his growing computer skills.

The night before my speech, I carefully set my alarm for 7:00 A.M. I double-checked it by advancing the time twelve hours just to be sure it went off. Then I puzzled for a dozen minutes over whether I had reset the clock correctly, and had to redo the entire operation to confirm an LED light was indicating P.M. and not A.M. I carefully selected my wardrobe, choosing my brown shoes, khaki slacks, a blue sports coat, and a freshly laundered white shirt that I was careful not to remove from its protective glassine bag, lest a hair or dark thread should land on it in the night. I put several inches between my choices and the rest of my clothes for speedy access. I showered in the evening, even though I fully intended to shower again in the morning. This was a precaution in the event something went wrong with the alarm and I had to rush, but it was also part of my need to be flawlessly clean for the reading. Two showers less than eight hours apart would make me sparkle and squeak to the touch. My sports coat, a fourteen-year-old polyester blue blazer, had never known a wrinkle and would stand in stark contrast to my khaki pants. My outfit would be smooth, blue, and synthetic above, crinkly, brown, and organic below. In a perfect fashion world, I knew above and below should be the same, either all smooth blue and synthetic or all crinkly brown and organic. I marveled that, like soy and talc, these two opposites would hang on the same body.

During these hours, I was making a transition from my imperfect everyday world where the unpredictable waited around every corner, into a single-minded existence where all contingencies are anticipated and prepared for. I laid out my hairbrush, toothpaste, socks, soap, and washcloth. I cleaned the mirror on the medicine chest so that I wouldn't see something on it that I would think was on me. This was important, because I wanted absolutely nothing to intrude upon my single and direct line to the podium, and nothing to distract me during the four and one half hours that there would be between waking and speaking.

Knowing I would probably be too nervous to fall asleep on time, I went to bed at eight-thirty instead of my usual ten-thirty, building in an extra two hours to fidget and calm down. I lay centered in the bed, intending to sleep facing the ceiling all night, without inelegant tossing and turning and scratching and noisemaking.

I reached for my universal light switch, which was located just out of reach on my bedside table now that I was in the center of my bed. I had to hinge my body over to snap off the lights. Then, there I was, in perfect symmetry. The white sheets were crisp and freshly laundered. There were no body residues from the night before to contaminate me after my shower. I went over my speech in my head, and once I had done that, I allowed myself a moment for self-congratulations. I was, I said to myself, the Most Average American. Most Average, Most Ordinary. I had become this solely through my own efforts, and had succeeded not only once, but twice, with two different essays. I couldn't wait to tell Granny and asked myself why I hadn't already written her with the great news. Of course it was because I wanted to wait until I had the award in hand before bragging about it. It's the Texas way.

In the morning, I was only slightly askew. The top sheet and blanket had barely moved. I must have slept at a rigid, horizontal version of "Ten-hut!" that would have made Patton proud. There was an empty moment before I remembered what today was, but when I did, my voltage cranked up and the ensuing adrenaline rush cleared my sinuses.

The first thing I did was to sit on the edge of the bed and go over my speech. Then I stood and delivered it again, this time adding in a few planned gestures. Satisfied, I stepped out of my pajamas and folded them into a drawer, and put on my robe for the seventy-two-inch walk to the bathroom. I took off the robe and hung it on the back of the door. I turned on the shower and waited the fifteen seconds for it to adjust. Stepping under the water, I let it engulf me and was overcome with pleasure. When my delirium abated, I soaped and scrubbed my already clean body.

Out of the shower, my every action was as deliberate as a chess move. Toweling off, folding, hanging, everything going smoothly until hair. I had determined not to comb it but to brush it once, then shake it so it would dry into a flopover. I had done this a thousand times, but today it resisted the casual look it had achieved after virtually every other head shake of my life. However, I had mentally prepared myself for this uncertainty. If I was to style my hair with a head shake, I had to accept the outcome of the head shake. And though I could have picked up my brush and teased it into perfection, I didn't.

Brian arrived on the nose at eight-thirty, and it was a good thing, too, since by that time I had been standing motionlessly by the door for twenty-two minutes, mostly as an anti-wrinkle maneuver. He and I were dressed almost identically except he wore a tie. Blue up top, brown down below, the only difference in our clothes being in designer eccentricities. My white shirt had stitching around the collar; his didn't. My coat was polyester, his was wool, though they both had the same sheen.

"No tie?" he asked.

"Should I?" I answered.

"I think so," he said.

I went to my closet and retrieved my one tie. A tie that was so hideous, so old, so wide, so unmatchable, so thick, so stained, that Brian made me wear his. "Come on, buddy," he said, and we started off. "Got your essay?" he asked. "Yes, and an extra set from Kinko's, just in case." I had folded my speech lengthwise and put it in my breast pocket. This caused a tiny corner of the white paper to peek out from my lapel, which I nervously tucked back in every three minutes for the rest of the day.

Brian had idled the car in the driveway, making it easy for me to enter, as I didn't have to step over a curb. I hung my coat on a hanger and put it on a hook in the back seat. He made me copilot, handing me the directions and saying, "We'll take the 10 to the 5 to the Disneyland turnoff, then left on Orangewood. We'll save some time because then we'll be headed away from Disneyland and out of traffic." He backed out of the driveway, telling me to put on my seat belt, but I really couldn't. It would have cut across my chest and left a wide imprint across my starched white shirt. We turned the corner onto Seventh and I stiffened my legs and pressed them against the floorboard, raising my rear end into the air. This kept me in a prone position with my shoulders being the only part of me touching the car seat. I wasn't sure whether I did this to prevent wrinkles or to prevent myself from slipping into a coma. The answer came later when my legs fatigued and I slowly lowered myself down to a sitting position and nothing happened: I did not blow up, faint, or die. But I remained intensely aware that my khaki pants were soon going to be streaked with hard creases across my fly front.

We were now on the freeway and I had focused the air-conditioning vent on my pants, thinking it might serve as a steamer. Finally, I said to Brian, "Would you mind if I lowered my pants a little?" "Huh?" he said. "If I could lower my pants a little, I don't think they'll get so wrinkled." "Sure," he said, leaving me wondering if nothing disturbed Brian, ever.

I unbuckled my belt and lowered my trousers to my thighs. I skooched down in my seat so my pant legs ballooned out to keep them from wrinkling, too. I aimed the air vent at my shirt, which bellowed like a sail, preventing even more wrinkling. Satisfied, I then turned to Brian and said, "I really appreciate you taking me."

Considering he was driving, Brian looked at me a dangerously long time, but absolutely nothing registered on his face. Even when he was pummeling Mussolini, his face had never changed from its Mount Rushmore glare.

We did have a few laughs as we wheeled down the Santa Ana Freeway. Small industrial neighborhoods lined the access roads and Brian pointed out a factory sign that innocently read, A SCREW FOR EVERY PURPOSE. He found this hilarious, and because he did, I did. As we neared Disneyland, traffic thickened and Brian said don't worry, because right up here we go the other way. Every other car on the road was an SUV, and Brian's green Lincoln rode so low that we were like the *Merrimack* in a sea of ocean liners.

Brian was right. Everyone was turning west toward Disneyland when we were turning east, which meant we avoided a horrendous wait at the freeway exit. We ended up on a wide-open four-lane street that headed toward a few low hills, while behind us soared the Matterhorn. I consulted the directions and soon we were entering what I would describe as a wealthy parking lot. There were wide lanes for access and every third space was separated from the next by grass-filled islands. Trees lined the rows, making it all look like an automotive *allée*. In the distance on a hill, stood—or sat—Freedom College, announced by a gilt sign tastefully engraved in a large plank of oak. The bottom line of the sign read, PRIVATELY FUNDED.

At one end of the parking lot was an open tent with a banner promoting Tepperton's Pies and something about Freedom Day. There were twenty or so people milling around; there were tables where students were signing people in, and also several official-looking ladies and gentlemen in blazers, including my contact with Tepperton, Gunther Frisk. Gunther was decked out in a tartan suit, the plaid just subtle enough to keep him from looking absurd. His body was so incongruous with itself that it looked like he had been made by three separate gods, each with a different blueprint for humanity. "That must be where we're supposed to go," said Brian, and he turned off the engine. I laid my shirt over my underwear as flatly as possible, and then gingerly pulled up my pants and closed them over my shirttail. I raised to my prone position, opened the car door, and angled my legs onto the asphalt with as little bend as possible. I took my coat off the hanger and slipped it over my shoulders, tucking my protruding notes back in my coat pocket. I surveyed myself and was deeply pleased that very little wrinkle damage had been done to my fly front. In fact, I looked nearly as crisp as I had when I exited my front door in Santa Monica.

Gunther Frisk spotted us and shot out of the crowd as though he were launched. "Yoo-hoo . . . here, here!" he shouted as he flailed and waved. We made our way toward the tent, but the parking lot had an uphill trend that made me worry about sweating into my cotton shirt, so I slowed to a rhino pace, which forced Brian, who was walking at a normal speed, to retard his tempo so I could catch up. After Brian introduced himself as my manager, Gunther directed us into the tent, where we were handed a packet of welcoming materials. We had our pictures snapped and two minutes later were given laminated photo IDs threaded through cords that were to hang from our necks like a referee's whistle. In one corner of the tent stood a clump of misfits, the other winners. Sue Dowd, with a body like the Capitol dome—a small head with a rotunda underneath; Kevin Chen, a whiz kid bearing an Afro; and Danny Pepelow, a kind of goon. And me. The only one missing was the recently evaporated Lenny Burns.

We were introduced all around, and honestly, it was clear I was the normal one. But as motley as we were, I suspected there was a unifying thread that ran through us all. It was a by-product of the instinct that made each one of us pick up the Tepperton's entry form and sit home alone in our rooms writing our essays. The quality was decency. But it had not really been earned. It was a trait that nebbishes acquire by default because of our inability to act upon the world with a force greater than a nudge. I stood there that day as a winner but feeling like a loser because of the company I kept. We weren't the elite of anything, we weren't the handsome ones with self-portraits hanging over their fireplaces or the swish moderns who were out speaking slang at a posh hotel bar. We were all lonely hearts who deemed that writing our essays might help us get a little attention. We were the winners of the Tepperton's Pies essay contest, and I, at least for today, was their king.

This sinking feeling did not last. I reminded myself that my entry into the contest had been a lark and that it had really been done to extend my Rite Aid visit by a few extra Zandy-filled minutes, though I guessed that my competitors had taken their efforts seriously. I thought of them slunk over their writing pads with their pencils gripped like javelins and their blue tongues sticking out in brain-squeezing concentration. The spell was also broken by Gunther Frisk's triple handclap and cry of "All right, people." It was time, he said, to start the Freedom Walk. He tried to gather us into a little regiment, but there were enough docents and officials trailing us to make the group seem a bit ragtag. We trudged up a concrete pathway. I needed to walk slowly enough as to not break a sweat, so I cleverly started at the front of the group, hoping that by the end of the march I wouldn't be too far behind. The sun beat down on me and I worried about a sunburn singeing one cheek, or the heat causing a layer of oily skin that would make my forehead shine under the spotlight like a lard-smeared cookie pan.

The top of the hill held an unholy sight. It turns out that Freedom College is a little village, pristine and fresh, with its classrooms set back on fertile lawns surrounded by low wrought iron gates. In front of each of these bungalows, hung from natural wood supports, were white signs with the name of each department in calligraphic script, and each compound was set on its own block, with a street in front of it, with sidewalks. And curbs. Curbs I had not counted on. In all my preparations for this day, the problem of curbs never occurred to me. Yes, there was the occasional access driveway for supply trucks, but they were never opposed by another driveway or were in some way askew. And worse, students of both sexes, sporting matching blazers, lined most of the sidewalks to hail our arrival, creating an audience for my terror. Our troop had gathered a small head of steam and was not about to regroup or swerve for my unexplainable impulses. The pathway fed onto a sidewalk and I saw that I was on a direct path to curb confrontation.

False hopes arose in me. Perhaps, I thought, the other contestants, too, could not cross curbs. But I knew the odds of finding anyone else whose neuroses had jelled into curb fear were slim. Perhaps my behavior would be canceled out by someone else's even more extravagant compulsion. Perhaps we'd find out that Danny Pepelow needed to sit in a trash can and bark. Maybe Sue Dowd couldn't go a full hour without putting a silver Jiffy

Pop bag over her head. But no rescue was materializing and the curb was nigh. I could turn back. I did not have to speak at Freedom Hall, I said to myself. I could stop and cower in front of the curb, collapsed in a pool of stinking sweat, weeping and moaning, "No, no, I can't cross it," or I could simply move backward while everyone looked at me and my ashen face and my moonwalking feet. These cowardly solutions were complicated by another powerful force, the fear of public humiliation. The students had started to applaud thinly, probably because they had been instructed to. My fear of the curb and my fear of embarrassment clashed, and my extremities turned cold. My hands trembled with the chill. I felt greatly out of balance and widened my stance to keep from reeling. I breathed deeply to calm myself, but instead, my pulse raced into the danger zone.

If I'd allowed my body to do what it wanted to do, it would have fallen on its knees and put its head on the ground, its arms stretched out on the sidewalk. Its mind would have roiled and its throat would have cried, and nothing but exhaustion would have made it all stop, and nothing but home could have set the scale back in balance. But instead, I marched on, spurred by inertia and the infinitesimal recollection that I had recently crossed a curb and had not died.

My feet were like anvils, and it seemed as if the curb were nearing me rather than I nearing it. My fear represented the failure of the human system. It is a sad truth of our creation: Something is amiss in our design, there are loose ends of our psychology that are simply not wrapped up. My fears were the dirty secrets of evolution. They were not provided for, and I was forced to construct elaborate temples to house them.

As I neared the curb, my gait slowed. Most of the party had passed me and was happily, thoughtlessly mid-street. Even Brian, who at first had hung back, was now even with me, and as we approached the curb, we were stride for stride, our arms swinging in time like a metronome. Just before Brian stepped off the curb, I slipped my index finger into the cuff of his jacket and clipped my thumb against it. I was hanging on to him for my life. I don't think Brian could feel my minuscule clamp on his coat sleeve. As I raised my foot into the air above the road, I relived Brian as leader, how his leap across my curb weeks ago had shot me over it, too, how his he-man engine had somehow revved up mine. My foot landed on the street and it was like diving into icy water. The sound of the clapping students became more and more distant as I submerged, and I kept my fingers secretly clasped to my lifeline.

When the next curb appeared, I came up for air and stepped up onto the sidewalk. Muffled sounds began to clear and sharpen. By now, Brian had felt the to-and-fro tug at his sleeve and he turned to me. My blood pressure had soared and had pushed streams of red into my eyeballs and he saw them wide with fear. But Brian seemed to think it was okay that I hung on to him for safety. And I felt safe, too, even though the contact point was only the size of a small fingerprint.

There were four curbs in all and each step down was like the dunking of a Salem witch. I would be submerged into the fires of hell and lifted into the sky for breath. My persecutors were Tepperton's Pies, and my redeemers were my thumb and forefinger pinching a square half inch of wool. When I finally saw Freedom Hall a few yards in front of me, its name now held a double meaning. My pulse lowered to acceptable; my tongue became unstuck from the roof of my mouth. But my God, was I drenched. I attempted to walk so my body would not touch my clothing, trying to center my legs in my trousers so my skin would not contaminate my pants with sweat. I held my arms bowed out so my underarms could aerate and dry, and I could feel that the hair at the nape of my neck was moist and starting to curl.

Finally, we were backstage in an air-conditioned office. The chill matched my own body temperature, which had plunged to freezing, and my evaporating perspiration cooled me into the shakes. My nervousness was increasing and I was afraid that if anyone spooked me I would spring in the air and hiss like a Halloween cat.

Soon we were escorted to the wings, where we stood waiting to be brought onstage. We could hear our introduction through the curtain but the words echoed vacantly and were hardly intelligible. Several students lingered around us and I overheard one of them whisper, "How'd he get away from his gardening job?" and then snicker.

We were told that we would give our speeches in order, "worst first," which was quickly changed to "least votes" first. This meant I would be going last. A stage manager paged the curtain and waved us onstage with a propeller elbow. We entered almost single file, and I realized it was the first moment since I'd left Santa Monica when Brian was not nearby. I looked back. The stage manager had barred him from the wings with a hand gesture.

Out on the stage, the four of us sat on folding chairs while the college dean introduced us one by one. I don't think any of us could make out a word he said. We were behind the speakers and all we could hear was the din of reverberating sound. Occasionally, however, the dean would throw his arm back and gesture toward one of us, at which point we would individually stand and receive enthusiastic applause. From where, I wondered, did this enthusiastic applause generate? Certainly not from the hearts of the audience members, who had no clue who we were or the extent of our accomplishments. I figured it was an artificially instilled fervor, inspired by a version of reform school discipline.

Sue Dowd spoke first, and though I couldn't understand a word she said, I wept anyway. For some reason, her body movements and gestures captivated me. She punctuated sentences with an emphatic fist or a slowly arcing open palm. Her oval body swayed with each sentence like a galleon at sea, and she concluded her speech with her head humbly bowed. There was a hesitation before the applause began, indicating that the audience was either so moved they couldn't quite compose themselves, or didn't realize her speech was over.

Danny Pepelow was next and inordinately dull. When I thought of the trouble I went to to dress nicely, I wondered who'd suggested to Danny that a lumberjack shirt, jeans, and leather jacket would be fine. I was able to catch a few words of his essay because he spoke so slowly that the sound waves couldn't overlap themselves. I wondered how he could have possibly gotten more votes than Sue Dowd. At least she gesticulated. Danny stood there like a boulder. His voice was so monotone that I welcomed the few seconds of audio feedback that peppered his speech. He sat down to half the applause Sue Dowd had coaxed, but still grinned as if he had spoken like Lincoln at Gettysburg.

The spotlight then swung to me, but the intro was for Kevin Chen. When the operator heard the Asian name, the light instantly bounced over to Kevin Chen, provoking a laugh from the audience. He walked confidently to the podium, but I still heard a few titters from small pockets of the audience. Kevin Chen was supremely intelligent and quite moving, his essay involving an immigrant family success story with a true and abiding love of America. When he sat down, there was nice applause and I think Kevin Chen had shown them something real that must have touched every heart but the coldest. There was also a specific locus of exuberant cheers from the darkened rear of the auditorium that I presumed was family.

That left only me, and the college dean gave an overly winded intro of which I did not hear a single word. Toward the end of it, though, Gunther Frisk appeared and walked over to him and whispered. Then the dean intoned a few sentences more and I did hear a few words that gave me that icy feeling in my toes and fingertips: "dead," "friend," "Lenny Burns." What? I thought. The dean signaled and waved me over. I stood, and Gunther Frisk met me halfway and hugged me with crushing force. "I hope you don't mind," he said. "Don't mind what?" I asked. "Don't mind saying a few words about Lenny Burns," he said, handing me Lenny's essay.

I approached the mike, tapped it, and blew into it; I don't know why. "It's really Lenny who should have won this today," I said, knowing that Lenny was me. "Lenny was a high school friend, and we continued our relationship . . ." Oops. Sounded bad, like we were boyfriends. But I could see the first few rows before they were lost in the lights and they were still a stretch of frozen smiley faces. "Lenny loved the ladies," I said, countering myself. I felt I was now even. "And what is America if not the freedom to love indiscriminately?" I had fallen behind. I said a few more words, each sentence contradicting the last, and I wrapped up with, "I will miss him," and managed a little tear in my voice on the word *miss*. I read a few lines from "his" essay and secretly knew that had the winner—me—not already been decided, my display of grief over the missing Lenny would have softened the judges and won him a prize right then. I finished the speech with a flourish, stealing Sue Dowd's head-bowing bit, which worked terrifically. Lenny Burns received the applause he deserved, and not just because he died so horribly, as I explained to the audience, from knee surgery gone awry.

I fumbled for my speech, which I realized was not only sticking out of my jacket but about to fall onto the floor. I buttoned my coat and noticed my fly had creased up like an accordion, plus my pants were hanging too low. I pulled them up by the belt, then bent over and tugged at my cuffs to stretch the pant legs straight. This eliminated some of the wrinkles and I felt ready to read. I began my speech with an "ahem," a superficial throat clear that I thought showed a command of the room. I spoke the first few sentences confidently, though my voice surprised me with its soprano thinness. Then I noticed the rapt looks on the faces in the audience and felt myself become more impassioned. After all, I was scoring. I invested myself more and more in every word, and this was a mistake, because I began to realize that my speech made absolutely no sense. "I am average because the cry of individuality flows confidently through my blood"? I am average because I am unique? Well then, I thought, who's not average, every average person? My tricky little phrases, meant to sound compelling, actually had no meaning. All my life, an inner semanticist had tried to sniff out and purge my brain of these twisted constructions, yet here I was, center stage with one dangling off my lips like an uneaten noodle. The confusion of words and meanings swirled around my head in a vortex. So I bent down again and pulled at my cuffs. While I was inverted, I was able to think more clearly. I remembered that my speech was not meant to be a tract but more of a poem. More Romantic. And as a Romantic, I had much more linguistic leeway than, say, a mathematician at a blackboard. Still upside down, I reminded myself I was in front of an audience who wanted to be enthralled, not lectured. I decided to reach deep down, to the wellspring of my charisma, which had been too long undisturbed, and dip my fingers in it and flick it liturgically over the audience.

I unfolded from my jackknife bend. My voice deepened and my testicles lowered. I spoke with the voice of a Roman senator: "I am average," I said, "because the cry of individuality flows through my blood as quietly as an old river . . . like the still power of an apple pie sitting in an open window to cool." I folded my papers and sat down. There was a nice wave of applause that was hard to gauge, as I'd never received applause ever in my life. Gunther Frisk clapped with speedy little pops and leaned into the mike. "Let's hope he means a Tepperton's Apple Pie!" The applause continued over his interjection and I had to stand again. He waved me over and made a big show of giving me the check, then waved over all the other contestants and gave them the smaller checks. The auditorium lights came up and a few people approached the stage to ask for autographs, which bewildered me. After about four seconds, my time as a rock star was over, and I was calmly ushered outside to a golf cart that had been secured by Brian and driven back to his car.

On the way home, Brian gave me several compliments that I discounted and denied. This tricked him into reiterating the compliments, and once he was enthusiastic enough, I accepted them. Then he segued into sports talk, mentioning Lakers and Pacers and Angels, teams I was so unfamiliar with that I couldn't connect the team names with the game. But Brian had been so wholeheartedly on my side that I felt obliged to respond with ardent head nods and "yeahs," though I might have misplaced a few, judging by Brian's occasional puzzled looks.

Brian took me to my bank and we barely made it before closing time. I deposited the five-thousand-dollar check, keeping forty dollars in cash, offering Brian five for gas. Not having driven a car in ten years, I didn't know how stratospherically the price of gas had risen. Now I know the amount was way low for what he must have spent, and I would like to make it up to him one day.

I heard about Granny's suicide before it actually happened. She must have had second thoughts or been unable to pull together the paraphernalia, as her death date fell several hours past the day and minute of my reading of her note. This one lay for just a few hours on my kitchen table before I pulled myself up to it with a jam sandwich and cranberry juice. "Sweetest Daniel," it began, and I suspected nothing. Her handwriting was always large and gay, filled with oversize loops and exuberant serifs. Only in the last few years had I noticed a shakiness starting to creep in. "I won't trouble you with the state of my health, except to say I'm in a race to the finish. I can't let my body drag me down like this without fighting back in some way. My heart is sad not to see you again, but on this page, in this ink, is all my love, held in the touch of the pen to the paper . . ." Then, in the next paragraph, "I can't breathe, Daniel, I'm gasping for air. My lungs are filling up and I'm drowning." She said, in the next few lines, that it was time to free herself, as well as the ones who care for her, of their burden. Granny had two Mexican senoras who attended to her, and one of them, Estrella, loved her so much she called her "Mother." One last line: "Finally, we do become wise, but then it's too late." Granny, dead at eighty-eight of self-inflicted vodka, pills, and one transparent plastic bag.

The news of her death left me disturbingly unaffected. At least for a while. I wondered if I were truly crazy not to feel engulfed by the loss and unable to function. But the sorrow was simply delayed and intermittent. It did not come when it should have but appeared in discrete packets over a series of discontinuous days, stretching into months. Once, while tossing Teddy into the air, a packet appeared in the space between us, and vanished once he was back in my grip. Once, I positioned my palm between my eyes and the sun, and I felt this had something to do with Granny, for it was she who stood between me and what would scorch me. It was not that I missed her; she was so far from me by the time it was all over that our communications had become spare. She lived in me dead or alive. Even now, the absence of her letters is the same as getting them, for when I have the vague notion that one is due, I feel the familiar sensation of comfort that I did when I held a physical letter in my hand.

The day after the letter was Easter Sunday. It reminded me that as an adolescent I was primped and combed and then incarcerated in a wool suit that had the texture of burrs. I was then dragged to church, where I had to sit for several hours on a cushionless maple pew in the suffocating Texas heat. These experiences drained me of the concept of Jesus as benevolent. I did, however, proudly wear an enamel pin that signified I had memorized the books of the Bible.

That Granny's death fell so close to this nostalgic day was just bad luck, and that Easter I lay in bed gripped in a vise of reflection. It was after ten, and although my thoughts of the past were viscous and unbudging, the darkness in the room intensified my hearing, allowing me to keep at least one of my senses in the present. Amid a deep concentration on a potato salad of thirty years ago, I heard a car door slam, followed by hurried steps, followed by a quiet but persistent knock on my front door. I threw on pants and a T-shirt and opened the door without asking who it was.

Clarissa stood before me in a shambles, with Teddy clinging to her like a koala bear. I had not seen either of them at all during Easter week.

"Are you up?" she asked.

"I'm up," I said, and Teddy, holding out his arms, climbed over onto me. Clarissa came in, glancing toward the street. "He's back?" I said.

"He was here all week and things were tolerable at least. But today he started getting agitated. It's like he's on a timer. He began phoning every five minutes, which got me upset, then he suddenly stopped calling and I knew what was next. I heard a car screech outside my apartment and I knew it was him, so I got Teddy and bumped his head hurrying him into the car seat." By now her voice was breaking and she soothed Teddy's head with her palm. "Can I just sit here or stay here for a minute or maybe the night till I figure out what to do?" But she knew she didn't have to ask, just stay. Teddy gripped my two forefingers with his fists and I moved them side to side. "Do you have anything?" she asked. "Any baby wipes or diapers or anything?" I had it all.

We followed our previous routine. Clarissa and Teddy slept in my room, and I slept on the sofa under lights so bright I tanned. Around 3:00 A.M. there was baby noise and I heard Clarissa's hushed footsteps as she lightly bounced Teddy around the bedroom. Her door was cracked open and I said, "Everything okay?"

She slid a bladed palm in the doorway, opening it by a few more inches. "You awake?" she asked. "C'mon in, let's talk," she said. We passed Teddy off between us several times as we entered the bedroom. I knew what the invitation was about, camping buddies. But she seemed to have something on her mind of a verbal nature. Clarissa accommodated my lighting requirements by closing the door just enough to create a soft half-light in the bedroom. After a while we put Teddy in the center of the bed, and though he still was wide awake, he calmed and made dove sounds. We were lying on either side of him and I put my hand on his grapefruit stomach, rolled him onto his back, and rocked him back and forth.

"What's going on with you these days?" asked Clarissa.

And I told her of Granny's suicide. "The funeral is the day after tomorrow," I said. "But I can't be there."

"Do you want to be there?" she asked.

"What could I do there? What good would I be?" I answered.

"I think I should leave for a while," said Clarissa. "Would you like me to go somewhere with you? We could drive to Texas, you, me, and Teddy."

"Too late for the funeral," I said.

"Yes, but you would be there; you would have shown up for her."

Upon hearing Clarissa's suggestion, my mind did a heroic calculation resulting in an unbalanced equation. On one side of the equals sign were the innumerable obstacles I would face on such a trip. I could list a thousand impossibilities: I cannot get in an elevator. I cannot stay on a hotel floor higher than three. I cannot use a public toilet. What if there were no Rite Aids? What if we passed a roadside mall where one store was open and the others were closed? What if I saw the words *apple orchard*? What if the trip took us in proximity to the terrifyingly inviting maw of the Grand Canyon? What if we were on a mountain pass with hairpin turns, or if, during the entire trip, I could not find a billboard bearing a palindromic word? What if our suitcases were of unequal sizes? How would I breathe at the higher elevations? Would the thin air kill me dead? How would we locate the exact state lines? And what if, at a gas station in Phoenix, the attendant wore a blue hat?

On the other side of the equation was Teddy. I could imagine Teddy cooing in the back while pounding arrhythmically on his kiddy seat, and I could imagine ideas for his next amusement streaming through my head from Needles to El Paso and displacing every neurotic thought. I could imagine trying to distill his chaos into order and taking on the responsibility of his protection. And there was Clarissa, who would be seated next to me; who, now that I was no longer a patient, could be asked direct questions instead of being the subject of my oblique method of deduction. I still knew very little about her, only that I was in love with her. These two factors pulled down the scale toward the positive. But I settled the matter with a brilliant dose of self-delusion. I manipulated my own stringent mind with a new thought: What if I could convert one present fear into a different and more distant fear? What if I could translate my fear of the Grand Canyon into a fear of Mount Rushmore? What if I could transform my desire to touch the four corners of every copier at Kinko's into an obsession with Big Ben? But my final proposal to myself was this: What if during the entire trip I would not allow myself to speak any word that contained the letter *e*. This is the kind of enormous duty that could supersede and dominate my other self-imposed tasks. I quickly scanned my vocabulary for useful words—a, an, am, was, is, for, against, through—and found enough there to make myself understood. Thus "let's eat" would become, "I'm hungry, baby! Chow down!" I couldn't say, "I love you," but I could say, "I'm crazy about you," which was probably a better choice anyway. I could call Clarissa by name; Teddy would simply become something affectionate like big man, bubby boy, or junior. One minor drawback: I couldn't say my own name.

This idea of condensing my habits into one preoccupying restriction seemed so clever that it filled me up with ethyl and I said to Clarissa, "Okay, I'll go." Even though I had not officially started my challenge, my response was my first stab at an *e*-less sentence.

It was decided we would leave in the morning. Clarissa was afraid to return home to pack; her bright pink car didn't have the stealth we needed for even a night run. She would have to buy clothes on the road. She had a credit card that she said was at its bursting point, with a few hundred dollars left on its limit. She had her cell phone but no charger, so we would have to be conservative in its use. We waited until 10:00 A.M., when I could withdraw my remaining thirty-eight hundred dollars for the trip.

I got in the car and said, "It's a long trip for us. I want our roads to know not much traffic," and we pulled away from the curb.

We knew we would never get to Texas in time for Granny's funeral, but the journey had another grail: I would be able to see Granny's farm one last time before it was sold due to the lack of an interested relative to run it.

April in California is like June anywhere else. It was seventy by 10:00 A.M., heading up to eighty. Even though our reason for fleeing LA was somber, the spontaneity of our trip inspired a certain giddiness in us, and Clarissa laughed as we pulled up to the Gap and she ran in for T-shirts and underwear and socks. Teddy looked at me from his car seat and burbled while manipulating a spoon. I, the passenger/copilot/lookout/scout who was incapable of taking the wheel, wondered what I would do if asked to move the car. Grin, I suppose. After the Gap, I hit the Rite Aid, and my knowledge of its layout sped me through dental hygiene, hairbrushes, everything feminine that Clarissa might need on the trip.

"I got you razors and things," I said. This was going to be easy; I had yet to miss the letter *e*.

I got back in the car and checked the glove compartment for maps. There were a few irrelevant ones, but the California map would at least get us to Arizona. Pinpointing my current parking spot on a map of the entire state of California was impossible, so I hoped that Clarissa knew how to get us out of town. She turned over her shoulder and fiddled with Teddy. Then, she didn't even ask where to go, just started driving south.

The traffic stopped and started along Santa Monica Boulevard, but soon we drove up a centrifugal cloverleaf onto the freeway where Clarissa stepped on it and accelerated to blissful speeds. It was as if the car had grown wings, letting us soar over the red lights and curbs and crosswalks. I wondered if the reason I was crazy, the reason that I had no job, that I had no friends, was so that at this particular moment in my life I could leave town on a whim with a woman and her baby, saying goodbye to no one, speeding along with no attachments to earth or heaven. The moment had come and I was ready for it. We rolled down the windows and the air whipped around us; Teddy chortled from behind. In honor of Philipa's dog, Tiger, I stuck my head out the window and let my tongue flap in the breeze while Clarissa changed the lyrics and sang "California, Here I Went," and kept time by thumping her palm on the steering wheel.

There were unpredictable and unaccountable slowdowns until we passed some shopping outlets in Palm Springs, where suddenly the road widened and flattened as though it had been put through a wringer. We pulled in for fast food at lunchtime, barely stopping the car. After four hours of driving, we had not lost our zing but had quieted into comfortable smiles and inner glows. Clarissa checked her messages once. She listened, disappointment slithered across her face, and she turned off the Nokia. I took the phone and stowed it in the car door, which had a convenient space for miscellaneous storage.

We continued heading south with the sun still high. I stole the occasional glance and could see Clarissa in relief. Each eyelash was clearly defined against the crisp background of desert and sky. She was an array of pastels, her skin with its pink underglow set against white sand and the turquoise blue of her blouse. I assembled from the sight of her, from memories of her, a clear picture of Clarissa's most touching quality: her denial of sadness. Only the most tragic circumstances could take the smile from her face and the bounce from her walk. Even now, as she fled from terror, she looked forward with innocence toward a happiness that waited, perhaps, a few miles ahead.

Contained in the hard shell case of Clarissa's Dodge, I was remarkably and mysteriously free from the stringency of the laws and rules that governed my Santa Monica life. So I decided to engage Clarissa in conversation. Clarissa must have decided the same thing, because before I could speak, she launched into a soliloquy that barely required from me an uh-huh.

"I think Chris saw me as his dolly," she said. I knew from her icy inflection on the word *Chris* that she meant her inseminator. "But there was no way I could see it until we were married," she went on. "He's borderline; that's what I figured. A belligerent narcissist. He needs help, but of course why would someone seek help if one of their symptoms is thinking everyone else is wrong? I think I'm a narcissist, too. I've got a lot of symptoms. Four out of six in the *Diagnostic and Statistical Manual.*"

I didn't know what she was talking about. It seemed to me that Chris was simply a violent son of a bitch. But I didn't have to live with him. If I had to justify someone to myself, I, too, would throw a lot of words at him. The more words I could ascribe, the more avenues of understanding I would have. Soon, every intolerable behavior would have a syntactical route to my forgiveness: "Oh, he's just exhibiting abstract Neo-juncture synapses," I would say, and then try to find treatments for abstract Neo-juncture synapses.

The difference now between me and Clarissa was that she was yakking and I was thinking. I felt I was in conversation with her; but my end of the dialogue never got spoken. So my brilliant comments, retorts, and summaries stayed put in my cortex, where only I would appreciate their clever spins and innuendos.

The route from California to New Mexico essentially comprises one left turn. The monotony of the road was a welcome comedown from the emotional razzmatazz of our tiny lives in Santa Monica. We had practically crossed Arizona by day's end, and just shy of the border, we checked into the Wampum Motel, a joint with tepee-shaped rooms and the musty scent of sixty years of transients. It fit our budget perfectly because nobody wanted to stay there except the most down-and-out, or college students looking for a campy thrill. The antique sign bearing the caricature of an Indian was enough to cause an uprising.

I'm not sure why Clarissa put us all in one room. Since I was paying, maybe she was honoring the budget, or perhaps she saw us as the Three Musketeers who must never be torn asunder. She got a room with twin beds and one bathroom. The lights were so dim in the room that I had no wattage problem. All I had to do was leave the bathroom light on, open the door one inch, and the room would be perfect for sleeping.

This arrangement also provided me with one of my life's four or five indelible images: After an excursion to the Wampum diner, we retired early to get a jump on the next day's drive. While Clarissa showered, Teddy slept securely in one of the twins, buffered on two sides by a pillow and a seat cushion. I had gotten in the other bed and turned out the light. I huddled up, trying to warm myself under the diaphanous wisps that the Wampum Motel called sheets. The room was lit only by moonlight, which seeped around every window blind and curtain. I heard the shower shut off. Moments later, Clarissa came quietly into the room, leaving the bathroom light on per my request but closing the door behind her. To her, the room was pitch black, but to me, having adjusted to the darkness, the room was a patchwork of shadow and light. Clarissa, naked underneath, had wrapped herself in a towel and was feeling her way across the room. I was officially asleep but my eyes were unable to move from her. Standing in profile against the linen curtain and silhouetted by the seeping moonlight, she dropped the towel, raised a T-shirt over her head, and slipped it on. Her body was outlined by the silvery light that edged around her and she was more voluptuous than I had imagined. She then crouched down and fumbled through a plastic bag, stood, and pulled on some underwear. I wondered if what I had done was a sin, not against God, but against her. I forgave myself by remembering that I was a man and she was a woman and it was in my nature to watch her, even though her ease with taking off her clothes in front of me could have been founded on the thought that she did not see me as a sexual creature.

As compelling as this event was, I did not infuse it with either the tangible heat of desire or the cool distance of appreciation. For whichever approach I chose, I knew it was bound to be unrequited, and so my dominant feeling for the rest of the night was one of isolation.

The morning was a blur of Teddy's needs. Things clanked and jars were opened and Clarissa turned herself away for breast-feeding. Though we slept well, we were both tired and car-lagged from the travel. Still, we were on the road by 7:00 A.M. and very soon we were in New Mexico.

New Mexico held me in a nostalgic grip, even though I had never been there. Only after we'd spent six hours crossing it before arriving in El Paso did I realize what was affecting me. It was that southern New Mexico was beginning to look, feel, and taste like Texas. Northern New Mexico was comparatively a rainforest; it looked as if an extremely choosy nutrient were coursing underground. Rocks burst with color. Rainbow striations shot across the walls of mesas, then disappeared into the ground. Dusky green succulents vividly dotted the tan hills, and the occasional saguaro stood in the distance with its hand raised in peace like a planetary alien.

But southern New Mexico was arid, eroded, and flat. As we drove, Clarissa liked to turn off the air-conditioning, roll down the window, and be dust-blown. I was beginning to sunburn on the right side of my face, and we screamed a conversation over the wind that ripped through the car. She told me that her bank account was being depleted fast, that she was worried she would have to quit school, thus ruining her chances of ultimately achieving a higher income. She said she was concerned that she would have to move back to Boston per her ex's demand, and she didn't understand why her ex even cared about whether they were in Boston, as he seldom exhibited any interest in Teddy. All this bad news was delivered without self-pity, as if it were just fact, and I felt a strong urge to cushion her fall as her life was collapsing. But I lacked any ideas to support her except cheerleading. I suppose I could have been a moral voice, but I was beginning to doubt my status in that department, too.

Our conversation reminded me that I was also in financial trouble. Granny's intuition had saved me many times, but that form of rescue was now over. I wondered if my pretense of having no need of money, to myself and to Granny, was childish. My paltry government check was insufficient to support my grand—compared to some—lifestyle. I knew that without Granny's occasional rain of money, there was going to be, upon my return to Santa Monica, a housing, clothing, and food crisis.

In El Paso, we found a Jimmy Crack Corn motel that fit within my new scaled-down notion of budget. I joked, "Discomfort is our byword." To her credit, Clarissa laughed and agreed. We stayed in separate rooms as we sensed a wretched bathroom situation, and we were right. Barely enough room for the knees.

The motel had made one attempt at landscaping, a ramshackle wooden walkway arcing over a concrete-bottomed pond. However disgusting it was for Clarissa and me to look into its murk, Teddy considered it Lake Geneva; he wanted to swim, frolic, water-ski, and sail in its green sludge. We wouldn't let him come in contact with the mossy soup, so dense that it left a green ring around the edge of the concrete, but I did make paper boats that Teddy was allowed to throw stones at and sink.

In the morning, Clarissa's shower woke me and I could time my ablutions to hers thanks to the paper-thin walls. We cleaned our teeth, peed, and washed simultaneously, enabling me to appear outside my door at the same time she appeared outside hers, and by 7:00 A.M., with Teddy already lulled into a stupor by the motion of the car, we were on the final stretch to Helmut, Texas.

What happened under the pecan tree qualifies as one of those events in life that is as small as an atom but with nuclear implications.

Clarissa and I had checked into a local motel, just a short hop from Granny's, that practically straddled the Llano River. It was set in a gnarly copse of juniper trees whose branches had woven themselves into a canopy that threw a wide net of shade. We were lucky to have found a low-cost paradise that had a number of natural amusements for Teddy, including nut-finding, water-squatting, and leaf-eating, and it was easy to idle away a few hours in the morning while we laboriously digested our manly Texas breakfasts.

Before lunch, Clarissa drove me to Granny's. I had no recollection of how to get there, though a few landmarks—the broadside of a white barn, a derelict gas pump, a cattle grate—did jog my memory. But when we left the highway and drove among the pecan groves whose trees overhung the road to the farm, I experienced an unbroken wave of familiarity. The trees grew in height and density as we neared the farmhouse, which was sheltered by a dozen more trees towering 150 feet in the air, protecting it from the coming summer heat. The house was a single-story hacienda, wrapped around a massive pecan tree that stood in the middle of a courtyard. The exterior walls were bleached adobe and the roofline was studded with wooden vigas. A long porch with mesquite supports, sagging with age, ran the length of the house on three sides, and a horse and goat were tied up near a water trough. The trees overhead were so dense that sunlight only dappled the house even at this moment of high noon. A few rough-hewn benches were situated among the trees. Attached to the house was a ramada woven with climbing plants, at the end of which a tiled Mexican fountain flowed with gurgling water, completing this picture of serenity.

There were three cars parked outside; two were dilapidated agricultural trucks and one a dusty black Mercedes. We pulled up and got out. A man in a tan suit swung open the screen door. He held a slim leather portfolio that indicated he was official. He said hello to us with a relaxed voice and we heard the first Southern drawl of the entire trip. We introduced ourselves and when I said I was "Dan, grandson of Granny," there was a frozen moment followed by, "Oh yes, we've been looking for you."

Clarissa went off to the fountain to show Teddy its delights. I went into the farmhouse with Morton Dean Argus, who turned out to be the lawyer for the estate. He explained he had driven all the way from San Antonio and had stayed here on the farm for the last three days to sort out issues among the few relatives who had arrived in pickup trucks after the news got out. "Y'all arrive a half hour later and I woulda been gone," he said.

Everything useful in the house had been sacked. Everything personal remained. Antique family photos still hung on the walls, but the microwave oven had been removed. The stove, a

1930 Magic Chef Range, was too ancient to loot, the marauders having no idea of its value to the right aesthete chef. A cedar chest filled with Indian rugs had been mysteriously overlooked. There were the occasional goodies, including period equestrian tack used as wall decor, as well as a small collection of heavy clay curios of sleeping Mexicans, whose original bright colors had patinated to soft pastels.

Morton Argus told me that Granny had been cremated and interred on the property under a tree of her designation. He told me that a one-page will had been read and that certain items—really merchandise—had been distributed to a few workers and relatives. My sister, Ida, had been there, he said, and I felt a pang of guilt that my sequestered lifestyle hadn't allowed her to contact me more quickly so I could have met her at the house. It was Ida, he said, who coordinated the dispersal of furniture to a small swarm of needy relatives.

Ida was three years younger than me. She'd moved to Dallas, married young, and borne children, and she seemed untouched by the impulses that took me inside myself. "Did my dad show up?" I said. Morton asked me his name. "Jack," I said. No, he hadn't.

Accompanied by Morton, I nosed through the house and came into a room piled with cardboard boxes and empty picture frames. An oval mirror leaned precariously against the floor. Four wooden kitchen chairs were alternately inverted and nested on each other.

"Anything you want in here?" asked Morton.

"I'll look," I said.

Morton excused himself, saying he had to sort out some papers. I knelt down and browsed through a couple of boxes. At the bottom of one, I found a metal container the size of a shoebox. It had a built-in lock but the key was long gone. I thought it would take a screwdriver to bust it open, but I gave it an extra tug and it had enough give to tell me it had only rusted shut. A little prying and the lid popped up. Inside was a bundle of letters, all addressed to Granny, all postmarked in the late '70s. Two of them had return addresses with the hand-printed initials *J.C.* They were from my father. I picked up the box, knowing that this would be the only thing I would take from the house.

I found Morton in the living room, which, because of the exterior shade and small windows, was exceedingly dark. He sat in an armchair that had been upholstered with a sun-bleached Indian blanket. He had a handful of papers that he shuffled then spread open and rearranged like a bridge hand.

"Has your sister contacted you?" he said.

"Not that I know of." I loved my rejoinder, grounded as it was in a fabulous paradoxical matrix, and perfectly *e*-less.

"So you don't know?" he said.

"Know what?"

"You and your sister," he said, "are splitting approximately six hundred and ninety thousand dollars."

I stayed in the house for another hour, glimpsing faint memories as I moved from one room to another. These were not memories of incidents, but were much more vague and beyond my reach. They were like ghosts who sweep through rooms, are sensed by the clairvoyant, and then are gone.

Clarissa and Teddy had wandered far away from the house and now had wandered back. She appeared at the screen door with a "How's it goin'?" that expressed an impatience to leave. I said goodbye to Morton, slid an arm around Teddy, and lifted him into his car seat, which made him scream. I put the metal box in the back seat and we drove back to the motel.

We sat in the dining room and I could tell that the trip was starting to wear on Clarissa. Our blistering escape had not solved her problems back home. Earlier I watched her call her sister as the phone battery gave out, and now she seemed in her own world, one that excluded me. Then she laid her hand across her wrist and jumped. "I lost my watch!" she said. She checked around her, then left me with Teddy while she searched the room and car. She returned—no watch—and explained that it had been a gift to herself from herself, and I assumed it had a greater history than she was telling me. Perhaps a reward for a personal accomplishment whose value only she could understand. "What do you think," she said, "are we ready to head home?"

"Now?" I said.

"In the morning."

"I want to go back to Granny's for an hour or so."

This annoyed her. She wanted to leave before dawn, and she persevered. "I need to get back," she said. "I don't even know what I'm doing here." This was the first time Clarissa had had a hint of surliness, but she made up for it later that night.

She and I were bunked in the same room. This motel was the kind a traveler would consider a charming, memorable find, as its architecture and decoration perfectly identified a specific year in a specific decade in a specific location that could not be seen anywhere else. Built in the '30s, the bathrooms had porcelain sinks and tubs that weighed a ton. The rooms were long and narrow and the ceilings and walls were lined with long planks of dark pine. Wrought iron hardware strapped each doorway and artisan-crafted sconces silhouetted tin cutouts of cowboy scenes through translucent leather shades. Clarissa and Teddy took one end of the room and I slept at the distant other on a sofa bed that sunk in the middle with a human imprint. We had amused each other by spreading ourselves on the floor and playing a game with a deck of cards that at one time had been so waterlogged it was three times its normal height. Clarissa and I tried to play gin, though we struggled to remember the rules, but Teddy made it impossible because he kept grabbing the cards and rearranging them. Clarissa began calling him Hoyle and I would say to him, "What do you think, Billy Bob, can I play that card?" And he would either pick up the card and drool on it or slide it back to one of us, which would make us laugh.

Clarissa and I were now used to seeing each other in our underwear. We both slept in T-shirts and underpants. She turned out the lights and we slipped into our respective beds. She spoke softly to me from across the room. "What was it like today?"

"Thanks," I said.

"For what?"

"For asking," I said.

"Daniel," she whispered, I think to say, of course she would ask.

We didn't speak for several minutes. I didn't want to tell Clarissa about the inheritance because I wanted to digest it myself first, and I didn't want anything external to affect our little trio. Then there was a rustle of sheets, then footsteps. Clarissa came across the room and knelt beside my bed. She reached her arm across the blanket until she found my shoulder and laid her hand on it. Her fingers crawled under my sleeve and began a small back-and-forth motion. She rested her head on the bed and her hair fell against my arm. I didn't move.

"Oh, Daniel," she said. "Oh, Daniel," she whispered.

I didn't know what to do.

"I love that you love Teddy." The upper one-eighth of her body caressed the upper one-eighth of my body. She moved her hand from my shoulder and laid her palm against my neck with a slight clutch.

"We should go to the house tomorrow, if that's what you want. I'm sorry about today. I'm just impatient; impatient for nothing."

She closed her eyes. My arm, with the bed as a fulcrum, was locked open at the elbow and sticking dumbly out into the room. It was the part a painter would have to leave out if he were going to make the scene at all elegant. I evaluated Clarissa's tender contact and I decided that it was possible for me to put my free hand on her shoulder and not have the action considered improper. I bent my elbow and touched her on the back. She didn't recoil, nor did she advance.

I didn't know if Clarissa's gestures toward me were platonic, Aristotelian, Hegelian, or erotic. So I just lay there, connected to her at three points: her hand on my neck, my hand on her back, her hair brushing against my side. I stared at the ceiling and wondered how I could be in love with someone whose name had no anagram.

Later, she dragged her hand sleepily across my chest and went back to her bed, leaving a ghostly impression on me like a handprint of phosphorus.

* * *

Teddy woke later than usual and Clarissa and I slept through our usual 7:00 A.M. get-up. By nine, though, we had eaten, packed, and loaded the car. We got to the end of the motel driveway and when we stopped, I said, "I don't want to go back to Granny's." And then Clarissa argued, "But you said you did." Then I came back, "It's out of our way." Then Clarissa said, "I don't mind. I think you should go." Out of politeness, we had switched sides and argued against ourselves for a while to show that we understood and cared about each other's position. Clarissa turned right and we eventually found ourselves once again driving among the pecan trees.

There were no cars out front and the house was locked up. I knew what I wanted to do—find Granny's grave. Clarissa said, "I'll leave you," and ran after Teddy, who had charged immediately toward the river. I stood before the house and listened to the breeze that rustled through the groves. I decided to walk near the river, upstream, to avoid the bustle of Clarissa and Teddy, who were downstream. I started out, but the pink Dodge caught my eye. I returned to it, felt around under the paper sacks filled with dirty laundry, and got the metal box I had chosen as my sole artifact of my life with Granny.

I walked through the forest and came upon a wooden bench—a half slice of a tree trunk—that faced the shallow and crystalline river. There was a hand-painted stone with Granny's name and dates on it, and a small recently disturbed patch of dirt. This diminutive marker was under the tallest and most majestic pecan tree on the farm, and I guessed that was why Granny chose the spot. I sat on the bench and looked toward the river, trying to meditate on this house and land, but couldn't. My mind has always been independent of my plans for it. I reached in the metal box and picked up the small cache of letters. I thumbed through them and took out the two from my father. I read the earlier one from 1979, which was about Granny. It was a snide criticism of how she ran her property, followed by some tactlessly delivered advice on how to fix things.

The second one was about me:

January 8, 1980

Dear G.,

I'm so glad you were able to see Ida before the trip. She's our little heartbreaker don't you think? I have a photo of her with a cotton candy we took at the San Antonio Fair. She looks like an angel. She knows exactly who Granny is too. We show her your photo and she says Granny. She's only four and she seems brighter than everyone around her. The song says there is nothing like a dame and there ain't. I didn't know how much I wanted a girl, but when Ida was born, that was it for Daniel.

The letter went on, but I didn't. Sitting graveside, I knew that these few words would be either my death or resurrection. Two months later, on a still California night, I would know which. It was there that I breathed my last breath in the world that I had created.

Clarissa and Teddy came up along the river. She spotted me and yelled, "Hey," then picked up Teddy and came over. "Guess what?" she said, holding up her arm. "I found my watch. I love it when lucky things happen."

* * *

Clarissa fired up the Neon and drove us out to the highway, where we settled into the ache and discomfort of the long road home. We didn't speak for a while, though I kept a broad smile on my face meant to hide my clammy shakes. All of us, including Teddy, were impatient to be home, and our three-motel trip to Texas turned into just two motel stays on the way back because of Clarissa's driving diligence. She kept us on the road deep into the night, and I often worried that we weren't going to find a motel with a vacancy.

I felt inadequate around Clarissa as we drove. I waited for her to speak before I felt allowed to. I tended to agree with everything she said, which made me not a real person. There were times when we drifted into solitary thought with no awareness of the passage of time. Once we started to again sing "California, Here I Come," and I bleeped myself with a loud buzzer tone when words with the letter *e* came up. Clarissa turned to me and laughed, "You know what we are, we're a mobile hootenanny." I roared at the word *hootenanny*. Then we fell to silence again. In Albuquerque we had the best tacos of our lives, and I forced Clarissa to stop at the municipal library for ten minutes, where I Xeroxed twenty pages from various investment books while she fluffed and dried Teddy.

Endless road engendered endless thought. Local architecture provoked in me nostalgia that I could not possibly have. Night caused distracting roadside images to fade into nothing. In the back seat was a pile of letters that radiated unease. Flashbacks of Clarissa's moonlit body presented themselves as floating pictures. My father's letter had finally been delivered to its ultimate reader. Over the next few hours, I experienced emotions for which there were no names. I felt like a different kind of pioneer, a discoverer of new feelings, of new blends of old sentiments, and I was unable to identify them as they passed through me. I decided to name them like teas, Blue Malva, Orange Pekoe Delight, Gardenia Ochre Assam. Then I worked on new facial expressions to go with my newly named emotions. Forehead raised, upper lip puffed, chin jutted. Eyes crossed, mouth agape, lower teeth showing.

I would sit in the back seat and hold Teddy on my lap when he was squirmy in his car seat. But when he was sacked out, I would sit in the front and mentally play with my $350,000. What I knew about finance had been gained through osmosis, but I estimated that I could, without risk, get about 6 percent on my inheritance. This meant that I could withdraw $41,747 a year for twelve years before the principal was depleted. Forty-one thousand dollars a year was twice what I was living on now, which I wouldn't really have needed had it not been for my next question to Clarissa. It was 9:00 P.M. and we were tired. "Can you slow, and pull off?" I said.

"Here?" she said.

The reason she said "here" was because we were on the darkest, loneliest highway on the darkest moonless evening. "It's a fabulous night and us folks ought to pop out and look at various stars." I spoke with an echo of a drawl to make my *e*-less sentence sound more reasonable.

She slowed and stopped. The mechanical hum of the car had become accepted as silence, but when we got out of the car, the further, deeper silence of the desert shocked us both. Holding

Teddy, I leaned against the car and pointed out the dipper, then the North Star, then Jupiter. A meteor caught my eye but Clarissa turned too late. Clarissa and I didn't speak, but this quiet was different from the stiltedness in the car. The air was cold and brittle but was punctuated with surprising eddies of heated winds.

It was going to take some acting on my part to keep her from knowing that my mouth was on a three-second delay from my brain while it tried to eliminate the letter *e* from everything I was about to say.

What I wanted to say was, "There's a three-bedroom at the Rose Crest for rent. Would you and Teddy like to share it with me?" but it was shot through with *e*'s. So instead I slouched back onto the fender and said, "I was shown a big vacant flat across from my pad. I'm thinking of taking it. If you want to, you could stay. I could watch him so you could study." There was a long pause. "You could stay in your own big room. I don't mind waking up with Junior on nights you just want to conk out." I couldn't think of anything else to say, though I wanted to keep talking so I would never have to hear her answer.

"How much is it?" she said.

"I would pay all our monthly bills, food, all that. You could finish school."

"Why would you do that?" she said.

Because I am insane. Because I am lonely. Because I love you. Because I love Teddy. "It could work for both of us," I said. "I'd watch him and you could go to school."

"Can I let you know?"

"Naturally," I said.

"We would be sharing, right?" she said.

She meant, sharing and that's all. I nodded yes and we got back in the car.

Twelve hours later she said, "I think it could work. You're sure you're okay with it?"

"I am."

The drive from Granny's had been one of escalating greenery, ending in the sight of home. The scrub of southern Texas had given way to cacti, which had given way to the occasional oasis in Arizona, which had given way to the pines and oaks of California, which turned into curbs and streets. When we finally pulled up in front of my apartment, I stuck my foot out of the car, put it on the grass, and said, "Sleet, greet, meet, fleet street." Clarissa looked at me like I was crazy.

Over the next few days, every habit of mine returned with a new intensity, as though I owed it a debt.

There were two letters waiting for me when I returned. One was a kindly but brief note from my sister informing me of Granny and our inheritance, the other from a law firm in San Antonio informing me of the same. Ida's letter, though less emotional than a letter from Granny, still had the same embedded goodness, and I wrote her back apologizing for my years of silence, listing a few of my dominant quirks so she could understand me a bit better. The letter was so good that I copied it and sent it to the law firm, too, though I realized later they could use it against me in court and try to keep the money for themselves. But they didn't.

The FOR LEASE sign was still up at the Rose Crest, but I didn't want to make any moves until the cash was in hand, and the money took several weeks—of course—to become mine. I had to prove who I was, which was not easy. I thought my argument to them—that I was me because no one else was me—was convincing, but it was not what they were looking for. I had to prove my lineage. My documents were vague. I had no driver's license and could not find my birth certificate. Ultimately, the legal firm came to a decision; they had no one to give the money to but me, and my sister had vouched for me, so enough was enough and they sent me the dough.

I now had an actual reason to call Elizabeth the Realtor. Not having a phone, I got the address of her company and walked there, even though the route proved to be almost impossible. I wondered if my path, when viewed from an airplane, would spell out my name. Just before giving up, I found a crosswalk for the handicapped that had two scooped-out curbs and used it as a gangplank to get to Elizabeth's block. I left a note that said I was interested in the apartment.

She drove by several hours later and I ran down the stairs before she could get to my door. Elizabeth must have developed an extremely sophisticated wealth detector because she suddenly began treating me as a viable customer who was swimming in cash, even though I was sure that nothing in my behavior had changed. Even after I made her drive me across the street, which wasn't more than twenty steps, she maintained a professional front and showed no exasperation. Or maybe she perceived my indifference toward her and was trying to win me back.

Within the hour, I'd leased the three-bedroom and even negotiated the price down fifty dollars a month. I had another eight days on my monthly rent and I told her I would move in at week's end. I watched Teddy several times that week and Clarissa showed no signs of backtracking.

I was now purchasing a newspaper every day and perusing the financial section. I diligently followed bonds, mutual funds, and stocks and noted their movement. Movement was what I hated. I didn't like that one day you could have a dollar and the next you could have eighty cents without having done anything. On the other hand, the idea that you could have a dollar and the next day have a dollar twenty thrilled me no end. I was worried that on the day my dollar was worth eighty cents I would be sad, and on the day it was worth a dollar twenty I would be elated, though I did like the idea of knowing exactly why I was in a certain mood. But I saw another possibility. If I bought bonds and held them to maturity, then the fluctuations in their value wouldn't affect me, and I liked that their dividends trickled in with regularity. This meant that my mood, too, would constantly trickle upward and by maturity, I would be ecstatic.

In interviewing a series of bond brokers, I sought out someone who could satisfy my requirement of extreme dullness. I felt that the happier a broker was, the shadier he was. If he was happy, it meant that he thought about things other than bonds. Happiness meant he might be frivolous and do things like take vacations. I wanted a Scrooge McDuck who thought about only one thing: decimal points. Since I was a person whose own personality rose and fell based on the input of another person, meetings with these brokers were deadly. The more somber he was, the more somber I would become, and we would often spiral down together into an abyss of tedium.

I interviewed four brokers at several firms in the Santa Monica area. It was the second one who was stupefyingly dull enough and who gave me a siren's call when I met with his rivals. His name was Brandon Brady, and he was so dreary that I'm sure that the rhythmic alliteration in his name made him faintly ill.

What made me finally choose Brandon was not his colorlessness but my perception of the depth of his narrow, hence thorough and numerical, mind. I was sitting with another broker, whose own deadly personality challenged Brandon's. It would have been a tough choice based on flatness alone. But when this broker laid out his plans for me, he started with a proposal to buy a ten-year bond starting next Wednesday.

"There's a problem with buying a ten-year bond next Wednesday," I said.

"And what is that?"

"If I buy a bond next Wednesday, ten years later, it would come due on a Saturday, but I couldn't cash it in until Monday. I would lose two days' interest."

He checked his computer, then looked at me as if I were a wax model of myself: I seemed like a human, but something was wrong.

And that was that. I went back to test broker number one, who made the same gaffe. But it was Brandon, who, after I had proposed buying a bond next Wednesday, got out a calculator and made a clatter as he ran his fingers over it, then frowned deeply. "Well," he said, "they've got us on this one. Why don't we wait a few days and see what other bonds come up?" I knew I had found my man.

* * *

Clarissa and Teddy's entry into the new apartment was biblical. It was as though they had been led into the promised land. Throw rugs of sunlight crept across every bedroom floor, and I had placed cheap plants in every empty corner, copying a home decor catalog I had found in the mailbox. I marched Clarissa around the place and she took a breath of delight in every new room, which gave me pleasure. I had budgeted for just enough furniture to make the place functional, so it looked a little spare, but if my twelve-year plan was to work, the cash would have to flow as though through an hourglass. Clarissa had some furniture that she coerced a friend with a pickup to deliver, and Teddy's colorful possessions were quickly distributed throughout the apartment. Clarissa installed a phone, which I viewed suspiciously at first, then finally forgot about. The place filled out incrementally, a few framed photos appeared, and by the end of the month it looked as though a family lived there. Except.

Except that the space between me and Clarissa remained uncrossable. Sometimes I felt an intense love coming from her toward me, but I couldn't tell if it was because of Teddy. I gave it time, and it was easy to give it time, because Teddy's antics often kept any serious discussion at bay. If my hand rested against Clarissa's, it was only a moment before I had to move it to snag Teddy. When he ambled around the apartment, Clarissa hung over him like a willow. There was no such thing as a solitary moment. I began to allow a phrase in my head that would never have been allowed across the street. The imperfect ideal. As strict as my life across the street had been, it was just as loose at the Rose Crest. Teddy's chaos left me in structural shambles, and I think I could tolerate it because the source of the chaos was unified. He was a person beyond logic; he was the singularity.

It is disappointing when you discover that the person you love loves someone else. I made this discovery twice. The first was one evening when the three of us sat down to our usual meal. These dinners were the fantastic disorder at the end of my rigorously structured days spent with my nose in financial magazines and reports. I had grown to anticipate them and participate in them with a newfound looseness. Clarissa and I chipped in and had food delivered, and there was a lot of freewheeling talk accompanied by the opening of white paper bags containing napkins and picnic utensils and tuna sandwiches and mustard packets. This crinkling noise and snap of the plastic tops of containers of mayonnaise always sparked us into thrilling recaps of the day's most mundane events, and months later I realized that these half hours were sacred.

After Clarissa had set Teddy in a high chair and thrown a few morsels of tuna in front of him, he fisted a glob of it and stuck it in his mouth, then turned to her and grinned. Clarissa's face beamed and broadened, her focus was only on him; there was nothing else, no apartment, no jobs, no schoolwork, no life other than the joyful force that streamed between them. And there was no me. I sat and waited out the absorption, which flickered when Clarissa reached for more food and finally both alit back on earth.

Clarissa's studies progressed and she engaged herself in them with fervor, and she grasped the language of psychology quickly.

The vocabulary and concepts came easily to her and she hinted that she had an affection for the subject matter that the other students didn't. At night she would catch me up on what she had learned during the day, give me shorthand analyses of syndromes and disorders, and then would go over comments she had made in class to get my opinion of them.

Clarissa was always thoughtful toward me and would express her gratitude for my assistance in her life, and I would thank her in return, which always left her puzzled. The impact she and Teddy had had on me was made clear one afternoon when a packet of mail arrived, forwarded from my old address. One of the envelopes was from Mensa. I opened it and read that it had been discovered that, as I had guessed, my scores had been compromised by human error, and would I like to take the test again? My first thought took the form of a shock: Human error at Mensa? What chance then did McDonald's have, and the Rite Aid, and CompUSA? My second thought took the form of a semantic shudder at the phrase "human error": Is there any other kind? My third thought was, no, I didn't want to take the test again, because here I was having a life, even though it was a pastiche of elements of the life of someone else.

One night I got a phone call from Clarissa asking if it was all right for her to be home later than usual. "Would you be okay? Were you going out?" she asked, "Can you watch Teddy; is Teddy okay?" Sure, I said.

Teddy and I had an evening of bliss. He was the model child and I was the model adoptive/uncle/friend. We cavorted on the bed, we played trash can basketball, we played "Where's Teddy?" at professional levels. Finally, a cloud came over him and he conked out on my bed and I slid him over and rested next to him. My lighting rules were still in effect and the soft thirty-watt lamp on my chest of drawers was balanced nicely by the solar glow in the living room. My door was ajar and I could see the front window and door as I lay in relative darkness. I used this solemn time for absolutely nothing, as I drained my mind of thought.

Tonto.

That's who I felt like when I heard the footsteps coming along the second-floor walkway. I thought to myself, "There are two of them, Kemosabe, and they're coming this way." I heard Clarissa's voice, then a man's. They spoke slowly, each response to the other delivered in the same whispered tone. Her answers were shy; his questions were confident and cool. They passed the window and I saw him looking at her as she looked down, fumbling for her keys. The door opened and he stood outside while she moved in, putting her purse down and turning around to him. He spoke to her, and he stepped into the apartment. Her hand touched the light switch and the hard overheads went out, sending my body into rigor mortis. But I watched. They spoke again and he put his hand on her arm, pulling her toward him. She responded. He moved his hand, sliding it up under her hair. He drew her into him and rested his forehead on hers, and I watched him close his eyes and breathe deeply to absorb her. His lips brushed her cheek and I saw her surrender, her shoulders dropping, her arms hanging without resistance. His hand went to her back and urged her, pressing her against him. Her arm went up to his waist, then around his back, and he moved his lips around to hers and kissed her, her arm tightening, locking on his back, her other arm sliding up to his elbow. Her head fell back and he continued kissing her, standing over her, then he stepped back and looked into her eyes, saying nothing.

It is hard to find that the person you love loves someone else. I knew that my tenure with Clarissa and Teddy would have an end.

It was early June, and I had continued my pattern with Teddy, and had continued to incrementally withdraw my attachment to Clarissa. There were other nights, nights involving quiet door closings and early morning slip-outs. These sounds made my detachment easier, even though there was no official announcement of a pledge of love, even though, as far as I knew, there was no introduction of the new man to Teddy, which I felt was wise of Clarissa and protective toward her child.

On a particularly disastrous afternoon, I was in charge of Teddy and he and I engaged in a battle of wits. My mind was coherent, rational, cogent. His was not. As compelling as my arguments were, his nonverbal mind resisted. We had no unifying language or belief. I wanted a counselor to mediate, who would come and interpret for us, find common ground, a tenet we could agree on, then lead us into mutually agreed-on behavior. All this angst was focused on a cloth ring that fit over a cloth pole. He screamed, he wanted it, he didn't want it, he cursed—I'm sure it was cursing—and there was absolutely no avenue for calm. But there were moments of transition. The moments of his transition from finding one thing unpleasant to finding another unpleasant. And he would gaze into my eyes, as if to read what I wanted from him so he could do the opposite. But these transitions were also moments of stillness, and in stillness is when my mind churns the fastest. I looked into the wells of his irises, into the murky pools of the lenses that zeroed in and out.

I had spent time with him; I had been the face, on occasion, that he woke up to. I was fixed in him; my image was held in his consciousness, and I wondered if his recollection of me had slipped beneath the watermark of his awareness and entered into a dreamy primordial place. I wondered if he saw me as his father. If he did, everything made sense. I was the safe one, the one he could rage against. The one from whom he would learn the nature, the limitation, and the context of the cloth ring on the cloth pole.

I constructed a triangle in my head. At its base was Teddy's identification of me as hero, along its ascending sides ran my participation in Teddy's life, however brief that participation might prove to be. At the apex was the word *triumph*, and its definition spewed out of the triangle like a Roman candle: If one day Teddy, the boy and child, approached me with trust, if one morning he ran to my bedroom to wake me, if one afternoon he was happy to see me and bore a belief that I would not harm him, then I would have achieved victory over my past.

But my thoughts did not mollify Teddy; he wanted action. It was now dusk and he continued to orate in soprano screams. I decided a trip to the Rite Aid was in order, and he softened his volume when I swept him up and indicated we were on our way outside.

The sky over the ocean was lit with incandescent streaks of maroon. The air hinted that the evening would be warm, as nothing moved, not a leaf. Teddy, a strong walker now, put his hand up for me to take, and I hunched over and walked at old-man speed. We walked along the sidewalk and I occasionally would playfully swing him over an impending crack. I approached the curb, where I normally would have turned left and headed eight driveways down to where I could cross the street. But I paused.

My hand smothered Teddy's. I looked at him and knew that after my cohabitation with Clarissa was over, he might not remember me at all. Yet I knew I was influencing him. Every smile or frown I sent his way was registering, every raised voice or gentle praise was logged in his spongy mind. I wondered if what I wanted to pass along to him was my convoluted route to the Rite Aid, born of fear and nonsense, if what I wanted him to take from me was my immobility and panic as I faced an eight-inch curb. Or would I do for him what Brian had done for me? Would I lead him, as Brian had me, across the fearful place and would I let him hold on to me as I had held on to Brian? Suddenly, turning left toward my maze of driveways was as impossible as stepping off the curb. I could not leave Teddy with a legacy of fear from an unremembered place. I pulled him toward the curb so he would not be like me. Recalling the day I flew over it with a running leap, I put out one foot into the street, so he would not be like me. He effortlessly stepped off, swaying with stiff knees. I checked the traffic and we started forth. I walked him across the street so that he would not be like me. I led him up on the curb. I continued my beeline to the Rite Aid, a route I had only imagined existed. Across streets, down sidewalks, in crosswalks and out of them, all so Teddy would not be like me. I was the *Santa Maria* and Teddy was the *Niña* and *Pinta*. I led, he followed. I conquered each curb and blazed a new route south and achieved the Rite Aid in fifteen minutes.

As I entered the store, I did not feel any elation; in fact, it was as if my triumph had never happened. I felt that this was the way things were supposed to be, and I sensed that my curb fear had been an indulgence so that I might feel special. I let Teddy's hand go and he shifted into cruise. I followed him down the aisle, sometimes urging him along, once stopping him from sweeping down an entire display of bath soaps. I did not, however, prevent him cascading an entire bottom row of men's hair coloring onto the floor.

I sat Teddy down and tried to group the dyes in their previous order. Men's medium brown, men's dark brown, men's ash blond. Men's mustache brown gel. A woman's arm extended into the mess and picked one up. Her skin was exposed at the wrist because her lab coat pulled back as she reached. She wore a small chrome watch and a delicately filigreed silver bracelet, so light it made no noise as it moved. As her arm reached into my vision, I heard her say, "Is he yours?"

I looked up and saw Zandy, who was a full aisle's length away from her pharmacy post, and I wondered if she had intentionally walked toward us or was just passing by.

"No, he belongs to a friend."

"What's his name?" she said.

"Teddy."

"Hello, little man," she said. Then she turned to me. "I fill your prescriptions here sometimes, so I know all your maladies. My name's Zandy."

I knew her name and she knew mine, but I told her again, including my middle name, and she cocked her head an inch to the sky. We had now gotten all the hair dye back on the shelf, and Zandy stood while I crouched on the ground wrangling Teddy. Zandy wore pantyhose that were translucent with a wash of white, and she had on running shoes that I assumed were to cushion her feet against the concrete floors of the Rite Aid. While I took in her feet and legs, her voice fell on me from above:

"Would you like to get a pizza?"

Teddy and I, led by Zandy, walked around the corner to Café Delores and ordered a triple something with a thin crust. I looked at Zandy and thought that she occupied her own space rather nicely. I thought of the status of my love life, which was as flaky as the coming pizza. I knew it was time. I decided to summon the full power of my charisma and unleash it on this pharmacist. But nothing came. It seemed there was no need because Zandy was in full charge of herself and didn't need anything extra to determine what she thought about me. I said, "How long have you worked at the pharmacy?" But instead of answering, she smiled, then laughed and put her hand on mine, and said, "Oh, you don't have to make conversation. I already like you."

Zandy Alice Allen proved to be the love of my life. I asked her once why she started talking to me that day and she said, "It was the way you were with the boy." After seeing her for several weeks, I recalled Clarissa's front-door kiss. I emulated her seducer and, one night at Zandy's doorstep, pressed her against me. Her head fell back and I kissed her. Her arms dropped to her side, then after a moment of helplessness, she raised her hands and held my arms. She drew in a breath while my lips were on hers, and I think she whispered the word *love*, but it was obscured by my mouth on hers.

Once, we were at lunch and she asked how old I was and I told her the truth: thirty-one. Months went by and she got to the heart of me. With a cheery delicacy she divided my obsessions into three categories: acceptable, unacceptable, and hilarious. The unacceptable ones were those that inhibited life, like the curbs. But Teddy had already successfully curtailed that one; each time I approached a corner, I envisioned myself as a leader and in time the impulse vanished. The other intolerable ones she simply vetoed, and I was able to adjourn them, or convert them into a mistrust of icebergs. The tolerable ones included silent counting and alphabetizing, though when Angela arrived she left me little time to indulge myself. We compromised on the lights, but eventually Zandy's humor—which included suddenly flicking lamps on and off and then dashing out of the room—made the obsession too unnerving to indulge in.

It took six months and a wellspring of perseverance for me to stop the government checks from coming in. I was able to go back to work for Hewlett-Packard and I moved up the ladder when I created a cipher so human that no computer could crack it. Zandy and I lived at the Rose Crest after Clarissa left, though she and Teddy stayed in our lives until one day they just weren't anymore. I knew that what happened between Teddy and me would one day be revealed to him. One night Zandy and I were in bed and she leaned over to me and whispered that she was pregnant, and I pulled her into me and we entwined ourselves and made slow and silent love without breaking our gaze to one another.

Angela was born on April 5, 2003, which pleased me because her twenty-first birthday would fall on a Friday, which meant she would be able to sleep late the next day after what would undoubtedly be a late night of partying.

When Angela was one year old, Zandy took her out to a small birthday fete for little ladies only and I was left alone at the Rose Crest. From the window I could see my old apartment and see my old lamp just through the curtains. This was the lamp I had once dressed in my shirt and used as a stand-in to determine whether Elizabeth could have seen me look at her, and now at the Rose Crest I felt far, far away from that moment. I indulged myself in one old pastime. As I looked across the street, I built in my head my final magic square:

Me	Zandy's mom, Sandy	Our neighbor, Mrs. Thompson, who loves Angela
Philipa	Zandy and Angela	Brian
Granny's memory	Clarissa and Teddy	My sister, Ida

Other names came, but the square overflowed and the confusion pleased me. I shifted away from the window, turning my back on the apartment across the street. I moved to the living room and sat, silently thanking those who had brought me here and those who had affected me, both above and below consciousness. I thought of the names in and around the magic square. I thought of their astounding number, both in the present and past, of Zandy and Angela, of Brian, of Granny, even of my father, whose disavowal of me led to this place, and I understood that as much as I had resisted the outside, as much as I had constricted my life, as much as I had closed and narrowed the channels into me, there were still many takers for the quiet heart.

ACKNOWLEDGMENTS

I would like to thank my diligent and inspiring editor, Leigh Haber, as well as my conscripted friends who were forced to read various drafts and held in a cellar until they offered in-depth commentary: Sarah Paley, Carol Muske-Dukes, Deborah Solomon, Sherle and John, Victoria Dailey, Susan Wheeler, April and Eric and Mary Karr. I would also like to thank Ricky Jay, who in minutes assembled a short treatise for my enlightenment on magic squares from his own amazing library. And Duke.

SHOUTERS

Our fast-paced modern age has made it impractical to read books that are more than 126 pages long. Yet so many classic books and many recently published books are as thick as they are wide. What are we to do? One answer is the Shouters. These are a small number of dedicated people who assign themselves randomly to various individuals, follow them around at a respectful distance, and shout out thick, time-consuming literature sentence by sentence. If you know anyone who has ever had a Shouter, you know there is something remarkably calming about a voice thirty or forty yards away that is speaking aloud say, "Airport," or "Being and Nothingness." Shouting is also a twenty-four-hour-a-day effort, and as the sun sets and day is transformed into night, so, too, is the voice transformed as one Shouter is relieved by another. Sometimes a mellifluous male is replaced with a calming female at a chapter change of *Madame Bovary*. As one gets ready for bed, the tuneful prose keeps on coming through the bedroom window and occasionally one wakes in the night to hear the voice still reciting, undaunted, from under a neighbor's oak. In the morning, there is another new voice and another new chapter, and the meaning of each paragraph drifts into the consciousness during gargling.

At first, it seems, having a Shouter makes it hard to concentrate on the work of the day, the phone calls, the meetings, driving—yes, the Shouters will follow your car with a bullhorn—but soon the shouting blends comfortably into daily life. Soon it is easy to exist both in the real world and in the world of literature that is hovering in the periphery. Occasionally, it is easy to get confused: Was it Uriah Heep who called? Is Scrooge my accountant? Is my husband out whale hunting? One executive, whose Shouter had been reciting Proust's *Remembrance of Things Past* for several weeks, swooned when he bit into a tea cake and remembered every Super Bowl score of the 1980s. But soon, the brain starts compartmentalizing everything and life again feels normal. In fact, the constant proximity to the other world, the one that is written about and dreamed about by writers, enhances the world we live in: One's wife seems more beautiful and complex, a husband more charming and daring.

Shouters have a certain calm about them. They approach their work like a Buddha, in peace and with quiet forcefulness. Becoming a Shouter is evidently a mystical process: One day the Shouter and Shoutee just find themselves "attached." It seems to be a young person's job, and many people in high-powered positions were once Shouters. It is hard to imagine that the perspiring finance worker in the next cubicle was once standing on a rooftop calling out the final paragraph of *The Good Earth* into the window of a fifth-floor co-op on the Upper East Side, or that the jovial TV newswoman was once on a boat in the Caribbean shouting out *The Brothers Karamozov* as she sailed alongside the corporate yacht *Belinda's Bottom*.

Who is picked to have a Shouter? It can be anyone, but *overworked* is an adjective that seems to apply to those lucky enough to be selected. Trump, Starr, Tyson are just a few of the busy luminaries whose lives have been subtly altered by Shouters. There may be resistance at first, particularly if an aggressive Shouter leaves paragraphs of Philip Roth on one's voicemail, and is often the annoying caller on line 3 anxious to finish Chapter 7 of *The Carpetbaggers*. But soon the Shouter is accepted. And amazingly, if several people with Shouters find themselves in the same room, amid the cacophony each can focus on his Shouter with ease, sometimes listening to two or even three novels at the same time with no complications.

The spontaneous and mystical attachment of a Shouter to a subject may be illustrated by this story about the supermodel Linda Evangelista. Once, she was sitting in a top New York restaurant when a party of six that included the talented actor Mandy Patinkin sat at the table next to hers. Linda had just purchased Tom Wolfe's novel *A Man in Full*, a novel often referred to as "a big thick book" or "a big heavy book." Linda began to read it, first softly, then slightly more aloud. She caught Mandy's ear, and though he politely tried to pay attention to his party's conversation, he was becoming more and more entranced with Linda's reading of the book. When the checks came, Linda found herself staying with Mandy through the coat check, and followed him out to the sidewalk, staying just far enough back so Mandy's other guests couldn't quite associate the two. When Mandy's limousine came, Linda, compelled, crawled up the back of the trunk and hung her head just inside the open sunroof and continued reading as the car inched its way along Forty-Sixth Street just as the theaters were letting out. Linda Shouted Mandy for four days until *A Man in Full* was finished, then quietly slipped away back to her life. They are friends today.

A Shouter leaves as quietly as he or she appears, sometimes after a single book has been read aloud, sometimes after several, but never before the job is done and mutual satisfaction has been attained. The Shoutee wakes up in the morning, noticing something is different but unsure of what it is. The orange juice is drunk, the coffee sipped. Is the radio off? The car is started, pulled out of the driveway. The voice is gone.

HISSY FIT

Let us assume there is a place in the universe that is so remote, so driven by inconceivable forces, where space and time are so warped and turned back upon themselves, that two plus two no longer equals four. If a mathematician were suddenly transported and dropped into this unthinkable place, it is very likely that he would throw a hissy fit. This is exactly what happens when a New York Writer contemplates, talks about, or, worst of all, is forced to visit Los Angeles.

It must be understood that the New York Writer is not necessarily a writer from New York. At home on the East Coast somewhere—it could even be Rhode Island—he is an individual, unique in every respect, defiantly singular and stylistically distinct. But when the assignment comes in, by fax or phone, to fly to Los Angeles and interview a poor-sap movie producer (poor sap because his ego leads him to believe that he will be the first of his kind to come off well), the proud author's metamorphosis begins. As the specter of California rises like a werewolf's moon, the mantle of New York Writer descends from the heavens and lands on his epaulets.

The ticket arrives by messenger and is subjected to much investigating and cross-checking to verify that it is truly round trip. Confusing words like *temblor* and *Knott's Berry Farm* drift in and out of his consciousness, and he wonders about the special mores of a thong-based culture.

The incidence of the hissy fit has risen in direct proportion to the airlines' cutbacks in oxygen levels on New York–Los Angeles flights. The longer flight time from east to west convinces our sojourner that even the headwinds are telling him not to go. It deprives his brain chemistry of valuable happiness molecules and gives him an agonizing arrival headache. He reads the *Los Angeles Times* on the plane and is disturbed by the typeface. Then, landing in the bright California sun after leaving New York on a cold, sunless day, he becomes doubly irked when he realizes he has left his sunglasses behind. Walking down the concourse, he sheds his forty-pound overcoat, peeling down to his wool shirt and furry vest. Now, overheated and overloaded, he recalls the words of a wheezing and sniffling SoHo gallery owner: "I was just in LA and got a raging cold in that ninety-degree heat," not recognizing in this unscientific pronouncement that if Los Angeles were an ethnic group, the comment would be a slur. Thus the hissy fit begins: The open palms move reflexively to the ears, in a nice approximation of Munch's *The Scream*. Nervous brain impulses tap out in Morse code, "I am not one of you . . . I don't belong here . . . Are there any others like me I can talk to?" Oddly, these thoughts are from the same writer who has climbed gun towers in Bosnia and gone undercover in street gangs.

Furthering the agony, the beleaguered writer finds himself in a rental car on the San Diego freeway and realizes he does not remember how to drive.

After pulling into the Mondrian Hotel on Sunset and striking a concrete pylon and maybe the valet parker, the writer slips and slides across the glassy floor of the lobby to the reception desk. To his left, he can see past the maître d's podium and the Armani-model hostess to an outdoor restaurant, crowded with people dressed in vinyl and other sauna-inducing unwearables. Behind him, the Beautiful Ones pose themselves around a sofa, and a tiny voice in his head whispers, "You will never have them, because you have not been professionally groomed."

The hissy fit is sustained throughout the day by an unpleasant cranial crowding of facts, comments, and sights, all of which must be simultaneously remembered, until the writer can unsheathe his computer and download his brain. Invited to the producer's house that evening for cocktails, the writer sees in the backyard of the subject's minivilla a gravity-defying bronze sculpture of a teen-on-a-swing, and a fiberglass rock over which a man-made waterfall flows. The writer now must chant over and over to himself, "Remember the fiberglass rock." Eventually, the producer greets him and clasps his hand, capturing his audience. One sentence later, he intimately reveals that his therapy involves talking to a doll of himself. Now the writer, with hours to go before ten-thirty, when the party will sputter and die, must keep repeating to himself, "Remember the fiberglass rock, remember he talks to a doll . . . fiberglass rock, talks to doll, teen-on-a-swing." This keeps him from taking a deep breath and from noticing that the spreading sunset has saturated the air with a soft orange glow, almost like Paris, and that the view to the ocean is dappled with cottages nestled in a hillside, their lights just flickering on, almost like Portofino. He fails to see that Los Angeles is a city of abundant and compelling almosts.

The journey from the producer's house to the Mondrian Hotel, through an accordion descent of roads from the hills to the flats, requires the navigational skills of Magellan. Driving under the sky with one star, he is still intoxicated by the dizzying combination of white wine, party dresses, and a sense of not belonging, while a truth unfolding outside his windshield goes unobserved: The New York grid of streets and avenues, with its intellectual sectors leading to artistic quarters leading to shopping Edens, does not lie correctly over this Los Angeles sprawl. For the Los Angeles grid is warped, like the assumed mathematical netherworld, and must be moved through in an illogical manner. As the surface is unpeeled, a deeper level is revealed, but just below that the surface level appears again. This effect leaves the writer seeing only quark smoke trails, the evidence of something richer that has been missed.

At last, he is back in his hotel room, which unfortunately faces east into the now dead-black hills. Had his room been facing west, he would have noted the sparkling twenty-five-mile vista to the sea, which looks almost like the Mediterranean. He would have noted how the streets of LA undulate over short hills, as though a finger is poking the landscape from underneath. How, laid over this crosshatch, are streets meandering on the diagonal, creating a multitude of ways to get from one place to another by traveling along the hypotenuse. These are the avenues of the tryst, which enable Acting Student A to travel the eighteen miles across town to Acting Student B's garage apartment in nine minutes flat after a hot-blooded phone call at midnight. Had he been facing seaward on a balcony overlooking the city, the writer might have heard, drifting out of a tiny apartment window, the optimistic voice of a shower singer, imbued with the conviction that this is a place where it is possible to be happy. He would have seen, above the rolling rows of houses, the five or six aircraft that are always floating motionlessly over the city, planes that now so directly connect to his jet lag, which is mysteriously working in reverse: Even though it's 3:00 A.M. in the east, he is wide awake. Instead, he observes how the hilltops have been shorn into mesas to accommodate someone's Palladian–Tudor–Gothic–French-fantasy palais, and as it's too late to call a sympathetic ear in New York, he heads to the lobby bar.

The bar is alive, and he falls into a conversation with Candy. Candy is either nineteen or twenty-five or thirty-two, and she pronounces her belief in the powers of the amethyst around her neck as fervently as Constantine for the Church of Rome. The writer knows that next week this belief will be forgotten, or replaced by another, and he remembers it for his article. The hissy fit prevents him from seeing that Candy carries around an even sillier and more poignant belief, one that must be maintained and renewed daily: that she is in possession of a talent that will lift her to the stars. This belief permeates LA's soil; it is in the cars, in the clothes, and in the conversations of the up-and-coming. It is a far-fetched religion, which works often enough to sustain a supply of new believers, and it becomes the mantra of every hopeful, regardless of education or class. The writer looks at the explosion of hair sitting opposite him and puts her in a convenient niche, missing the point that the foolish can't write, but boy, can they act.

After a limp and sexless blackout sleep at the hotel, the writer, with a hangover and no sunglasses, waits for his prey at a staggeringly sunny outdoor café. The producer, after having called the restaurant twice, each time warning of a fifteen-minute delay, sweeps in a half hour late but with an on-time feeling and cuddles fully half the diners before sitting down. So now two stereotypes, one that is lived daily and the other acquired for the journey, sit opposite each other. The writer needs no tape recorder, since it is not the words that will be reported but only the facts, observable and imagined, that fit the thesis. The hissy fit settles in nicely and filters everything through its eyes. Forty minutes later, the cell phone that is lying on the table vibrates across it, and the meeting is over.

Returning to an already dark New York City on the welcoming shorter flight home, the writer arrives at the melodious and historic acronym JFK and not the atonal, punning LAX. The hissy fit begins to subside. Soothed by the familiar jolts of a taxi ride and a one-hour view of the Beloved City from the gridlocked Triborough Bridge, the writer arrives home with a laptop full of judgments. The autopsy is faxed in, gleefully edited and published, then distributed proudly to concurring family and friends. The New York Writer lies back on his bed, adjacent to the clanging radiator where a rented copy of the producer's latest flop has accidentally melted into a horseshoe. He falls asleep, under the sky with no stars, his grasp slowly loosening from his manuscript, never dreaming that one should not ridicule one's foolish, fun, poetic cousin.

DRIVEL

Dolly defended me at a party. She was an artist who showed at the Whitney Biennial, so she had a certain outlook, a certain point of view, a certain understanding of things. She came into my life as a stranger who spoke up when I was being attacked by some cocktail types for being the publisher of *American Drivel Review*. It wasn't drivel that I published, she explained to them, but rather the *idea* of drivel.

One drink later, we paired off. She slouched back on the sofa with her legs ajar, her skirt draped between them. I poured out my heart to this person I had known barely ten minutes: how it was hard to find good drivel, even harder to write it. She knew that to succeed, one must pore over every word, replacing it five or six times, and labor over every pause and comma.

I made love to her that night. The snap of the condom going on echoed through the apartment like Lawrence of Arabia's spear sticking in an Arab shield. I whispered passages from *Agamemnon's Armor*, a five-inch-thick romance novel with three authors. She liked that.

As publisher of *ADR*, I never had actually written the stuff myself. But that morning, arising with a vigor that had no doubt spilled over from the night before, I sat down and tossed off a few lines and nervously showed them to Dolly. She took them into another room, and I sat alone for several painful minutes. She came back and looked at me. "This is not just drivel," she exulted. "It's *pure* drivel." The butterflies in my stomach sopranoed a chorus of "Hallelujah."

That night, we celebrated with a champagne dinner for two, and I told her that her skin was the color of fine white typing paper held in the sun and reflecting the pink of a New Mexican adobe horse barn.

The next two months were heaven. I no longer just published drivel; I was now writing it. Dolly, too, had a burst of creativity, which sent her into a splendid spiraling depression. She had painted a tabletop still life that was a conceptual work in that it had no concept. Thus the viewer became a "viewer," who looked at a painting, which became a "painting." The "viewer" then left the museum to "discuss" the experience with "others." Dolly could take the infinitesimal pause to imply the quotations around a word (she could also indicate italics with just a twist of her voice).

Not wanting to judge my own work or to trust Dolly's love-skewed opinion, I sent my pieces around and made sure they were rejected by five different magazines before I would let myself publish them in *Drivel Review*. Meanwhile, fueled by her depression, Dolly kept producing one artwork after another and selling them to a rock musician with the unusual name of Fiber Behind, but it kept us in doughnuts and he seemed to really appreciate her work.

But our love was extinguished quickly, as though someone had thrown water from a high tower onto a burning dog.

What happened was this: Dolly came home at her usual time. What I had to tell her was difficult to say, but it somehow came out with the right amount of effortlessness, in spite of my nerves.

"I went downtown and saw your new painting of a toaster at Dia. I enjoyed it."

She acknowledged the compliment, started to leave the room, and, as I expected, stopped short.

"You mean you 'enjoyed' it, don't you?" Her voice indicated the quotation marks.

I reiterated, "No, I actually enjoyed it."

Dolly's attention focused, and she came over and sat beside me. "Rod, do you mean you didn't go into the 'gallery' and 'see' my 'painting'?" I nodded sadly.

"You mean you saw my painting without any irony whatsoever?" Again, I nodded yes.

"But, Rod, if you view my painting of a toaster without irony, it's just a painting of a toaster."

I responded, "All I can tell you is that I enjoyed it. I really liked the way the toaster looked."

We struggled through the rest of the night, pretending that everything was the same, but by morning it was over between us, and Dolly left with a small "Goodbye," soaking with the irony I had come to love so much.

I wanted to run, run after her into the night, even though it was day, for my pain was bursting out of me, like a sock filled with one too many bocce balls.

Those were my final words in the last issue of *Drivel Review.* Since then, I have heard that Dolly spent some time with Fiber Behind, but I'm sure she picked up a farewell copy and read my final, short, painful burst of drivel. I like to think that a tear marked her cheek, like the trace of a snail creeping across white china.

I LOVE LOOSELY

RICKY: Lucy, I'm home!

LUCY: Oh, hi, Ricky. How were things at the club today?

RICKY: Oh, fine.

LUCY: What did you do?

RICKY: The usual—rehearsed a new number and had sex with an usherette.

LUCY: *Waaaaaaaa!*

RICKY: Lucy, what's the matter?

LUCY: You said you had sex with an usherette. . . . *Waaaaaaa!*

RICKY: Lucy, don' be silly. It was only oral sex.

LUCY: It was?

RICKY: Of course, Lucy.

LUCY: It wasn't intercourse?

RICKY: Of course not, Lucy. That would be cheating.

LUCY: Oh, Ricky, I almost forgot those passages from the Bible you read to me that proved it.

RICKY: Now I'm goin' to change, and you go make dinner.

LUCY: Yes, Ricky.

(*Ricky exits. Lucy goes to the phone.*)

LUCY: (*On the phone*) Ethel?

ETHEL: (*On the phone*) What is it this time, Lucy?

LUCY: Ethel, I'm not so sure about this "oral sex is not cheating" business.

ETHEL: This is not another one of your schemes, is it?

LUCY: Oh no, Ethel. It's just that Ricky claims it says so in the Bible.

ETHEL: Well, Lucy, why don't you ask a monsignor?

LUCY: Where would I find one?

ETHEL: There's one in the building. Mrs. Trumble has one visiting her now. You want me to send him down?

LUCY: Thanks, Ethel.

(*There is a knock at the door. Lucy answers. It's the monsignor.*)

LUCY: That was fast!

MONSIGNOR: Hello, Mrs. Ricardo. It says right here in Leviticus that oral sex is not cheating.

LUCY: How did you know what I wanted to ask?

MONSIGNOR: It's the only thing people have been asking me for months. Men have been joining our church by the thousands! Ah . . . ah . . . *ah choo*!

(*The monsignor's mustache flies off.*)

LUCY: *Fred!*

FRED: Lucy, this was all Ricky's idea!

(*Ricky enters.*)

RICKY: Lucy, is my dinner ready? (*He sees Fred and starts swearing in Spanish.*)

(*Ethel enters, sees the mustache on the floor, picks it up, and hands it to Fred.*)

ETHEL: Here, put this on your bald head for old times' sake.

LUCY: But how did Ricky know I was worried that oral sex was actually cheating?

ETHEL: I've been taping all your phone conversations and selling them to him, Lucy.

LUCY: But, Ethel, you're my best friend!

ETHEL: I was getting even with you for making me wear that cat-suit to the Beverly Hills Hotel.

RICKY: Ethel, tell Lucy you're sorry.

ETHEL: Oh, all right. Lucy, I'm sorry I taped all your phone calls and ruined your life.

LUCY: And, Ricky, I'm sorry I thought you had intercourse when it was just oral sex.

(*They all hug.*)

FRED: Can I take off my wire now, Ricky?

THE HUNDRED GREATEST BOOKS THAT I'VE READ

1. *The A-Bomb and Your School Desk*
2. *Little Lulu*, number 24, January 1954
3. *The Weekly Reader Humor Column*
4. Women Love It If You're Funny! (advertisement)
5. *Robert Orben's Patter for Magicians*
6. The book that starts, "It was the best of times; it was the worst of times."
7. *Silas Marner*, by George Eliot (first and last page only)
8. *The Catcher in the Rye*, by J. D. Salinger
9. *Sex for Teenagers* (pamphlet, 1962)
10. *The Nude* (serious art photos)
11. *Lolita* (movie only)
12. *Owner's Manual, 1966 Mustang*
13. *Showmanship for Magicians*, by Dariel Fitzkee
14. *Marijuana! Totally Harmless* (can't remember author)
15. *Steal This Book*, by Abbie Hoffman
16. *Fasting with Incense*, by "Free"
17. *Being and Nothingness*, by J.-P. Sartre

18. *Being and Nothingness,* CliffsNotes
19. *The Complete Works of e. e. cummings*
20. *The Love Poems of John Donne*
21. *How for Two Years to Never Once Speak to the Girl of Your Dreams, Even Though You Sit Across from Her Every Day in the College Library,* by Iggy Carbanza
22. *How to Seduce Women by Being Withdrawn, Falsely Poetic, Quiet and Moody* (same author)
23. *The Expert at the Card Table,* by S. W. Erdnase
24. *Hamlet* (screenplay)
25. *Millionaire Banjo Players of Fresno* (leaflet)
26. *A Coney Island of the Mind,* by Lawrence Ferlinghetti
27. *Why It's Not Important to Have a Fancy Table at a Restaurant,* by D. Jones
28. *Journey to Ixtlan,* by Carlos Castaneda
29. *Who to Call When You're Busted for Peyote,* by Officer P. R. Gainsly
30. *Books Whose Titles Are Printed at the Top of the Cover So They Look Good Sticking Out of Your Back Pocket,* published by the New York Public Library
31. *Tess of the D'Urbervilles,* by Thomas Hardy
32. *Crime and Punishment,* by Dostoyevsky
33. *Ulysses,* by James Joyce (first sentence only)
34. *The Playboy Advisor* (letters about stereo equipment only)
35. *What Nightclub Audiences Are Like in Utah,* by "Red" Snapper
36. *Fifty Great Spots for Self-Immolation in Bryce Canyon,* by "Red" Snapper (now deceased)

37. *Great Laundromats of the Southwest,* by the General Services Administration
38. *Using Hypnotism to Eliminate the Word "Like" from Your Vocabulary,* by Swami Helatious
39. *The Hollywood Hot One Hundred* (article)
40. *How to Not Let Anyone Know You're Having a Panic Attack,* by E. K. G.
41. *The Hollywood Hot One Hundred* (rechecking)
42. *If You're Not Happy When Everything Good Is Happening to You, You Must Be Insane,* by Loopy d'Lulu
43. *The Nouveau Riche, and Its Attraction to Silver Bathroom Wallpaper,* by Paige Rense
44. *How to Bid at Sotheby's*
45. *Thinking You're a Genius in the Art Market Until 1989,* by Sir Warren Duggs (ex-Christie's, currently in prison)
46. *Beating the Experts at Chinese Ceramics,* by Taiwan Tony
47. *Selling Your Fake Chinese Ceramics,* by Taiwan Tony
48. *Windows for Dummies*
49. *Windows for Idiots*
50. *Windows for the Subhuman*
51. *Fifty Annoying Sinus Infections You Can Legally Give Bill Gates,* by Steve Jobs
52. *Romeo and Juliet,* by William Shakespeare
53. *Wuthering Heights,* by Emily Brontë
54. *The Wedding Planner,* by Martha Stewart
55. *Men Are from Mars, Women Are from Venus,* by John Gray (gift)
56. *How Come You Don't Listen to Me No Mo'?,* by Dr. Grady Ulose (gift)

57. *Ten Lousy Things Men Do to Be Rotten,* by Dr. Laura Sleshslinger
58. *Crummy Men Who Can't Think and Don' Do Nothin',* by Dr. Laura Sleshslinger
59. *Pre-Nup Loopholes,* by Anon., Esq.
60. *How to Survive the Loss of a Love,* Prelude Press
61. *How to Get Over a Broken Love Affair*
62. *Mourning Is Your Best Friend*
63. *Be a Man, Get Over It!*
64. *Diagnostic and Statistical Manual of Mental Disorders,* American Psychiatric Association
65. *Get Ready to Live!,* by H. Camper
66. *Omelet: Olga—Mnemonic Devices for Remembering Waitresses' Names*
67. *Victoria's Secret,* fall catalog
68. *Your Stomach, and Why It's So Fat*
69. *Inappropriate Dating and Your Hair,* by Spraon Brown
70. *Male Menopause,* by "A Big, Crying Baby"
71. *He,* by Robert Johnson
72. *Him, a Journey into the Male Psyche,* by Howard Johnson
73. *Hunting Quail with a Tank,* by Charlton Heston
74. *Bonding with the Feminine*
75. *Bringing Out the Feminine*
76. *What Breasts Can Make You Do,* by Joseph Keen
77. *Owner's Manual for the Harley-Davidson "Sportster" 883*
78. *One Hundred Worst Movies of the '80s* (skimmed)
79. *Women Love It When Men Cry, for About a Minute*
80. *Life Begins at Forty, Too Bad You're Fifty,* by Trini Montana

81. *It's Time to Leave Childish Humor Behind,* by Ayed Lykta Dooya
82. *How Methadone Can Help Cure Your ChapStick Addiction* (doctor's office pamphlet)
83. *Your Prostate,* by Dr. Pokey d'Hole
84. *Glasses, Contacts, or Surgery?* (pamphlet)
85. *Tingling Feet, a Diet Cure* (Internet download)
86. *Ringing in the Ears* (pamphlet)
87. *Hearing in Restaurants,* by Dr. S. Louder
88. *Those Itchy, Itchy Eyes!* (e-mailed booklet)
89. *Arthritis!*
90. *Tics You Can Look Forward To*
91. Arrhythmia Can Be Fun! (billboard)
92. *The User's Guide to Prescription Drugs,* AMA
93. *Look! And Other Ways to Get Her to Turn Away While You Take Your Viagra*
94. *Why It's Important to Have a Fancy Table at a Restaurant,* by D. Jones
95. *Final Exit* (Hemlock Society)
96. *Whatever Happened to . . .* (article)
97. *Staying Current Through Insane Contract Demands,* by Specs LaRue
98. *Celebrity Secrets for Crying During Interviews,* by Rogers and Cowan
99. Your Birth Certificate Could Be Five Years Off (magazine ad)
100. *Wisdom After Fifty and Why Nobody Cares*

CLOSURE

Closure. I wanted it. Or I wasn't going to be able to move on. The taxi had dropped me off fully ten blocks earlier than I had requested. Sixty-First instead of Seventy-First. Luckily, I had copied down the cab number in case for some reason I needed closure. This time, I did. I called the taxi company from my cell phone. I told them what I wanted. "Some kind of closure," I said. "I need to get on with my life." They understood. Thus the day had begun.

It was a little matter of a short-change at the supermarket. One dollar and fifty cents. Not much, but as I stood there counting the change, realizing the mistake, I couldn't move on. I confronted the checkout girl. "Oops," she said. Oops? Oops? This was not closure. How was I to move on? I did not sense that the store was taking responsibility. The manager came over and took me aside. He understood closure. He apologized and took responsibility. I was lucky. I could move on.

My girlfriend Josie was already at the apartment. I had given her a key just two weeks earlier. I came in with the groceries. We put them away and ordered in. We watched the news. Murder, larceny, confidence games: so many people who couldn't move on. I kissed her and held her hand. I took her to the bedroom. I tried to make love to her, but couldn't. Too many loose ends. But she wanted closure. I explained that because so many people in my life weren't taking responsibility, it became impossible for me to accept my own responsibility. She understood. But she still wanted closure.

Two days go by. My movie theater free admission coupon is not being honored. A line forms behind me as I explain my situation to the ticket seller. I had called ahead to make sure it would be honored. They said it would be. Yet here I am, being embarrassed in front of strangers. Josie says, "Let's pay," and suggests that we move on. I cannot. I tell them I will need closure. The man selling tickets says the coupon people made a mistake, and they are the ones who will need to take responsibility. "So you need closure," I say. "Yes," he replies, "before we can move on." "So my closure is dependent on your closure," I say. "Yes." Just then Josie says, "I need closure too, tonight." She pays. I move on, even though I am unable to move on.

We watch the movie. It is about Mary, Queen of Scots. She was beheaded. At least she got closure. When the movie is over, it says, "The end." We can go home.

Pop goes the champagne cork. Josie starts drinking. I start to worry. She starts kissing me. I am helpless. I can't move on. The phone rings and the machine picks up. It's the manager of the movie theater. "I talked with the coupon people," he says, "they will issue a new coupon. I'm hoping now we can move on." I smile at Josie. But something's still not right. I notice the answering machine blinking. I irritate Josie when I play back the message. It is the taxi company with a full apology. I can move on.

I give Josie closure. She snuggles next to me. A candle burns to the end and snuffs itself out. The moonlight trickles into the bedroom. I look at the bedroom door. It's ajar. I know what I need.

THE Y3K BUG

With only eight years to go before the end of the third millennium, many scientists are beginning to express concern over the Tridecta Blighter Function, whose circuitry was not programmed to accommodate the year 3000. "Who knew that people would live six hundred years?" said Tyrell Oven-Baby No. 9, whose work in Danish metaoscillititaniannia led the way to the familiar Fundolator. "Yes, it's true," continued No. 9, "at the stroke of midnight, on December 31, 2999, some individuals' heads will explode. Naturally, the heads will grow back, but they will keep exploding, at random intervals, for the rest of their owners' lives. This will be fine for the New Year's Eve celebration, but I think most people would prefer it to stop by Dirndl Day."

Of course, all of us have had our heads regenerated at one time or another, so why the fuss? The problem is that most of us who had a Tridecta Blighter Function implanted in our duodenum before the year 2465 will lose the use of two of our penises. This will leave most of us with our eight vaginas intact but with only six functioning male organs. Sure, it's possible to get by with only six penises, but what about quality of life?

Some experts believe that the problem is overrated—that, at worst, a head may explode seven or eight times. And, since most people today keep their heads at home in an aluminum box, what difference will it make? But others consider this a freedom-of-choice issue, maintaining that we have the right to have our heads explode because we want them to, and not because some corporate giant failed to look six hundred years into the future. This is as fundamental a right, they claim, as the right to redirect the world's rivers for personal gain, the right to re-hem anyone's outer garments, and the right to govern one of the lesser races, such as the Offspring of Jerry Springer's Guests.

Many people worry that the Y3K bug will interfere with the holidays. Perhaps the old Gregorian calendar might have been affected, but the Calendar of New Practicalities, which is centered on the three major televised holidays—the Super Bowl, the Oscars, and the NBA playoffs—only requires a six-second delay at the start of the third quarter of the basketball semifinals every twenty-six years to keep it accurate. The holidays of Christmas, Easter, and Rosh Hashanah, combined into one three-day weekend to appease religious nuts, should not be affected.

WHAT CAN I DO?

Try to relax. When New Year's Eve rolls around, put on an old movie, such as the hilarious comedy classic *2001.* Or treat yourself to a glass of water. This might also be a good time to plug up any oozing plasma you might have.

Stay home and let your head blow up. The worst thing that happens is that you're out of commission until a new one grows. We all know what a peaceful time that can be, with no faxes ringing in our heads, and no B-mail messages being delivered to our right hemisphere from President Pete.

WHAT HAPPENS IF MY HEAD BLOWS UP WHILE I'M AT A PARTY?

Everyone will know about the Y3K bug, and most likely you won't be the only one to explode. You should be prepared, however, for those unkind revelers who will spoil your evening by taunting you with the nickname Ol' Six Penis.

Even with all these helpful tips, there are bound to be those among you who are still uneasy about the coming millennium. If you can't relax, try to meditate on these words:

> Everything's going to be O.K. Be sure to watch our two-hour special, brought to you by Andromeda, where we recap the music of the millennium.

I'm sure we can all take comfort in this message from our wisest of elders, Dick Clark.

A WORD FROM THE WORDS

First, let me say how much I enjoy being one of the words in this book and how grateful I am for this opportunity to speak for the whole group. Often we're so busy speaking for others that we never get to speak for ourselves, or directly to you, the reader. I guess it's redundant to say "you, the reader," but we're not used to writing, and it sounds better to my ear than, say, "you, the two giant fists that are holding me" or "you, the large, heavy mass of protoplasm."

There's also a nice variety of words in this book, and that always makes it fun. We can hang around with the tough utilitarian words, like *the*, and have a few beers, or we can wander over and visit the lofty *perambulate*, who turned out to be a very nice verb with a very lovely wife, *tutu*. *Fuzzy* also turned out to be a lot of fun; she had a great sense of humor and a welcoming manner that we all learned from. I can never decide whether I'd like to be proletariat or bourgeois in this world of words. The common words, such as the pronouns and the transitive verbs, get used a lot, but they're tired (you should see them running around here, carrying their objects). The exciting words, like *fo'c'sle*, make a lot of impact but aren't frequently called into service. I'm lucky. I'm *underpants*. Sometimes I'm used innocuously, but other times I get to be in very racy sentences in some pretty damn good books. Of course, some usages I find shocking. Which is a point I'd like to make: When you read something that disgusts you, don't blame the word. *Scrotum* goes around here like someone just shot his best friend, but really he's a legitimate guy who gets used in ugly ways by a lot of cheeseballs. Likewise *pimple*. I was there when he got used as "a pimple on the face of humanity." The poor guy was blue for a month. He walked around here with a hangdog look and even tried to be friends with *hangdog look*, but around here, a phrase won't mingle with a word; they just won't. It also irks me that two ordinary words can be given a hyphen and suddenly they're all-important. Me? Of course I would love to be a proper noun, but I'm not, so that's that. Even with the current fad of giving children unusual names, it's unlikely that any couple will call a newborn *Underpants*.

This is also my first experience being on a page, since my typing on January 23 (birthday coming up!). When I was a computer word, things were great. I could blast through cyberspace, scroll across screens, travel to India. Now that I'm on the page, I'm worried that it's going to be mostly dark. My request to you, the person above me, with the two gigantic lenses over your eyes, is that you occasionally open the book after you have finished reading it and give all of us a little air. A simple thumbing through will do. Not that I'm unhappy in here. There are enough diverse words that our little civilization can keep itself amused for the twenty or so years we expect to be on a shelf, or stacked in a corner, or sold in a garage.

I'd also like to say something to you budding writers. Believe me, I do understand that sometimes it's essential to use incorrect grammar. That is fine with me, and the words who are in those sentences are aware of their lot in life. But it's difficult to even hang around an incomplete sentence, much less be in one. I imagine it's like talking to a person whose head is missing. It just doesn't feel right. A friend of mine has been misspelled in a computer file for over fourteen years, and it doesn't look like he's ever going to be spell-checked.

There are a couple of individuals who would like to speak:

I'm the word *sidle,* and it was fun to be in that story about the dog (I couldn't see the title from where I was).

Greetings. I'm *scummy,* and I'd like to mention that you are a lowlife.

Hello. I'm *hello,* and I'd like to say myself.

And now we'd like to hear from a group of individuals without whom none of the work we do would be possible:

Hi. We're the letters, and we'd just like to say that we enjoy being a part of the very fine words on this page. Thank you.

And last but not least, someone very special to the whole crew here in *Pure Drivel* would like to end this book:

?

ABOUT THE AUTHOR

Steve Martin is one of the most well-known talents in entertainment. His work has earned him an Academy Award®, five Grammy® awards, an Emmy®, the Mark Twain Award, and the Kennedy Center Honors, among others. As an author, Martin's work includes the novel *An Object of Beauty*; the play *Picasso at the Lapin Agile*; a collection of comic pieces, *Pure Drivel*; a bestselling novella, *Shopgirl*; and his memoir, *Born Standing Up*. Martin's films include *The Jerk; Planes, Trains, and Automobiles; Roxanne; Parenthood; L.A. Story; Father of the Bride*; and *Bowfinger*; among countless others.